Some
Like It
Scot

Some Like It Scot

DONNA KAUFFMAN

BRAVA

KENSINGTON PUBLISHING CORP.
www.kensingtonbooks.com

BRAVA BOOKS are published by

Kensington Publishing Corp.
119 West 40th Street
New York, NY 10018

All Kensington titles, imprints, and distributed lines are available at special quantity discounts for bulk purchases for sales promotion, premiums, fund-raising, educational, or institutional use.

Special book excerpts or customized printings can also be created to fit specific needs. For details, write or phone the office of the Kensington Special Sales Manager: Kensington Publishing Corp., 119 West 40th Street, New York, NY 10018. Attn. Special Sales Department. Phone: 1-800-221-2647.

Brava and the B logo are Reg. U.S. Pat. & TM Off.

ISBN-13: 978-0-7582-5087-2
ISBN-10: 0-7582-5087-8

First Kensington Trade Paperback Printing: June 2010

10 9 8 7 6 5 4 3 2 1

Printed in the United States of America

For Brian
For the encouragement, support, and timely distractions

I would also like to acknowledge the many wonderful weavers from the world of basket-making who have helped to educate me about the intricacies of this complex and stunningly beautiful craft. Special thanks to Joanne Howard and Linda Hovermale for your time and enthusiasm and all of the hands-on instruction. Please excuse the artistic liberties I've taken, and know that any mistakes that were made are surely my own.

Chapter 1

Graham MacLeod needed a bride.

Not that he wanted one. But there were extenuating circumstances.

"How about Bitsy?" Roan said, clicking away on his computer keyboard, resulting in a steady stream of photographs parading across his monitor.

Graham did not want to know what site his friend was on, much less who any of those women were. He was hardly going to choose a mate from a website catalog.

Roan barely paused on any of them more than a second or two, then kept clicking, while faces kept flashing.

Graham turned and looked out the office window, wanting no part of any of it, truth be told. He should be out in the fields, running tests, checking the fresh growth. Not wasting time on some four-hundred-year-old wild goose chase.

Roan took a short break, sighed, and plowed his fingers through his hair, then went back to tapping keys, a resolute expression on his normally genial face. "I mean, there is that unfortunate skin condition, and I'm no' too certain she'll be willin' to leave the family homestead, carin' for her great auntie's cats as she does." He paused briefly to shoot a wry smile in Graham's direction. "Not to mention carting her over the threshold might take the wind out of your sails a wee bit."

Graham glanced over at him. "Bitsy is your cousin. Have a care."

"She's routinely pulled pranks on us since we were wee lads," Roan reminded him. "And no' the gentle, affectionate kind, either, if you recall. I still bear the physical scars. Just last week she thought it would be the height of amusement to con Henrietta into addin' a heavy starch to my laundry. The laundry in question was my boxers."

Shay snorted from where he sat at the other desk, across the room. "So you're sayin' your cousin gave you a stiffie?"

"That's no' amusin', Shay, no' in the least," Roan shot back.

"And he wants to marry her off to me," Graham said to Shay. "With friends like that—"

"It's a friend like me who's going through all the trouble of helping you out in the first place, don't forget," Roan said. "I wouldn't have suggested her, but she's the only available McAuley lass of age left on the island."

Graham turned fully back around. "That canno' be true."

Roan laughed. "Ye've less than four hundred of us to see after, perhaps twice as many sheep, but I'll bet you know the sheep's lineage better than your own. You spend far too much time out in the fields, running tests, measuring soil—"

"Probably sending longing looks toward the sheep," Shay interjected, but was studiously going over papers when Graham shot him a dark look.

Roan laughed. "Perhaps I should send them a warning. You've been quite the hermit far too long."

"Veritable monk," Shay added, distractedly. "It's not natural."

"Yes, well, as you both are fully aware, given you face similar circumstances, the list of available companions on Kinloch is a rather short one past blood relatives of one sort or another."

"Aye, but we're not tied to a clan law that forces us to marry one of them in order to carry on our work," Roan said, not remotely put off by Graham's deepening scowl.

"Nor are you tied to only finding a suitable McAuley on this island," Shay reminded him. "Which is why God made ferry boats. Perhaps you've heard of them, big seafaring vessels that can transport a man to the mainland—and heaven—in a matter of hours."

"He only goes to the mainland for science and farming symposiums," Roan reminded Shay. "And a veritable smorgasbord of sweet, young flesh to be found at those functions, I'm sure."

"Actually, I think horn-rims on a woman are rather sexy," Shay said, pausing in his reading as if to give that matter serious thought.

"Only as you're sliding them off her, so she canno' see you so clearly," Roan joked. "Blurry up your bits a little. 'Things are larger than they actually appear, darlin', and all that."

"He's really no' that amusing after all, is he?" Shay said to Graham in that flat, dry manner that was distinctly his, before going straight back into the stack of legal documents he was poring over.

Graham gazed at his two closest friends. He and Roan McAuley had been best mates since they'd both been in nappies. Shay Callaghan had popped up during their seventh summer, when his mother dumped him on Kinloch to be raised by his father before leaving for parts unknown. It had come as a particular surprise to Callaghan senior, as he hadn't known he was a father until that fateful day. The three youths had muskateered up pretty much immediately, and had been quite the reckonable force ever since.

As young men, they'd left their tiny Hebridean island, heading to university on the mainland—Graham in Glasgow, Shay and Roan in Edinburgh—each in pursuit of very different dreams. But fate's quirks had eventually brought all three back to their rustic, rural home, where they remained, each with a vested interest in bettering the life for their fellow clansmen and islanders.

They were an odd mix. Shay, always the pragmatic, level-headed one, was the natural born mediator and solver of problems. He'd become a barrister, just like his father, though their relationship had always been a rocky one. Aiden Callaghan had been gone close to six years, an early heart attack taking him far before his time, leaving Shay, freshly minted degree in hand, as the most recent Callaghan man to handle all matters of legal import, for the Kinloch residents, as his forebears had done for centuries prior.

Roan, on the other hand, was the one with the ready wit and easy charm. Inventor, dreamer, and electronics genius, once he'd found computers and the Internet, there had been no stopping him. While Shay kept the peace, Roan was often called upon to use his droll and easygoing nature to keep his more serious and focused compatriots from growing too stodgy and dour.

Graham was a scientist by nature and degree. He was happiest when he was out in the fields, and the only technology he cared about was the kind that would help him nurture the unique Kinloch flaxseed crop that his clansmen's entire economic existence depended upon. In addition to being a scientist and a farmer, he was, and had been for several fortnights now, the laird of the MacLeod clan, as well as current leader of the dual clanship—with the McAuleys—that comprised the citizenry of Kinloch.

Or he was until the autumnal equinox, anyway.

At which point he needed to be married to a McAuley, or the leadership would pass to the other side. In this case, it would put them into the hands of a man who didn't even reside on Kinloch, who very likely wasn't even aware of the daft ancient island law, much less his possible pending inherited title.

"Do you really think all this is necessary?" Graham asked, yet again. "Ualraig was single for as long as most everyone on the island can remember. I don't recall them nudging him to tie the knot after my dear grandmother departed."

"But it was precisely because he had wed your dear grandmamma when he became laird and leader, that it wasn't a concern," Shay noted. "No' a legal one, at any rate."

"But how legally enforceable is a four-hundred-year-old marriage pact? Surely there isn't a man, woman, or sheep, for that matter, who sincerely wishes me to stop moving forward with our crop growth. We've turned things around substantially in the years since the blight, and in the past three we've seen significant progress, but no' enough as yet to guarantee the rest of us won't be fleeing to the mainland to look for new livelihoods. We've already lost people more than we should have, though I can hardly blame them. But if we're to ultimately survive, we need—I need—to keep pushing and doing whatever it takes to get us back to one hundred percent growth. Hell, seventy-five percent would allow us to take advantage of our full market potential. We can't promise that right now, so we have to turn new interests away. We're at sixty-two percent. Sixty-two! With winter howling at our backs. We've no time for silly games."

Graham waved a hand at Roan's laptop, which might as well be umbilically attached to the man, he was never separated from the damn thing.

Roan headed the island board of tourism—which was actually just Roan and auld Liza MacLeod, who came in thrice weekly to do minor bookkeeping and the odd secretarial job. But he also took care of marketing Kinloch Basketry, which was the far bigger and most important job. The unique artisan baskets were woven from the waxed linen threads made from the rare, if small, flax crop that grew on the island.

There was no denying it had been Roan's marketing genius and "big-picture strategy," as he'd called it, that had moved them from merely selling their one-of-a-kind baskets in the U.K., to competing in a global marketplace . . . and competing quite famously.

Much like Harris tweed, which had been borne on one of their sister islands, theirs was a cottage industry—literally— that single-handedly kept the island economy afloat and, like its tweed weaving counterpart, could continue to do so for generations, if not for one wee problem.

"If we don't grow the flax, we can't weave the bloody things! That is where my energies should be directed," Graham said. He paced Roan's small office, trying to stay calm in the face of the ridiculousness of it all, but losing the battle handily. At barely thirty-one, he'd already worked too hard, for too long, taking up where Ualraig had left off, fighting the foul whims of Mother

Nature. They were all working hard, and the stakes were bloody damn high.

The blight that struck their island home close to a dozen years back had made it a struggle to take full advantage of the increased interest Roan's online marketing campaign had brought them. The impact on the wee island's economy had been so severe, at their lowest points, it had looked as if the centuries strong MacLeod-McAuley clan alliance might finally be forced to a sad, ignominious end.

But Graham's hard work and dedication to finding solutions to the ongoing struggles they faced by growing a unique crop on such unforgiving land was beginning to pay off. Harvest percentages were climbing—slowly—but the increase was constant, with no decline at all for the past three growth cycles. With enough consistency, they could accept more contracts for their baskets. There was real hope, and his clansmen knew it and supported him wholeheartedly. Not that he wanted their gratitude, but due to the situation at hand, surely now that he was clan chief in full, they weren't going to hold him hostage to some centuries-old, outdated tribal law.

Shay cleared his throat. "I've studied the original documents until my eyes are crossing, Graham. I'm sorry to report that I don't see any way around it."

"We'll simply overturn it, then, right? As clan chief, don't I have a wee bit of say in how the island laws are maintained? Surely—"

"According to what was written, the law was purposely created so that no individual clan chief could abolish it," Shay explained. "Its sole purpose was to keep the clans united against—"

"The insurgency on the mainland, which, I might remind you, hasn't been an issue for quite some time. Just what are we protecting ourselves from, by forcing the sitting chief to legally bind himself to the other clan by marrying it?"

Shay held him under a steady regard. "We're a wee spit of land located not only a fair distance from our mother land, but also from the rest of our sister islands, all situated between us and its bonny shores. We've no cause to have ever been the stronghold we've succeeded in being, for any amount of time, much less centuries of it. Clearly the pact has done what it set out to do. It has worked. I dinnae believe it matters, Graham, that the wars that provoked its evolution have ended. Look at the American constitution and how it has managed to guide a country to power, despite being written so long ago that the creators of the document couldn't possibly have foreseen how it would be applied in times such as the ones we live in now. And yet," he added, mildly, "they seem to be doing okay."

Graham lifted his hands, then let them fall helplessly at his sides. "I understand the sentimental reasons why everyone wants to hew themselves to the auld rituals. But it's no' practical any longer, to force my hand, especially in something as sacred as marriage, all to appease a ruling that we no longer need abide by to survive. What we need to do to survive is to grow the flax, increase our industrial output. If we're going to focus on sentiment, then let it be the pride of the fact that we create the most intricately woven, beautifully artistic, unique baskets in the world. It's history, it's art. It's the—"

"Harris Tweed of craftsmanship," Roan finished with him, then sighed. "We've heard the speech, Graham."

"Then you already know that it's that very history we should be embracing, and working toward maintaining, to keep us a thriving island stronghold. Not worrying about whether the MacLeod laird has taken a McAuley bride within some ridiculous and entirely nonsensically determined period of time. I don't believe in it and I refuse to follow it."

Graham thumped Roan's desk with his fist to underscore his words, though Roan barely raised a brow at the action, despite it being well out of character. "I'll take it up in a town meeting if need be. Gain a consensus vote. Surely if everyone says aye to abolishing the thing, it must be rendered no longer legally binding. We could rid ourselves of it and get back to focusing on what's important." He smacked the desk with both palms, then pushed off and strode across the room to look out the front window and down the main lane of the village. "There will be no sham wedding on Kinloch." He turned back to face his friends. "I have your support in this, am I right?"

Both Roan and Shay continued to stare at him for several long moments, before finally looking at each other.

"I'll expand the search to the mainland," Roan said.

Shay nodded. "I'll write up the banns that are to be posted as soon as an agreement with the bride has been reached."

Graham looked at them both incredulously. "Did ye no' hear a word I just said?"

"We did," they both said in unison, neither one so much as pausing as they continued going about whatever it was they had to go about to see Graham lawfully wed to an eligible member of the McAuley clan before the end of the autumnal equinox. Being as it was mid-August, that was little more than a month away. Giving him roughly forty days to find a bride.

Heaven help them all.

"I'm going to call the town council," Graham stated, not giving up just because the two men he regarded as brothers had already done so. "In fact, I'm going to call an island tribunal. If we get a consensus then, as far as I'm concerned, legal or no', that's all the support I need to continue on and be done with this wild goose chase."

"It's no' just a consensus, Graham," Shay told him. "It has to be one hundred percent. They all have to say aye."

Graham spun back around. "Really? So there is a solution! Why didn't you say so? I'm certain I can and will have that. Who would say nay?"

"I can think of a few," Roan said. "Like Dougal. And auld Branan, for certain."

"They're not the only elders who will hold out," Shay agreed. "They love you, no doubt, but they'll stick with tradition."

"Even over what's best for the island? If we let someone else, an outsider no less, come here and begin making decisions regarding our well-being—surely even the oldest resident wouldn't chance that."

Roan shrugged. "Perhaps they think you'll persevere with your crop management whether you're laird or no'."

"What if I have no say in the matter? What if this"—he turned to Shay—"what's the bloke's name?"

"Iain McAuley."

Graham turned back to Roan. "Iain. What if this Iain has other ideas about our little island industry? He's never so much as set foot on our soil much less worked it with his own hands. Who knows what he'd decide to do. We can't risk that."

"He may not even want it," Roan reminded him. "In fact, he probably won't. Who would?" He looked to Shay and grinned. "We're no' exactly the Fortune 500 of inheritances, you know."

"He'll probably be begging you to take it over." Shay agreed, then leaned back in his seat and folded his arms. "Besides, if he wants to be laird, he'll have to honor the marriage pact law as well."

Graham pumped an air fist. "Right! He'll have to marry a MacLeod! I'm betting he won't be any more enthusiastic about that than I am. Hell, for all we know, he's already married."

Shay shook his head. "He's no'. He's thirty-two, unwed, living in Edinburgh. Works for an investment firm. Quite the bright and shiny diamond, too, from what I've dug up."

"Still—"

"There is a much longer list of eligible MacLeod lasses," Roan pointed out. He shrugged when Graham shot him a dark look. "I'm only stating the truth here. I mean, aye, he could find the whole thing tiresome and a waste of his time, but what do we know? Maybe he'll think it quite the lark. Shay said he already has more money than Croesus—from his job, as well as a few trusts and such from his mum's side of the tree."

"He could marry just to lay claim to the property and the title," Shay said. "The wealthy generally don't mind accruing more things."

"This would hardly be a feather in his asset list."

Shay shrugged, and Roan said, "I don't think we should chance it," before going back to his search.

Graham turned to Shay, who merely lifted a brow. "He's right," he added, as Graham began swearing under his breath.

"I'm still calling the island tribunal," Graham insisted. "If I get the damn law overturned, there will be no title inheritance. Kinloch will remain under my governance as long as her people wish me to lead."

"You'll have forty days to campaign, get them all to agree," Shay reminded him.

"And that's the same forty days you'd also have to find a bride," Roan added. "I dinnae think it's a wise bet to divide your energies."

"I need to try. Especially given that even if I was willing to follow the law, there doesn't seem to be anyone eligible to marry anyway."

Both of his friends sighed, then nodded, knowing, as they must have all along, that he wouldn't go down without a fight. To that end, Graham turned on his heel, determined to do whatever it was going to take to set the proceedings in motion. His hand was on the knob, when Roan hooted.

"What do ye know. I think I've found her!"

Graham turned, knowing he had to at least ask. "Found who?"

"Your wife."

"Roan—"

"I expanded my search to the mainland, and, well . . . I had to search a wee bit more widely, but I plugged the McAuley name into Facebook, then backtracked the names to the tree list that Shay has drawn up, and"—he turned his laptop around and gestured with a flourish—"voila! A connection to our own McAuley tree, albeit a wee bit distant one. But it only matters that the connection is there."

Graham wasn't about to take a single step closer, much less look at the poor woman Roan had targeted. He already felt trapped, bound, and tethered by an archaic clan law . . . and he'd grown up knowing about it. He couldn't fathom broaching the subject with someone who knew nothing of him, nothing of

Kinloch, much less of the ridiculous MacLeod-McAuley marriage pact.

Roan looked at him triumphantly. "It just took a little determination."

"How do you know she's linked with our McAuleys? Just becaue her surname—"

"That's the beauty of Facebook, my friend. Her whole family history is documented, mostly as it pertains to their family industry, but there it is," he added with a bit of dramatic flair, squinting back at the screen, tapping some keys, and scrolling some more. "Shay and I already drew up a lineage of everyone on Kinloch, going back several generations, so all I had to do was extend the branches out on those who have left the island over the past, say, fifty years. He spun the laptop back around again so the monitor faced Graham. "There's a direct link. She's the veritable needle in a haystack." He grinned, quite self-satisfied. "And we found her."

A knot fisted tightly in Graham's gut. It felt a lot like a noose, tightening around his neck. "Even if I was willing to remotely consider the idiotic idea of pursuing the poor lass—and I'm most emphatically not—what on earth could I say to her that wouldn't make me sound like an utter loon? I mean, consider it, Roan. Truly. I approach a total stranger, and propose marriage, and if that same well-documented family of hers has even the slightest bit of protectiveness, they'd have me in a white jacket, locked in the nearest tower. And I could hardly blame them."

He turned to Shay, needing the voice of reason he would surely provide. "Tell him this is utter lunacy."

Shay didn't so much as glance at Roan. "You should at least consider it," he said, leaving Graham momentarily speechless. He lifted his hand before Graham could regroup and lecture them both on the rest of the vast and varied reasons why considering it was the very last thing he was about to do. "Think of it as a contract, of sorts. In fact," Shay said, his aristocratic features lighting up in a way they rarely did, "I'll gladly draw up a legal agreement that you can propose with. Approach it like a business deal."

"Because every woman dreams of being proposed to with a legal document," Graham said darkly, unable to truly believe he was even having this conversation. "You two canno' be serious."

But it only took looking at them to prove that they couldn't be more serious.

"You have to at least try," Roan said. "I mean, we did find a candidate. That's a start—more of a solution to all this than we had before."

"You've both gone stark ravers. Mad as hatters."

"If you don't at least try," Shay said, "there will be nothing to stop Iain from taking over Kinloch, if he decides to show up and claim a MacLeod as a bride. Then everything we've all worked for will have been for naught."

"You were right when you said this wasn't just about you," Roan added. "It's no' like we all don't have an ancestor or ten who've had to make far greater sacrifices in the name of clan unity and prosperity."

"Besides," Shay went on, "there's nothing in the law that says you can't dissolve the union at a later time."

"How much later?" Graham asked, still not actually considering following through on it. He was more set on getting the island to turn the law over than ever before. When he was done, not only would he not have to face the ridiculous stipulation, but neither would any MacLeod or McAuley after him. And it would effectively render Iain's claim on Kinloch null and void as well. Win-win, the way he saw it.

"The original documents don't address the topic directly. I suppose because divorce or dissolution of a marriage, especially an arranged one between two clans, wasn't something that happened often, if ever. Especially in our case, where there was too much riding on the union to allow the participants that kind of luxury."

"You're saying none of them ever did? Divorce or dissolve, I mean?"

"I've gone all the way back," Shay said. "Traced it all, looking for loopholes or precedent." He crossed his arms and leaned back in his chair. Then shook his head. "No' a single union ended in anything other than death."

"And no," Roan said archly, "you can't dump her off the cliffs."

"Very funny." Graham shook his head, then swore under his breath. "So you're saying I could dissolve the union, but that I'd be the first in four hundred years to do so. Brilliant."

"Well, you're talking about dissolving the pact itself," Roan said. "Surely if you think our fellow islanders will agree to such a thing, then they'd be equally amenable to you making a mockery of the law all together."

Graham ducked his chin. He'd never once, in all his years, felt his birthright to be a burden. It was a vital, albeit sometimes difficult life path, but a challenging one he'd taken to with dedicated interest rather than complaint. Yet, in that moment, he'd be a liar if he said the mantle didn't weigh heavily on his shoulders . . . and he wished he were merely the scientist farmer he felt himself to be.

"You truly dinnae think they'll agree to abandon the law, do ye?" he said quietly, as the most likely eventuality sunk in and took hold for the first time. "Even though it might mean the very survival of this island?"

Both Shay and Roan shook their heads. "You could try," Shay said.

"But, as I said, you'll be wasting time that could be spent courting one"—Roan shifted the laptop back around and peered at the screen—"Katie McAuley."

"Which isn't a guaranteed win, either," Graham reminded them. "I'm either asking my own clansmen to abandon the auld law, or allow me to make mock of it by finagling a marriage agreement from a woman I've never even met."

"Ye'd hardly be the first in our history to do that," Roan said. "And she's no' exactly hard on the eyes, lad. Have a look. Besides," he said, his mischievous charm surfacing, "you were the one blessed with the MacLeod good looks and charm. We'd place our bets that you'd be able to win her over. Who knows, perhaps it wouldn't be in name only. You would make quite the bonny couple."

Graham scowled at him. He felt far from charming at the moment.

"Go on," Shay urged. "Have a look. Then decide."

"I can even pinpoint an exact location and time for you to meet," Roan said.

"And however would you know that?"

Roan nodded at the screen. "She's chatted about it with some of her girlfriends."

"How is it you're suddenly privy to chats she's had with her mates?"

He sighed and rolled his eyes. "You really should consider using your own computer for something other than research. Perhaps if you had, we'd already have solved this problem." He sighed when Graham merely continued waiting a response. "Facebook," he explained, with exaggerated patience. "It's all there on her wall."

"Her what?" Graham waved a hand. "Truly, don't elaborate. I dinnae want to know. There is work to be done. I can't be dallying about on some online site, trolling for . . ." He shuddered, just thinking about it. "Ualraig is likely rolling in his grave right now and I couldn't blame him. We havnae struggled and fought and worked so hard to have it all hinge on"—he waved his hand in the direction of the laptop—"that. Her."

"Katie McAuley," Roan supplied helpfully, clearly undaunted in the face of Graham's disgust. "She'll be at the St. Agnes chapel Saturday hence. Half past two. I'd strongly suggest you be there a might bit earlier."

"At a chapel?" Shay asked.

"Mm hmm," Roan said briskly, looking back at the screen,

tapping the keys again. A moment later the printer started churning. "Wedding."

"How poetic," Shay said, his mouth curving in a wry grin. "Perhaps witnessing the vows will soften her up some, eh, Graham?"

"You need to talk to her before that," Roan said, pulling the sheet from the printer and handing it to Graham. "After the ceremony people head in all different directions, and there is no telling how closely monitored the reception might be. The church is your best bet."

Graham took the paper without even looking at it. "I canno' believe you're both serious. You truly believe I should travel all the way to the mainland, to—" He glanced down at the map printout Roan had given him, then squinted and looked at it more closely, before looking back at his oldest, dearest, and quite possibly soon to be dearly departed friend. "It says Annapolis. Maryland. Which, the last time I checked, wasn't on the mainland, it was—"

"Oh, but it 'tis," Roan said, his single dimple deepening with obvious glee. "Just happens it's the mainland of America."

"Now you truly have gone off your daft." Graham turned to Shay. "I'm not heading across the pond to chase this"—he shook the paper as fury, along with a good amount of fear, knotted the words in his throat. "This is the most outrageous, preposterous—" He stormed to one end of the office, then back to face them. He had to make them see, make them understand. "We simply have to gain support for abolishing the law. That's all there is to it."

A light tap sounded on the door directly behind Graham. He'd barely moved out of the way when it swung open to reveal the stout form of Eliza McAuley. "Ye've a visitor, just in off the ferry."

"Eliza, it will have to wait," Graham said. "We're in the middle of a very important discussion. We—"

"I've two perfectly good ears, Graham MacLeod. I can hear quite well what's going on in here, and let me tell you," she said, stepping up to him with a fiery light sparking her faded blue eyes to life, "Roan is correct. You'll find little support for your abolishment scheme amongst the elders on this island. Don't think we'll stand by while you attempt to undermine what our ancestors set about creating. We're still here four hundred years later largely due to their foresight." Then she pinched his cheek, as she'd done since he was a wee lad. "Don't think we dinnae love you, because we surely do, spoil you, we do. Doted on ye since ye were but a wee lad, traipsing along after your grandfather. And we're proud of you now, we are. Fiercely so. We raised ye to be the man ye are, have no doubt of it. And are quite content with how you turned out. But you need to be sensitive to balancing your new ways with our auld ones."

"Eliza," he said, working his jaw slightly when she released his face. The pinch wasn't any more enjoyable now than it had been in his youth. "Do you mean to say that you honestly believe it's in our best interests for me to bind myself to what amounts to a complete stranger?"

Eliza's smile was wide and confident. "Darling lad, weren't ye listening to Shay? We've been arranging marriages for quite a long time. I'm no' thinking your argument there will hold much weight."

Had the auld woman had her ear to the door the entire time? "But—"

"But perhaps I should introduce the young man waiting patiently in the outer office. He might be the one to change your mind."

"We don't have time right now to—"

"Oh, but ye'll make the time for this." Eliza had already shifted back and a moment later a tall, blond-haired, nattily dressed, rather dashing-looking fellow entered the room in such a way as to say that he was quite used to making an entrance, and equally confident that folks would react favorably when he did.

"I say," he said, skimming his gaze past each of theirs, then sticking his hand out. "Which of you is Graham MacLeod?"

"That would be me," Graham said, stepping forward. "What can I do for you, Mr. . . ."

The man chuckled, displaying a marquee poster set of teeth a blinding shade of white not often seen on that side of the pond, and extended his hand for a brisk, firm shake. "Iain. Iain McAuley, and I've come to claim my island. And my bride." His grin widened, revealing two perfectly formed dimples. "I daresay, not in that particular order."

Chapter 2

Forty-eight hours later

Graham shifted gears with his right hand as he jerked the steering wheel with his left, guiding his vehicle wildly back to the right side of the road. Which was the wrong side of the road, as far as he was concerned. It had been tricky enough getting the hang of shifting gears wrong-handed, while operating the pedals correctly, sitting on the wrong side of the car, and driving at high speeds on the wrong side of the road. Not a single roundabout to be found, either. The Yanks had been there several hundred years, and still had no idea how to manage traffic in an orderly fashion.

Of course, the traffic he was generally used to navigating through had four stubby legs and a rather sturdy bleat for a horn.

He crossed over a stone and white fence bridge and drove into the historic, older section of Annapolis, Maryland. Though delighted to finally enter a roundabout, with what appeared to be cobblestone streets extending out in key points around it, he counted wrong and exited down Main instead of Duke of Gloucester. He found himself at the waterfront moments later.

As a village, Annapolis was picturesque, and he certainly appreciated the view of the bay. It didn't make him feel entirely at home, what with all the gleaming yachts and soaring schooners moored about. Kinloch didn't favor too many of those. None, actually. But Annapolis was a seafaring village nonetheless and both the layout and the buildings reminded him of home. Certainly the only time he'd been reminded of it since landing at the chaotic airport in Baltimore earlier. So Graham tried to embrace what good there was to be found.

It was a sincerely positive way to look at things, considering his chances of embracing anything—or anyone—else in the near future, were unlikely in the extreme. He shifted in his seat, uncomfortably warm and not a little itchy in his formal wear. Given the lack of planning time, he hadn't many flight options and had known the window for making it to the church before the ceremony would be brief. Hence the quick change in the airport bathroom and the unfortunate substitution of a small, standard transmission economy rental over the larger utility vehicle Roan had promised he'd reserved. There'd been no time to argue, however, so he'd crammed his broad frame into the tiny piece of tin and barreled off.

He'd arrived, mercifully if not surprisingly, still in one piece after the harrowing journey along the highway. The likelihood of a successful mission seemed even more far-fetched than it had when he'd boarded the ferry in Kinloch. He was there to convince a complete stranger to not only leave with him and go to Scotland, but to bind herself to him in matrimony. What sane person would do that?

What had he been thinking, allowing Roan and Shay to convince him to do this?

Iain McAuley's smug, impossibly perfect visage swam through his mind. Again. Graham renewed his efforts. He had to do his best to find a workable solution. Everyone was counting on him and he couldn't let them down. He definitely couldn't return home to face that imposter who would call himself a clan laird as anything other than the rightful successor himself.

And, to do that . . . he needed a bride.

Bloody hell.

He miraculously discovered a connecting street that put him

back on the right path, and there, looming straight ahead, was the tall spire of St. Agnes parish, accurately resembling the one in the picture Roan had printed off the Internet. There were only two other like-size churches in the historic section and he'd passed them both going through the roundabout and getting lost on the waterfront. So it had to be the one. The massive, redbrick building butted right up against the road, leaving no room for parking, although he did spy a sleek black town car, idling at the curb at the far end of the building. He assumed, given the flowers and ribbons tied to the back, that it was the car the newly wedded couple would get in upon exiting the chapel, and though he was tempted to park in front of it in order to get inside the church as quickly as possible, he couldn't risk coming out later to find his car had been towed away.

There wasn't a soul outside the church, which meant the ceremony had probably already started. If he stationed himself in one of the rear pews, he would have a good opportunity to scan all the guests as they filed out behind the bride and groom, and hopefully gain the attention of Miss Katie McAuley.

He turned into a small alleyway just before the church, hoping to find parking, and, to his relief, there was a car park just beyond the stonewalled prayer garden situated at the rear of the church. He managed to make the turn without careening into anything, although an older woman walking a very small bundle of fluff had looked quite alarmed for a moment. She'd all but yanked her little lap rat clear across the road when he'd turned a bit wildly at the last moment. He would have waved an apology, but he was using all his available appendages to maneuver the vehicle safely through the narrow alley and into the car park. He crawled through each and every row of the sizable lot looking for the first available space—which wasn't to be found.

"Who's marrying here, royalty?" he muttered, then finally spied a wee area at a vee in the rows. Grateful for the size of his car for the first time, he managed to nudge the tin can into the narrow slot and exit without doing any further damage to himself or the cars on either side.

He winced a little as he straightened out his limbs and spine, and adjusted what needed adjusting. He patted his *sporran*, which contained his wallet, passport, and the picture of Miss McAuley, then locked the thing up before heading across the paved lot at a fast lope.

He thought about slipping in through a rear door, but not being familiar with the church, with his luck he'd pop in right at the pulpit, or something equally unfortunate. So, after a glimpse up the path that led into the beautifully sculpted prayer garden, he opted to take a fast jog along the cobblestone walkway that led around to the front entrance of the main chapel. But his plan faltered before he could take off—when he heard the swearing.

It was coming from . . . the prayer garden? He took several steps along the hand-laid stone pathway. Weeping he could understand in such a place . . . but swearing? An argument perhaps? Either with God himself or someone mortal, he didn't know. Either way, it wasn't his concern, but he didn't turn back right away. The voice grew louder. Just one. A woman. A very unhappy woman from the sound of it.

He'd never been one to turn his back on another person's troubles. If there was a broken-down car along the lane, he stopped to help get it back up and running. If a visitor to the island got lost out on one of the trails, or . . . anywhere, really, he guided them back to the familiar. Of course, given the entire loop around the island was just shy of ten kilometers, perhaps that wouldn't exactly earn him sainthood, but ignoring a plea for help went against his grain. Only . . . the woman in question wasn't pleading so much as . . . ranting. In fact, he couldn't recall ever hearing a member of the opposite sex use such an . . . inventive string of invectives such as was being issued forth.

He definitely had no business intruding, and no real desire to confront a distraught woman, but found himself pausing another second longer when there was a break in the rant. *Probably to regain her breath,* he thought, somewhat uncharitably, but waited to see if there was another party as equally invested in the . . . conversation . . . as she was. How the other party would respond to such an outpouring, he had no idea, but he doubted it would be received all that well—which meant he'd be put in the position of deciding whether or not the woman could use a little . . . what did the Yanks call it? Backup?

But there was no second voice. And the woman didn't start up again. He let out a little sigh of relief. He needed to get inside the church without further delay. But before he could change direction, a vivid swirl of white satin and lace whipped out past the end of one of the tall, manicured hedgerows. Quite an abundance of it, actually. It disappeared swiftly, as if snatched away.

He was truly torn. If he wasn't mistaken, the ranting woman was the bride. An exceedingly unhappy bride, from the sound of it, which, again, was not his concern. His job was clear and quite tightly focused. Find Katie McAuley, convince her he wasn't a madman, but a man with a problem only she could help him solve. On the interminably long flight over, he'd decided his best bet was to follow Shay's advice and put the entire thing forward to her as a business agreement. In fact, he had the preliminary documents Shay had drawn up, in the car with him.

He was planning to use them only as talking points, a guideline of what he expected, but if she agreed to help him, pretty much everything was open to negotiation. He'd make sure she was adequately compensated. If there was such compensation for legally wedding a complete stranger to keep him from losing his land and his people.

Now Graham was the one swearing, albeit under his breath. There had to be some other way to thwart Iain McAuley's threat. Of course, right that very second, the smarmy horse's arse was quite likely using that genetically blessed visage of his to court any number of available MacLeod lasses. The MacLeods had been quite prolific in their ability to procreate members of the opposite sex . . . unlike the past generation of McAuleys. And while Graham liked to think he had the loyalty of his people locked up tight, it would only take one lass whose head could be turned by that pretty face of Iain's to ruin it all. Given the challenges the young people of Kinloch had finding someone on the island to date, much less marry—someone who wasn't already a relative—aye, but he couldn't imagine it would be all that hard a task for the newly transplanted McAuley.

To Graham the idea that his fate and the future of his homeland lay in the hands of a complete stranger and a young, vulnerable woman was disturbing to say the least.

He purposely didn't contrast and compare how equally disturbing his specific mission was. After all, his goal was nothing if not purely motivated. He had no idea what Iain McAuley's goals or motives were—something Shay and Roan were supposed to be digging into during his absence.

So, the very last thing he should be concerning himself with, was the trials and tribulations of the woman presently stalking about the prayer garden. Except if she was indeed the bride, then the ceremony certainly wasn't taking place at that particular moment, which bought him time to find Katie. Though it was doubtful he could have any meaningful conversation with her regarding his mission—not while crammed into a pew, shoulder to shoulder, hip to hip, with other complete strangers—he could possibly secure a moment of her time once the ceremony was completed.

Which it wouldn't be . . . as long as the bride was out there muttering and swearing. So, he could either go and take advantage of the time stall . . . or offer whatever assistance he could. Those were his options, which were rendered moot a moment later when he heard the first sniffle, followed by a stifled sob.

Bollocks.

Crying women were near the top of the list of things he would rather not deal with. But only a complete cad would leave a bride sobbing behind her own wedding chapel—even if he didn't know her, or a single member of the wedding party personally. Or course, that didn't mean he had to be happy about it. Muttering under his breath about the utter ridiculousness of stupid clan laws, wild goose chases, not to mention crashing the wedding of complete strangers, he strode deliberately up the garden path. At the very least, he could find out what was going to happen next. Perhaps the wedding was to be called off. Then he'd have to find Katie and get her to listen to his proposition while possible chaos reigned supreme inside the church.

That would be so . . . fitting . . . given how ludicrous the whole excursion had been thus far.

He slowed as he came to the hedge where he'd seen the fluff of bridal gown. Exactly what he thought he was going to say, he had no earthly idea, but so what else was new? As it happened, a steadying breath and a straightening of the shoulders was as far as he got in figuring it out. As he stepped around the corner of the hedge, intent on announcing his presence and inquiring if he could be of any assistance, the bride came barreling around the opposite corner . . . and plowed directly into his chest.

"Ooph!" she grunted as she went wheeling back again.

Graham instinctively reached for her to keep her from going over backwards as she tripped over the long train of her dress. He got a fistful of veil and satin, along with her slender arms, but managed to steady her without crushing the garment—or her—completely. She was a wee thing. Though, compared with his somewhat overly tall and broad frame, most women were. Perhaps it was the voluminous dress and veil, but she was virtually lost amidst the yards of satin and tulle.

As soon as he felt she was steadied, he gently released her. "I'm very sorry, I only meant to inquire—"

"Wh-who are you?" she stuttered, her voice raw and thick with tears. He couldn't get a good look at her face, covered as it was by waves of netting. A sparkle of blue and a slash of red lipstick were the only things he could determine. Being quite a bit shorter than he was, he had to crouch a bit to peer through the netting to get to her face. He couldn't see her hair, pinned up as it was beneath the cap of the veil. It looked as if the thing were about to swallow her whole.

"Graham," he responded automatically. "Graham MacLeod. I—are you okay?" Stupid question since she was clearly not okay, but as an invitation to offer assistance, it was all he knew to say.

"Are you a friend of Blaine's?" She looked him up and down, somewhat bewildered. "No, I know everyone Blaine knows. Did he . . . hire you? Or something?" She looked past him.

"Hire? For what?" he asked, looking behind him as well, truly baffled, but seeing nothing but the empty garden path.

"Bagpipes? Riverdancing? I don't know. My ancestry is Scottish and given the getup . . ." She gestured to the tartan he wore wrapped around his hips and over one shoulder. A white linen shirt, along with the black knee stockings, though strained a bit over his muscled calves, were properly tied and tasseled. Heavy soled, hand-tooled black leather shoes, with buckles passed down through the generations, as was the sporran he wore strapped to his waist, completed his formal clan attire.

Life on Kinloch didn't demand an extensive wardrobe. He only dressed up for weddings and funerals, which meant . . . pretty much donning exactly what he was wearing right then. He'd never gotten around to purchasing an actual suit. He'd never been in need of one. Even at university, he'd spent all his time in classrooms, or doing course work in the fields. Of course, at home, all the other clansmen would have been similarly garbed at such an event. Other than his size, he'd have hardly stood out. But there was little he could do about that here.

"I'm afraid I'm no' a piper. Were ye expectin' one?"

"No. Of course not." She laughed shortly, though there was a bit of an hysterical edge to it. "Although, that would certainly cap things off. They had them at my grandfather's funeral recently, and I thought they were the saddest sounding things I've ever heard. So ethereal and echoing through the mists and all."

She lifted her slender shoulders in a shrug and Graham honestly didn't know if she was going to laugh or sob. She did a little of both. "Perhaps they'd be even more appropriate today."

"I'm terrible on the pipes," he told her, tugging his handkerchief from his chest pocket and handing it to her. "Never had an affinity for it. I'm sorry, though. About your grandfather."

She nodded and he thought he detected a bit of a sniffle. "Thank you," she said, and somehow managed to get the square of linen under her veil to dab at her eyes and nose. "He was the best. My grandfather. I loved him very much. He was the only one who understood, who encouraged me to . . ." She trailed off, then shrugged as if unable to continue, sniffling again into his handkerchief.

"I lost my own grandfather, no' too long ago," he confided, not knowing what else to say. "We had pipers there, too. But it was more celebration than dirge." His mouth curved. "We Scots enjoy any excuse for music and spirits. Auld Ualraig would have enjoyed every minute."

He thought he saw a ghost of a smile through the veil. "That would have suited Grandpa far better than the somber affair we had, but God forbid my family do anything that might be taken as unseemly or improper."

"You don't have wakes here?"

"Oh, we do. But my family would not. Funerals aren't celebrations, but very serious occasions, with lengthy, self-important soliloquies detailing all the life achievements—which are meant more to impress than to provide any comfort—and, of course, only restrained emotions are allowed, if at all. There will be no weeping or wailing. Breaking down in public would be considered a serious breach of family protocol."

"Even at a funeral?"

"At any event, for any occasion. It was stunning, really, that they allowed the pipes to be played. But my grandfather had that much stipulated in his will. They didn't want to hang that up in any kind of legal red tape." She lifted a shoulder. "So, at least he was sent off with the music he wanted most to hear echoing through the air."

"Your grandfather, he was of a different stripe? Than your family, I mean. Though no', perhaps, from you."

Her nod was accompanied by another small sniffle. "Different stripe, different drummer. He was that, in spades. He did his best to turn them all on their ear every chance he got. He was the only one who could shake things up. My great-aunt and uncle—his siblings—tried for years—unsuccessfully, thank God—to unseat him from the family board and take away his voting stock. If only he'd been able to control a percentage or two more, he might have really made a difference. At least one that lasted longer than the time it took to bury him."

She crossed over to a low, stone bench, and sank down onto it, heedless of her train, miles of satin, and God knew whatever was underneath that made the skirt span out like Little Miss Muffett.

"I'm sorry," he said, "for reminding you of a sad thing." She was clearly already miserable enough.

She shook her head. "No. He's exactly who I should be thinking about. He didn't want us railroaded into this anymore than we did. If he were still here, maybe I'd have the strength to do the right thing." She followed that with a very unladylike, self-deprecating snort. "I should have the strength regardless."

"Us?"

She lifted her gaze. "What?"

"You said us. And we. Do you mean your fiancé isn't happy with the planned nuptials either?"

She dropped her chin, then shook her head. "No. No, he's not."

Graham didn't think he'd ever seen a more miserable person. He didn't know her, but wished there was something he could do to lighten her load. "I'm sorry you're upset. No bride should be sad on her wedding day." He realized the utter hypocrisy of what he'd just said, given what he was trying to accomplish.

"I appreciate the sentiment," she said.

"I meant it," he said truthfully. "It should be the most joyous of days, entered into willingly and happily."

"If only life were that simple."

"Aye," he said, thinking of his own immediate future, more than hers. "By any chance . . . do you know Katie McAuley?"

"I—what?" she said, frowning in confusion, then looked at him more closely. "Yes, of course I do." She paused for a moment, then asked, her tone far more wary, "Who did you say you were again?"

"Graham MacLeod. I've come quite a long way to meet her."

"You have? Why?"

Graham felt like a cad for bringing it up. But, for once, she was focused on him, and not so much on her own worries. Perhaps the distraction would give her the needed time to pull herself together. Or at least make him feel less guilty for badgering her when she clearly didn't need any more of that in her life. He surmised her family was behind the wedding. He knew a little about the pressure family could bring to bear. In his case, the "family" extended to every man, woman, child, and sheep on Kinloch.

"Does she know you?"

He looked to her again, telling himself he needed to keep his own obligations in mind. "No, she's never heard of me." *What the hell*, he thought, and went with the truth. "I've come to ask her to marry me."

The bride gave a short, spluttering laugh that ended with an alarming choking noise, prompting Graham to sit next to her. Gently, but firmly he patted her on the back. "Careful, now. Careful. Ye've a big moment ahead of you."

Wrong thing to say.

She immediately withdrew and shifted away from him. "Yes. It's just the wrong big moment."

He thought she was going to dissolve into sobs again, or start another rant, but instead, she lifted her head and looked back at him. "Why do you want to marry a woman you've never met? Who has never met you?"

"It's . . . complicated. It has to do with our dual ancestry and a ridiculous ancient clan law that I'm forced to abide by if I want to succeed my grandfather as MacLeod laird."

"But she's a McAuley."

"Aye. We're destined to always be joined. Four hundred years runnin'." He lifted a hand. "I know, I sound like a lunatic—standin' here in full clan regalia, lookin' to propose to a complete stranger. Trust me, no one is more aware of that fact than I. But I've no choice other than to try. Too many people are countin' on my success, and to do anything less would be a disservice to their loyalty and faith. Both to me and our joined ancestors. Beyond that, it's a long, tedious story. And, to be sure, ye've better things to be doing at the moment than listenin' to me."

"I'd like to hear the story."

"Shouldn't you be gettin' inside the chapel?"

"I should be runnin', screamin' from the chapel," she said, lightly mocking his accent, which made his lips quirk, and hers too, he thought, as it appeared the red slash beneath the veil had curved a little.

"Actually," she said, gesturing to herself and their surroundings, "I guess, in a way, I have. Halfway, at least."

"What's keepin' you from runnin' the rest of the way? In, or out? Your fiancé, is he a bad sort? Are you two ill matched, then? Is that the worry?"

"Blaine?" She laughed as if the very thought was unfathomable. "No, far from it. He's the perfect man. With the perfect pedigree, from the perfect family."

Graham was heartened by the news that she wasn't about to legally bind herself to a scoundrel. Though why it mattered to him at all, he couldn't have said.

"Both our families came over on the Mayflower," she continued. "And it seems we haven't managed to get away from sailing ships or each other, ever since." She smiled then. "Perhaps it's like your clan law thing. Only, in my case, it's more of a clan curse."

"In what way?" he asked, curious to hear her take on arranged marriage, given that's what it sounded like.

She waved a dismissive hand, and promptly got it tangled up in her veil. He helped her extricate her slender fingers but it took a bit longer to get the netting untangled from her diamond ring.

"That's . . . quite a stone," he said, trying to gently work the mesh free.

She held her hand up, as if to admire the setting. "It would have been unseemly to give me anything less obscene."

He paused in his ministrations and glanced at her, but could only see the barest hint of her chin as she'd averted her gaze once again. "I dinnae understand your meaning. I thought women loved diamonds."

"Yes, of course. Women are supposed to swoon over the three Cs." When he merely stared at her, she went on. "Cut, carat, and clarity. Me, I could give a rat's patootie."

He grinned before he could check the reaction, but she waved off his impoliteness, which just tangled her hand all over again. She tugged it free from his grasp. "Don't worry about it. I'll . . . figure it out later."

He rather liked having her hand in his, something he wasn't aware of until his own were free and he couldn't seem to figure out what to do with them. He thought about that, a slender hand, delicate fingers adorned in diamonds, clasped in his, then glanced up at the church, and thought about the unsuspecting woman who waited inside.

"You're really just going to up and propose?" she asked, following his gaze.

He jerked his gaze back to her, then to the ground, then finally lifted a shoulder. "I'll introduce myself, explain my reason for being here, but . . . in the end, yes. I mean, it's more a business dealing, no' a true life commitment. But a commitment all the same, for whatever duration. Of course, I'd make the sacrifice worth her while, in whatever way I possibly could. All things considered . . ." He drifted off. Talking about it made the whole mission sound all the more ridiculous and hopeless. But one thing hadn't changed. He still had to try.

"How well do ye know her?" he asked, glancing sideways at his bench companion.

"Are you asking me to tell you how best to get her to agree to your . . . proposition?"

"Never mind. That's no' fair, and ye've certainly got more pressing issues to deal with." He started to rise. "I should leave you to them. I'm sorry I intruded."

She impulsively grabbed his arm and tugged him back down on the stone bench. "Don't leave. Yet."

He looked at that same pale hand, still tangled in her veil, clutching his arm, and felt something clutch inside him. Very likely it was his heart constricting at the thought of another woman's hand, similarly garbed, doing the same thing forty days hence.

She pulled her hand away. "Sorry. I just . . . I don't want to be alone with my thoughts quite yet." She paused, then looked at him. "Do you mind?"

He looked up in time to see, more clearly than he had, the sparkling blue eyes hidden behind the layers of white tulle. They reminded him of the water on the sound off Kinloch west, on a cloud-free day. "No. I dinnae mind," he said, and realized as he said it, that he spoke the truth. "Not a'tall."

"Thank you."

"You're welcome." They stared at each other for a beat longer, then another one, before she finally turned her face away, and stared at some unknown point in the garden beyond. He turned his head, too, and gave himself a stern, silent lecture on getting his mind back on the matter at hand . . . and off the compelling woman sitting next to him. The woman who was about to be married. Unhappily, but that only made the strange, sudden attraction even more impossible. Not to mention he was there to coax another woman entirely into being his bride.

He made a small sound and she briefly rested her veil-wrapped hand on his wrist, before pulling it back again. "I'm sorry," she said.

"For?"

"You're clearly no more happy in your stated mission than I am in mine. Seems we're both here for reasons having to do with duty, rather than heart."

"Aye, 'tis true." He covered her hand with his, and pressed before she could pull it away, though he couldn't have said what, specifically, compelled him to do it. Perhaps it was simply the need to be in direct contact with the one person who could seemingly comprehend his fiendish dilemma.

"Is there any other way?" she asked.

He shook his head. "There is a time frame stipulated in the law."

"How much time do you have?"

"To be lawfully wed? A little more than four weeks hence."

He heard her slight intake of breath. "Wow."

"Indeed."

She slid her hand from beneath his as they sat quietly for a few moments. Then she said, "How long do you have to stay married? I mean, if you're proposing as a business arrangement, you can't mean to stay married."

"I've a friend, back on the island—Kinloch, where I'm from— looking into that very thing. I wouldn't tie anyone down longer than absolutely necessary. Of course."

"Of course," she echoed.

Silence once again descended between them—which he broke by abruptly announcing, "To make matters worse, there is another contender to take my place."

She looked at him and he could see her eyes widen. "He's coming here to ask the same thing?"

"No, no. He's McAuley—the direct heir to the title from the other side. He's back home, wooing any single MacLeod lass who might stray 'cross his path. Given his gene pool is quite favorable, as is his job title and the trust fund he landed at birth, not to mention there are far more available MacLeod lasses than there are McAuleys—of which there are none—I'm thinkin' he willnae face much of a challenge."

"Oh."

"Indeed."

"So . . . it's something of a race, then, to the altar."

Graham sighed. That sounded so . . . pathetic. "Aye. I suppose that's the truth of it." How in bloody hell had he found himself in that place? It was mortifying. He just wanted to go home. Back to his fields, his crops, his lab.

Her hand moved to his again, and she squeezed. "I'm rooting for you."

For some reason, that depressed him further. "Thank you. I'll take all the positive support I can get." He covered her hand with his own again, and met her eyes as best as he could, given the layers of veil between them. "I'll return the favor."

"I don't know what, exactly, I'd ask you to root for."

"Well, I can either escort you inside and see you safely wed . . . or you could take my rented motor car and make your escape complete."

She laughed. "Don't tempt me."

He glanced at the church again. "Will no one come to your aid? You've been out here for a wee spell. Surely someone inside is concerned for your welfare."

She lifted her gaze to the church and held it steadily. "I warned them not to, or I would bolt. I'm sure they're watching from one of the windows, stunned I had the temerity to do this much."

"Are you such a timid mouse then? Because you don't seem it."

He saw the red lips curve in earnest. "Thank you. I think that's the nicest thing you could have said to me. I'm not a mouse. At least not in here." She tapped her head. "Or here." She laid her veil-wrapped hand against her chest. "I couldn't do my job well if I was. And, heaven knows, I'm very good at my job." She sighed, not sounding particularly thrilled about that fact.

"But ye don't make a stand when it's family. Is that it?"

She looked at him, though what she could see through all that netting, he had no idea. "No," she said. "I don't. Can't. No, that's not true. I could. But I don't. It's . . . complicated." She continued holding his gaze. "But something tells me you, of all people, might understand where I'm coming from."

"Aye," he said quietly, thinking they were both idiots for allowing themselves to get into such a quandary. But what else was he to do? Perhaps she was facing the similar lack of options. "I believe I do." He looked up toward the stained glass arched windows of the church that looked out over the garden. If there were family members inside, watching her . . . he wondered what they thought of him. His appearance. Not to mention their conversation, complete with hand-holding. Perhaps the fact that they were sitting and talking, which meant she wasn't running away as yet, was enough to keep them at bay.

Very abruptly, she slipped her hand from his and stood. "This is silly. Sitting out here being 'a petulant sulk' as Cricket so kindly called me, is only delaying the inevitable."

He stood. "Who is Cricket?" And why is it inevitable, he wanted to ask. But did not.

"Blaine's mother." The bride gave a small shudder. "Trust me when I say she's not remotely chirpy, so I don't know where the nickname came from. I'm just thankful I never got saddled with one. One that stuck."

He tilted his head and folded his arms. "Now you have to tell me."

"Tell you what?"

"Which ones didnae stick?" He held up one hand, briefly. "Before you accuse me of mockery, please be aware that we in the U.K. invented the hideously unfortunate nickname."

She folded her arms, heedless of the veil she was crushing, her tone amused when she spoke. "I'll tell you mine if you tell me yours."

"I don't believe I mentioned that I had one. I was speaking on behalf of my countrymen, and all our forebears who bore the brunt of such names as Squibs, Blinker, Duckie. Those are merely in my immediate branch of the auld tree."

She couldn't entirely stifle the snicker.

"See?" he said. "Your turn."

"Mine aren't nearly so . . . auspicious. I have a number of names in addition to my surname, so plenty to play with. Among them Katherine and Georgina. Family names."

"Both beautiful."

She smiled. "Thank you. Could definitely have been worse. But the nicknames just didn't suit." She sighed, then said, "Mostly various forms of Gigi and Kiki, all trotted out early on during my childhood and tried on for size."

"Hardly torturous, but how did you keep them from sticking?"

"I don't recall, actually, but my grandfather told me I simply refused to answer to them."

"Smart and confident, even as a child. Good for you."

"Smart, perhaps." She glanced at the church, and he could see a slight slump in her spine, even as she squared her shoulders. "As for the rest, well, I'm apparently still working on that part." She looked back at him and he could see the red lips curving more broadly, though her eyes were in shadows behind the tulle. "I should get inside—before I've used up whatever leverage I have left. I'm sure I'll need it just to get through the rest of today."

"Are you certain?"

"I've never been less certain of anything in my life. But I am certain my life will be made exponentially more miserable if I don't. And I don't want to hurt Blaine. He's counting on me. And, this way, I'm in some position of power." She took a step away from him and fluffed out her skirts, then straightened her veil, finally managing to extricate her ring finger from the netting. "Even if it's power I have absolutely zero interest in wielding," she added, more to herself, than to him.

She took another step, shook out a few more folds, then turned back to him. The sun chose that moment to shift out from behind a small cloud and beam directly upon her. She was radiant, bathed in the soft yellow glow. "You're a beautiful bride," he said. Truly the most stunning vision he'd ever seen. He felt that odd clutch again. "I wish there was more I could offer."

She stared at him. "You've offered more than you know."

Before he could respond—not that he had any idea what that response would have been—she turned on her heel and fled. Toward the church, he noted. And wondered why her choice depressed him so.

Selfishly, it meant the service would go forward, and he'd have ample chance to meet up with Katie and at least beg a moment of her time. The fact that a complete stranger was about to tie herself to a man she clearly didn't love, for reasons that had nothing to do with her own wishes . . . none of his business. Especially given he was there to embark on the very same business.

He'd never want anyone so unhappily bound to him. No matter the circumstance—which led him to decide, right then and there, that if Katie McAuley couldn't wholeheartedly agree to the business deal he was prepared to offer, viewing it as only such, then that would be the end of that. He'd have to find another way to thwart Iain's threat to his home, and his people.

He heard the loud reverberation of the chapel's pipe organ ring out the beginning of Mendelssohn's wedding march and he sprinted around to the front of the church. He slipped inside behind the bride, just as she began her walk down the aisle. His heart sank, but he shook off the disconcerting feeling and edged as quietly as possible into the end of the last pew once she'd made her way down the aisle. All eyes were on the bride. No one noticed the man in the kilt. He pulled the crumpled photo of Katie McAuley out of his sporran, and forced his gaze away from the bride and down to the picture in his hands. He needed to find her and start focusing on what he planned to do next.

He unfolded the photo . . . and frowned at the face smiling back at him. Blond tendrils were blowing wildly about her face, as were those of the brunette and redhead mates she was clutched between. All three women were laughing, smiling, as if enjoying a great lark. Or simply the company they were in, regardless of location or event. He couldn't fathom feeling so utterly carefree. Or so happy, for that matter. It was both an unsettling discovery, and a rather depressing one. He enjoyed the challenge of his work, but . . . was he happy? The carefree smiling kind of happy? He knew the answer to that. What he wanted to know was when, exactly, had he stopped having fun? He could hear Roan's voice ring through his consciousness, as if he were an angel—or more aptly, a devil—perched upon his tartaned shoulder. *"When did you ever start?"*

The pastor began intoning the marriage rites, and Graham's gaze was pulled intractably back to the woman standing in front of the altar. She turned to her betrothed and he lifted the veil. Graham felt himself drawn physically forward, the crumpled photo in his hands forgotten, as he shifted on his feet and tried his best to—finally—see her face. It was only natural, he told himself, to want to see what she looked like, after talking with her in the garden.

But why he was holding his breath, he had no earthly idea.

She turned her head, just slightly, and he swore she looked directly at him. His heart squeezed. Hard. Then stuttered to a stop. Only this time he knew exactly why. He looked down at the picture in his hand, and forced himself to draw in air past the tightness in his chest. He distantly heard the pastor urge everyone to be seated. One by one, everyone did.

Everyone, that was, except him.

He turned over the wedding program that had been handed to him as he'd entered the church. He looked at the lengthy name engraved on the front, then lifted his gaze to her. "It's you," he declared, his deep voice echoing loudly, reverberating around the soaring chapel ceiling. "Katherine Elizabeth Georgina Rosemary McAuley." Katie. The nickname that had stuck. He held up the photo, as if that would explain everything, while he stood there, acutely dumbfounded. His mind raced as fast as his heart, as everything suddenly made perfect sense. And no sense at all.

He lifted the photo higher, stabbing it forward, as if making a claim. And perhaps he was. He felt driven by something unknown, a force he could neither put name nor logic to. If he were honest, it had begun outside, in the garden. It was something both primal and primeval, driven by what could only be utter lunacy. Because clearly, he'd lost whatever he'd had left of his mind. Yet that didn't stop him from continuing. In fact, he barely paused to draw breath.

"You're meant to be mine," he declared, loudly, defiantly, to the collective gasp of every man, woman, and child lining each and every pew. He didn't care. Because he'd never meant anything more in his entire life. And he hadn't the remotest idea why. Yet it was truth; one he'd never been more certain of. It was as if all four hundred years of MacLeods willfully and intently binding themselves to McAuleys was pumping viscerally through his veins.

Clan curse, indeed.

Chapter 3

Graham's declaration rang out inside the chapel, echoing and reverberating, then arrowing straight through her—as if the angels and cherubs painted inside each of the pocketed, celestial domes above their heads, and sculpted atop the pillars that lined the interior of the old church, had all taken up playing their trumpets and strumming their harps at the same time—creating a cacophony inside her head . . . and heart.

Katie stared, her gaze locked on the wild-eyed man who was not proclaiming his wish to marry her as part of some family obligation, but staking his outright ownership of her. She should have laughed. Hysterically. Because her life was nothing if not ridiculous already, so why not have a mad Scot turn her A-list attended, excruciatingly planned-to-perfection, media-and-marketing-coup-of-the-century sham wedding into utter chaos? It was certainly the high point for her.

"Katie?"

Blaine gripped her arms, jerking her gaze from the kilted man who, not ten minutes earlier had unknowingly offered up a bizarre, yet tantalizing option to the immediate future she'd thought her only choice. Blaine held her gaze, but not her attention. Her thoughts were a complete scramble. Her stomach was a clutched knot, and her heart threatened to beat straight through the hand-beaded satin and Irish lace presently binding her chest and waist so tightly she'd been short of breath since being cinched into it.

She was very much afraid she might throw up. In fact, she wanted to throw up. Surely that would make her feel better. Or pass out. *Yes*. Passing out, quite dramatically, in front of the entire church assembly, would be perfect. Not to mention a clever way of getting out of dealing with any of it. At least right that very second, anyway.

Except hadn't she spent the past six months getting out of dealing with any of it? Hell, if she were honest—and why not, better late than never—her whole life had been an exercise in avoiding confrontation and doing whatever it took to keep the people in her life happy. And by people, she meant family. Hers, and Blaine's.

"Katie." Blaine shook her, albeit lightly. He would never harm her. Never. Poor, sweet, adorable, and adoring Blaine.

She forced herself to look at him directly, to focus. And struggled to find the words she knew—*knew*—she had to say. And had said, so many times, inside her own head, too afraid of subverting her entire life to contemplate saying them out loud. But being brave on the inside didn't count.

Hence her standing there, inside the chapel her family and Blaine's had attended since its earliest inception several hundred years earlier, in a wedding dress she hadn't picked out, carrying flowers she didn't know the names of, about to marry a man she adored above all others and had loved her entire life . . . like a brother. Not a husband.

"I'm so sorry, Blaine. I can't marry you." She held her breath, her pulse drumming so loudly she couldn't tell if she'd really said that out loud, or just imagined she had. Again.

He frowned, and looked confused, which meant she'd finally gone and done it. *Oh my God*. She tensed—froze really—but there was no going back. No taking it back. Even if she wanted to—which, of course, she didn't. She just had to figure out how to survive the next five seconds without having a heart attack or stroking out.

She kept her gaze pinned on Blaine and only Blaine, carefully keeping even so much as a glimpse of anyone else—especially the anyone elses presently crowding the front pews of the church—out of her range of vision. Just Blaine. Other than her grandfather, he'd been the only safe haven she'd ever had, the one port in the storm that was a constant in both their lives. The one person she could always trust, who would always be steady. Rock steady. Only she'd just cast herself off that steady rock, hadn't she? And her grandfather was gone. She was out to sea, with no port . . . and a very big storm brewing that was only moments from crashing over her.

"I'm am sorry," she whispered, never meaning the words more. "I can't. We can't. You know that, right?"

"I don't know anything of the sort. Katie, what's going on? Who is that guy?"

She had no answer for that, of course. Other than his name, she had no idea who he was. A lunatic, clearly.

And a port. If she dared.

But didn't leaping from steady rock to utter madness make her the lunatic? Clearly. Though who could blame her? Other than every member of her family, and Blaine's. Yet, given what she'd had to contend with, was it any surprise, she was having some kind of psychotic breakdown? It wasn't that farfetched—was it?—she'd finally hit her breaking point on her wedding day, standing in front of the pastor, God, and every single important person in her life, his life . . . and most importantly, because it was always most important, her parents' lives? Surely that was the case. What else could explain the fact that she was teetering on the brink of ruining the rest of her life . . . and possibly that of the only man she'd ever really loved.

"You know I adore you, Blaine. But we—I—can't do this."

"We don't have a choice," he whispered furiously and his grip grew surprisingly firm.

"Have you been working out?" she asked, shocked by his display of strength. "Did you finally call that personal trainer I told you about? Because, that's a pretty impressive—"

"*Katie*," he said, shaking her. "What in the hell has gotten into you?"

She was losing it. Rapidly. *Stop blabbering. Focus.*

"You know we shouldn't marry each other. I mean, we're supposed to, destined to since birth, blah blah blah. But we really can't. It's too much. Too far."

"We've talked about that," he ground out. "Endlessly. And we agreed—"

"You agreed," she corrected. "And I . . . was too afraid to go against you. Or, more to the point, them." She twitched her veiled head in the direction of the front pew. She could hear their guests getting restless, the murmuring growing. Time was running out. "I just want to be happy. You should want to be happy."

"Katie, we'll make it work. We always do. No one else could possibly understand what it's like for me—for us. You're the only one I can trust. Could ever trust."

She'd never seen him look so intense, so . . . well, virile. It was kind of hot, actually. Only she knew better than to let that affect her. Way better. "I'm not the only one," she said, hoping her gaze was as intense, as pointed. "And you know that. It's time everyone else did, too. There is another way. For you."

His eyes went from furious to terror-filled. "Don't," he said, more order than plea. "You wouldn't."

"Of course I wouldn't. But you should. You have to. So you can start living your life. I want to start living mine."

His expression turned heartbreakingly bleak when he seemed to realize she wasn't kidding. "Don't do this," he pleaded, his voice barely above a whisper. "I'll make it work, Katie. We will. I'll make your happiness my main priority."

"That's just it, Blaine. I want you to make *your* happiness your main priority. And that means not marrying me. If you really love me, really want me to be happy, then do this. For yourself. For me. Whatever it takes. This is ridiculous. You know that, right? They can have everything else they want. But they can't have this. It's too much. The price is too big. For both of us."

"But . . . there's a way. I know there is," he said, clearly panicked. "Katie, come on, it's too late now. We're here. It's all set. We have to follow through, then we can . . . figure things out."

"That's just it, it's not too late. And now is the only time we can fix this. I have to take a stand. I know I should have a long time ago. I'll regret forever doing this to you here, now, you know that, right? I didn't plan this. Any of this." Truer words had never been spoken. She looked past Blaine to his best man, Tag, who had gone completely pale, then back to the man who had been her best friend since birth. "We're allowed to be happy, Blaine. I don't know what—or who—will make me happy. But you do." She looked pointedly at the man standing behind him, who, by all rights, should be standing where she stood. "I want the chance to find out. Right now is your chance—which means this is our chance. Possibly our only chance."

"Katie, please," he begged, breaking her heart. "Don't. Don't ruin this. Don't ruin *me*. If you've ever loved me"—he framed her face with his hands—"you can't do this," he said, his tone somehow fierce and shattered at the same time. "I won't allow it."

To his shock, and certainly to hers, she smiled. It was as if a sudden, otherworldly calm descended over her. Her heart slowed, her mind cleared—like she was having an out of body experience and was floating overhead with the angels and cherubs, looking down on the travesty that her wedding day had become. Had always been, actually. "You don't get to allow or disallow. No one does. Just me. If you do trust me, then believe me when I say I'm doing us both a favor."

She turned then and faced their gathered families and invited guests . . . along with a certain uninvited one. She purposely looked beyond the front pews, where her parents, and Blaine's, were making noises that indicated her moment to finally stand up for herself was going to be very short-lived if she didn't act swiftly. She honestly had no idea what they would do, as she'd never risked finding out before. There always was too much at stake. Or so it had seemed. Funny, how standing there, with her own life and her very future at stake, it felt, for the first time, like hers was the more important one.

She looked past her family, and Blaine's, and found Graham. She spoke directly to him. "Did you mean what you said?" Her voice sounded far more steady and confidant than she felt. Her gaze remained locked on the Scot, who was easily head and shoulders bigger than pretty much everyone in the room. Her port, she thought, and felt oddly steadied by it. By him. She could certainly do worse.

He was still wielding some crumpled piece of paper, like a proclamation, in front of him. "Aye," he stated, that deep, gravelly burr ringing clearly and quite commandingly throughout the chapel, despite the fact that the hushed silence of a moment before had already begun erupting in small, little volcanoes of chatter . . . with the biggest eruption surging to the surface in the front row as her parents stood and took their first steps toward her.

"Then I accept."

Vesuvius McAuley-Sheffield blew approximately one second later as the entire chapel rose to its feet, as one, and looked ready to descend upon her. She went into survival mode, working off some instinct she'd never known she had. It was purely self-preservation, but when had she ever considered that an option?

When she finally put her own self first.

She turned to Blaine and slid the engagement ring off her finger. "You know I love you," she said, quietly and fiercely, as she pushed it into his palm. Then she stepped past the gape-mouthed Blaine, and thrust her ridiculously over-the-top bouquet straight into Tag's chest. She lowered her voice so only he could hear her. "You've officially caught the bouquet. You'd better stand by him and love him the best way you know how. Or I'm going to come back and personally kick your ass."

She turned back to Blaine, grabbed his face in her palms and kissed him soundly on the mouth. "I love you, Sheffie. More than life."

"Mac," he choked out, using his own childhood endearment for her, tears swimming in his beautiful brown eyes. "Don't leave me."

She held his cheeks more tightly. "You don't need me. You only need you. Now go, be happy, dammit."

Her mother rushed toward the stairs as Katie turned, a rather terrifying expression carved into her already rigid features. Her father was right behind, looking equal parts exceedingly angry and deeply disappointed. He'd had plenty of experience with both of those expressions where Katie was concerned—where all the women in his life were concerned, actually.

Well, she was about to give him one less woman to concern himself with.

She made a quick sidestep and danced around the pulpit. "Sorry, Father Flaherty, I really, truly am. Say prayers for me. I'm going to need them!"

Her Scot—at least he wasn't anyone else's—had worked his way quite easily through the guests thronging into the aisle and had made his way to the base of the deep blue carpeted steps leading up to the altar. She hadn't noticed, in the prayer garden, how big he truly was. So tall. And brawny. She might have thought it a trick of the plaid that cascaded over one shoulder, only he made everyone in the growing chaos surrounding him look small and ineffectual by comparison. There had to be something to that.

"Katie," he said, his voice rising easily above the din. He reached for her.

Without a second's hesitation, she launched herself off the top step, knowing he would catch her. And he did.

"Oh!" she gasped, as strong arms closed instantly around her. He shifted her into his arms, dress cascading over his arm, as if they'd rehearsed it dozens of times, to get the timing so perfectly right. If it weren't for the abject terror starting to creep in around the defiance and righteous moxie she'd been filled to overflowing with the past few minutes, she might have felt positively princess-like. "We need to get out of here," she whispered fervently. "Fast."

"Wait just one minute there!" Her father, sounding superior and autocratic. Like a king, ruling his subjects, expecting total obeisance—or off with their heads. He'd had lots of practice with that.

To her surprise, her rescuer actually paused. "No, no! Keep going. This is my only chance." She looked up at the length of chiseled jaw, then he looked down, and their eyes met, close up, and just like that, the rest of the world fell away.

"You are a woman grown, aye? Of legal age to decide for yourself your course of action?"

"You don't understand, it's . . . complicated. So very, very complicated. I need you to get us out of here, before—"

"Katherine Elizabeth, what on earth do you think you're doing? Do you realize what you've done? You've made a spectacle of yourself. And of us. That's what you've done." Her mother had somehow managed to wedge her svelte, size two frame squarely in front of her daughter's Scot. How a woman who was easily a full foot and a half shorter—even in her one-of-a-kind, Ferragamo, hand-dyed satin pumps—than the man presently towering over her, managed to look down her perfect, aquiline nose at him, Katie would never be able to figure out. Her mother was a force of nature. Rather like a tsunami. Or a monsoon. Sweeping in, blowing down, and drowning anything that got in her path.

"Now you'll kindly get back up on that dais, apologize—profusely—to everyone here, and proceed with this wedding. I'll make certain none of this . . . incident . . . remains digitally viable with any of our photographers."

She turned slightly and raised her voice. "If anyone here even thinks about using their phones, or breathes a word of this outside this chapel . . . well, surely that's not something anyone has any interest in doing." She looked back to her daughter. "We can salvage this. *I* can salvage this. But it will take some doing. Now, for heaven's sake, let's get back to business here." She clapped her hands together, as if expecting time to spin backwards and all to be as it was five minutes prior. Katie wasn't entirely sure her mother couldn't do just that.

"You'll kindly use a different tone when speaking to your

daughter," Graham quietly informed Mrs. McAuley, making the room gasp collectively. "She's made her decision, and while I understand your disappointment, you've naught to do but accept it. Now, if you don't mind. We 've a plane to catch."

"A plane!" her father blasted. He was more thunderstorm than monsoon. Lots of wind and booming noises. Occasionally incinerating things with blistering bolts of lightning. "If you think you are taking her out of this chapel, much less out of this town, you are—"

"Going to be late," Graham replied, seemingly unfazed— which was shocking all on its own, but then, he wasn't from here. He had no idea who he was dealing with.

"Graham," she said, keeping her voice low. "You rock in ways you don't even know. But we might want to move it along, before—"

"How could you! How dare you humiliate my darling son!"

Mrs. Sheffield gets here, Katie finished silently, somehow managing to stifle the deep, shuddering sigh that accompanied the thought, along with the much desired eye roll. Katie was a master of the stifled eye roll. Along with the imaginary foot stomp, finger-down-the-throat gesture, forefinger pistol, and the ever popular middle finger salute. "Graham, really, we have to—"

"I'm gettin' the general idea," he said, his words quiet and meant only for her.

Something about that accent did all kinds of delicious, tingly things to her insides. Possibly enhanced by the fact that she was being held in his rather brawny arms, and could feel his heart beating just below her cheek. In fact, were he to turn, and lower his mouth just a scant few inches . . . she could find out what those lips of his tasted like.

Her own parted, without permission, then snapped shut again as his gaze lowered to hers. His dark pupils punched wide, swallowing up that crystalline gray, and broadcasting what looked like a very similar desire.

Oh. Oh my. Her heart fluttered, then she shut that down, too. *So inappropriate, Katie!* It was probably nothing more than a

panic reaction to the pandemonium she was in the midst of—
that she'd created. But still, no point in compounding things
further.

Oh God, she thought, as her mind—and heart—raced ahead
again. *I'm really doing this!* Reality started to crash in, along
with the rest of the wedding party and most of the guest list. It
was when the first flash went off that Graham finally took action.

"Pardon me, ma'am," he said, ever so politely, as he gently
but firmly bullied his way, shoulder and kilted hip first, past her
gaping mother and furious father, past a mottled-faced Cricket,
past the wedding photographers and videographers, who Katie
prayed weren't the ones using the flash. They'd never work in
Annapolis again if that were the case, and were already going
to be out a tidy sum for the event.

It should have been more difficult, but somehow Graham
had them at the soaring chapel doors seemingly seconds later. It
wasn't until he pushed through them, launching them into the
streaming sunlight and fresh air, that she realized she'd been
holding her breath the entire time. She was gulping in air like a
beached fish.

"Hold on," he instructed.

Like she was going to do anything else. Her dress wasn't exactly made for expedient transportation on foot. "Where are
you going?" she asked, as he ducked left.

"My car is in the park, in the rear."

"Limo. Curbside. Much closer."

"But—"

Just then the doors burst open behind him, purging a throng
of satin- and suit-clad people from the inner sanctum of the
chapel.

"Limo it 'tis," he said, and carried her down the stone steps
with both a speed and agility that, at any other time, she'd have
paid proper homage to, but at that moment, just hung on for
dear life and prayed they made it to the limo in one piece. "Sir,"

Graham shouted at the driver. "If you could be so kind as to start the car!"

The driver, who was leaning against the far side of the car, smoking a cigarette glanced up, his eyes widening in surprise— which wasn't all that odd, considering the spectacle they were making. His eyes widened farther as he spied the throng descending behind them.

"Right now, if you dinnae mind," Graham shouted, as he closed in on the rear, curbside door.

The driver finally snapped to attention, automatically moving around the back of the car, ostensibly to open their door, as he was trained to do.

"I have it," Graham assured him, as he held Katie more tightly with one arm. He fished his other hand out from the sea of streaming satin and lace to grapple with the door handle. "Just drive. Due haste, man."

Katie wasn't sure if it was the accent, the outfit, or both, but the driver sketched a quick salute and dashed for the driver's side door. "You can put me down," she told him. "I can manage the dress, if you'll just—"

But he'd gotten the door open by then, and after a quick look past her shoulder, turned and all but stuffed her into the back seat. "Sorry," he said, clambering in behind her. And there was a lot of him to clamber.

She was sorry the sudden waterfall of veil that flipped down over her face prevented her from getting a glimpse of what he wore under that tartan. Not that she'd been thinking about that. Of course she hadn't. She'd just run out of a church. On her wedding day. Creating chaos and leaving her poor, beloved Blaine behind to handle God knew what. The very last thing she had any business thinking about, even in the most abstract of terms, was whether her partner in crime was going commando under his kilt.

She fought her way clear of the veil as the driver peeled away from the curb, sending her sprawling toward Graham, who was getting his own self situated on the seat next to her and couldn't brace himself for the collision.

"Oh!" she gasped, planting her hands on his chest—his broad, well-muscled chest. How was it, back in the garden, she'd thought him a kind of gentle giant, albeit a bit of an odd soul as well, who'd just happened across an angry bride and tried his best to console her? Because the man who'd stood up inside her family church and loudly proclaimed her to be his, who'd caught her in his arms, then boldly confronted her parents before making his way through an angry throng, leaping down old stone steps and carrying her swiftly to their escape chariot . . . wasn't anything like that guy in the garden.

"Sorry," she said, trying to extricate herself, but her veil was hopelessly caught and knotted on the giant sword he had pinned to his plaid, keeping the tartan from slipping off his shoulder. Like it would dare.

"Stop squirming for a wee moment," he instructed, trying to blow the netting off his face. "Just—"

She reached up and tugged the whole thing off her head, sending a number of pins and clips flying. She didn't care, although she was certain her veil-hair look was ever-so-delightful. But it wasn't like she had to worry about the after-ceremony photos. "There," she said, thrusting it at him. "It's not like I need it anymore." Then it hit her, all over again. What she'd done.

Had she really, truly, just done that? Walked out on her family?

How wrong was it, that on her wedding day, when she'd left a man standing at the altar—a man she did love—it was leaving her family that scared her more.

Graham took the veil from her, frowning, and held it in his hands, not looking at it, but staring at her.

She noticed, and paused in her attempts to tame the skirt of her dress into something she could actually sit in, while simultaneously keeping her tightly laced boobs from not cutting off her breathing entirely. "What?"

He snapped out of his reverie, and ducked his chin as he

went to work, carefully untangling the veil from his sword. "Nothing, nothing a'tall."

He sounded like the man in the garden—which would be interesting at any other time. She dared a glance out the rear window as the limo careened around the corner, mercifully cutting the church from view. She let out a deep sigh of relief, which did absolutely nothing to quell the wave of nausea climbing rapidly up her throat. "Driver! Pull over! Pull over!"

The driver immediately swerved to the nearest curb, sending her once again sprawling across Graham's lap. She shoved the door handle and pulled herself straight over him, just in time to get her head past the running board, and . . . nothing. Dammit. She'd feel so much better, so much . . . freer, if she could just—

She froze when she felt his fingers moving along her spine. "What"—she cleared her throat, and it had nothing to do with the tightness of her dress or the urge to toss her cookies—"are you doing?"

"Ye canno' breathe in this . . . contraption," he said, and went to work unlacing the back of her dress.

"Seriously, you can't do—oh." She stopped speaking as her ability to take in a deep breath became a possibility. She breathed deeply twice more. Then sighed—heavily, for a change—in abject relief. "Thank you," she said, never more sincerely. "But . . . you need to stop, uh, or I won't have—"

"Give me a moment," he said, every bit as calm and collected as he'd been in the garden.

Her port in the storm, indeed.

He tugged gently on the laces, but not so much that she felt constrained. He fiddled about a moment longer, then said, "There. All set."

She fumbled and reached behind her, then struggled to sit back up. He helped her by all but lifting her from him and settled her back in her seat. The way one might a stuffed doll. Albeit a doll one had affection for, as he'd done it as gently as possible.

"Thank you," she said again. "I can—" She paused, breathed, and realized she didn't feel nauseous anymore. "Thank you," she repeated.

"Are ye all right?" Graham asked. He had one steadying hand on her shoulder. And it was steadying. Also distracting.

"I'm sorry for the drama there. I thought I was going to . . . you know."

"And are you?"

She shook her head. "I just wanted to." Right before curling up into the fetal position and doing her damndest to forget the entire day had ever happened. "I'm good now. It was the dress, I guess."

Graham tapped on the divider window with his free hand, and the town car pulled away from the curb and resumed their journey. He lifted his hand from her shoulder and pushed the tumble of hair from her face. "I'm certain it was more than the dress. But I'm glad that much has been resolved."

He pushed the last wayward strand from her cheek, which was such a soothing gesture, she caught herself pressing lightly against the palm of his hand. It was hard, and callused . . . but also warm, and gentle despite being broad enough to cup most of the side of her head in his palm alone. The acid wave in her gut was gone. Instead she had to contend with a sudden burning sensation behind her eyes. No. She was not going to get emotional. McAuleys didn't get emotional.

Though she'd always thought that rule was restrictive bordering on cruel, especially when she'd been a youngster, all that training should be good for something. Right then, crying was not going to do her any good. Later, when she was alone, it was going to be the sobfest of the century, accompanied by a gluttony of chocolate if she had anything to say about it. And possibly large quantities of whatever adult beverage she could get her hands on.

But not yet. She'd done the hard part. Okay, so part one of the hard part. Certainly there was worse yet to come. She could not allow herself to fall apart at the first sign of someone showing concern or caring. She'd just claimed her independence, literally in front of God and everyone. She was on her own, her own woman. Hear her roar.

And though she hadn't been in that new stage of her life very long, she was pretty sure being independent precluded leaning on anyone. Certainly not inside the first five minutes, anyway.

"I'm okay," she said, forcing the words past the lump in her throat, then forcing that down, too. She removed herself from his warmth and care and concern. It would be her undoing if she allowed herself even a second more of it. It was all catching up to her in a giant rush of reality and she wasn't prepared to deal with that part yet. Truth be told, she wasn't sure she'd ever be ready.

"Where to, sir?" The driver's voice crackled through the intercom. The glass partition between them was smoked, making the driver nothing more than a shadowy figure on the other side.

"Airport," Graham said. "Baltimore."

Katie didn't argue. In fact, hearing the word *airport* helped yank her brain back to the matter at hand. She had not a prayer of figuring out what to do with the rest of her life, much less the catastrophic ramifications of what she'd just left behind— especially during a hell-for-leather limo ride in her half undone wedding dress, with a gigantic, mad Scotsman who claimed he owned her, as her only support system. That would not be happening. All she really had to do, right that very second, was figure out what to do next. The rest would work itself out in time.

An eon or two should do it.

She had no idea what Graham had in mind, although she assumed it was a flight back to the U.K. Scotland, however, was not on her itinerary. Not that day. Not ever. She and Blaine were supposed to be flying to Italy for an extended tour through wine country, followed by a river cruise through the Gota Canal in Sweden. She had all the tickets and documents tucked in her bags in the trunk of the limo. While a part of her wished, badly, that she could have somehow gotten Blaine out of the country and away from the fire and brimstone and hell hath no fury that was surely happening back in the church, she also knew that by leaving her family behind, she'd had no choice but to also leave Blaine. They couldn't continue to be partners in crime if only one of them wanted the prison break.

She had realized for some time, their co-dependancy was the biggest part of the reason why they'd put up with their families' respective crap as long as they had.

So she'd go to Italy. Alone. And maybe Sweden, too. Though the canal part had been for Blaine. He was an engineer trapped in the body of an heir to an empire he didn't want. Seeing one of the great wonders of the engineering world was to have been her wedding gift to him. It was as close as he would come to re-alizing his own dream of designing new infrastructure systems to help solve engineering issues in underdeveloped countries. Maybe she'd overnight his tickets to him from the airport. En-courage him to go on his own. Or take Tag. Whatever. Maybe he'd embark on the new chance she'd given him by finally, mer-cifully, breaking them both free.

She wondered if he was doing that . . . or if he was already struggling to patch things up. At least, leaving as she had, clearly showing that he'd had no knowledge of it, he could be the poor victim, and martyr the whole thing. If he wanted to go that way. She fervently, fervently, prayed he would not. If he didn't use her escape to break free, she knew he never would. And he'd spend the rest of his life living a lie. Multiple lies.

She wasn't doing that. Not anymore. She'd go to Italy, soak up lovely scenery, drink copious amounts of alcohol, eat an ob-scene amount of pasta, and figure out what a woman did who'd just turned her back on every scrap of support she had—on her family, on her entire life. If that wasn't enough of an emotional whirlpool, she was also going to come home to the stark reality of no roof over her head, no bank accounts she could access, and surely no job to report to. And most likely no one to turn to while she got on her feet. She doubted her friends would stand up to the pressure her family was certain to bring to bear on them. She couldn't blame them for that. Her only true friend was Blaine. And she doubted he'd be opening his door to her after what she'd just done to him.

It struck her then. So obvious, and yet previously so unthinkable. But . . . What if . . . Could she just . . . never go home?

She stifled an urge to gasp. But the skies didn't open, terror didn't reign down. She wasn't even struck by lightning for daring to have such an anarchist thought.

Wow. Could she really not go home? Actually, now that she thought about it, did she really have a choice?

She rubbed a spot over her heart, the pain there like a sharp stab. But what other choice had there been left to make? Her family hadn't left her much of one. Yes, she should have planned a better exit strategy than bailing out on a lifetime commitment to the joint family empire then ditching it and running away from it on her wedding day.

But . . . too late! There was no turning back, no do-over.

So, okay. Fine. Good. She'd spent the past six years since completing her MBA making sure that McAuley-Sheffield, a company that employed hundreds of people, ran like a tightly oiled machine. Surely she could figure out how to run a tightly oiled company of one. She'd just pick some new place and . . . start from scratch. She was educated. She had skills. She had dreams. Okay maybe not actually fully realized ones, like Blaine had, but that was only because she'd been too busy being self-protective. Don't allow yourself to want what you can't have, and life went a lot more smoothly. With her thirtieth birthday in viewing distance, she was finally daring to dream.

So what if, at the moment, it felt a lot more like a hallucination.

The idea should have terrified her, or at the very least caused a case of semi-hysterical giggles. Instead . . . it excited her. In a terrifying, semi-hysterical way. The kind that didn't so much make her want to giggle as to throw up again, but she could work on that part. It was early yet.

She looked at Graham, who was still unknotting her veil.

More likely he was simply politely leaving her to gather herself, and her thoughts. She appreciated both. She looked away from him and through her passenger window as her beloved waterfront hometown passed by in a blur. There was a slight prickle behind her eyes again. Nothing was ever going to be the same. Would she ever walk the docks there again? Eat ice cream at Storm Brothers? Chat up Dixon over at Waterbend? She might have issues with her family, but she loved her hometown. Deeply. In many ways, it was her only other true friend. She fought back the tears, but her deep sigh brought Graham's head up.

"Ye've done the right thing, you know." He said it with quiet confidence, as if she'd just carried on her entire internal debate out loud. It was exactly the kind of unquestioning support she needed. Except he was a complete stranger and had absolutely no idea the enormity of what she'd just done.

"I dinnae claim to understand what all you're dealing with," he said, as if reading her mind. "But you wouldn't have been out in that garden, so angry and upset, if being inside and saying your vows was the right thing to do." He tucked the netting in one hand and reached out with his other. "I know what I said, back in the chapel, must ha'e sounded like the rantings of a lunatic. I-I honestly don't know where that came from. Heat of the moment, perhaps. I did mean what I said in the garden, though. I promise you, we'll talk it all through, come up with a working plan, that does the best by both of us. You've my word on that."

He laid his hand over hers then, and she wanted to yank it away, to tell him right then and there that while she might have agreed to things back in the chapel, she had no idea what she'd been saying either. Guilt took the place of the sadness of watching her hometown fall into the distance behind them. But she couldn't let that undo her.

She'd thank him for getting her out of there, and make it worth his while, if there was any possible way to repay a man for saving her life. But she wasn't going to Scotland with him.

And she certainly wasn't going to marry him. She'd just run from one arranged marriage.

She'd have to be crazy to even consider running toward another, regardless of the reasons behind it.

But she didn't yank her hand away. Nor did she tell him any such thing. Instead she lifted her thumb and stroked the sides of his warm, strong fingers, guiltily allowing herself, for those few moments, to drink in his easy strength, his confidence.

He was both haven and shelter. He was on her side. It was wrong of her to take that shelter and not tell him the truth. She knew that. But she had no one else. Very soon she wouldn't have him, either.

She'd already used up all the backbone she had in her for the day. Possibly a lifetime, comparatively speaking. It was purely about survival. She'd apologize for that, too. Later. As soon as they got to the airport and escape was in sight.

After all, she'd already left one man at the altar. How hard could it be to leave another at a ticket counter?

Chapter 4

"Thank you," she told him. "For the support. I know you don't understand why I'd even put myself in that situation. It's—"

"Complex," he finished. "That, I understand. We are oftentimes at the mercy of our duty to others. I'm no' passing judgment, sitting as I am, on the outside looking in, anymore than I'd want anyone judging me." He gestured between them, smiling. "Given the circumstances."

She relaxed a bit further, and he was glad he'd cleared the air somewhat. After their rather dramatic exit from the church, changing the topic to the matter at hand—at least where he was concerned—wasn't an easy task.

"I appreciate that. I-I should have never let it get that far."

He lifted a shoulder. "Easier to say now that you've gotten away."

"If I'd had the nerve, from the very start, to stand up to them, to stand up for myself. And Blaine. To just stand up at all, frankly. Life would have been different. And it wouldn't have come to this."

"Your grandfather, wasn't he of any help?"

"Oh, he was my biggest motivator. And instigator," she added, with a smile that was sad and affectionate all at once. "But I wasn't like him. Or not enough like him, anyway. I didn't relish the skirmishes like he did, didn't enjoy the battle royale, much less the stormy aftermath of war. It didn't even faze him. I think he actually enjoyed it. He used to say he could gauge his success by how many members of the family he'd managed to piss off, on any particular venture."

"Business venture? Or family?"

"There is no separation between church and state in our McAuley clan. So family is business and vice versa. Same with the Sheffields. I've often thought it was amazing that we'd managed to live in separate households—us and the Sheffields, I mean—the way they micromanaged everything and everyone else. Their presence was constant, as if they were always in my backpocket. Or on my shoulder."

"Sounds rather oppressive. Why didn't you move out, get your own flat?"

She made a snorting sound, as if he'd asked why hadn't she merely sprouted two heads. "Moving out on my own would have been tantamount to . . . well, what I did today. If a might less dramatic."

"What about university? Did you go away to school?"

She sighed, but there was a smile on her face. "Best years of my life. I'd have gone for my doctorate if I thought they'd let me stay away another few years. I made it through one round of post grad though."

"Did you ever think of no' going back home? After you got your degree?"

"Every day," she said with a dry laugh, then sobered. "But I wasn't prepared to do that. To suffer the consequences. I loved the autonomy of being on my own, although, don't get me wrong, they watched over me. Closely. Despite not wanting to go home to them, I did want to go home. To my home. I love Annapolis, love everything about it."

His shoulders rounded a bit as he thought of Kinloch, and how much he loved it. And there he was, asking her to give up a place that was equally important to her. "Will you go back?" he asked. "I mean, when we've sorted things out, and you've had some time away after . . . you know."

"I honestly don't know. I can't imagine not going back, so at some point, I'm sure I will. I just—I have no idea how all that will play out. Not yet."

She was talking, and he heard every word, but his thoughts, not to mention a good part of the rest of him, were all caught up in the touch of her soft fingertips, stroking the sides of his not-so-soft hands. He wondered if she realized her hand was still touching his.

He certainly hadn't forgotten.

His gaze was drawn to her slender fingers, tipped with perfectly shaped nails. His gaze fixed on the impression her engagement ring had made on her ring finger, and had him wondering how long she'd worn it. Her fiancé hadn't looked like a bad sort. Quite the opposite, actually. Sort of like an affectionate puppy, eager to do the bidding of whoever would feed it.

If anything, she'd seemed truly heartbroken to leave him behind. So it wasn't the fiancé she didn't love, in some fashion, anyway, but perhaps what the marriage itself represented. She'd alluded to being in much the same situation he was in— which, quite frankly, made it all the more stunning she'd agreed to his offer. Of course, her forced arrangement likely came with all sorts of attendant commitments that made the entire proposition untenable—even if there was honest affection, or true love between them. Whereas his arrangement with her would be cut and dried, business only. They didn't even have to like each other.

"I've faith ye'll figure it all out," he told her. "Time has a way of providing perspective."

She nodded in agreement, as a weary sigh escaped her lips. She'd either worn off, or more likely chewed off, most of her lipstick. While the red had been an alluring slash when playing peekaboo behind layers of netting, he thought she'd be even more beautiful without any of that artifice. In fact, it was tempting to take his kerchief and blot off the rest, and the smudge of mascara beneath those beautiful blue eyes as well.

Causing much greater disappointment than was proportionate to their short acquaintance, she slid her hand from his and scooted a little more toward her end of the seat. "I appreciate your confidence in me. It's nice to hear it from someone."

"Even if that someone is a complete stranger," he said, dryly.

"I wouldn't say a complete stranger. Not at this point."

"Aye. It was, admittedly, one of the more interesting ways I've ever made someone's acquaintance."

She smiled a little at that. "Are you referring to finding the bride swearing a blue streak in the garden? Or carrying her out of the church where she was to be married, less than an hour after meeting her?"

"I would have to say the tale should be recounted in its entirety, to do it full justice." He grinned, then, and a little more of the anxiety and tension ebbed away. Only to be replaced with an entirely different kind, when she grinned back.

"So," she asked, "do you have a pub back on your island, where the locals down pints of Guinness while regaling each other with such tales or is that just a cliche?"

"No' a cliche, I'm afraid. Have no worries, I wouldnae sully your good name by retelling the tale and castin' you in a bad light in any way."

"How many people are on your island?"

"Three hundred and sixty-seven. Sixty-six at the moment," he said, gesturing to himself.

Her smile turned wry. "Then you won't have to tell the tale. It will get around all on its own. Or perhaps you should tell the tale yourself. At least give it a chance to be properly told once." She shook her head. "Three hundred and sixty-seven. We have over thirty thousand, just in my hometown of Annapolis."

"Aye, a thriving metropolis we are no'. It's certainly a different way of life, but it's peaceful and the men and women there have the best hearts you will ever encounter. You'll have time to regroup, and think."

"You are the leader of their clan, hauling me back from

America as your bride and wife. Do you really think they won't be just a wee bit curious about me?" She said it good-naturedly, as if it were still rather surreal to her.

He supposed it had to be, at this point. "Aye, they'll be that and more. But they'll be welcomin' ye and lookin' to make ye as comfortable as can be."

"You make it sound like a sort of Brigadoon."

"Don't worry, Katie. I've a wee bit of pull around the place. I'll make sure yer comforts are seen to. I promise ye that."

She shook her head. "I appreciate that, I truly do. But I think the key for me now is to handle things on my own. I've allowed others to steer the course for far too long. Forever, actually. I need to captain my own ship." She laughed a little at that, and the sound was a mixture of both amusement and sadness. "If anyone should know how to do that, a McAuley should, right?"

Roan had done a little digging on Katie before Graham caught the ferry off the island. Her family and their business had always been based in the historic town of Annapolis, and centered around ship design and building. Originally, sailing vessels and ships of commerce. These days their inventory leant itself more toward sleek, sailing boats and very large yachts. The privately owned company was partnered with another equally old Maryland family, the Sheffields, which Graham now knew was Katie's fiancé's family. Ex-fiancé.

That was all Roan had a chance to learn before Graham left Kinloch. It was an imposing enough dossier, so he'd purposely kept himself from reading anything else Roan had sent during his transatlantic journey. He'd wanted to meet Katie first, then tackle the learning curve. He wished he'd learned as much as possible, earlier.

He felt the weight of his cell phone, currently in the sporran strapped across his chest, but didn't dig it out to look through those messages. Beating all the odds, he'd succeeded in his mission. Thus far, anyway. Katie was with him, and they were heading home. That was a better start than he'd realistically allowed himself to hope for. Getting back to Kinloch was going to take time, so there would be plenty of opportunity to learn more from Katie directly.

"Your family builds boats, is that right? Yachts and the like?"

She looked surprised for a moment, then her expression turned downright wary. "Right. With all the rest . . . I forgot. I, of all people, should know better." She shook her head, and her slight laugh was self-deprecating at best. "Wow, I'm just making one good decision after another." She looked to him. "After all, you were hunting me when you arrived, uninvited, to my wedding. Just how much do you know about me? My family? How did you find me? And how, exactly, do you know I'm related to the McAuley's of Kinloch? I can't believe I'm just now asking you this."

Graham immediately lifted his hand in a sign of peace. "Please, ye've nothing to worry about on that score. I'm no' a stalker. It wasn't you specifically we were searching for when we found ye. You were just the—"

"First one to pop up?" she finished, then shook her head and rolled her eyes briefly upward. "Of all the gin joints in all the world," she murmured. "Well, I don't suppose I can be too offended by that, given that it worked out well for me, at least in the immediate short term. But, let me ask you, would it have mattered who your friend had tracked down? You know, age, location, family situation, children, appearance? Or was the only prerequisite that she be single?"

"I'm no' marryin' for love here," he stated, partly to ease her mind, and partly because hearing it stated so baldly didn't make him feel the least bit better about the situation. "I never intended to put it forth as anything but a business arrangement. So . . . no. In that regard, it wouldn't have mattered, at least no' enough to keep me from making contact. Beyond that, I would have made a decision—"

"On a case by case basis?" She laughed shortly, but there was no humor in it. "I'm sorry. I'm the last one who should be giving you a hard time about the situation you've found yourself in. But, surely you knew this was coming."

"I did, aye. But I suppose I wasnae actually thinking I'd have to do anything about it."

"You mean you thought your—the people on your island—would have let it slide?"

"Other issues are taking precedence at the moment. I felt like our energies and concerns would be focused there, and on my work in that regard. So . . . no, I honestly didn't think, when it came down to it, that they'd mind if I took my time and married because I wanted to."

"So why did they—oh, wait, I remember now. You mentioned that there's someone else, trying to beat you to the altar."

He was feeling exponentially worse about the entire scheme than he had at any previous moment—which was saying a great deal. But just the mention of Iain shifted things back toward the focus they needed to be in. "Aye. Iain McAuley. I've no idea his agenda. He's no' from the island, but a distant relation of my departed grandmother. He was only discovered after my grandfather's death. And, rightly, at least as the law is written, he's given the chance, too."

"Okay," she said. A "for now" clearly followed that, but remained unspoken. "So, how do you know I'm related to your McAuleys?"

"My friend, Roan, takes care of all the tourism and marketing of our island trade. His research skills are legion. He was trying to track down any McAuley relation to those on our island, and though I don't know exactly how he came to discover you, he does have the lineage all mapped out. Your family, from what I understand, has been well documented on your side of the pond, which made it much easier for him to chart. I'll show you when we get there. You might find it interesting, learning a bit more of your family tree on our side. Has your family ever discussed your Scots heritage?"

"Often," she said, not entirely fondly, "and generally only as it pertains to increasing their bottom line and making them more marketable. I'm sure your friend is amazing at his job, but you haven't seen marketing until you've witnessed the McAuley-

Sheffield branding machine in action. Beyond what they regale the public with, however, I don't know much. You're right, it is literally centuries back before a member of my direct family actually lived in Scotland. So it wasn't an immediate feeling to me, as it might have been if we just came over to America a generation or so ago."

"We use our own lore as part of our industry as well, but our history is our industry. One wouldn't thrive or continue without the other. Still, I can understand that it feels less than special, or personal, when you're only reading about your own history on the back of a brochure, without the added benefit of hearing those same stories, with all their affectionate embellishments, handed down from storyteller, to storyteller, generation to generation."

She sighed and looked a bit wistful at that. "That, I'd have enjoyed."

"Well, I can't say that you won't be overrun with McAuley history while on Kinloch, because you'll be literally overrun with McAuleys. So you may have the chance to catch up a wee bit on those very anecdotes."

"Would this be in between all the peace and quiet I'm going to have?" she asked with a laugh.

He laughed with her. "They'll respect your need for privacy and a chance to explore at your own pace."

There was a pause, then she said, "Really?" quite dubiously.

He tried to maintain a straight expression, but the grin wouldn't be contained. "No' a hope in hell, actually. But once I set some boundaries, they'll contain themselves." *Or answer to me*, he thought, but didn't say to her. She was very much in a place where her independence was at the forefront of her mind, and he respected that. He'd do what needed to be done behind the scenes as much as possible, and allow her to find her own way. At least where she could. At the very least, he'd attempt to allow her to steer the course, as she'd called it. It was important to her, and it was of utmost importance to him to do what it took to keep her happy. And willing to marry him.

He leaned back in his seat a little, as the enormity of that little bit of reality sunk another layer deeper into his psyche.

"I know I joked about it," she said, her voice barely a soft intrusion into the growing silence, "but . . . do you plan to tell them?"

"Tell who about what?"

"Your people. Your . . . clan. About where I was, and what I was about to do, when we decided to join forces?"

That gave him pause. "I-I hadn't really thought about it."

"You really didn't know, did you? That I was the bride. Or that the bride was the woman you'd come to find and whisk away to your ancestral home."

"No, I had no idea. I'm certain if Roan had mentioned that little tidbit, I'd have never boarded the ferry."

"So, your friend, he knew?"

Graham nodded. "Oh, I'm certain of that, aye. He was quite explicit about arriving at the chapel before the ceremony began. Better to search out my target, he explained. It truly never once occurred to me you'd be the bride herself. I presume it was your online interaction with friends and family regarding your impending nuptials that made you easier to track down, along with the lineage."

"Yes," she said, her thoughts appearing to drift as the whole thing likely played through her mind. "You're probably right."

They fell into silence again for a moment or two, then she said, "So you know my lineage, at least as it pertains to yours. And you know about the boats, as you call them. What else do you know?" The wary edge in her tone returned, and he couldn't fault her for it.

He'd all but abducted her, albeit willingly on her part, from her own wedding. He could understand how she might have come to realize, now that things were calming down enough to think clearly, that perhaps she'd leapt from frying pan to fire. He tried to calm her concerns before she edged toward panic and demanded the driver pull over and let her out.

"Rest assured, I've no interest in anything your family has, or that you have, for that matter, other than a legal tie to your last name. And then, only as it pertains to what I need it for at home. I'm no' in need of anything more, Katie, on that you've my word."

She nodded, but the wariness remained. He'd merely have to prove to her he was a man of his word.

"You mentioned your family has similar ties to the Sheffields, as mine does with your clan. That would be your fiancé's family."

Her expression grew decidedly more agitated. *Brilliant strategy, there, MacLeod.*

"Former fiancé," she corrected, sadness filling her crystal blue eyes, making him feel even worse. "Yes, we are as connected as we can possibly be and have it all be legal and genetically sound. And would continue to be, if I'd stayed and done my part."

Graham didn't ask her to elaborate, but rather tried to move her back to more neutral ground, if there was a such a thing. "Your two families have built a very successful industry together, aye?" Her gaze grew more shuttered, so he braced his hand on the back of the seat and turned to face her more directly. "I'm only tryin' to make conversation, to get to know you. I canno' be more sincere when I say, I dinnae care about your family industry as it pertains to their wealth, Katie. I have my own ancestry, my own people."

"Your own wealth?"

"By my measure, I am the wealthiest of men. But not because of what's in the bank's coffers."

She folded her arms, her expression sliding from distrustful to merely annoyed. It was a step. "So you're broke."

"Hardly. It's no' your personal money I'm after, either. As I said, only your name, and only as it relates to mine."

She spurted a wry laugh then. "Good thing. Because my name is all I will have. I can guarantee you that before we even arrive at BWI, any access I have to any account, credit, bank, or otherwise, will have already been frozen."

Graham frowned. "Surely they wouldn't be so punitive as

to—on your wedding day. I mean, I know they are upset, that's understandable, but—"

"But nothing. You don't know my parents. Or Blaine's. Trust me. I thought you weren't interested in my money?"

He reminded himself again that it was perfectly normal for her to be reacting that way, but he wasn't used to being questioned on his moral standing and he was becoming a little impatient in getting her to see that, to believe it. "I'm no'. I was concerned for your sake. You've just made a daring choice, and it seems like a big enough hurdle you're leaping, without the added burden of losing what security you have left."

She kept her arms folded, but didn't say anything to that.

"Don't worry about finances. At least, no' now. I know ye want to do things on your own, and as you can, please do as you will. But allow me to at least make you welcome, as my guest, for the time being. I will make sure you want for nothing. I—it will likely not meet the standards to which you're accustomed," he added, for the first time in his life feeling a bit abashed about his actual standing. He didn't much like that, either. "It's no' very posh, I admit, or at all, really. A bit rustic, comparatively speaking, I'm certain. But I promise to keep you warm, dry, fed, clothed, and as happy and content as I can."

"I appreciate the gesture, Graham, I do, but I'm not going—"

"I don't take your agreement to come with me lightly. Far from it. In fact, because of your kind, generous nature in even considering my offer, you could be the one that saves my clan from possible economic ruin, which is the same as the ruination of Kinloch. Ye're our angel of mercy. I've no intent on treating you ill. As I said in the garden, I will offer an agreement that will be as good an advantage for ye as I can make it. On that you have my word. And while ye havnae come to know it yet, my word actually means something to me."

Her folded arms loosened a bit and her shoulders lost some of their stiffness as he continued to hold her gaze quite directly.

"I—thank you," she said, somewhat stiltedly, as if she was suddenly the one at a loss for the right words to say. "I didn't mean to insult you. It's just . . . you have to understand, coming from the life I had, the family I'm part of, most men I meet—it was one of the main reasons, I think, that Blaine and I stuck together like we did. There were a lot of things he could never be to me, but the one thing I know, as deep in my heart as I could ever know, is that I can trust him." Her words were filled with the same sadness and deep affection he'd heard in her voice before. It was hard not to be moved by it.

"You love him," Graham stated, not as a question, for it was clear on her face, and in every word she spoke.

"I do."

"So why no' marry him?"

She looked down at her hands as she twisted her fingers together. "He's family to me. In many ways, the only real family I have, if you're talking about the loving, supportive kind. And I am that for him. We grew up together, more like puppies from the same litter. It was always assumed, for as long as I can recall, that we'd end up together. Our families openly wanted that and acted accordingly."

"And you and Blaine?"

"We went along, at least at first. It was a grand game as children, then a trusted bond as adolescents."

"And as teenagers?"

She ducked her head again. "That's when it became something of a challenge. But we'd agreed for so long, allowed them to mold us, push us, for so long, mostly because it was just easier that way. We always thought we'd each meet someone, and take our stand when it finally mattered. Only we never did. Or I never did. Blaine didn't want to push it, and so we never said anything, never told them . . ."

"What? That you were more siblings than romantic partners in your feelings for each other?"

"Oh, they knew that. Anyone with eyes in their head could see we had no romantic interest in each other."

"Yet they continued to presume—"

"Oh, you have no idea how presumptuous they can be. My

parents as well as Blaine's, are both in marriages that are and always have been far more advantageous business arrangements than love matches. They see that kind of dispassionate union as powerful, because you're not compromising any part of yourself, while acknowledging that the whole is stronger than the sum of its parts—particularly as it applies to the company bottom line. When it comes to McAuley-Sheffield, it's always about the bottom line. So it wouldn't have mattered if we'd hated each other on sight at birth, the outcome would have been all the same. In fact, I'm sure they saw our tight bond as a detriment, only because that kind of thing clouds good judgment."

She recited that last part as if she'd heard it quoted to her on a frequent basis. Given her rather chilling description of her family, he wouldn't doubt that she had. He could also see why she'd clung to her childhood friend for so long. He'd been the one source of unconditional love she'd had.

"It does sound quite dispassionate, aye, but then my country's history is rife with far more arranged marriages than no'. On my very own island, our own history is much the same. Though I'm fortunate enough to have been raised by parents, at least early on, and grand and great grandparents, each of whom made a fully committed love match, that just also happened to fulfill clan laws."

"But not you?"

"Well, I wasna exactly focused on looking. My efforts and energies have been focused elsewhere for a long time, in service to my clan, and to our future."

"Even when you knew it was coming? Or did your turn as . . . what is it called? Island leader?"

"Clan chief. Laird."

"Right. That. Did that come suddenly?"

"No' entirely, no. But everyone knows my heart is fully dedicated to seeing us through, to better times."

"If this other person, Iain, did you say? If he hadn't shown up, do you think you'd still be stuck with fulfilling the law?"

"I had thoughts on how to get past it."

"How?"

"The law is outdated, kept more out of sentiment than need. I thought to get them to vote it out of existence."

"Would they have?"

He lifted a shoulder. "I canno' say, but the vote had to be unanimous, so it would have taken some doing with the elders on the island."

"But that would have bought you time, either way."

"Aye."

"And then this guy shows up. Do you know what he wants with the island?"

"None, other than he has no qualms over fulfilling the requirements."

"Surely, if your island is so small and closeknit, no one would agree to marry—"

"There are far more MacLeod lasses on Kinloch, than McAuleys of the same sex and age. Luck of birth. Our Mr. Iain McAuley, most recently of Edinburgh, appears quite able to offer a life far different than our humble island home provides, to the lucky lass whose eye he catches. So nay, I canno' trust that they'll no' agree to his proposition."

"If you could get them to repeal the law before he finds someone to marry him, would that solve the problem?"

"Likely, aye, but as I said, 'tis a gamble, and no' one I'm certain it would be wise to take. Just like our culture still embraces the Gaelic language of our ancestors, along with many of the traditions and methods, I've been made to realize, despite the challenges that face us as an island dwelling clan, as a whole, we're no' so progressive as all that. It matters no' to them if Iain beats me to the altar. He'll be the clan laird in name and deed, and, saddened or no', they'll honor that." He lifted his gaze to find hers on him. He found her remarkably easy to be candid with. In fact, he couldn't recall a time when he had been such a chatty fellow. "I suppose that is the final irony."

"What is?"

"I do take the vows of marriage quite seriously. I didn't want the law repealed because I didn't believe in the union, or what the true strength of such a bond could provide, both for me personally, and for the clan, on numerous levels. I just wanted the freedom to—"

"Choose your own mate, on your own schedule, your own way," she finished, then sighed. "I understand. Fully."

"Aye," he said, quietly. "I imagine you do."

Silence fell again, only this time it was easier. When she reached out and covered his hand with hers, he couldn't help but think that the irony was still not complete. Her hand in his. As it would be, in marriage. How the both of them, only wanting that true bond of love and marriage . . . and look where they sat. He became quite specifically aware of how her skin felt beneath his fingers as he turned his hand and slid his through hers. Odd, he thought, how such slender fingers, almost fragile in appearance, belonged to a woman with such grit and determination.

He wondered if she knew, given how long it had taken her to speak up for herself, and her childhood mate, how strong she truly was. But he'd heard it, in her tone. Seen it, in her eyes, the set of her jaw. She might have taken awhile to leave the cocoon, but he was witnessing the birth of the butterfly, right in front of his eyes.

How on earth was he going to keep her from wanting to fly away? Could his heart and moral conscience stop her from seeking her freedom, if she did?

Chapter 5

"We're quite the pair, aren't we?" Katie said, meaning to sound wry, but sounding rather wistful, instead.

Her gaze shifted to their joined hands, but she didn't pull hers away, though she knew it was well past time to start squaring her shoulders, and distancing herself from him, physically and emotionally, in preparation for what came next. But now that they'd talked, that he'd shared some of himself, of what was going on with him and what he faced when he returned, it was harder to separate and compartmentalize her emotions like she knew she had to. Perhaps, like her, he was finding the contact between them grounding in some way. Telling herself that she was only keeping her hand in his in order to soothe him was a lie even she couldn't make herself believe.

"It took a lot of courage to do what you did today," he said, sounding both admiring and perhaps a bit wistful himself.

Yep. It wasn't going to be easy, walking away from him. He was compelling to her on many levels, their lives intertwining as they were, in ways both interesting and a bit fantastical.

"After watching you in the church," she said, "I don't think it's a lack of courage that's keeping you from telling your people to take their ancient marriage law and shove it."

He chuckled, and she liked the natural, vibrating warmth of it. His deep voice reflected his broad, sturdy build, his wide, strong hands. And legs that were hewn like tree trunks, she noted. How was it she hadn't noticed all that leg earlier? Well, she had, perhaps, been a wee bit distracted by other things. But now that she was noticing . . . damn.

She tried to casually shift her gaze away and up, toward the rear window, somewhere, anywhere, but directly at him. She had no business noticing, much less feeling that ping of attraction, no matter that even his knees were pretty damn sexy. How was that possible?

She sighed.

"We'll figure it out," he said, mistaking the sigh for something else.

She wasn't mistaking it, though. That sigh was coming from a deep, deep well. A well of unfulfilled . . . things—lots of things. Lust, for one. Lust, unsated needs, and every delicious thing that went with that combination.

Needs she was not going to be fulfilling with Graham MacLeod. On his island. Or in the backseat of the limo. There would be no slaking of needs, no pursuing lusty thoughts. It was the time for taking action to get her life in gear. Not the time to see if she could get a little action with her very own Scottish hunk.

Though, now that she'd thought about it, she had to admit, it was damn tempting. In fact, her palms were sweating. Just a little.

No. No, no, no. They'd had an interesting conversation, and she'd been quietly intrigued, and surprisingly comforted by him. But that couldn't deter her from what she knew she had to do—and what she knew she *couldn't* do. And that was go to Scotland. Or allow him to believe she was going to be the one to solve his problems. He still had time. Not much, but some. She had to tell him immediately, so he could move on. Maybe his friend—Roan was it?—maybe he'd found other candidates. Graham could go track them down. What were the chances that at least one of them would be more than happy to run off to some small island off the coast of Scotland with a guy that did the kind of things for a kilt that shouldn't be legal?

So . . . why can't I be that person? What, really, was stopping her? It wasn't like she had a finite amount of time to kick-start her new life. Not like the deadline he was operating under. Would it be so wrong to just . . . go for it?

No. Stay focused.

She really couldn't allow her little voice to subvert her any-more. She'd been subversive enough for one day, following the urgings of that very same little voice. Since she'd given it reign, it seemed it was turning into a much bigger voice. Quite the nag, in fact. A big, fat nagging voice that was prodding her to consider—truly consider—that maybe she should run off with Graham. After all, other than using one half of her honeymoon tickets, what options did she have right then in the immediate future? Even that solo honeymoon would come to an end.

Her time on, what had he said it was called? Kinloch? That was an open-ended invite. Definitely a place no one would ever know to look for her.

"Katie?"

She looked from their joined hands, to his face. He really had such a good face, didn't he? It was rugged, chiseled even, with the tiniest hint of a cleft in his chin. Or was that a scar? Ei-ther way, it was sexy as hell. Dangerous, even, a little bit. There was nothing remotely dangerous about Blaine. Graham, on the other hand, made her body vibrate a little when he smiled. Or laughed. Or . . . breathed.

The thing that really got her? Not the sexy cleft, or the sex-ier knees. It was his eyes. He had such—contemplative, yes that was exactly it—contemplative eyes. They weren't exactly a color. Gray, kind of, except when he was really looking at her and all intense, then they were almost . . . lavender. That wasn't even an eye color, was it? But with that dark, wild hair of his, and dark slashy eyebrows, they were almost . . . spooky. Ish. Like he could look at her and see into her . . . and beyond her . . . all at the same time. He was part warrior, in build, and part poet, in expression and thought.

She shook her head, and realized she was staring at him, at his eyes, and—

"I willnae allow anything to happen to ye, Katie," he said. "Trust that, if naught else."

That voice, deep and solid, but somehow gentle and confident all at the same time. And that accent. Seriously with that— swoonable.

"I-I can take care of me," she said, hearing the unsteadiness in her voice, but unable to do anything about it. Likely he'd just blame it on her unstable emotional state. Her perfectly understandable unstable emotional state. He didn't have to know he was the cause—mostly—not the fact that she'd just run out on her family, and Blaine, the best friend she'd ever had. Any second, despite being a sane, rational, overeducated adult, she was pretty sure the earth was going to swallow her whole, or the sky was going to shoot down a lightning bolt to strike her dead. Surely, at the very least, something earth shattering, life rendering, was going to happen.

It certainly had always felt that way before, whenever she'd even contemplated letting the little voice take over.

But, instead, she was sitting in the limo. With Graham. And there was a whole new life—well, okay, not a life, or a future even—but certainly a new adventure. And time. Precious time. To figure out what her future was going to be. She'd help Graham achieve his goals. And she'd figure out what her new goals were going to be.

Win-win, really.

"I know ye can take care of yourself. I just witnessed as much," he said. "I'm only sayin', we're not going forward independent of one another. The legal union may be in name only, but there are all kinds of bonds, Katie. So I'm givin' you mine, in my word."

"I—" She didn't know what to say. Neither did her little voice, apparently. Silence from both sides. "There's a lot still, that we need to—"

"Discuss, I know. I'm simply—thank you for being willing to have that discussion. When we get to Kinloch, you'll see. And you'll know. And then you can decide. I realize the timing of this, given your own situation . . ." He broke off, and sighed, and she could see that he felt truly torn in what he was asking of her. "I won't abuse your goodwill, and your generosity. That much I can also promise."

Her heart was pounding, as she stared into his eyes. How had this day, a day of both dread and exhilaration, led her to this moment, with a complete stranger? A stranger who made her feel safe, and secure. Her mad Scot. How was it even possible? How was it even sane?

She'd have to figure out how to shield herself from his influence. She needed to stand on her own feet, form her own educated opinions, and make her own choices. She'd broken free. She had to move forward. Not sideways. And certainly backwards.

But, right that very second, as long as she was aware of all that . . . would it really cause any long-term harm if one of her first independent decisions was to indulge in a few moments of this? His strong, broad hand covering hers. Those kind, steady eyes shoring up her own defenses. The confidence in that chin, the strength in those broad shoulders.

Those oh-so-incredibly well built, muscular legs.

Who knew a skirt on a guy could be so damn hot?

"Thank you," she replied, hearing the hint of huskiness threading through her voice. Sheesh. If he had any clue the thoughts that were running through her mind, he'd begin to wonder if maybe he was the one making the giant mistake. He was consoling the poor, crazy, runaway bride and she was wondering— again—what he was wearing under that kilt.

Clearly she was suffering some kind of post-traumatic stress. She had killed a wedding, after all. It wouldn't be that farfetched.

Her hand trembled a bit in his, and he lifted it between them. She experienced the oddest sensation as he looked from their joined hands to her eyes. It didn't make any sense, the feeling that there was, indeed, a very powerful connection between them. One that went far, far deeper than any solace or emotional haven he may be momentarily providing. But it was there, for her, anyway, pulsing beneath the surface. She recalled his raw exclamation in the chapel. What she felt was every bit as primal and intense as that. What was going on?

"We'll figure it out," she said finally, her thoughts and emotions a complete jumble, as were her intentions to leave him at the airport and strike out fully on her own. As long as her hand was in his, she was having a hard time thinking straight.

Her fingers had stopped trembling, but her breath tightened in her chest as he shifted his hand and she thought he was breaking the . . . connection they were sharing, for lack of a better way to describe it. It was ridiculous, that the very *thought* that he might break the connection had her holding her breath. Especially since she'd hoped he'd be the one to do it, because she clearly could not. But it wouldn't explain the anxiety that spiked inside her, or the unexplained certainty that if he broke the bond, it would somehow prove an irrevocable action.

She had well and truly lost her mind.

Instead of pulling away, he shifted his hand so their palms mated together, and drew their joined hands closer to his chest.

Suddenly it seemed like there wasn't enough air to breathe, and not enough space between them. Or was there too much space between them? Her head was swimming, and it was hard to put her thoughts in any rational order. She wanted to squeeze her eyes shut, regroup. She wanted to think, to be in control. It was the whole point, wasn't it? But, once again, she did none of those things.

Only it wasn't because of external pressures, and certainly not for the greater good of her family, Blaine, or even McAuley-Sheffield. There wasn't even a particle of a thought about any of them in her head at the moment—which, she supposed, should be seen as some kind of triumph . . . but she was too busy being avidly intent on her sudden connection to her mad Scot to find much reward in the realization.

The moment between them extended, and her heart began to

pound more rapidly. Her pulse felt like a live wire, twitching beneath her skin, plucking at her most sensitive spots.

His eyes were like deep pools of lavender-gray that had gone all turbulent and stormy. Not with anger, but with a ferocity that only served to further heighten every sensation she was experiencing. Gone was the man who had helped calm her nerves in the prayer garden. Returned was the wild Scot who had stood inside the chapel of her ancestors and claimed her as his own, much as his own ancestors might have done in centuries past. He came from a place that was somewhat uncivilized given their adherence to an ancient clan law, a place still strongly connected to the Celt and Gael roots that her grandfather had spoken about the few times he'd tried to teach her about her ancestors.

Up close, she saw how truly rugged his features were, the lines that fanned out from his eyes and bracketed his mouth, proving he either smiled and laughed often, or, more likely, given his island home, spent a great deal of time outside. The idea of him living in such elemental surroundings, the very idea of what kind of man that type of life must have forged, only added to those raw, visceral undercurrents.

It was a scar, she saw, not a cleft, that divided his chin. She had to curl the fingers of her free hand to keep from reaching out and tracing its grooved, jagged path. *Insane, insane, insane.* The word echoed like a litany inside her head, ironically her only proof that she was anything but. Surely a truly insane person wouldn't be aware of their own lost grasp on reality, right?

Her attentions moved to his mouth, and it was hard to stay focused on that rational train of thought. She'd heard lips referred to, in fiction, as being chiseled, but hadn't quite been able to picture it. Until now. For as rugged and wind-hewn as his face might appear, his mouth was perfectly etched as if from marble. She'd seen his lips curve in a smile, widen in laughter, and knew them to be inviting and warm, but, at the moment they looked as if they had indeed been carved from granite.

His hair was shaggy and long by any corporate standard, even one such as McAuley-Sheffield, which still retained at least a modicum of its earthier connections to the more bohemian style of sailors and captains of the sea. Perhaps not anyone on the payroll, but certainly a familiar enough sight haunting the office hallways as they came in to discuss the details of their new racing slew or transatlantic yacht. Looking like they'd just rolled out of their hammock and slid their feet into a pair of Tevas, yet quite likely carrying a discreet card in their wallets containing offshore account numbers in the Caymans, where they had funds enough to purchase entire fleets of original, one-of-a-kind designed McAuley-Sheffield crafts.

She doubted Graham sported such a card in his wallet. He'd claimed to be the wealthiest of men, but not necessarily by count of the almighty dollar. Or British sterling, she supposed, in his case. Rather than be put off by the distinction, it drew her more fully into the circle of . . . whatever spell it was he was weaving around her. Perhaps he wasn't human at all, but some kind of Celtic faery.

If Celtic faeries came in the form of six-foot-plus rugged hunks in a kilt, it would explain a lot. And she'd be quite willing to believe if it got her own questionable sanity off the hook. But the idea that the man would go so far out of his way to act on the convictions of his beliefs to take care of his people was intensely attractive to her.

She had no business being attracted to anyone. Her wedding might have been a complete sham, but she still had a number of things to work out, before even thinking about someone else. But she *was* thinking of someone else. A very specific someone. Her eyes widened as she watched that someone shift ever-so-slightly closer. Like some invisible beam was pulling them toward each other, that neither had the power—or, okay, inclination—to resist. Was he really—did he think it was remotely appropriate to—she was wearing a wedding gown for God sake. Surely he didn't intend to—and she certainly wasn't prepared to allow him—

"Katie," he said, with a fair bit of gravel to his tone, which only engraved that accent of his even more deeply into her psyche. If that's what she was calling it at the moment.

"Yes," she whispered, as breathlessly as any helpless heroine who'd ever traipsed across a windswept moor toward her certain doom—and was perfectly happy to do so if it meant one last, swooning moment in the arms of the ruggedly handsome, but impossibly, untamable Scottish hero.

"Rest stop, just ahead." The direct voice of the driver injected a cold shock of reality into the otherworld that the rear compartment in the limo had become. "Should I pull in?"

"Uh"—she cleared her throat, more than once—"yes," she managed, sounding choked. "Please. Good idea."

She would have tugged her hand free then—surely she would have—and damn the irrevocable consequences her fantasy-saturated brain had dreamed up. But his grip actually tightened and held her in place.

Just like that, she was back in the netherworld. Helplessly stranded on the moors, but not trying too awfully hard to look for an escape route.

"It's no' just me," he said, a hint of earnest wonder in his tone. Possibly a bit of worry, as well. Maybe more than a bit. She chose to focus on the former.

"Is it?" he asked. "Ye do feel it?"

She could only stare, rooted to his gaze, his touch. He reached up then, and brushed his blunt fingertips softly across her cheek.

"Do ye, Katie?" he urged, sounding every bit as confused as she felt.

"I-I don't know what I feel," she said, which was partly true. She felt like pressing her cheek against the work-roughened fingers stroking her soft skin. She felt like pulling the palm of his hand down and placing it over the hummingbird speed pulse of her heart.

He brushed his thumb across her lips, making her shudder as a sharper sensation of pleasure arrowed straight through her. She closed her eyes, tilting her head back as he pressed harder on the softest part of her lower lip, and clenched her thighs to-gether against the sudden, very insistent ache that bloomed there.

The instant she shut her eyes, his finger still caressing her lip, she was suddenly, and very intensely assaulted with vivid im-ages of two bodies, passionately entwined, limbs twisted in linen sheets, skin sheened with sweat, as the man—beautifully sculpted, perfectly naked—pistoned himself into the woman beneath him, her long, slender legs wrapped around his hips, blond hair spread out on the mattress beneath her.

That was no random mental scenario she was dreaming up. It was far too vivid, filled with sights, sounds, scents . . . happen-ing right in front of her—except it was only in her mind, and not for real. Or was it? It felt real, sounded real . . . she wasn't making it up. It was as if the entire thing had been put directly into her brain, like a memory of something that had already happened, something she was simply recalling.

The man in her vision started to climax, arching his back, groaning, his voice so deep and guttural it made Katie gasp. When he rolled off the woman, Katie gasped again. The woman was her. The man was Graham. Only neither of them looked exactly . . . as they did. But it was her. And him. Only . . . dif-ferent.

"Katie?"

She snapped her eyes open and the vision vanished.

Of course it did. And of course it had been her, with Gra-ham. She'd been the one to think it up, hadn't she? It might not have felt that way in the moment, but maybe she was in some kind of subconscious denial of how badly she was wanting the man presently stroking her bottom lip.

And leaning his head closer, she realized, as her own eyes widened.

"You do feel it, then?" he said, his voice barely more than a dark whisper. "No' only me."

The town car pulled off the interstate, and the slow swerve pitched Graham slightly forward, and her back. She realized their hands were still linked when he tightened his grip, pulling her forward to keep her from falling backwards. Only to lean her back slowly and follow her down.

She should be stopping him, squirming, pulling away, telling him to knock it off. She'd just been an almost married woman. But that was ridiculous. He'd been there. He knew the whole thing had been a sham.

Still . . . who made out in the back of a limo wearing the wedding dress bought for another man? Even if the man was just Blaine?

"Miss?" the driver's voice intruded. "We're here."

"Graham—we shouldn't—"

He immediately pulled back and tugged her upright. "I'm sorry," he said, steadying her, then abruptly letting go of her hand. "I—I dinnae know what came over me."

"No, no, don't apologize. I . . ." She stopped before she said something even more foolish—like he shouldn't apologize because she'd wanted it every bit as much as he did.

He was still looking at her, but his expression, for once, was shuttered. "Was I alone in that moment? Be honest with me, Katie."

Lie, she told herself, knowing it was the wiser course. Even as she knew she couldn't. He'd asked her, several times, while she was having heart palpitations and sex dream visions, if he was the only one feeling it. He'd just wanted to know if she was feeling the same urge to kiss. Didn't he? Because it wasn't possible that he'd been experiencing the same out-of-body—but totally in body, her body!—sensation she had. Was it?

Some latent sense of self-protection finally, mercifully kicked in and she shook her head. "I don't know what that was. But I can't—we can't—it's . . ." She shook her head, then tucked her hands around her waist and hugged herself as she turned to look out the passenger window as the driver pulled alongside a low stone building. A rest stop. She was going to go into a gross, highway rest stop, in a twenty-thousand-dollar wedding dress. Her mother would die.

Of course, it had been her mother who'd ordered the dress that Katie'd never wanted in the first place. Her mother wasn't there, was she? Nor would she ever know what had happened in, to, or with the dress.

Feeling almost jubilantly emancipated by the very thought—and clearly clinging to any thought that had to do with the part of her life she fully understood . . . and not the inexplicable, hormone-laden insanity that was the present moment—she shoved the door open and slid her slippered foot out. Then looked back at Graham. "It's been a long day. I just need some time. To sort things out."

"Of course," he said, lifting his hand as if to dismiss the subject between them, his expression even more shuttered, if that was possible.

As she looked at him, it was difficult to believe just moments ago they'd shared . . . whatever the hell that had been.

As she reached over to haul the length of train up to her lap, so she could turn and slide the rest of the way out of the limo without tripping over it and face-planting on the pavement, he said, "I'm—I was simply curious. I won't speak of it again."

His quietly spoken words pulled her right back in. She paused, and looked over her shoulder, but she didn't say anything. Frankly, because she wasn't sure what to say. That she'd touched him, felt some really weird connection to him, then closed her eyes and imagined them writhing naked in some big, ancient bed? Right. It was clear he was flummoxed by whatever was bothering him. But it was probably just guilt overcoming on to her after promising things would be just business between them. She was sure there was no way it could have anything to do with the same stress-induced, feverish sex scenario that had played out inside her own mind.

"I need to get inside to change," she said, rather abruptly, but she had to do something. Anything. "So we don't miss our flight," she added, though she was once again questioning what her best course of action should be. She'd been all decided on going with Graham. Only . . . maybe that wasn't the wisest move if she truly did want time and space to sort through things. Whatever their connection was or wasn't, one thing was clear: they were both feeling it. That could only spell one thing. Danger, danger.

"Do ye need any further assistance?" He gestured. "With the dress, or whatnot?"

She shook her head. "But—my suitcases are in the trunk. The outfit I was going to wear when we left the reception is back in the dressing room, so I'll need to dig something out to wear." Another thought occurred to her. "My purse. My phone, cards, all of it, back in the dressing room." She barked a short, humorless laugh. "Probably just as well. I do not need to see what kind of calls and messages are being left on my phone. I imagine the only thing still valid in my wallet is my driver's license—and that's only if Father hasn't figured out how to revoke that, too." Her eyes widened further. "Crap. That means I don't have identification."

"Passport?" Graham asked.

She had to stop and think for a moment, then sighed in relief. "With our travel documents, in the valise in the trunk. Oh, thank God." It only took a moment for her to also realize that Blaine's passport was in that same valise, and his clothes were all neatly packed back there, too. Well, she could always send the limo back to the church. Or to the Sheffields' home. She doubted Blaine was going to need it right away.

"Good," Graham said. When she started to slide out again, he added, "Just hold there for a moment." He opened his door and got out, then came around . . . and lifted her straight out of the car into his arms. "No need to ruin the dress."

There was a sudden burst of clapping from behind them. They turned to find a trio of college age coeds, grouped together by their SUV, cheering and clapping for them.

"That's so romantic!" one girl gushed.

Another threw a wink at Katie. "Your new husband is one hot Scot."

The last of the three sighed and held her hand to her chest.

"Your dress is stunning, and that outfit..." She fanned her face as she looked quite openly at Graham.

Who, Katie could see from her close vantage point, was actually blushing just a little. It surprised her when he gave them a brief smile and salute. "Thank you," he said, then carried her around to the rear of the town car, and the trunk that had already been popped open.

"Oh my God!" one of the girls squealed. "Did you get a load of that accent?"

Katie didn't bother correcting their assumption either. It seemed easier to let it go. "You can put me down," she said, so only he could hear. "I need to get in my suitcases."

"And ruin the show?" His smile grew, but that bit of a blush was still there.

He let her slip to her feet, but took the train balled up in her arms from her. "Allow me."

Embarrassed, she thought, *but still gallant*. She could have told the coeds he was every bit as swoonable as they thought he was.

"Should we send the car back with your—with Mr. Sheffield's luggage?" he said, noting the number of bags arranged neatly inside the trunk.

"What?" she said, still distracted by him. "Oh." She peered inside the trunk to point out which were hers. "Hmm. These are all mine. I guess Blaine's hadn't arrived yet."

His eyes widened slightly, but he didn't comment.

"I'm not as high maintenance as this would indicate," she assured him. "If it were up to me, I'd go with a duffel bag and a backpack."

"It was no' up to you? It was your honeymoon, was it no'?"

"No," she said, "it was no'." His brow lifted a bit at her mocking of his accent, but she smiled at him, and the amusement was immediately returned if the light in his eyes was any indication. *Thank goodness he has a sense of humor*, she thought. He could appear quite stoic, she realized, but that steady, focused exterior hid a very complex and thoughtful man. At least that's what she was coming to understand about him.

"It was a McAuley-Sheffield honeymoon—which was far more a European marketing campaign than any kind of celebration of a new marriage. Of course, the marriage was about the business anyway, so this was not exactly a surprise. But I'd have been expected to make at least several wardrobe changes a day, and I certainly wouldn't have been seen in the same thing twice."

"Certainly," he said, the deadpan undertone making her dart a look his way. He looked completely innocent. But when her own mouth quirked a little, that twinkle surfaced again.

She liked his quiet humor. And that he got it, but in such an understated way as to make it feel like something intimate and personal, shared only between them. She and Blaine had many such little private jokes and understandings between them, borne of a lifetime spent in close cahoots with each other.

But this had an entirely different feeling to it. Intimate in a way that wasn't just cohorts-in-crime . . . but partners in . . . well, a lot of things that weren't just about friendship. She realized she really liked it. A lot.

She got caught up in that twinkle for another moment or two, then, feeling a little flustered when those other images danced around the edges of her brain again, she turned back and busied herself digging through the first bag she could reach. She quickly slid out a pair of navy slacks and a soft, silky, umber-toned pullover. She spared a second thinking about the undergarments she wore, which were more about the foundation of a wedding dress than for everyday comfort, but she was not going to dig for a more appropriate bra or undies in front of him. Not with the way her mind was working at the moment.

She zipped up the bag. "Okay, I'm good," she said, and stepped back so he could lower the trunk lid that he'd been propping up with one hand.

He lowered it and snapped it shut, as she turned and tried to gather the train in one hand and keep from completely crushing the clothes she'd just gotten out, in the other.

"Just hold on to the clothes."

She shifted them against her chest and turned, as he scooped her up again and flipped the long train into her lap.

More clapping, oohing and ahhing followed.

"Most romantic thing ever!"

"I know!"

Katie felt her cheeks heat and started to correct them. "It's really not what—"

"Shh, let them have their fun," he said quietly, so only she could hear.

She looked up at him as he carried her to the curb and, to her utter surprise, sent the growing cluster of women a smiling wink. She shook her head, but smiled. He was such a contradiction. Concerned and gallant one moment, bold, claiming warrior the next. Embarrassed center stager, and . . . irrepressible flirt. She wondered what it would be like, to have him relaxed and flirting like that with her.

She became suddenly more aware of how his arms felt supporting her, and how hard and broad his chest was, as he held her against it.

"You can put me down now," she said, as they reached the walk leading to the rest stop building.

"I realize there may be little sentimentality to this dress," he said, "but I'll get you to the restroom door so you don't have to wrestle with it any longer than necessary."

He did just that, and paused to the side of the wide entrance-way.

She looked up and instead of finding that twinkle, or even an amused look on his face, she was surprised to see him looking quite serious. "What is it?"

"I'm sorry," he said.

Her brows lifted. "For?"

"This day."

"What have you got to be sorry about? If anything, you rescued me from this day."

He didn't say anything to that. Then he gently put her feet on the ground. She clutched her clothes to her chest, suddenly feeling a bit wobbly, though it had nothing to do with her dress or narrow-heeled slippers.

"You're beautiful, Miss McAuley. And ye did the dress justice. Though I'm no' sure there's a dress that's been made that can do you the same." Then, while she gathered the wits he'd just so easily and thoroughly scattered, he turned away and busied himself lifting her train, and gathering it into a loosely folded bundle. As if the moment had never happened, he handed the soft bundle to her to keep it off the ground. "Can you navigate from here?"

"I—" She had to clear her suddenly thick throat. She couldn't recall anyone ever saying anything quite so lovely to her. "Yes. I'll be fine."

He studied her for a moment, then nodded. "I believe you will, Katherine Elizabeth Georgina Rosemary McAuley. I believe you will."

Completely nonplussed, she didn't know what else to do but head inside to finally, mercifully, get out of the dress.

"You deserved a better day than this," she thought she heard him murmur behind her.

She hustled the rest of the way inside, suddenly impatient to have the thing off of her, to put the day, and all that it meant, behind her. To be Katie McAuley, new woman, and not Katie McAuley, joke bride.

Fortunately, Graham had done all the difficult work when he'd loosened the dress in the limo earlier. She could reach around and get to the rest of the stays, though it took a few minutes to orient her fingers properly to unhook them all. Once done, she was out of it and free, in record time. She laid it over the swinging door and piled the train on top of it, letting it hang over both sides of the door. She peeled off garters and hosiery. Shoes. She'd forgotten to get different shoes. Shrugging, she slipped on her pants and adjusted her strapless bra a time or two, then gave up. She put on the pullover before stepping back into her satin pumps, and leaving the stall entirely.

She gave herself a cursory once-over in the wall of mirrors that ran opposite the stalls. Her hair was a mussed-up disaster. She could only imagine what the coeds thought they'd been doing in the back of that limo. Then she thought about what they'd almost done—or started doing—and realized that if the rest stop had been any further away, that supposition might not have been so far off.

She raked her fingers through her hair and tried to smooth it into some semblance of order, then just gave up. "Well, it's a start."

She smirked a little at the added lift and fullness to the front of her pullover, provided by the engineering feat that was the bra she was wearing. She turned for a side view, and her eyes widened a little at the pronounced curves. Something that wasn't exactly synonymous with her usual look. The old Katie McAuley dressed down her femininity, partly because she wanted to be taken seriously, working in a male-dominated field, and partly because that was the kind of woman she was. Not an uber girly-girl. Much to her mother's endless dismay. Come to think of it, that might have been half the reason she wasn't one. Asserting her rebellious, independent tendencies in the small ways she could.

But she was the new Katie McAuley now. Or, perhaps, the real Katie McAuley. She posed a little, pronouncing the curvy look. Her thoughts went to Graham, and the reaction her appearance might get from him. "Yep, I'm keeping the bra." Then, a little stunned at herself, and not a little excited by the idea there might be other sides to her she'd never explored before, she turned and looked at the hunk of white dress hanging over the swinging stall door. She was tempted to leave it right where it was, but decided against it. After all, it was hardly the dress's fault. So, she hauled it off, then rolled it up in a bundle in her arms. She didn't want it, but she wouldn't abandon it to a roadside rest stop fate.

You did the dress justice. Though I'm not sure there's a dress that's been made that can do you the same. Graham's words echoed in her mind as she left the restroom. To her surprise, and definite dismay, she felt her eyes burn a little. She purposely did not look at the bundle in her arms, but thrust it straight into his as soon as she exited the building.

He said nothing as he clutched it to his tartan-covered chest to keep from dropping it.

She went straight to the limo and tapped on the trunk. The driver popped it for her and she made quick work of finding something better to wear on her feet.

She straightened to find him standing behind her, still holding the dress. "I don't care what you do with it. But I don't think I want to see it again."

He simply nodded.

Thankfully the coeds had apparently driven off. But there were one or two other looks from passersby. Mostly at Graham, as he was still in full kilt regalia. She ignored them and climbed unceremoniously into the back of the limo. She heard the trunk click shut a moment later, but didn't look to see where the dress had ended up.

She had only a second or two, before he climbed in behind her, to gather herself and get some kind of grip. She decided she needed to keep some space between them. That was first and foremost. Then she needed to decide exactly what her strategy would be at the airport. Free of the dress, free of the day that had led her to that point—for that matter, the life that had led her to that point—she had to decide what she was going to do next. Would she free herself of him, too?

The other door opened, and the size of the back of the limo shrunk swiftly as it was filled with the oversized Scot.

Italy? Or Scotland?

Maybe she should choose another destination entirely. One that wasn't connected to any of the men in her life. Yes. That was probably the best thing to do. Then her shoulders—and her bravado—slumped a little. She hadn't any funds, or connection to any funds, that would allow her the luxury of buying another ticket.

Graham was right. Everyone she knew or was connected to her old life in any meaningful way, knew she had tickets to Italy.

No one knew she had a ticket to Scotland.

"Are ye okay, Katie?" he asked, as if reading her thoughts, once again.

"Fine," she said, then straightened and settled herself in her seat. She set her shoulders, crossed her legs, and set her sights not on him, but forward instead. Where they should be. And where they would remain. Her options, as she saw them, were few. He wanted a wife in name only. She needed a ticket out of her old life. All the rest of whatever the hell had been going on between them before they'd pulled off to the rest stop . . . well, she didn't know what that was. Residual insanity from a long emotional day. But that was also in the past.

It was all business going forward. He was offering her a deal. A favorable one, he'd said. She had a new life to build, and only one way to fund it, as far as she could see.

"So," she said, smoothing her hair from her face, then folding her arms in the same manner as she might have if she were sitting in the corporate meeting room. "What time is our flight?"

Chapter 6

Graham kept his own counsel, and his distance, on the re-mainder of their ride. Something had changed when she'd removed the wedding dress. As if she'd shed the old, and was now girded for the new.

He respected that, and allowed her the time and space to prepare herself for what came next. He thought about what she'd asked him previously . . . what was he going to tell every-one when they returned? Had Roan already let it slip that he was, for all intents and purposes, stealing a bride from the altar?

Not that it mattered, he supposed. There were no secrets on Kinloch. The story would come out. He had to figure out how best to protect her from his well meaning, but naturally nosy clansmen. Once things calmed down and settled a bit, he wanted the two of them to sit down with Shay and go over the pro-posed joint venture.

Joint venture.

He dipped his chin a little bit, feeling somewhat shamed by the whole thing, which was frustrating to him. He wasn't doing anything his own ancestors hadn't done. Given no choice in the matter, he was being up front and dealing with it, in the most honest and direct way he could. Certainly no one on the island would fault him for being so cold and clinical about it. They'd be humbled, or at least he hoped they would, that he was willing to make that kind of sacrifice in order to continue working for the greater good of them all.

Yet, none of that rationale made him feel the least bit better about the plans he was making for his immediate future. It wasn't who he was. Neatly typed legal documents, duly signed by two willing parties or not, it felt . . . wrong.

His gaze slid to Katie, who had her hands folded in her lap, her gaze pointed somewhere beyond her passenger window. She wasn't as tiny or delicate as she'd seemed while in that voluminous dress. He still towered over her, but he towered over pretty much everyone. She seemed sturdier . . . stronger. Certainly more capable and far less fragile in her current ensemble than she had in yards of satin and tulle. However, she looked every bit as stunning. Her blond hair tumbled around her face, softening the impact of the neatly designed, perfectly fitted clothing she wore. Well-made pieces, even he could see that, but there was nothing frilly, or even particularly feminine about them.

Yet her beauty shone bold and bright, like a beacon of light. Perhaps it was her hair, which looked like the sun itself had kissed every strand. He had spent very little, if any, time around someone with blond hair. Male or female. There were a few fairer haired souls on the island, but the shade would be considered pale red, at best. Nothing like the light-infused waterfall of sunshine that seemed to hold him so transfixed.

Another, far more unwelcome visage swam through his mind. Iain's dashing prince charming good looks were also topped with a thick, blond mane. Wonderful. If the women on Kinloch were a tenth as transfixed as he was by Katie's golden goddess tresses, his challenge was only greater than before.

"We've arrived," came the driver's voice over the speaker.

Graham was pulled from his darkening thoughts to the world outside the limo. They were parked in the midst of the bustling departures lane at the airport. Up to that point it had all been talk and conjecture . . . interspersed with a few intensely shared moments he hadn't allowed himself to dwell on since leaving the rest stop. Those would explain themselves—or not—as time went on. At least, that's what he'd told himself. It was better than torturing himself by trying to figure out what had truly been going on between them.

But once they stepped from the limo . . . once they checked in luggage and boarded that plane, it was far more real than it had been in the safe little microcosm their world had become in the back of the limo. Conjecture and what ifs were about to become reality—or at least take a huge step toward that possible outcome.

He looked to Katie, who despite her often asserted wish to be in charge of herself and her destiny, at the moment looked more than a little uncertain at the prospect of her immediate future and what her initial independent decisions had caused her to do.

"I'll no' force you, or coerce you, into doing anything ye dinnae want to do, Katie. We'll go to Kinloch, and you'll have time, and space—I'll see to that—to think things through, thoroughly and completely, before we take any additional steps. This is just the first one, but I'll no' rush you beyond it."

She lifted her gaze to his, and for once, he couldn't tell what she was thinking. She'd worn her emotions fairly clearly on her face and it was a bit disconcerting to suddenly feel disconnected from her. It occurred to him just how connected he had, indeed, felt, since . . . well, since first entering the prayer garden, if truth be told.

"Thank you," she said. "I just—I want you to know I considered not going. I mean, I've thought about leaving you here, and using my tickets to go to Italy and onward. To just be alone. I've thought about it a lot."

His gut tightened, but it was the squeeze of his heart that was the most painful. And disturbing. He wasn't thinking so much about Kinloch and possibly losing his one chance to legalize his standing there. No, he'd been thinking he wasn't ready to say good-bye to her yet. Couldn't imagine that she'd simply cease to be in his life.

He'd only just found her.

Visions flickered at the edge of his consciousness, but he purposely blinked them away.

"Graham?"

He looked directly at her, forced himself to focus on what he knew to be true and real. That he needed her, but only as it pertained to him achieving his goals. Her goals were not his, nor would they ever be. If she agreed to help him, it would be as big a sacrifice for her as it was for him. He'd make sure to do everything he could to honor that sacrifice.

And do nothing to exploit it.

"I understand. I know you want to step into your new life. No' into a life with me. I can only . . ." The words drifted off as he continued to look into her eyes, as sparkling as the sea break. He heard himself say what was in his heart . . . not what was in his head. "I can only say that I don't want you to leave. I want you to come with me to Kinloch. I dinnae rightly know why it's so important that you do. But it is. And no' just for the official reasons I need your hand in marriage."

He let the statement hang there, and damned himself for even attempting to put into words the inescapable things he'd been feeling since they'd joined forces, even before entering the chapel.

"I'm no' tryin' to scare you away." Although he was doing a bloody good job of it, if her guarded expression was any indication. "I'm simply speaking of what is. I don't want to say good-bye to you. But I'll stand by all that I've said. No coercion. You have my undying gratitude for being willing to travel with me thus far. 'Tis certainly far more than I'd hoped for when I boarded the ferry, what seems like forever ago now. Please, come home with me. I'll see that, beyond all else, ye don't regret it. You're free to leave at any time, of course. In fact, I'll purchase you a ticket back home when we go inside, dated the day we'd need to—"

"Seal the deal?" she said, no inflection in her tone at all.

She held his gaze, hers still closed and wary. He could kick himself, but what was done was done. He couldn't explain what more there seemed to be to their union, as he had no explanation for it. He meant what he said, about being grateful for anything she was willing to concede, to the greater good of his people. But at that moment, breath held in his chest, it sure as bloody hell felt like a whole lot more was at stake as he awaited her response.

"Aye," he said, determined to shut the hell up.

"I have no other prospects," she finally said. "A trip to Italy might be as good as any to gather my thoughts and plan my next step, but I'd have no means beyond hotels that are already bought and paid for, and excursions already planned with no further balance due." She lifted her shoulders, and for the first time, he saw the true trepidation that lay just beneath the surface of her apparent calm acceptance of her current situation. She truly was bereft of all she'd known, all she'd ever had.

"You're not only offering me an all expenses paid get-out-of-my-life free card, but I'm assuming there is some financial compensation coming my way if I agree to . . . lend you my name."

His heart grew cold and tight at her detached and clinical calm. Though he certainly couldn't fault her for behaving in such a way. Yet it hurt, all the same. He was not that man. That was not how he conducted business, much less his own personal life.

"Katie . . ."

She lifted a hand. "I'm not saying I agree. Yet. I'm saying I'll go with you. To Kinloch. I'll consider your offer, as I also take the time to consider all my options, whatever else they might be. I just want you to understand where I am, and why I'm considering it. It's purely business, Graham. And it needs to remain business."

He nodded. "Understood."

Yet their gazes held for several moments longer than strictly business dictated.

Then the driver was tapping on the window, startling them both into action.

"I'll come around," Graham said.

"I'm fine," she responded, and they both climbed out of their respective sides. The driver assisted Katie as Graham went to the back and started unloading her luggage.

She met him there. "I'm sorry for all this. If I could remember which thing was in which bag, I could consolidate, but—"

"Maybe it's best to take everything you have with you."

She glanced up at him, and read his meaning. "You make a good point. I'm glad we didn't end up booking *my* chosen honeymoon destination."

"Which was?"

"Bora Bora. Also known as the furthest known spot from McAuley-Sheffield as I could get without going somewhere really cold."

"I don't know that I'd have minded that wardrobe so much, but perhaps you have a point." He smiled and was gratified when she did the same in response. "Here, let me help."

She reached for another bag, but he motioned her away. "I've got it. Which one has your travel documents? Passport?"

"They're in that one," she said, pointing to the stitched leather, wheeled carry on, which matched all the other hand-stitched leather bags lining the curb. Two deep.

An airline attendant approached and Katie smiled. "Thank goodness for curbside check-in, huh?"

Graham smiled and turned to greet the young man. "I'll need to book additional passage," he said. "Miss McAuley will be accompanying me." He withdrew his passport from his sporran and wasted a brief moment wishing he had his own knapsack and a change of clothes, but he'd suffer far worse to see the whole thing move forward. "I'll need to change my ticket as well. Here's the information."

Within minutes they were ushered inside and had everything taken care of. The booking agent had managed to maneuver them into seats next to each other. The first leg would take them overnight to Heathrow. From there to Glasgow, then a train ride up to Oban and the first ferry. He turned to Katie as she tucked her own documents in her bag. "We should be on Kinloch by late tomorrow night," he told her.

He spied the weariness creeping in around the edges of her eyes and mouth as she smiled. "Not as far, technically, as Bora Bora, but perhaps equally distant from known civilization. At least the civilization known as my family."

"'Tis a wee bit of an adventure, aye, but worthwhile in the end."

They spent the next hour going through the rigors of security and making their way to their gate.

"We have some time before boarding. We should eat."

She shook her head. "I'm not hungry but please go ahead." She gestured to the row of empty seats lining the plate-glass window that served as one wall of the waiting area. "I'll be over there when you get back."

He thought about skipping the food and staying with her, but his stomach was growling. Loudly. He also suspected she could use a few minutes of solitude to gather her thoughts without him hovering about. "I'll return shortly. Can I bring you anything?"

She shook her head. "I'm fine, really."

He headed off toward the food vendors, thinking he should use the time apart to call Roan and update him on what was going on. And likewise get an update on what was going on back home. He was certain they were anxiously waiting to hear a progress report. But he was oddly reluctant to share the news with them as yet. They'd be thrilled. Then the real circus would begin, and . . . it seemed as if there'd been enough circus for one day. Katie needed some respite. And so, for that matter, did he. There hadn't been time for jet lag to creep in and he was already winging his way back home. Preferable, to be certain, but perhaps he needed some time to collect his thoughts about the whirlwind his life had become every bit as much as Katie did.

He found a small coffee vendor, and decided to get her a cup and a muffin. She'd need something other than airplane food to see her through the long flight. He stopped and picked up some trail mix, a couple bottles of water, and tossed in a bar of chocolate as well, before heading back to the gate. He scanned their seating area as he crossed the passageway to their section, then slowed as he spied her. She had her small roll-on propped next to her, and was leaning against the pillar next to her seat. Sound asleep, from the looks of it.

Seeing the weariness and fatigue lining her lovely face, even in sleep, had him acknowledging his own exhaustion. Mentally, physically. He wouldn't mind checking out for a few hours, either. Instead, he carefully set her coffee and muffin on the table next to her, then took the seat next to hers, leaned back while sipping his cappuccino . . . and watched over her.

By the time he'd drained the cup, he felt at least a semblance of humanity seep back into his system. They had several hours before boarding. He didn't want to disturb her, but didn't feel right sitting there, leaving her slumped uncomfortably against the hard pillar. He shifted a little and eased her slumbering form toward him.

She rustled a little, and murmured something drowsily.

"We don't have to board yet," he said quietly. "Just rest awhile. I'll wake you when it's time."

She nodded a little, murmured something that sounded like "that's good," then snuggled against his shoulder and dropped back to sleep.

He slid his arm around her and was surprised to discover that, perhaps, he was the more comforted one. It felt quite normal, having her nestled there, as if she'd done so many times before. Flickers of images danced around the periphery of his consciousness, much as they had in the limo, but as he'd done then, he purposely shut them out, focusing instead on brushing the hair from her cheek with his fingertips, and allowing himself the luxury of simply drinking his fill of her.

Hell of a day, he thought, but it was ending quite nicely.

He dozed briefly, but spent most of the next few hours watching her sleep . . . and imagining what it would be like, life on Kinloch with her in the mix. In his life. The boarding announcement was finally made, mercifully ending his prolonged game of What If. He gently nudged Katie awake. "They're calling for us to board," he said quietly.

She nodded, yawned, then carefully extracted herself from his arms and sat up. If she'd been surprised to learn she'd been sleeping half sprawled against him, she didn't show it. But it took her a moment or two to blink fully awake. He wondered if she was like that in the morning, in bed—then shut that image out of his mind.

He stifled a sudden urge to yawn, and wished he'd spent more of the past few hours sleeping. She hadn't needed watching over, she wasn't a child. It was interesting to him, that protective streak he had with her. He'd never particularly felt that way about any one individual before, though he certainly had felt it collectively where his clan was concerned. Maybe it was just an extension of that.

Except it certainly felt more . . . personal. Like he was very specifically charged with seeing to her happiness and well-being. Which, if she had even an inkling of that, she'd be the first one to tell him where he could stuff those Neanderthal tendencies.

He'd told himself, while sitting there with her in his arms, it was strictly the notion that she was the one making the sacrifice for him, so naturally he felt responsible for her in return.

Aye. He didn't believe that. And yet, what else could it be?

They boarded the plane, stowed Katie's carry-on, and settled in their seats. Graham pulled down pillows and blankets for them both. And though he'd thought the intimacy of the plane, flying through the night, would give them a chance to talk further about what lay ahead and how best to handle it, both of them were fast asleep before the first bag of pretzels was served.

It was light outside when he opened his eyes again. He thought the captain had just announced their descent into Heathrow, but he might have dreamed it.

What was not a dream was the fact that Katie's face was

pressed against his shoulder . . . and their hands were joined, fingers twined. He was already smiling before he could figure out what his reaction to that should be. She'd made it perfectly clear they were to progress forward as an all-business agreement, putting aside whatever it was that had been going on in the limo. And now . . . well, they'd both been asleep. It was simply comfort seeking comfort.

Yet he did nothing to disengage his hand from hers.

How was it that less than twenty-four hours ago, he hadn't known her, and the idea of holding her hand while she slept made him happy? Happy. Apparently he did still recognize the emotion.

She was right, smart even, to insist on a business-only arrangement. Not simply because of the crossroads she'd come to in her own life, but because there was simply no other way to approach it, given what they had to do in order to make it legal. They were, for all intents and purposes, still complete strangers.

Sitting there, still not sliding his hand from hers, he was quite content to know she'd sought the comfort of him while she slept.

She didn't feel like a stranger to him. Holding her hand, listening to her steady breathing, feeling the warmth of her, nestled against him, he relived in his mind, their time in the garden figuring out what she should do next, telling her why he was there. He thought of standing up inside the church—her church—and claiming her as his own, rescuing her from the ensuing mob that consisted mostly of her very own family members, carrying her to a waiting limo—in a wedding dress—a dress meant for another man. He pondered lowering her to her back inside that limo, intent on claiming her in another way entirely, feeling things that made absolutely no rational sense, but that had never felt more right inside that exact moment.

It was far more madness than any semblance of reality or normalcy. It begged for a business-only arrangement between them, for both their sakes. Anything else would be tempting all sorts of trouble, from a wide variety of sources.

Yet, sitting there, thinking quite clearly back through every second of time they'd shared, he thought what she felt like to him was . . . right. Just . . . right.

It was as if there was, deep inside him, a sense of . . . relief. That was the word, the feeling, that resonated inside of him. He couldn't explain it, not in any rational sense. Nor could he discredit it. He felt it. Purely, simply.

The pilot announced again their impending descent. Katie rustled a little beside him. He rubbed his thumb along the side of her fingers where their hands were joined, in an instinctive move to soothe her, as if he'd done it oftentimes before.

She woke more fully then, and sat up straight as she blinked herself into awareness, slipping her hand from his as she reached up to rake her hair from her face. He wasn't sure if she realized they'd been holding hands, which was okay with him. He knew.

"Are we—?"

"Almost there? Aye. We'll be landin' in a few minutes."

She looked up and saw the seat-belt sign wasn't on yet. "I need to . . ."

He shifted out of his seat, grunting a bit under his breath as his body protested stretching after sitting so long in one position.

Katie skimmed by him and headed to the back of the plane without saying anything else.

"No' a morning person," he murmured, smiling briefly as he watched her retreating form, thinking back to how groggy she'd been waking up in the airport.

He rummaged in the overhead bin, then moved a bit as she returned, looking a bit fresher of face and light of eye. "Good morning, sunshine," he said, smiling.

"Amusing," she said, dryly.

He settled next to her again and offered her a piece of chocolate. "You are to me. Want a bite?"

She eyed him warily, then the proffered candy bar. "Chocolate?"

"We'll stop and get a full meal once we've gotten the next leg settled, but in the meantime, with no coffee, I thought this the next best substitute. Actually," he said, snapping a bite off the end, "I'd choose this every time if I could."

"Don't talk with your mouth full," she said, somewhat grumpily, but snatched the chocolate from his hand when he started to move it away.

"Ye're welcome," he said, as dryly as she had, when she closed her eyes in momentary bliss as the chocolate melted in her mouth.

"Mmm-hmm," was her only response. She cracked one eye open as she finally swallowed. "Don't tell me, you're one of those unbearable morning people. You probably don't even drink coffee."

"Cappucino, but aye, I'd rather have tea."

"Tea." She made the word sound like something one might scrape from the bottom of her booted heel.

"I am from the U.K., after all."

She nodded and slumped back in her seat. "Aye," she said, her imitation of his brogue getting better with each go. "That ye are." She rolled her head so she could make eye contact with him. "So, what is the next leg of our adventure, oh kilted one?"

He'd never heard her sound so cavalierly insouciant. Not that he'd had extensive exposure to her. She had been swearing quite the blue streak before their paths had literally crossed in the churchyard the day before. But, in both instances, rather than being off-putting, he'd found her lack of pretension rather charming. "You really do need coffee, don't you?"

However, as he wanted to keep his manhood intact, he refrained from sharing that with her. He knew that much.

"Like a sailor needs a strong breeze," she responded, with the kind of conviction only a true addict could convey.

"Well, I canno' claim that we make the best of the regular brew here, but if you don't mind something a bit stronger, we are quite adept at making cappuccino."

"How strong?"

"How does black as pitch sound?"

"Heavenly."

"Then we shall have some as soon as we step foot on solid ground."

"Bless you."

He smiled at her. "You're welcome," he said, quite sincerely. He enjoyed making her happy, though he couldn't have said why exactly. Certainly there was the pending agreement to be signed, but he was already quite well aware he'd have felt that way about her regardless.

"What is the next leg, anyway? I can't believe I slept all the way from—well, from the limo onward, for all intents and purposes."

"It was a pretty big day yesterday. Emancipating oneself from a previous life can take it out of a person."

"That it can," she said, the words trailing off as her expression turned largely internal.

He wondered at her thoughts, and wanted to ask if she was experiencing any morning-after regrets. But he wasn't fully prepared to hear her answer. As she'd already proven, he doubted she'd dodge the direct question.

"But I did it, didn't I? I mean, here you are, and here I am. No longer in Annapolis. Not married to Blaine. I didn't dream it all, right?"

He shook his head, holding her gaze. "No, no you didn't."

She smiled then, and it was as if the sun itself had come out to bathe him in its radiant warmth. "Good."

"Aye," he said, and smiled back.

Chapter 7

Katie followed in the natural wake Graham made through the throngs at the airport in Glasgow. She felt like she'd been on the lam for days now. But at least the fatigue of it kept her from thinking too much. Or, thinking more than she had to, which was still more thinking than she wanted to do.

Up until the day before, she'd understood her life plan—as it had been presented to her. Admittedly, one she'd signed off on, versus dealing with the alternative. Until then, she'd been a rational, educated, engaged-to-be-married, hardworking business-woman, dedicated to the greater good of family and company. Given they were synonymous in her world made achieving that goal much simpler.

In a matter of just under twenty-four hours, she'd become a jobless, homeless, disinherited, single renegade, on the run with a man she'd just met, who was wearing a kilt, and who she'd promised to form a legal bond of matrimony with, in a foreign country.

Totally sane.

She lugged her heavy roll-on behind her, wishing she hadn't been so adamant about dragging it herself. Graham was so tall it had bounced behind him like a child's pull toy. Besides, he'd done an amazing job getting her mountain of luggage moved from one arrival destination to the following departure destination, like a pro who traveled often, which he'd assured her, he was not. And she was, after all, an independent woman. Hear her roar.

She sighed. And kept lugging.

They still had a train ride and a ferry boat adventure ahead of them. They wouldn't reach Kinloch until after midnight. She wasn't sure how she felt about that. Part of her hoped Graham could secret her onto the island and tuck her away, where she could sleep for a day or ten, then emerge when she was well rested, clearheaded, and had at least partially regained her agile mind and sharp intellect. She'd settle for sanity. But the businesswoman who had spent years knowing it was best to tackle a problem head-on, find out up front what all the particulars were going to be, so she could hit the ground running, thereby creating the greatest opportunity for success . . . that woman wanted to debark from the ferry into the throng of MacLeod's and McAuley's and learn straight off what lay in store.

At the moment, she was leaning—heavily—toward the first part.

"Almost there," Graham assured her.

She felt like—and knew she looked like—a rumpled rag doll who had seen better days. Months. Graham, on the other hand, looked like a cavalier, devil-may-care clansman off to meet his band of merry men. He was steady, solid, always had a smile for her, and a supportive hand to her elbow or the small of her back. He was never patronizing, nor had he invaded her personal space unless no other option presented itself.

He'd never once mentioned that each time she woke up from another doze or sleep fest, she'd been all but wrapped around him. Given her ultimatum at their arrival at BWI—was it only yesterday?—he'd had every right to call her on it. But he'd been the consummate gentlemen. Of course, he wanted something from her. A big something. So, it was imperative he treat her with the utmost respect.

It was therefore intensely perverse of her to be feeling a little bit put out with him for not being more . . . whatever it was he'd been back in that limo. God knew she'd seen herself in the mirror in the ladies room upon arrival. She was hardly enticing. But . . . if the truth were to be told, she hadn't exactly sought him out only in an unconscious state. More than once she'd been well aware of where she was, and who she was leaning on . . . and who was gently stroking her fingers after she'd "sleepily" woven her hand in his.

Perhaps not the coolest thing she'd ever done, but dammit, she was embarking into a whole new world. She was not going to apologize for taking a bit of solace and steadiness where she could find it.

She watched him stride ahead, her gaze raking him from head to toe, completely unaware of the crowds of people jostling by, her focus narrowed down to his shaggy hair, ridiculously broad shoulders, lean hips, fine ass—from what she could tell—and amazing calves. What red-blooded woman wouldn't want to lean on that? Just for a bit?

Once she'd gotten settled and her feet under her again she'd be fine completely on her own. Surely. She had to be.

"Here we are," he said, turning to her with that easy smile, and those kind eyes.

There was absolutely no reason, none at all, why those kind eyes frustrated the ever living hell out of her. Where were those intense lavender eyes from the limo? Raking over her like he wanted to devour every inch of her? Where was that guy from her stress-induced—she was convinced—hallucinations? The one rolling her around on sheets of fine linen . . . pumping himself into her like the world was going to come to an end if he didn't find that explosive climax between her thighs.

"Are you okay?" he asked, looking quite concerned.

She pulled to a stop beside him. "Yes. Why?"

"You groaned a little. I know it's been a long journey and we've a ways to go. Are you sure I can't take that for you?" He reached for the rolling bag.

She yanked it closer to her, like it was some kind of stuffed bear. "No. I have it."

He lifted his hands. "Fine, fine."

She blew out a long breath. She was being a bitch. A totally uncalled for, unfair bitch. "I'm sorry. I'm just—"

"Tired, I'm sure," he said, with sincere understanding, ever the solicitous one. "It's okay."

"It's not okay. I've slept almost every minute since we left the States. I have no excuse. I travel all the time for my job. This is nothing."

He turned toward her, creating an intimate little circle, making her realize that people were staring and perhaps, just perhaps, she'd been raising her voice a tiny bit.

"You're emotionally exhausted, and your life is not the same one it was when you were traveling for business. It's okay, Katie. Truly. Let me help you."

It's the least I can do. He didn't say it, but she heard it nonetheless. The perversity continued as she didn't want him to be Mr. Understanding. She wanted him to tell her to knock it off, then put his hands on her face and look at her the way he had in the backseat of that limo . . . only she wouldn't push him away.

Man, she really needed some fresh air, decent food, and some time completely alone. She was losing it.

"Thank you," she said. Again. "I—why don't I go check on the train situation?"

"Why don't you wait for the bags and I'll handle that. You don't have—I'll need to be the one to do that."

Right. She'd forgotten. All she had to her name was her passport. And suitcases full of clothes. No phone, no cards, no cash. "Okay, no problem. I can do that."

Graham turned and secured the help of a skycap with a big cart, then walked back to her. "I won't be long. I just need to book passage and get us transport to the train station."

"Do you—have you called anyone? Called home?" She'd been dying to ask. He hadn't said a word, so she'd put it off. But the time to keep her head buried in the sand, or in sleep, had come to an end.

He shook his head. "I will."

"Do you know what you're going to tell them?"

He stared at her for a long moment without saying anything, then the luggage carousel kicked on, startling them both. "I'd better go get things settled," he said.

She noticed no one in particular paid any attention to the man in the kilt. Not like in Baltimore. They were in Scotland. He was home. Not that there were many kilted men strolling about the airport, but she assumed it wasn't exactly an oddity in these parts. Scotland. She hadn't seen any of it, yet. She wondered what the train ride would be like. Would there be wonderful countryside vistas? Time for her to really regroup and settle herself?

"Miss?"

She turned to see the skycap gesturing to the moving luggage belt.

"Do you need assistance there?"

"No, no, I have it, thanks." She wedged herself into the crowd that clogged the line along the moving track, wondering if they had to do customs again. "Never again will I travel with so much stuff."

The irony was that until she sorted out things at home, it was all her stuff. As in *all*. It would quite likely accompany her anywhere and everywhere she went—at least for the time being.

Graham returned as the skycap was rolling their luggage-laden cart away from the conveyor belt. "This way," he said.

She merely nodded and followed. Once they were settled on the train, she'd talk with him. About everything. She needed a plan, and to make a plan, she needed information. Most immediately, she needed to know exactly what to expect when they arrived on Kinloch, exactly what his plans were where she was concerned, especially as they pertained to her being his guest. Where was she staying? With him? With relatives? In a hotel? Did they have hotels on Kinloch? He'd made it sound pretty rustic.

Once all that was settled, they needed to talk about what he would expect from her in regards to the deal. What he was willing to offer her, and what, specifically, would be required of her if she agreed to go through with it.

That was just to start.

But it was one train ride. If she could get that much information, she'd be happy. She knew it was her last chance to have him exclusively to herself. Once they were on Kinloch, once he was home, all bets were off, and her standing would be far more subjective. She had no idea how easily influenced he might be by his friends, or the people he was doing this for. She understood that. At least where the business dealings were concerned, she understood that. She used to make her living understanding that.

As to the rest, to the personal part . . . she had not the first clue. She wanted it to be all business. But in their case, business meant marriage. How were the island folk going to react to the "business arrangement"? And how, exactly, was that arrangement going to work between them?

She'd kill for her BlackBerry. She needed to make notes, make sure she didn't forget to cover anything pertinent.

"Katie?"

"What?" she said, a bit distractedly. When nothing else was forthcoming, she glanced up to see they'd come to the taxi queue outside the airport. "Oh."

She turned to the skycap, who, along with Graham and the driver, had loaded one of the cute little traditional British cabs to the hilt with her bags, including inside. It was a small miracle there was room left for the two of them. "Thank you," she said, automatically reaching for her purse, to tip him, only to realize, then flush a little as she had to step back while Graham took care of it. "Thank you," she said again, humbled anew at her circumstances. It would be temporary, she'd already determined that. Some way, somehow, she was going to earn her own keep. And not just by signing some damn marriage contract.

She'd call home. At some point. Maybe not right off. She didn't want to risk anyone tracking her down until she was good and ready to risk being found. One thing she had concluded was they might cut her off from the family trust, but she had her own money—money she'd earned working for McAuley-Sheffield. It was a blip on the chart of what she'd been technically worth before she'd been carried out of her own church, but it was enough for her to start over. Or to *begin* starting over.

It was a start, dammit.

She refused to be dependant on Graham's kindness and generosity a moment longer than she had to. She had two feet. And she planned to stand on them.

So it surprised a squeal out of her when she found herself suddenly scooped up in Graham's strong arms and carted around to the other side of the cab. She'd forgotten about the wrong side driving.

"What are you doing?" she spluttered, as the rain she hadn't noticed was falling, caught her full in the face. "Oh!"

"Puddles. Deep ones. Mind your head," he said as he gently stuffed her inside the backseat of the cab and followed her in. It was no limo, and though she scooted over as quickly as she could, they were all but in each other's laps once he was safely inside and the cabbie had shut the door. Graham had to duck his head and slouch a little to fit.

"Sure ye don't want to sit up front here?" the driver asked as he jumped into his seat and closed his own door.

"No," they both said simultaneously, then caught each other's gaze. And smiled.

It was the first truly personal moment she'd felt that they'd shared since leaving the States—if you didn't count the times she'd woken up snuggled next to him, hands entwined.

Times she supposedly didn't recall because she was groggy with sleep.

She sighed a little, and concern caused those sexy little creases at the corners of Graham's eyes to crinkle up a bit.

"It's no' too far to the station. The train will be a lot roomier than the planes have been. You'll be able to stretch a bit. And walk about, if you want. We'll get something to eat after we get underway."

She wanted to tell him to stop taking care of her. Despite allowing her parents and Blaine's to run roughshod over her life plans, she wasn't exactly coddled in her day-to-day life. She worked. Hard. And took care of herself. Okay, perhaps not so much her living space, which was her own private suite in the family homestead, and it was true she'd rarely cooked for herself. But at work, she ran the show in her division. No one tended to her.

But Graham did. He thought he had to, she realized. But he didn't. She should tell him to stop it. And she would.

Except it was kind of nice to think that someone would want to do that for her, just because. She'd done that for Blaine—because she loved him, and because, frankly, he needed a keeper. He had definitely been the skirt in the relationship. So . . . it was kind of nice to be the girl. Not so much pampered, as . . . tended to. Like there was some honest affection there.

Business deal, she reminded herself. He needs you in good spirits, thinking kindly of him at all times.

"That sounds pretty good, actually," she said, realizing as she said it she was feeling a bit ravenous. Finally. Maybe getting to her destination country, truly in a place no one would think to look for her, had settled her nerves enough to allow the knot in her stomach to unclench a little.

"Good," he said, smiling. "I was getting a bit worried about you."

Business deal, she repeated to herself, while smiling back at him. "No need. I can—"

"Take care of yourself. I know," he said, and there might have been a bit of an eyeroll, but the smile was sincere.

"I'm aware I keep saying that," she said, "but trust me, as soon as I'm able I plan to practice what I've been preaching."

"I've no doubt," he said, sounding as if he truly meant it. "In the meantime, I'm no' patronizing you by being concerned about your general welfare. It's sincere."

"It's business," she said, not meaning to say it out loud. Too late.

His smile smoothed a bit, in that it no longer reached his eyes. "Is that why you think I'm being solicitous?"

"I think it makes sense to keep the client happy. At least, that's how I conducted business."

"I don't generally have to concern myself with conducting business, as ye call it. I don't have clients. No' in the way ye do."

"Still—"

"Still, when I say something to you, it's because I truly mean it. No' because I'm watching out for my potential investment." He lifted a hand to stifle her protest. "I'm no' being cavalier with you, true. But I wouldn't be, no matter the circumstances. That's no' who I am."

"No," she said, "I don't imagine it is. You'll have to forgive me. I've been swimming with the sharks, often under my own roof, for so long now, I forget there are decent fish in the sea as well."

He smiled again. "Shark bait, I presume."

She laughed at that. "Possibly. Okay, okay, probably. But I'd like to leave the shark tank behind completely. How are the waters in your part of the sea?"

"Well, there's one shark in particular at the moment I'm a bit concerned about."

"Iain?"

He nodded. "I should have already called, gotten an update. I'll try once we're on the train."

"Why haven't you tried before?" she asked, truly curious.

"Honestly? I haven't known exactly what I wanted to say. They're all going to be very curious about how things went, and when I tell them, they'll be curious about you. And . . . I suppose I havena' wanted to share you as yet."

His answer surprised her. Made her feel all warm and glowy.

"I know that sounds odd," he added quickly, clearly seeing

he'd flustered her a little, "but this whole escapade falls under that banner headline." He lifted his hands. "Despite my sentiments where you're concerned, I do understand your business-only preference."

"Graham—"

"To that end," he went on, talking over her protestations, "I'll want to do what's necessary to make your entry into and subsequent stay on the island as smooth as possible. Everyone will be excited to meet you."

"I was thinking about that, too. Maybe on the train—I think we need to talk, go over things, before we get there."

"Agreed."

The taxi lurched around a corner, sending Katie sprawling forward. Graham caught her arms and braced her so she wouldn't pitch headfirst into him, but once they'd regained their seating, he didn't immediately let her go.

She reached up to brush her hair from her face, which was only a few scant inches from his, she realized as she untangled the mess. Then their gazes got all tangled up, too.

Her breathing grew a little ragged as the moment spun out a little longer, and a little longer still. His pupils slowly expanded, swallowing up the gray irises. Maybe it was the gloomy skies, but she could swear there was a tinge of lavender glow there, too.

"Graham," she said, surprised at how throaty she sounded.

He blinked, as if he'd been jerked out of a moment, but when he straightened, to let her go, Katie instinctively put her hand on his chest, stilling him. There was no doubt about that lavender flash, as he continued to regard her in silence.

"You asked . . . yesterday, in the limo. If I—if I felt something . . . different. Between us."

"Aye," he said, his own voice rougher than normal.

The sound of it shot a thrill straight through her.

Ill advised, her big ass little voice shouted. *Business, business, business.*

But there was another fledgling little voice, that new one she'd given life to when she'd stood up, literally in front of God and everyone, and staked claim to a new life. That little voice was a champion for a new life. And it was saying . . . *tell him*. Be honest. For once, be open. To new things. New ideas.

New people.

"I did," she told him, and watched, as another hot thrill drilled her, when those eyes went to that dark, stormy, intense place. "It's like . . . I can't explain it. But it's not normal. For me, anyway. It almost feels a little . . . out-of-body." That was as close as she could come to telling him about the visions. That first one in particular. But they'd come to her in her sleep, too. Different visions, same theme. Same two people. Could simply be dreams. Daydreams . . . night dreams. But they'd felt pretty damn real. And more highly realized, more detailed, each time she slipped into one.

"Does if feel as if you're reminiscing about something that has actually happened?" he said. "Or is it more like dreaming of something you want to happen?"

Was he reading her mind? Her breath caught. No. It was wild enough that she had them. It wasn't possible that he—"Do you have them, too? These . . . reminiscences?"

His eyes flashed even darker. "You have them, then? The visions? Like suddenly you're watching a movie, only it's no' a film. You're seeing a different place and time, but the two people you're watching are—"

"Us," she choked out. Her body was a wild combination at the moment, both tensing in fear at the inexplicable thing they were experiencing together . . . and feeling hot, bothered, and more than a little twitchy-needy at the thought of actually doing anything she'd pictured in those . . . reminiscences. With him. She nodded her head. "Yes."

"Doing . . ."

She nodded a few more times, incapable of filling in the blank any more directly.

The intensity in his gaze increased. Something she hadn't thought possible. His body was heavy, warm, and broad as it loomed over hers, pulling her slowly down behind the stack of leather suitcases, out of the driver's view. And, heaven help her, she didn't even care. She wanted him heavy, broad, and naked, on her. Dear Lord it was hot in that taxi.

"What do you think it means?" he asked.

"We're both under . . . a lot of stress," she managed, though the words were almost a raw whisper. Her throat was tight, as were the tiniest of muscles between her thighs. Gone was any sense of the weariness and fatigue she'd felt had been plaguing her. She was feeling quite energized at the moment, thank you very much.

"So, we're just . . . imagining things?" He kept most of his weight up on his elbows, but he didn't shift off her. "The exact same things?"

"We don't know they're exactly the same things," she whispered. He felt so incredibly good, even partly on top of her. She couldn't think straight. The scent of him sent an arrow of lust straight through her.

"In your visions," he persisted, making her focus when all she wanted to do was sink fully into the oblivion he was offering.

"Are you seeing a heavily carved headboard, broad like—"

She impulsively reached up and pressed her fingers to his lips before he could say another word. The result of touching him was like being in the middle of a sun flare.

He shifted his weight to one side, and covered her hand with his own, but instead of pulling her fingers away, he pressed them more firmly against his lips. He was not only heavy and warm and perfect on top of her . . . he was also aroused. Fully, from the feel of . . . things.

She couldn't help but think how easy it would be, with him wearing that kilt to just—

"Train station, coming up!"

Graham jerked upright so fast he rapped his head on the roof of the taxi.

Katie quickly righted and settled herself as well . . . and purposely did not make any effort to look up front at the driver and risk meeting his gaze in the rearview mirror.

She glanced over at Graham, at the same instant he glanced at her. Instead of flushing furiously, which would have been her expected reaction . . . she smiled. He surprised her by smiling back. Then she snickered, not intentionally. She couldn't seem to stifle it. He had that twinkle in his eye and she was feeling quite twinkly herself. A second later, he followed suit, until, like two partners in crime, they both burst out laughing, and continued to laugh until they were holding their sides, wincing.

"You know," he said, when they finally got themselves under control, "I'm beginnin' to think I canno' be inside a conveyance of any type with you, without things getting out of control."

She barely stifled another snicker. "I know! I was just thinking the same thing."

"I probably should be reassuring you I am relieved there has always been a driver present, playing chaperone between us."

"Probably, you should be doing that, yes," she said, barely keeping a straight face.

He looked at her, then turned to stare straight ahead again. But she saw the slow smile curving his lips. "Aye. Probably should."

And then did no such thing.

She turned and looked past her mountain of luggage, out her window. She was smiling, too.

"Departures," their driver said, as he pulled to the curb in front of the busy Queen Street station building.

"I'll come around," Graham said, and climbed out his side of the car.

Katie would have protested the need for it, as she would have felt silly sitting there waiting for him to come open her door, but with the luggage between her and her exit, it was wait or climb out his door after him and go around. The driver was already out and had closed Graham's door behind him as there was traffic going past on that side. So she sat where she was, and used the scant minute of time to regroup, to decide what in the hell she was going to do, after that little revelatory moment between them. What in the hell did all that mean?

Sure, the guy was getting to her, and she was having ridiculous, insatiably hot daydream fantasies about him—who wouldn't?—but the idea there was something else going on, something she couldn't put a name to? Mystical? Spiritual? Neither of those suited. What she'd seen, or felt, or imagined had been pulsing, primal, and far too visceral to be either of those things.

She thought about the moment after they'd revealed their shared visions, the intimacy in sharing a private laugh. It had felt good. Better than good. Better, almost, than the damn visions that had started the whole conversation.

Almost as good as he'd felt pressed down on top of her. The weight of him had felt so . . . well, *primal* was again the word that came to mind.

Other than with Blaine, she'd never really laughed with anyone, in that shared, only-we-get-it kind of way. It turned out that sharing that kind of moment with a man while simultaneously wanting him deep inside your personal space—deep in a lot of spaces, actually—was significantly more intriguing.

She wasn't quite sure what to do with that. Or with him—given the situation. She had no basis of comparison. No set plans or historical compilation of data on how to deal with that particular combination of events.

She was interested. So was he. Quite, from the feel of things. From what she'd felt, he seemed proportionate to his broad size, pretty much everywhere, and that was certainly skewing her reaction as well. Her life as she knew it might be DOA at the moment . . . but *she* most certainly wasn't dead along with it. Far from it if the tingly little sparks of awareness that skated quite pleasurably over her skin just thinking about him was any indication.

So, what do you do, Katherine Elizabeth Georgina Rosemary McAuley? What do you do?

The side door opened and between Graham and the driver, her mountain of luggage quickly became a molehill. Then it was time to take his offered hand and climb out behind them. And into the next stage in her new life. She was well aware the train ride was only part of it.

At least on a train, they'd have to remain civil and hands off. She doubted she'd have the luxury of simply sleeping through it, as she'd managed to do throughout the previous legs of their journey. They needed to discuss things, anyway.

But all she could think when she reached up and grabbed that warm, broad, work-roughened hand . . . was how it would feel caressing her skin. And cupping her—

"Katie?"

She realized she was staring at his hand in hers, scooted to the edge of the seat, and stepped out next to him. Quickly she disengaged her hand, then had to clear her throat when the words didn't move past the dry knot there. "So, where to next?"

"We take the train to Oban. From there it's a ferry ride out to Castlebay on the Isle of Barra, then another to Kinloch."

She didn't have her watch, so she glanced at the sky. "Will we make the last ferry?"

"Being summer, it doesn't get dark until close to midnight, and even then, it's no' a full dark. The ferry schedule is busier these months. We should make it." He paused for a moment and took a longer look at her face. "Were you . . . hoping otherwise?"

"No," she said quickly.

"But?"

She sighed shortly. "I've been thinking about my arrival. I can't decide if it would be easier to steal in during the night and hide until morning, have a chance to regroup. You know, put my game face on, then meet . . . whoever it is I'll be meeting. But I'm assuming I'll be a curiosity on an island your size, given the stakes. Everyone will know, right?"

He nodded. "Aye. No' much of a way around that. But I've told you—"

"I know, Graham, and I'm not questioning you or your word. But you won't be able to control everything, and so, I'm just . . . trying to gird myself, I suppose. I'm not even sure how I feel about all this yet, so I won't know what to say to them."

"Then tell them that. It's okay, Katie." Taking her arm, he pulled her a step closer as the cab pulled away from the curb and another gentleman started loading her luggage on a trolley. "I don't want you to put on some kind of act. I just want you to be you. Doubts and all, that's fine. It's to be expected. They'll respect your honesty."

She looked up at him. "I don't want to make things more difficult for you than they already are. And I don't want you to waste time with me if you think there is a sure thing out there you should be focusing your energies on." Even as she said it, something heavy and hurtful tugged inside of her, at the thought of him pursuing anyone but her, which . . . made absolutely no sense whatsoever. She had nothing invested in him beyond a two-day acquaintance.

And a few shared, exceedingly hot visions.

She studiously ignored that last thought.

He let out a short laugh. "I willnae be pursuing any other unwilling brides. It was quite out of character for me to come to you. I'm no' in the habit of begging for help, and certainly not traveling thousands of miles to do so. It was . . . an act of desperation. But if you find you canno' follow through, no one will blame you. Least of all me. I won't lie and say there won't be disappointment, but as a people, we've dealt with far greater disappointment than this. I have other ideas on how I will approach the issue, so while the two of us tying the knot would be the easier and swifter recourse, its no' the only one."

"You mean getting the vote to rescind it. So why not pursue that?"

"Because it has even less a chance of succeeding. And, because frankly this solution will make everyone the happiest."

"Except you," she said, studying his expression.

"I'm fine," he said.

She laughed. "Right. You mean that about as much as I do, all the times I've said it to you on this trip. Actually, I do mean it. I just wished I had stronger conviction in actually pulling it off."

He smiled briefly. "Then we understand each other quite well."

She smiled, too, though not with as much sincere warmth. She told herself it was silly to feel slighted that, to him, marrying her was a burden. Of course it was. She was a stranger. She knew the feeling came from having so recently abandoned her own wedding. When she married, she wanted it to be because her intended loved her more than air, as she would him.

A marriage to Graham was business, no different from marrying Blaine, she supposed. But at least no one was pretending otherwise. There would be no gown, no ceremony— She glanced up at Graham. "W-we wouldn't have to have a church ceremony, would we? If we . . . you know? That's not part of the law, right?"

"I honestly don't know. I'll have to ask Shay. But . . . I wouldn't think so. No."

She noticed he was eyeing her again. "I'm asking so I know. Not because I—"

"Katie, shhh. You're worrying this far too much. You're worrying this more than I am, and it's my problem. No' yours. Please know that. What happens, happens. What we decide works, will be what we do."

"I know, you said that, but . . . do you really believe the people on Kinloch won't pressure me? I mean, they want you to win, right?"

He visibly scowled at that. "Aye."

"I know," she said, putting her hand over the one he'd laid on her arm. "Everything about how this is playing out isn't what either one of us would want. Maybe both of us knowing that will make it easier to consider. I mean, it's not like one of us thinks this is anything other than what it is, right?"

He glanced down at her hand on his, then briefly at her face, then away, at the train station entry, though she doubted he was seeing much of it. "Aye. Come on, we've tickets to buy and a train to catch."

She thought he'd bring up the subject again once they were situated on the train, but he didn't. He went in search of food, then came back and cajoled her into going with him to the service car where they could sit and eat a real meal. Her first in what felt like weeks. She was surprised to find she was ravenous. Maybe she'd finally relaxed enough to accept her journey as an adventure. Or maybe his reassurances that she'd be left alone to come to her own conclusions about his proposition had made her more comfortable with the whole thing. Whatever the case, she all but inhaled the Shepherd's pie and baked apple dessert.

Neither had done much talking, other then exclaiming on their hunger and commenting on the food. When they were done, Graham didn't linger, but put his napkin on the table and stood, gesturing her to proceed him from the car back to their seats. She found herself wishing she'd bought a magazine in the train station, then was reminded once again that she hadn't any funds. Though she knew without a doubt Graham would have taken care of any request she'd made, she was glad she hadn't asked him for anything else. Since their little chat curbside, in front of the station, things, while not exactly awkward, were no longer as easy or congenial as they'd been.

Nor were they laced with that heady physical chemistry she'd been feeling pretty much every second of her time spent near him—pretty much every second of the day since their meeting in the prayer garden.

She leaned back and closed her eyes, and thought over that moment. What he'd said, how solicitous he'd been, despite the tension and stress he had been under himself. It said a lot about his character, as had pretty much everything he'd done and said since then.

Except perhaps when he'd been lying half on top of her in the limo to the airport . . . and again in the cab leaving Glasgow. She wasn't sure what that said about either of them.

Maybe it was just as well their time completely alone with one another was coming to an end. She opened her eyes just enough to steal a sideways glance at him. His head was tipped back and his eyes were closed. She wondered how much rest he'd gotten since leaving Kinloch.

She also wondered if she could fake sleep and shift her head to his shoulder all innocent like and enjoy his heat, and sturdy stability one last time. She closed her eyes and talked herself out of it. Playtime was over, as was the post-apocalyptic wedding limbo. Showtime was but hours away. She was going to have to stop thinking about Graham and his amazing wonder-kilt, and start thinking about his offer and her future, both immediate and distant. Where would she go after Kinloch? Where did she want to go?

Most importantly, what in the hell did she want to do with herself once she got there?

She had quite an arsenal of corporate marketing and sales skills, albeit in her case geared toward the ship-building industry, but still, management skills, both in education and in actual practice, had to count for something. She'd been very good at her job. Her family would have accepted nothing less. She'd find . . . something.

She let out a long, soft breath. The very idea of going back to anything resembling her old job bored the ever-loving snot out of her.

But what the hell else was she to do?

Not for the first time did she wish she'd let herself dream, like Blaine had. Like Blaine always had. Since they'd been little kids, he'd always had the ability to create the most imaginative alternate universes for them to inhabit. Always about as far away from the reality of their uber-controlled lives as possible. As they'd grown older, they'd come to appreciate what they did have, and tried like hell—she did anyway—to not resent what they didn't. Like having normal parents who loved them for who they were, not what they could bring to the eventual corporate table. She knew she led an otherwise privileged life. No one ever felt sorry for the poor little rich girl. She'd focused on making the best of the good and tolerating the rest.

Blaine, on the other hand, had always dreamed of what could be, what might be, if he ever had the balls to do something about it. Katie couldn't handle letting herself dream the unattainable. It made focusing on the positive that much harder and seemed, all in all, a negative track.

Not Blaine. He'd dreamed, and he'd dreamed big. Huge. His plans had only grown more detailed the older he got. He'd taken double major classes in college. Using money he earned on his own that his parents would never know about, he took additional classes toward the engineering degree he so wanted. Of course they'd found out. And of course they'd put an end to it. But not before making Blaine feel like the most ungrateful child on the planet for doing so.

Katie thought it was then he'd finally resigned himself to his fate. She didn't recall much time, if any, spent on dreaming big after that. His only big dream left was finding someone whom he truly loved, and who loved him back, which he had, in Tag.

No one knew better than Blaine how to conduct a discreet life. Katie had no idea if his family knew, or suspected. On the one hand, she thought if they did, they'd have made a major production out of it. On the other hand, she couldn't honestly imagine they didn't. She'd often wondered if they were just practicing a don't-ask-don't-tell mantra because, in the end, Blaine was doing as they wanted him to do.

She wondered what was happening right then, back home. Where he was, whether Tag had stepped forward. If her parents were so furious at what she'd done that they'd forgotten to be worried that she'd, essentially, gone missing. She made a face. No, they wouldn't be worried about anything other than how the sham of a wedding was going to play out in the press. She imagined the past day-and-a-half had been spent mostly doing damage control and ordering others to track her down and bring her to hand.

Well, that wasn't going to happen.

She'd circled right back around to what her next step was going to be. She only knew what it wasn't going to be.

She must have sighed, though she didn't recall doing so. Graham apparently hadn't been dozing after all. He reached over and took her hand, and tugged her gently closer, so her head angled toward his shoulder.

She shot him a glance, but he was still leaning back, eyes closed. She debated whether to take his lead, but who was she kidding? She gently leaned against him. He settled further into his seat, tugged her closer, and wove his hand through hers.

Maybe he's asleep, she thought, feeling the steady rise and fall of his chest below her chin. And maybe, it didn't matter.

She settled herself, too, and figured they both deserved what little comfort they could get before stepping into the next part of their joint venture.

It didn't take long for the steady cadence and rhythm of the moving train, the general peacefulness of the car they were in, and Graham's sturdy warmth to lull her into a doze. Just as sleep was claiming her, she could have sworn she felt him press his cheek—or were those his lips?—to the top of her head, and murmur, "It's all going to work out fine, Katherine Georgina. You just wait and see."

"Katherine Elizabeth Georgina," she murmured, making the correction automatically.

She felt him chuckle quietly, and knew then he'd never been asleep.

That made her smile. And sleep as soundly as she ever had.

Chapter 8

Graham hated to wake her, but they'd arrived in Oban and needed to hurry to catch the late ferry crossing to Castlebay. From there, service over to Kinloch was going to be tenuous, at best. Even in the fading light, the skies to the west didn't look too promising.

It had been an exhausting two days, and this after a matching day-and-a-half getting to Annapolis in the first place. Between the toll of travel by several modes of transportation, and the added stress of the reason for the trip in the first place . . . compounded by the fact that he was no longer traveling alone, and everything that went with that new reality had been way more than he could ever have predicted . . . it was all finally catching up to him. He'd slept better than he'd expected to on the train, but it was a small drop compared to what he truly needed to clear his head and be at his best upon his return.

Once they'd booked ferry passage, he'd call Roan. He knew, from checking his phone that he had a backlog of voice mail, e-mail, text messages, and missed calls that likely meant a less-than-lovely reception when he finally checked in. He didn't give a rat's patootie, as Katie would say, how Roan or Shay were holding up, especially given that Roan had known what he was sending Graham into, without the least bit of forewarning. He could leave them to stew with little guilt on his end. But their arrival was close enough that he had to start laying the ground-work for Katie's entree and subsequent stay.

He also needed to find out exactly what had gone on with Mr. Iain McAuley during his absence. Surely he couldn't have made much progress in a few days time.

Graham looked down at the woman nestled against his chest, and rethought that last sentiment.

"Katie," he said, keeping his tone quiet. "We've arrived. We're in Oban. You need to wake up now."

She moved a little, mumbled something under her breath . . . then snuggled in a little closer.

He smiled. It was strange to think he might actually miss wak-ing up while she slept, sprawled all over him, making one of his arms numb from leaning on it for hours. Though, he had no one to blame but himself. He'd just . . . hell, he wasn't sure why he'd pulled her close. But it was the last time, the last leg where they'd be seated together for a long stretch, and he'd just . . .

He'd just.

"Katie," he said again, shifting a little as he gently pushed her up and off of his chest.

As soon as her cheek moved past his shoulder, she blinked her eyes open.

He smiled. "Hullo, sleepyhead. We're in Oban."

She frowned. "What?"

"Ferry. Time for the ferry."

Her eyes opened wider. "We're here?"

He nodded.

She rubbed her face and raked her hands through her hair, then scowled again. "Please tell me there will be some place for me to make myself look like something other than an escaped convict before we arrive in Kinloch." She paused, then looked at him, quite seriously, and said, "Though, I suppose that's an apt description."

He'd noted she hadn't spoken much about what she'd left behind. He knew she had no phone, but she hadn't asked to use his. "Do you—is there anyone you think you should call? I have a phone."

She shook her head. "No. I'm not . . . no."

"Okay," he said, simply. "If you should ever want to—"

"Is there a place I could buy one of those pay-as-you-go phones? Wait, what am I saying?" She ducked her chin and busied herself by straightening her top and smoothing out her pants.

He wasn't sure why he did it, but he reached out and tipped her chin up, so she looked directly at him. "I'll get you a phone. You can pay me back later. Or we'll write it into the agreement if you want. I know this is hard for you, a lot of changes, but I won't think less of you for asking for a little help until we get things settled."

"It's not your good graces I was worried about."

"Whose then?"

She tapped her chest. "Mine." She sighed and shifted back, away from his touch. "You wouldn't understand."

"On the contrary, I think I understand more than you realize." He stretched and stood. "Whatever the case, just know the offer stands. Come on, we need to go book passage."

She merely nodded, gathered herself, and followed him off the train without further comment.

They were both still travel weary. He knew that. The kind of tired sleeping while sitting up in a jostling mode of transportation didn't fix.

It took a bit to gather her mountain of luggage and get it redirected toward the ferry. Most of the ferry passengers were crossing with their cars, so it took him and Katie a bit longer to get situated.

"I'm sorry." She folded her arms and glared at her pile of matching Italian hand-stitched valises and trunks. "For the pain in the ass those have become."

"Stop saying—"

"No, I won't. Because *I'm* sorry. It's a pain in my ass, too."

He smiled at that. She was grumpy. And rumpled. And a little past the point of trying to hide it. He tried to put himself in her position, not only as a runaway bride, daughter, and corporate family pawn, but also as someone who was stepping way outside her comfort zone. It was a lot.

Besides, she made a cute grump.

Something he wisely kept to himself.

All that unruly hair, which had more curl to it than he'd realized, all done up under that veil as it had been, was clearly trying to revert to its natural state. And her face . . . it wasn't the lean, aquiline look of a woman born of wealth. She had a rather button-like nose, a rounded chin with a bit of a dimple, fairly pronounced cheekbones, a cupid bow mouth, and the thickest lashes he'd ever seen on a natural blonde. All of that bounty provided the backdrop to the bluest eyes he'd been fortunate to look into. She appeared quite like a woodland sprite, as if one had come to life in the form of a mortal woman.

He heard her grumbling under her breath, and his hidden smile spread to a grin as he preceded her along the railing to the front of the boat, where they could watch the sunset as they made their way across the Sea of Hebrides.

So what if she was a grumpy sprite. The underlying pallor to her skin and the smudges beneath her eyes kept him from trying to cajole her out of it. She needed a bed, and some alone time away from the rest of the world.

"The ferry is so much bigger than I'd expected."

"Aye," he said. "Caledonian MacBrayne is the main ferry service used to cross over to Uists. Here, further north in Mallaig, and even farther, from Uig on Skye."

"The Uists?"

"Part of the Outer Hebrides. Lewis and Harris is the northern most island."

"Harris. As in Harris tweed?"

He nodded. "As in exactly that. It is all woven there."

"On the island itself?"

He nodded. "By law, it must be woven by loom in the weaver's own home."

"Wow. That's—I had no idea."

He nodded again. "It used to be the wool was all sheared and spun on the island as well. They passed the Harris Tweed Act sometime back, which allows them to use wool from other places, but it must meet a strict set of standards. The resultant product is reviewed by inspectors from the Harris Tweed Authority—"

"Wait. They have tweed inspectors?"

He nodded, amused by her expression. "Aye. If it meets their strict standards, it receives the Orb Mark, which means it's acceptable for use in making Harris Tweed products. It's all highly regulated, but we take great pride in the result."

"I can well imagine. That's amazing, actually. That it still exists today, following the same standards, and hasn't been mechanized by modern technology. It's wonderful, really."

He smiled. "Aye, it is that and more. I'm glad you think of it that way as well. It will help you better understand my tie to Kinloch, both ancestral and personal. Harris Tweed is quite similar to our own, albeit much smaller industry. We are not bound by such a strict set of laws, but we have our own strictures and guidelines. We're likewise known for the quality control and the weaving itself, which is all done in similar fashion to the tweed—in the home of the weaver."

"You make wool fabric on Kinloch, too?"

He shook his head. "Our industry is artisan basketry."

"Artisan . . . baskets? Made out of wool?"

He laughed. "No, I've gotten ye all confused. Our baskets are made from linen, which originates with the flaxseed plant. After harvest, it's spun, dyed, and waxed, then run onto spools in a heavy thread form."

"You make baskets. From thread."

He nodded. "They are works of art more than for functional use. We still control every aspect of the process, right on the island. I'll be happy to show you, once we're home." In fact, he had every intention of showing her the foundation upon which he'd built his life. All his learning, all his energy and focus had revolved around maintaining and continuing the success of their heritage industry, to keep Kinloch thriving and to preserve what he saw as an important ancestral art.

"Oh, I want to see it. That sounds amazing."

"I happen to think it is, but you'll judge for yourself."

She turned back to the rail as the engines of the ferry revved strongly to life, indicating they were about to debark port. "I had no idea. Baskets. From linen thread." She looked up at him over her shoulder, where he'd moved in to stand closely behind her at the rail. "Why didn't you tell me?"

"Well, it hadn't come up as yet. I had every intention. It's the reason I came to find ye."

"The basket weaving?"

"It's the foundation of the economy on our island. We've struggled. I've devoted my life's work to finding ways to improve the consistency of the crop output and protect it from blight. My grandfather spent all his later years trying to get us back after a particularly harsh blight almost brought life on Kinloch to an end. I'm still helping us rebound, and trying to keep it from happening again, so we can confidently solidify our hold on the market. Using the modern technology we can employ, namely the Internet, we're growing to a worldwide market."

She shook her head, appearing a bit in disbelief. "It's an incredible story, Graham."

"I don't know about that, but it is my story."

The boat moved just then, and while he was prepared from past experience, she wasn't. So when there was a tug and a jerk as the boat began its progress away from the slip dock, Katie was forced to grab the rail momentarily to steady herself.

Graham immediately took hold of her shoulders to assist her, but after she righted herself, he found himself reluctant to release her.

So . . . he didn't.

And she didn't move away.

He wondered what excuse he would find to touch her, hold her, when they weren't at the mercy of unpredictable vehicle movement. He continued to brace her as they proceeded slowly across the harbor, toward the strait that ran between the mainland and the outer islands, which were becoming more visible in the distance.

He looked down at Katie as she watched the world unfold in front of her. His world. She was a stranger to him, and to the island way of life he held so dear. A way of life that she held in her slender hands. He watched as she looked back at the very picturesque Oban harbor town of Port Appin, with its rows of old stone homes and shops that lined the shore. They scattered up into the hills, the crest of which was topped by the coliseum-style remains of McCaig's Folly.

"It's truly beautiful here, Graham," she said, with sincere awe in her voice.

Her comment spurred the pride of his homeland that always coursed through him, but, on that occasion, he felt it a bit more keenly. "It will be far more quaint when we ferry from Castle-bay over to Kinloch. You'll get your more traditional boat ride then." He smiled. "You might wish you were back on the Cal-Mac."

"Possibly," she said, but it was clear she was still distracted by the view. She turned her head the full range until she'd taken in the entire skyline. "It's lovely. Absolutely breathtaking."

He smiled, happy that she was taken with the view. He found it irresistible, but then he was somewhat biased. "Wait until ye see the outer islands, Barra, Vatersay, then Kinloch. I think you'll see why I'm going to such lengths to preserve our way of life there." At least he hoped so.

She turned just enough to look up at him. It moved her more deeply into the protective stance of his body, which stirred instantly and quite insistently to life. He shifted, just a bit, but kept his gaze on hers. And kept his lower body just out of accidental brushing range. More stimulation was unwise at the moment—especially seeing as he apparently had no consistent discipline whatsoever where she was concerned. At that very moment, he still had his hands on her, and she was allowing the contact to continue.

"I know I might not seem it," she said, mercifully drawing thoughts away from the insistent state of his body. "But I am looking forward to seeing it. All of it. I know the circumstances of why I'm here are a bit daunting to me, and I'm guessing to you as well, so I'm sorry for being anxious about all that. But the rest, if it looks anything like this . . ." She let her words drift off as she once again took in the harbor view, and beyond to the islands in the west.

He leaned down so his head was more on par with hers, and reached past her shoulder to point. "Those are part of the Inner Hebrides. Mull and Lismore. Once we're past that into the Sea of the Hebrides, you'll get sight of Coll, and your first look at Barra, and when we're a bit closer still, you'll see Kinloch to the south and west."

"I can see why this place calls to you," she said quietly, as they continued slowly chugging their way up the channel between Mull and Lismore. "It's different in so many ways from Annapolis, and yet when I come home from being out on the water, there is such a pull there for me." She glanced up again. "So, I understand why there is one here, for you."

She hadn't even gotten to the outer islands, as yet, he thought. Castlebay was a comparatively large, thriving village. The journey beyond that point was going to be quite a bit more rustic compared to the view in front of her. Katie came from wealth and privilege. Though she seemed quite down to earth and pleased by the elemental aspects of what lay in front of her . . . he wasn't quite sure that pleasure would remain once she realized there wasn't a Mayfair hotel suite waiting for her at the end of their journey. Hell, there wasn't even central heating.

"Perhaps we do share that in common," he said, though privately he wondered if the similarity began and ended with their respective homes being waterfront bound.

"How does Port Appin here in Oban compare with Castlebay on Barra, or . . . what is the port town on Kinloch?

"*Aiobhneas.*" When her brow knitted, he clarified. "Gaelic. Roughly translated, it means joy."

"It sounds beautiful when you say it. I wouldn't even try," she said, with a self-deprecating smile he found charming. It deepened the hint of a dimple in her chin.

"Do you speak the language fluently?" she asked.

He nodded. "It's been an unfortunate victim of progress, and is dying on the mainland. Up in the western Highlands, and farther north, as well as out in the Hebrides, it's still a strong part of our culture and in many cases, especially with our older clansmen and women, the predominant language spoken. On Kinloch, you'll see, the road signs and local buildings, menus, and the like, will have either Gaelic only, or both Gaelic and English. Our local news and the paper are in Gaelic as well."

Katie sighed, but she was still smiling. "Great, something else to worry about."

"Dinnae worry," he said, with a laugh, "they all speak English as well. Though, perhaps, a very heavily accented version to your ears. You'll be able to make yourself understood."

She smiled, then turned back to look at the view outward toward the sea, her body shifting ever so slightly closer to his. "So, compare Oban to Castlebay, and to . . . Port Joy," she finished with a laugh.

He laughed with her. "'Tis a lovely ring to it. Oban is far bigger, with residents numbering in the thousands. Eight or more thousand, at least. Castlebay is the largest village on Barra, and the main port of call, but the island, along with its sister island, Vatarsay, totals little over a thousand people."

"Wow," she said. "Like I said, Annapolis alone is something like thirty thousand or so, and it's not considered a big city. It's hard to imagine even the eight or ten thousand in Oban. But the islands are really quite, well, I'm guessing rural isn't really the right word, but—what about Kinloch? It's smaller, I take it, than Barra?"

He smiled and nodded, even while inwardly wincing. What would she think when she discovered just how "rural" her new home would be? Temporary though it may be, he didn't want it to be any more temporary than necessary. Meaning he needed her to stay at least as long as it took for her to make up her mind about him. About his proposal, he mentally added. It wasn't him she was judging, but what he was offering her.

He was actually glad their manner of exiting the chapel had prevented her from retrieving her purse and any real access she had to other people or to personal funds. Not that he considered her imprisoned by any stretch, but, at the moment, he wasn't unhappy with the reality that she was somewhat beholden to him.

He was well aware, however, how much she loathed being beholden to anyone at that particular juncture of her life, so he wasn't going to take too much comfort in the setup the fates had so kindly handed him. But he did plan to take as full advantage of them as he could.

As the ferry moved out into the sea, and he could barely see home on the horizon, he felt that primal tug toward his singular place on earth. He was reminded anew of what was at stake, and what his priorities were.

His hands tightened on her shoulders, and she lifted one of her own from the rail, covered his, and squeezed. "You haven't been gone all that long, but you miss it, don't you?" she asked, looking ahead, not at him. But leaving her hand covering his.

He nodded, then realized she couldn't see the gesture. "Aye," he said, his voice a bit more guttural than he'd expected. It had been an emotional couple of days. Months, actually, if he factored in the turmoil since Ualraig's death.

"Will ye miss your own place in the world, Katie McAuley?" he heard himself ask. It was an unwise thing, to plant any seed of homesickness in her head, or in her heart. But they'd be there regardless. At the moment, he was feeling a particular kinship with her that was hard to ignore, so the question just came out.

She nodded, and squeezed his hand harder.

Quite instinctively, he stepped up and pulled her more fully into the shelter of his body. "I understand. And I'm sorry."

He thought she might have sniffled, but she merely nodded, her head bobbing beneath his chin. "Thanks," she said, her voice barely carrying above the thrumming engines of the ferry.

He nestled her against his chest, and slid their joined hands around her waist, matching it with his other arm, until she was ensconced inside them. He felt, rather than heard the sigh that preceded her relaxing back against him, taking his comfort, and perhaps, borrowing from his strength as well.

She wanted independence and autonomy, he thought, and understood the desire. But, at the moment, she fit quite perfectly where she stood. As he found comfort and strength in their joined embrace, he didn't think she'd given up so much of either, as it was more like they shared them with each other.

He thought of the things he wanted to say to her. Tell her about Kinloch. His friends there. The islanders who were both his extended family and his responsibility. He had a sense she would understand him, understand the dual pressures, possibly better than anyone he'd met. Not because she understood his culture, as their differences were vast. But because she had faced that same duality of purpose and expectation in her own life. Though, for him, it was more welcome task than unwanted burden.

She leaned a bit more heavily into his arms as they entered the open waters, heading toward Castlebay. The sun was setting, the air was warm, but the wind crossing the bow of the ship made it feel a bit more brisk than it actually was.

"I wish I could paint," she said.

"Paint?" he asked, confused momentarily as he was pulled from his ruminations about her, his future . . . and what role she was going to play.

"You know. Oil on canvas kind of paint. That is a pretty stunning view, with the sun setting, all the colors and hues. I don't think a photograph alone could do it justice. I'm not bad with pen and ink, but that . . . needs to be painted." She laughed shortly. "My skills run more toward using rulers and T-squares. Not exactly the most elegant art."

"Did you help design your family's sailing boats?"

"When I was young, before I went off to college, I fancied myself as a future designer of high-end racing sloops and fancy yachts. Not so much the engineering aspect of how it sat in the water, but the look of it, the style."

"Sounds like a perfect fit with the family business."

She sighed and he tucked her more fully against him. He'd have said it was to keep the wind from tossing her hair about and into her face as she spoke. But he knew it was every bit as self-serving as it was to afford protection from the elements.

He was feeling very . . . elemental at the moment. But the wind, the deepening colors of the sky, the churning waters, and the beautiful vista ahead of the peaks of Barra had little to do with it.

"I'd have thought so, too. But my father made it very clear that my talents were to be focused on the pragmatic and practical, not the whimsical. After that I tried to win him over to the idea of letting me get into the marketing end of things. I thought I would simply move toward a graphic artist approach and help advertise our business, direct my focus to something that combined the art with the industry."

"And?"

"Shot down. My mother, actually, was the dream crusher in that instance. She had these kind of dueling desires for me. On the one hand, she pushed every bit as hard as my father did for me to be part of the business. I am their only child, much to my father's dismay, as he'd wanted a son to mold into a new version of himself."

"A daughter couldn't do the same?"

"Oh, he molded me all right. Eventually—when he accepted

that I was his only chance at industrial immortality. That was precisely why my mother was so torn. She was happy that he'd finally given up the idea that he'd have a male offspring to carry on his name and take over his share of the company. My mother was happy, I think, to have his disapproval over her inadequacy in childbearing off her shoulders. So she pushed the father-daughter bond every chance she got. No matter if she agreed with his plans for me, or not."

"Did she work for the company, too?"

Katie laughed, but there was little humor in it. "In her own way, I think she contributes every bit as much, if not more, to the success of the company than my father does. Only she's not on their payroll, no."

"So, in what way—"

"Our business relies heavily on perception. People with lots of money want to buy a product they see as top of the line, which ours is. But it can't just be well made, it also needs to be prestigious. My mother was nothing if not the best hostess, best corporate wife, best charity organizer, in terms of schmoozing the clientele. She dedicated herself to building McAuley-Sheffield into a very prestigious business, from the social end of things. It was no small feat, and led to her internal battle—let my father mold me, or groom me herself to be, well . . . her."

Graham nodded, stroked her arms with his thumbs, and let her keep talking.

"You see, there was a lot of pressure for McAuley-Sheffield to go public, not remain privately owned."

"Pressure from?"

"Blaine's father. He believed the time had come to take it in that direction, in order to keep the company thriving. My father disagreed."

"I'm assuming this dissension was part of why you and Blaine were pushed together?"

"Exactly. Finally, they had an opportunity to unite the company in a way they never had before. My dad was pushing me to learn the business so I could be strong enough to keep it private, as he wished. He knew Blaine wouldn't be a match for me in that regard, down the line. My mother, on the other hand, wanted me to marry Blaine and take over her duties, keeping the flames burning from the outside, the social angle. She couldn't do it forever, and she feared without that combination—"

"The business was equally doomed," Graham finished.

Katie simply nodded.

He leaned down to kiss the top of her head, as if that was something he did—often—and checked himself mid motion.

An odd sensation shot through him when he pulled back. As if he'd altered things in some way. Some wrong way.

"Anyway, that was more than you probably needed to know."

On the contrary, he wanted to tell her. It was exactly the kind of thing he wanted to know. She'd claimed the need to break free and stand on her own, be her own person, with her own mind. Only she hadn't once struck him as the kind of woman who'd tolerate anything less of herself.

He better understood why she'd been trapped as she had. It was rather astounding, actually, that on her wedding of all days, she'd finally taken that stand. He realized he might have played a small role, but she'd already been well pushed to the breaking point before he arrived, given the state he'd found her in.

"No," he said. "Thank you for telling me. I appreciate the trust."

"It's probably best you know, anyway. So you know what you're getting with me. And the potential for future, potentially ugly entanglements with my family, if we . . . you know."

His arms tightened around her in an instinctive need to protect. As if the very idea that someone would threaten her in any way was his sole and absolute duty to defend. So strong was the notion that he shook his head, as if he could so easily shake off the feeling.

It was merely her discussing their legal union, which was naturally fraught with all kinds of anxiety and concerns, some of them he'd surely not contemplated as yet. The reaction was purely a subconscious reaction to everything that was roiling about inside his head.

Except the ache he felt was centered in his chest.

It wasn't the sort of ache one would mistake for a heart attack. Not that his heart wasn't under attack, just that the war being waged was one he didn't fully understand. She wasn't clinging, though, and she most certainly wasn't pushing for, well, anything. In fact, she was one step away from turning tail and running. Or would be if she had her hands on her wallet.

Step back. That's what he needed to do. Take a giant step back. Both figuratively . . . and literally.

To that end, he loosened his hold on her, and was moving away when she gasped and pointed.

"Is that it? Is that Kinloch?"

He glanced outward, surprised to see they were closing in on Castlebay. The ferry had moved far enough leeward in preparation to enter the harbor via the deepest channel, which provided a glimpse of the island just beyond and to the west of Barra.

His island.

"Aye," he said, feeling the ache bloom anew in his chest, but the cause was entirely different. The source was not at all foreign or confusing. "That is home, Katie."

My home, he added silently, with intent. Because what he'd thought, in that instant, was *our home*.

He realized he'd not only not stepped back, he'd actually stepped up and tucked her into the shelter of his body once again. She turned just then, and even though it was nigh on to midnight, the glow of the setting sun, barely apparent over the horizon of Barra, appeared to set the tips of her curls afire. There was a light in her blue eyes, one he couldn't recall seeing before that moment.

"It's beautiful, Graham," she said, smiling up into his face. "I didn't expect the mountains and the—all of it. It's stunning."

Not, "wow, it's so tiny," or "how do you survive on such a spit of land." No, she'd gasped, smiled, and called it stunning.

As was she, he thought, lowering his head as he turned her more fully into his arms, his actions no longer under his control. Surely, *he* wouldn't be taking that step—not when he most needed to gird himself, and gather his wits about him.

But he didn't check the motion. Didn't even try.

The truth was, he'd wanted to kiss Katherine Elizabeth Georgina Rosemary McAuley since he'd first laid eyes on her—dressed to wed another man. A stranger. Yet it felt like he'd waited eons already, before he took what he knew to be his.

Chapter 9

Katie froze, just for a split second, as she tried to shift gears from her excitement at seeing the island, and focus on the idea, the possibility that Graham was going to—

"Oh," she said, rather breathlessly, as he slid his hand to the back of her neck and tipped her mouth up to his. "Graham—"

He paused. She hadn't really thought he would. There was that fierce light in his eyes again. She'd seen it in the chapel . . . and again in the limo . . . the taxi, too. They'd been interrupted, every time. Her grip on his shoulders tightened, which was when she became aware she'd grabbed hold of him. And not with the intent to push him away.

"Aye, Katie?" he said, his gaze so intently focused on her face, most specifically her mouth, that any intelligent response she might have given was rendered pointless.

She was too busy trying to shore up her suddenly wobbling legs.

"You—we—should we be . . . ?"

"Probably not," he said, his voice like a sanding block against teak, "but I'm no' thinkin' so clearly at the moment, *mo chridhe*. So if ye feel ye should stop me, say so now." He lowered his head another fraction of an inch.

She could feel the warmth of his breath mingle with hers, his lips were so close. So close she only had to lift the tiniest bit onto her toes to brush her lips against them. The yearning to taste him, to feel what it would be like to tap into that focus, that intensity, that . . . ferocity, all aimed so potently at her . . . by doing something as simple, as wonderful, as mating her mouth to his . . . was overwhelmingly powerful.

In the end, she decided the matter for him—and for herself. Lifting to her toes, she brushed her lips against his. Standing, as it happened, on her own two feet. Making her own choices. Taking control of her life. Taking, for once, what she wanted.

He let her kiss him, accepting without taking, and she felt his shoulders flex under the pressure of her fingers, even as she heard the soft groan come from somewhere deep inside his chest. "Katie," he murmured against her mouth. "*Mo chridhe.*"

She had no idea what that meant, but the way he said it made her toes curl. Something deep inside her began to unfurl, and her kiss grew more insistent.

An instant later she was cradled fully against his chest as he bent his head to hers and shifted the kiss to one of need and possession.

She had absolutely no problem with that. She was feeling a bit needy and possessive herself at that moment.

He slid his hands around to cup her face. His palms were broad, and warm, and callused. Strong and steady, they were like a sturdy frame she could center herself between. His lips were warm, firm, and tasted a bit salty from the sea spray and wind, making her wonder if she tasted the same to him.

She tipped up a bit more onto her toes, wanting more of him, feeling suddenly as if she'd been starved and had been offered an endless feast.

She supposed the description wasn't far from the truth. She and Blaine had never been intimate at any point in their lives, but despite knowing they'd end up bound forever in some way, they'd never been foolish enough to believe that their deep, abiding friendship would be enough.

That was why, when Tag had come along, she'd encouraged Blaine to pursue him. There had been others before, but they'd been teenage crushes or the shallow flings of the newly liberated college student. Tag had been the first serious threat to Blaine's heart and Katie had wanted him to follow that call. Even to the point of discussing his coming out, to his family, to everyone, so he could have what would make him truly happy. Men had given up kingdoms for love, surely the world wouldn't end if Blaine gave up McAuley-Sheffield for his.

Though he had fallen head over heels, he'd never found the courage to do what his heart begged him—what she'd begged him—to do.

In the end, he hadn't heeded either. His heart, because he'd wanted it too badly to risk losing it all. Or her, because he said she didn't really know what she was talking about.

She'd had her own schoolgirl crushes, and she'd thought she'd found love in college. In the end, it had just been convenient sex. She'd never found her equivalent to Blaine's Tag. After her college debacle, she hadn't been in any big hurry to repeat that painful mistake. Once she'd graduated and gone to work for the company, she hadn't been able to figure out how to conduct a private life that would remain truly private. Her parents could believe whatever they would about her relationship with Blaine. She'd never lied to them about her feelings for him. Whether they knew, or suspected what the full truth was, on either side, she had no idea. It wasn't as if they discussed intimate matters. But, to her mind anyway, it had to be painfully obvious to anyone who knew them, or spent any time with them.

Yet the farce continued. What mattered was what people assumed they knew, not necessarily what was actually true. What mattered was the face one showed to the world, not what one might privately feel. How many times had her parents drilled that into her? That it was all about projecting what you wanted the world to believe to be true. Perception was a reality you could control. So, no way would she have set herself up, much less someone else, for the potential scandal that would ensue if she'd been discovered to be "cheating" on Blaine.

So it was only natural, normal even, for her to be feeling like a sex-starved maniac. Because . . . wasn't she? Starving?

"Katie?"

She blinked her eyes open, to find Graham's face an inch or two from hers, his steady regard still intent, but combined with sincere concern.

"What?" she whispered, then lifted her hand to her face . . . and realized the salty taste hadn't come from the sea spray, or even Graham for that matter.

Mortified, she scrubbed away the trickle of tears, hoping beyond hope that he'd assume it was merely the wind stinging her eyes. How pathetic could she be? She hadn't thought she could be any more humbled than she'd felt before entering the church the first time . . . what felt like eons ago. She'd felt silly, and stupid and weak for not standing up to her family, or to Blaine. For not demanding the farce be brought to an end long before she committed the even more egregious sin of marrying a man she loved like a brother, in the presence of God and everyone else she loved and cared about.

She remembered wondering what in the hell she'd been thinking, to believe what she was about to do was actually okay. That she thought she'd been doing it for her family, or for Blaine, or for the greater good of McAuley-Sheffield was hardly a point in her favor. She thought of the pain and frustration that had coursed through her, literally shaking her, as she'd also been forced to confront the ugly truth that her very own parents didn't care she was about to commit what amounted to life perjury— as long as it got them the desired outcome. So why in God's name was she willing to do something so sacrificial for them?

She hadn't believed, hadn't been truly aware until that moment of understanding, some part of her—the part that was still their child—had hoped, prayed, when push came to shove, they'd step forward and tell her it was okay. They loved her and just wanted her to be happy. In that moment, she'd reckoned with the truth. They were never going to do that.

That soul-snatching epiphany is what had sent her into the prayer garden in a fit of self-directed fury. What an idiot she was. What a pathetic, sorry, blind idiot. Of all the people on the planet, she was the last one who should have believed her parents could ever be the loving, supportive image of parenthood they projected to the world. She was the one who knew, without a doubt, it wasn't true. Yet somewhere in her heart she'd wanted to buy what they were selling . . . just like everybody else.

Enter Graham MacLeod, with his ridiculously insane offer, his solid, sturdy presence, his unbelievable hotness in a kilt, all bundled up with that gentle warrior demeanor.

That same gentle warrior was brushing her hair from her face . . . but not releasing her when she tried to tug free of his arms.

"Ye dinnae have to flee. I promise I'll keep myself under better control. I—" He broke off, then looked down. "I'm definitely no' in the habit of forcing my attentions on anyone, but with you . . ." He looked to her again, and her heart squeezed at the true remorse and confusion she saw there. "I don't know what comes over me with you. But it's no' my intention to scare you with inappropriate—"

She impulsively grabbed his face and tugged his mouth to hers. He stiffened, but only for a moment. Then they were both kissing like it was the last feast they'd ever have. She broke the kiss off just as it was about to rocket beyond their control. Again. She felt a little lightheaded, and a lot breathless. "It wasn't inappropriate, Graham. I was most definitely not shedding tears because I was in fear of . . . anything. Except maybe myself." He started to speak, but she lifted her finger to his mouth . . . and felt that wham pow punch all over again.

His pupils had shot wide as well, giving her another glimpse of the desire barely restrained beneath the surface veneer of politeness. When she tried to snatch her hand away, he deftly captured it in his own, and held it between them, their gazes locked and . . . hungry.

"I'm expecting nothing, Katie," he said, and she could feel the words all but vibrate against her skin. "Yet I'm discovering I want . . . everything." He brought her fingertips to his lips, and kissed them, one by one, while keeping his gaze fixed intently on hers. "I know it's no' sensible, and that we've enough to handle in each of our lives, without further . . . complications." He nibbled on one fingertip and she thought she might expire right there from abject desire. "Yet, I cannae seem to bring it to any kind of order. In my head. Or . . . anywhere else."

"I-I know," she managed, her throat tight, every part of her throbbing with more bound up need than she thought it possible for one body to contain. "I-I've allowed my life to go so far afield, I no longer even know who I am, or what I really want. So, I know. I know it's not fair to start anything, or lead you to believe . . . anything. And yet . . ." She curled the fingers he held until she held his hand, then pulled it to her own lips, and softly placed a kiss on the back of it, all the while watching his eyes as they remained so focused on her own. "So, I do know, Graham. I just don't know what to do about it."

"And the tears?" he asked, lowering their joined hands between them, but trapping them against his chest as he tugged her closer.

"Utter confusion, and wishing I knew my own self better. Wishing that I hadn't ended up in a place where I don't know how to respond to what should be the most natural and wonderful form of human connection between two people who are attracted to each other." She tried to laugh, but it didn't quite come out that way. "I'm messed up, Graham. You don't need that. Or me." She broke their gaze then, and glanced away, anywhere, it didn't matter since she wasn't seeing anything outwardly at the moment. "I'm not usually pathetic. At least I never felt that way about myself. I knew my responsibilities and I accepted them. I was firm and decisive about how I dealt with . . . everything. Not remotely pathetic, but proactively dealing with what life had handed me in a specific, well thought-out manner. But I realize now . . . I've been pathetic the whole time." She laughed then, and it sounded sorry and sad, even to her own ears. Her throat tightened again, and she honestly didn't think she could bear being humbled any further, though perhaps there was no lower place to go.

"Katie."

He nudged her chin up until she looked at him. Her eyes were glassy and there didn't seem to be a damn thing she could do about it.

"You are decisive and strong. No' many could put up with the pressures and expectations you have, and handle them so well and so thoroughly. It's no' pathetic to come to realize that you've been looking at things in a way that might have been the best for others, but perhaps not what's best for you. You've been putting everyone else first. And you've finally come to know that, now, it's time to put yourself first. From the moment you reached that bit of knowledge, you acted on it. Firmly decisive—"

"If not particularly well thought-out," she finished, with a watery laugh.

He cupped her face again, smiling even as the intensity in his voice remained. "What matters is you did it."

His absolute belief in what he was saying was a powerful force, one that, standing in his arms, his gaze so focused on her own, the steady thrum of his heartbeat vibrating through her, was impossible to defend against. She found she didn't want to. She wanted to believe he was right. With everything she had, she wanted to believe it would all work out, that she hadn't jumped from frying pan to fire. Both in her own life, as it had been up to her church exodus, and standing, on a ferry boat bound for a remote Scottish island. But it was still all too surreal. She'd spent a lifetime wanting to believe things that weren't true. Wanting to believe that everything would somehow magically work out in the end.

And look where that had gotten her.

She ducked her chin away so he was no longer touching her face . . . but didn't extricate herself from his arms. She knew she had to . . . and she was working on it. "You're kind and generous, Graham. But you don't really know me. I may look like I'm all those things, but trust me. On the inside, I'm a disaster."

"Hardly that," he said, then cocked his head a bit, as if to look more deeply into her soul. She wasn't entirely sure he couldn't. "I know what I see, Katie. Maybe it's a bit of myself I recognize in you. I have something of a personal understanding of the matter."

"Meaning?"

"You're no' the only one who has woken up to discover that life was suddenly not going as it should, if there is ever to be real personal fulfillment involved."

"Have you ever wished you weren't in charge? That the burden of taking care of an island full of people had fallen to anyone else but you?"

"Fatigued by it? Aye. But truly wishing the burden away? No. I've had a lifetime to think on it, and to prepare. It's just that . . . my way of leading, of helping, has been to focus on the betterment of us all by making sure we remain economically sound, and therefore a viable, self-sustaining population. Ualraig, my grandfather . . . was wonderful in dealing directly with the people, handling the more political and personal conflicts that arise. It's during those times I feel inadequate and less than capable of the job that's been laid at my feet. I know how to take care of us as a whole, but I often worry I'm going to let them down in the other ways that matter."

"Do they make you feel this way?"

"No," he said, then paused, as if to truly contemplate that. "No, they don't."

"Well then?"

He shook his head, and his lips curved into a smile that fully reached his eyes as he continued to regard her. "Well then, indeed."

They smiled at each other for a few long moments, and she felt for the first time, a true bond had been forged between them. One that wasn't physical or hormonal. Or built on surface similarities. Or tied to the situation currently binding them together.

She realized, all the while they'd been deep in each other's personal space—kissed, even—she hadn't once had one of those vivid, erotically charged visions that had leapt so abruptly and intently into her mind's eye, like before whenever she'd had close contact with him. So maybe it really had been some sort of stress-induced hysteria.

Except maybe not—since he was seeing the same things she was.

She couldn't think about that. Or . . . any of it. "How much longer," she asked, remembering there was still so much more left to that day. She couldn't fathom it. She felt . . . tapped out. In every way.

"Longer?" he asked, looking confused. "Oh, until Castlebay." He looked across the rail at the horizon that was slowly coming closer and closer. "Another hour." He looked back to her then and his hold on her tightened briefly at what he saw on her face. "We'll stay in Castlebay tonight." When her eyes widened, he hurried to add, "In our own proper rooms. That's no' what I was aiming for. It's been a long two days. We should take a night, eat, sleep, regroup. It's no' going to matter if we get to Kinloch tonight or tomorrow. They can wait a wee bit longer, and we can get some much-needed rest."

She could have cried all over again, but it would have been tears of gratitude. "That sounds truly wonderful. Thank you. I'll pay you back, for—"

"Now yer just insulting me," he said, but kindly enough. "I've said my piece about this and I won't discuss it further. Ye ken?"

"I ken," she said, smiling, and feeling better for it. "I just—"

"You need to relax and think your own thoughts for the remainder of the night. Dinnae worry so much about what others are thinking, or might think. You're here for you, Katie. Keep yourself in the lead. Even with me. Maybe especially with me."

She tilted her head and studied him. "Is this some kind of reverse psychology?" she said, her tone wry.

He smiled. "I wouldn't begin to know how to apply it, so no. I'm wanting you to do what's best for you. I know what I want, and what I need, but that's up to me to think on, aye? I'm no' your responsibility. I can take care of me, just as you can take care of you."

"Okay then," she said, knowing she didn't need to hear that to know it was true . . . but it felt good to hear it nonetheless. Especially from him. She moved out of his arms and he didn't stop her. Step one, she thought, in regaining her perspective, and possibly whatever hope she had of regaining herself.

She was going to have a full night's reprieve to regroup, and that should be uppermost in her mind. A hot meal, a hotter shower, and a real bed sounded like nirvana to her. But those were still at least an hour or more away. "I think I'm going to take a walk around the decks. Breathe the air and enjoy the night that never gets dark." She smiled a little. "Think my own thoughts." *And be alone long enough to work that kiss out of my system before we walk into a hotel together*, she added silently.

If he was surprised or offended in any way at her sudden defection, he certainly didn't show it. Maybe he was relieved to get his own space for a time, too. It wouldn't be surprising. She was used to spending her days surrounded by people, and noise, and endless demands on her time and attention. Graham spent his time on a tiny island, stuck out at sea, overseeing fields of . . . whatever it was he said his baskets were made out of. Baskets. She was still trying to wrap her head around that one. Beside the point, he was used to the solitude. She wondered what he'd thought about how the past couple days had gone and she imagined he was every bit as done in as she was, only for different reasons.

"Probably no' a bad idea," he said, proving her right, if not, perversely, making her happy about it.

It was precisely why she needed some alone time—to regain some sense of perspective.

"I'll be calling home while you're having your stroll. Get a report on how things are progressing."

"You're telling them you're bringing me with you, right? I mean, we're not making this some kind of big surprise."

"No, nothing like that. And aye, I'll be telling them."

She didn't want to bring up the specifics again. As she mulled it over, she found she wasn't quite as concerned about who knew what regarding where he'd found her . . . and what she'd been about to do when he had, which must mean she was acclimating to her new circumstances. Or too numb to care. Either way, it felt better than the anxiety that had been plaguing her earlier.

Some apprehension lingered in her expression, because he went on to say, "When I left, only my two closest friends knew the circumstances under which we'd be meeting each other. I don't know who has common knowledge regarding that."

"Meaning you don't know if your friends told everyone about it?"

"No, they wouldn't. But it's a small island and news has a way of getting about. They wouldn't patronize or be malicious. But that doesna mean the knowledge hasn't spread anyway."

"Did they—meaning everyone—know what the purpose of your trip was? In general, I mean, if not specifically about me?"

"If you mean did they think I'd suddenly gone on holiday, no. They knew what my mission was. No' about you specifically, though."

"Do you do that? Ever, I mean. Leave the island on holiday?"

He shook his head. "No' much point in it."

"You don't believe in rest and relaxation breaks? Is it so demanding, being responsible for these people, they can't do without you for a short time?"

"No, it's no' that at all. I simply don't see the need to caravan about when there's work to be done."

"There's always work to be done. That doesn't mean you can't occasionally wave and say you're taking a little break. In fact, I'd bet it might even improve things, allow you to gain a fresh perspective on whatever the problem of the day is. Or month. Or year," she added, noticing his expression darken a bit.

"How often was it that you put into practice the advice you're giving in your tidy little speech?"

She opened her mouth, all ready to shoot him down, then stopped, and closed it again.

His knowing smile would have been irritating if it hadn't been so charmingly adorable.

"Okay, okay, touché," she said, before taking the mature path and sticking her tongue out at him. "But, unlike you, I actually wanted a break, wanted to take time off to explore and get away from . . . things."

"Understandable, given what I know of your situation. For me . . . if it took me somewhere to learn more about what it is I'm trying to accomplish, then the travel and time away would be well worth it."

"But you don't feel the need to just get away from it all? Even briefly? To some degree, you have to be in much the same situation, in terms of the constant inescapable demands of your position."

"It's no' that onerous a task, really. I know what I said earlier, about mediating issues, but we're a small population and generally just going about our business. Perhaps that's where we truly differ."

"I know we look differently at dealing with what's been expected of us, but—"

"I'm no' referring to that. What I meant was, it's more cultural. You live in a very busy, very high-volume world. Just driving to Annapolis from the airport was like being dropped on another planet. Even when I went to university on the mainland here, there was never that sense of absolute, live or die urgency to get anywhere to do anything. I've never been in such a palpably anxious environment. We're far more relaxed in going about our daily lives. Nothing is so urgent that we feel the need to be so tightly wrapped or tense about getting to the next thing. So perhaps I have less to want to get away from," he explained. "By and large, we're a happy people, but always aware that life is bigger than the task at hand. We appreciate what we have, what we've accomplished, and take pride in bettering our situations, but no' to the degree that we let it devalue the quality of the lives we're leading."

She'd like to take offense of his portrait of American life, especially her specific slice of it. She'd traveled enough to know, comparatively speaking, Annapolis had a far more relaxed and bohemian vibe about it than many other mid-Atlantic cities of the same or greater size. Mostly due to it being both a port and a sea town, complete with all the recreational sports that went with it. Overall, she suspected he was absolutely right. It was a little stultifying to think she was part of that cultural environment . . . but also intriguing to know she was about to get a chance to see what it was like to live in his.

"We take great pleasure in the small things, like time spent with friends, tipping back an ale or two, playing some music, dancing, singing and the like. As a rule, we dinnae work ourselves to exhaustion, nor do we feel compelled to do so time and again, without taking some respite."

She nodded, thinking the world he described sounded like a lovely place to inhabit. She'd long thought her own personal time clock was a bit out of whack, but between working with family and living with family, very little of her time could be completely claimed as her own. At work, there were constant business demands, and at home, constant social ones—which were usually business oriented. There wasn't much down time. Time spent with Blaine was usually her escape. Of course, they spent a good part of their time together bitching about that very life, so she wasn't entirely sure it could be claimed as an escape or true respite.

His expression shifted to one of amusement, and a very attractive twinkle sparkled in his eyes when he smiled. "You must think me—us—quite provincial and backward."

"No," she said, quite sincerely, "I think you sound healthy, happy, and well-balanced. I'm quite well aware of the imbalances in my life, but I don't know I'd ever thought of an alternative quite as lovely as the one you're describing."

"It is a rather bucolic lifestyle, and we are provincial in many ways because of it. Though I don't think of us as backward." His smile flashed wider for a moment. "Aye, so perhaps a wee bit, then."

"I'm sure you're not. Not if you're representative of the people on your island, anyway."

His smile grew again and she thought she might have seen a brief flush as well. Not used to being complimented, it appeared. She smiled to herself, rather liking that particular insight. In fact, she was liking most of the insights she'd gained where he was concerned.

"Okay," she said, thinking it was as good a time as any to take off on her own. "I'm off for a bit. Where should I meet back? And when?"

"You'll see us coming into port long before we arrive. Right here's as good a place as any. We'll go retrieve your luggage, but we won't have to do that until we're in the docking slip."

She groaned inwardly, thinking of having to drag all the stuff into town, then back out to whatever ferry they were taking the next day. Maybe there was some way they could store most of it at the docks.

"Enjoy your exploring," he said, then reached into the odd-looking pouch he wore strapped around his waist.

It amazed her that he still looked relatively fresh and crisp in his formal kilt getup. She was quite certain she looked anything but, and she'd had the chance to change clothes since leaving the church. He'd been wearing what he had on even longer.

"Here," he said, handing her some pound notes and a few Euros. When she stared at the money he was handing her without taking it, he added, "There's a place inside where you can get something to eat. It's possible we can find a pub still open in Castlebay, but it's been a long day with little to eat. No sense waiting when you can get something now."

She took the money, knowing better than to say anything about paying him back. But she took careful note of how much he'd given her, and mentally added it to her running tally. "Thank you," she said. "I think I will."

He looked both surprised and pleased.

"I'm not a complete ingrate, you know," she said with a laugh. "I can accept a helping hand now and again."

He nodded, and that twinkle surfaced again. They smiled at each other and it felt more intimate. Shared knowledge and shared experiences did that. It made her feel far too warm and fuzzy. She waved a hand, then turned in the direction of the rear of the boat, deciding she'd search out food first. Much better to formulate her game plan on a full stomach.

If only she had the first clue what her game plan was going to be.

Chapter 10

Graham orchestrated the removal of Katie's luggage from the ferry to the docks. If it wasn't for the fact that the pile of designer leather bags literally comprised everything she owned, he might have been a little more impatient with the process.

"If you'd like to go ahead to locate rooms, I can take care of this."

"What?" Graham realized he'd been checking his watch. He let his hand drop to his side. "No, no, it's okay. We're almost set here."

They stood off to one side as the bags went from the pier to the back of a lorry. Graham had tried to wave off any help and do it himself, but the lorry driver had recognized him as The MacLeod, due, Graham supposed, to the clan crest pinning his tartan in place, and had insisted on tackling the chore. Rather than make a scene, or inadvertently insult the man, Graham had stepped back with Katie, who hadn't said a word about what her opinion might be of the deferential treatment he was receiving.

She hadn't come back around to meet him until the ferry had begun docking. Other than a hello and asking about debarking arrangements for them, and for her luggage—which, to be fair, she was as annoyed with as he was—she hadn't said much. It made him wonder what she'd been thinking about for the past hour. He knew his thoughts had been far more on her than where they should have been—returning to the island and getting back to work. And continuing the ridiculous farce his trip had launched in the first place.

He was holding out hope that Roan or Shay had done as he'd asked before leaving, and continued to hunt for any loophole that would save him from having to actually wed Katie. Not that having her around was any kind of burden. He was quite thankful—perhaps too thankful—that she'd agree to stay. He couldn't kid himself any longer that his joy in the matter was based on her being the solution to his problem. If anything, that was the only part about her staying on that he truly hated.

The way they'd met had been anything but natural or normal, but what had happened since, as they'd grown to know each other—traveling day and night with someone can definitely expedite the learning curve—had all come along rather organically. They were one short hop away from home . . . and he didn't want her to be there for some contrived reason. He wanted her to be there because she chose to be there, because she wanted to be there.

Because she wanted more time with him, as he did with her.

For the first time in his life, he was actively engaged on every level with someone, and he wanted more. It was intriguing, enticing, and damn exciting. Of course he wanted more time with her.

The very last thing he needed was to screw it up by being forced to marry her.

He swore under his breath. The irony was more than maddening. It was sickening. It was all he'd thought about, during his time alone on the boat. No one should be forced to wed someone for what amounted to extortion. She'd just walked away from her entire family to avoid doing that very thing. That she was even considering his offer was mostly due to the fact that she was quite abruptly having to find a way to fend for herself. She'd been very direct about that fact. It was not what he wanted from her. He didn't want her as part of any bargain.

What did it say about him that he didn't have the kind of fortitude she did? Or the same kind of courage she had? The kind that sent her into the prayer garden, mad as hell, and ultimately out of her designated life.

That was the crux of it. Cast in that light, the burden weighing on him doubled in tonnage.

It was true there was more at stake than his own personal welfare and happiness. He doubted Katie had concerns that McAuley-Sheffield would fold without her on board. The same could not be said of Kinloch if he made a comparable departure from his obligations.

If he was willing to make the overall welfare and happiness of every one of his clanspeople his main priority and the focus of his life's work—happily so—was it asking too much of them to allow him to privately pursue his own happiness in return? He'd like to think it was the least they'd be willing to do, and happily so, as well.

How did he make them understand that was all he was asking for? All they had to do was rescind the bloody law, boot Iain and his infernal smugness off the island, and let their clan chief get back to work. Surely the pursuit of that goal was worthier than what he was about to propose to the near stranger standing beside him.

Then he could pursue her honestly, with no other agenda in play, and see where it led. Was that too much to ask? He was in the most perverse situation he could ever imagine.

He should have never bloody left.

He should have remained on Kinloch and fought for his vision of what the best future would be for both clans, and to hell with ancient clan law, and to hell with Iain McAuley. He'd panicked, it was as simple and as awful as that. He'd let Roan and Shay get inside his head, and Iain's Adonis-like perfection played right into his moment of weakness. So he'd panicked. And leapt at the chance to fix things by taking on the most ridiculous, foolhardy mission one could imagine.

He stood on the docks of Castlebay, a mere ferry ride from home . . . with the end result of that ridiculous, foolhardy mission standing beside him, watching as her entire worldly possessions were loaded into the back of a rented lorry. Possessions that were bound for Kinloch, along with their owner. Ironically he truly wanted that exact scenario to be playing out, but for the real reason a woman moved halfway around the world for a man.

Love. Not business.

So what in bloody hell was he doing?

He felt his heart thump a bit wildly, and sweat bead on his brow, and he worked to get himself under some semblance of control before Katie noticed he was not in his right mind. Because clearly, he *wasn't* in his right mind. How the whole world wasn't noticing that, he had no idea. After almost two full days spent avoiding communicating with Roan or anyone else back home, he wished quite fervently that he'd been able to talk with his good friend.

He realized the irony, given it was partly due to his good friend that Graham was in the current predicament he wanted his friend's help with. Of course, Roan wouldn't see it as a predicament that needed resolving, so much as a resounding cause for celebration. To that end, perhaps it was just as well Graham had neglected to turn off his mobile on the long train ride from Glasgow after the last time he'd checked his messages. The battery was dead.

His charger was with his other stuff in the rental back in Annapolis. He wasn't entirely sure how he was going to resolve the car issue, much less go about getting his stuff back. He had no acquaintances in the U.S., but that was the least of his concerns at the moment.

He planned on placing a call from the hotel once they had a bit of a warm meal and were settled into their rooms for the night, which gave him less than an hour or so to figure out exactly how he was going to broach the subject.

That subject being how to jointly explain to both his fellow clansmen, and to Katie, that he was not going to marry anyone he wasn't in love with.

He blew out a silent, if slightly shaky breath. There. He'd done it. He'd decided. And just like that, his pulse slowed, and a sense of calm came over him, along with profound relief. That alone told him, unequivocally, it was the right decision to make.

He also had to figure out how he was going to explain to everyone that, while he refused to marry according to some ancient tribal law, he had no intention of turning over Kinloch to anyone—much less someone without a single direct or personal tie to the place. If Roan and Shay truly were the bonded friends they'd always been, they'd turn their swift and ready attentions to helping him figure that out. If they bucked him again, as they had before, he'd point out he'd tried it their way. It was time to do things his way.

He glanced at Katie. The part about telling her of his decision would be exclusively on him. It was only fair. He was the one who'd asked—begged—her for help only she could give. And she'd agreed to come along, to consider it. He wondered how likely it was her reticence since returning from her stroll was an indication she'd been having similar regrets? It would certainly make their discussion go much more smoothly. Or would, perhaps, after a nice hot meal and a warm bed for the night.

In the same exact moment he'd thought the words "warm bed," Katie turned and put her hand on his arm.

Just like that, the images he'd thought were banished for good came rushing back, with twice the force as before. It was as if her touch had transported him, both physically and mentally, to some other place. Some other time, as well, if the vision before him was anything to go by.

There was no bed, no vision of him rapturously entwined with her. He wasn't in some omniscient viewpoint, looking down on the action below. He was in a bower, standing in a lush green glade, filled to bursting. The assault on each of his senses was so vivid, with bright poppies and lush orchids.

Just beyond the edge of the bower, the bountiful flora and the tumbling, rock-strewn thatches of vivid green grass gave way to the *machair*, and a sandy, pebbled beach. Farther away was the stone structure of a round corner turret, possibly the only thing remaining of what had once been a great walled stronghold. Upon further inspection, as his viewpoint crystallized, he realized it was actually an abbey.

He wanted to move forward—was compelled to—and learn more about the structure, but someone was talking to him. A woman was calling his name, and he turned back to find it was someone much like Katie. Her hair was the same shot-with-sunshine blond, and fell in long, swirling curls that drifted far down her spine, clinging to her derriere. Her body, that derriere, was lush and enticing. She was dressed in period garb, somewhere around the turn of the sixteenth century, if the memory of his beloved history lessons were serving him properly. Equally distracting was the fact that her clothing was rather in a state of dishabille . . . and if the knowing smile curving those cupid-bow lips, and the twinkle in her luminescent blue eyes was any indication . . . he thought he'd had something to do with her disheveled and flushed state.

She called his name again, and he moved toward where she lay on a woven blanket spread out across the section of the glade that cushioned the border between the machair and the denser jumble of stones that rose behind him as a mountain. As he opened his mouth to ask her who she was, and why he was there, she called his name again. Except . . . it was her voice, but her lips weren't moving. He paused as she reached for him and he was about to sink down on the blanket beside her. Her smile slipped . . . and the next thing he knew, he was standing on the dock in Castlebay, with modern-day Katie tugging a bit more insistently on his arm.

"Graham, the driver's ready to go. Graham? Are you okay?"

He couldn't rightly say what he was in that moment, other

than deeply confused. "Fine," he said, rather a bit more tersely than intended. Given he'd just been shot back a few centuries for no apparent reason, dazzled by a mysterious beauty who could be Katie's sixteenth-century twin, then jerked back to the present, he could be forgiven if he appeared a bit out of sorts. "Ye dinnae have to look at me like I'm daft. I was just . . . lost in thought there for a moment."

She studied him a minute longer, concern clear on her face, but mercifully she dropped her hand from his arm before he was forced to remove it for her. He wasn't sure which unnerved him more, that he feared her continued physical connection might possibly jerk him around the time continuum again . . . or that he was too much the coward to touch her hand himself to move it away, to find out.

Neither was a particularly reassuring revelation.

"We should go. It's late," he said, motioning her to lead the way.

She gave him a brief, rather incredulous look, then shook it off and turned with a smile for the lorry driver.

As they crossed the lot, she said, "Were you able to talk to your friends on Kinloch? Is that what gotten you so distracted? What did they say? Are things going okay? Is that other guy making any progress with his campaign?"

"I dinnae know," he said, his gut tightening up a notch as he thought about Iain McAuley and was reminded of the big decision he'd made just before he'd temporarily lost what was left of his mind. "My mobile battery died, so I'll have to wait to place the call once we find lodging." He'd never had reason to stay overnight in Castlebay, but he knew the village quite well, and had a place in mind.

The lorry driver waved them to the passenger side. "We're all set here, Mr. MacLeod." He sent a particularly twinkly smile in the direction of Katie as he opened the passenger door with a flourish. "Lassies first."

Katie shot a quick look at Graham, her smile a bit tentative. The accompanying eye roll, however, as she jerked her chin ever so discreetly in the direction of the old man, was purely the woman he'd come to know over the past two days.

At any other time that private gesture would have had him smiling quite naturally in return, but such a casual response was beyond him at the moment. He told himself it was because of the decision he'd made, and the talk he'd have to have with Katie at some point soon or first thing in the morning. It wasn't going to take place in earshot of the driver. He gestured her a bit impatiently, to follow the driver's lead. He got a raised eyebrow and a brief flash of annoyance for the effort, but he couldn't worry about that. He'd be lucky if it was the worst of what she offered him once he explained himself and his new course of action.

The lorry driver was short, stout, and balding, somewhere in his early seventies was Graham's guess. He still moved pretty swiftly though, as he scooted in to give Katie a boost up into the front seat. Graham happily deferred, just to avoid putting his hands anywhere near her for the time being. If that made him a coward, so be it.

"Just shift on over a bit," the old man instructed. "Your young man here is going to take up a bit of space. No' to worry," he added with a quick wink. "I'll part with some of my own for one so pretty as yourself."

Katie smiled in return, and said, "Oh, he's not my ma—" but broke off when she caught Graham's gaze over the driver's shoulder. Momentarily flustered for reasons he couldn't fathom given that his own dark mood had to be readily apparent, she nonetheless quickly looked back to the old man and said, "Thank you, I appreciate that."

Graham hadn't given any thought as to how they should best conduct themselves in public. For the moment, he didn't mind her allowing the driver to believe what he would. Any misconception about them would be clarified with their sleeping arrangements. And the fact that they would very likely be departing on opposite ferries in the morning. Not that anyone should care or notice, but the old man looked like the type to spin a tale or two over a pint of ale. Given the deference he'd granted Graham based on his leadership position on Kinloch, he doubted the man would pass up the chance to embellish on that a little. Nor would it surprise him for word of any or all of their visit to eventually reach ears on Kinloch. But between the call he planned to make later, and catching the first ferry over in the morning, he was doubtful anything would come of it before he reached home himself.

He climbed in the lorry after Katie, and though thankful for the offer of a lift into the village proper, Graham was grateful it was also a short drive. Space was at a distinct premium, and he quickly discovered spending an hour out of each other's eyesight after being joined at the hip for two long days hadn't given his body quite the respite it needed for him to regain control of his responses where she was concerned.

That moment out of time on the docks might have had a bit to do with it as well, but he was already trying to distance himself from that entire episode and remain steadfastly focused on the here and now. It was where his attentions had to remain if he had any hope of sorting out the best path to achieve his goals as he'd originally intended—before he'd allowed the insanity of Roan and Shay's idiot plan to sway him into such ill-advised action.

That particular part of his goal was impossible to achieve at the moment. Katie was all but plastered against him, knee to hip, elbow to shoulder. It had taken enormous self-control not to flinch like a startled tern when the door closed behind him, shoving him up against Katie in the tight space before he could brace himself against it. Not that it would have mattered. When the driver climbed in, whatever space Graham could have put between him and Katie was irrevocably taken away.

He sat there like a stupid git, feeling both ridiculous and mortified, but unable to stop himself from fearing that at any moment he'd be transported off to God knew where again. He had no idea what outward shift might have happened during that time, but given that he had absolutely nowhere to hide, he bloody well didn't want to find out.

Further disconcerting him was the way his body had chosen to respond to the continued forced contact with Katie. It wasn't bad enough he was grappling with an apparent mental defect, but he had to deal with a very . . . immediate and hard-to-hide reaction to her close proximity. Whether it was simply a continued response to the ongoing stimulation they'd shared between them during the entire journey, or some leftover effect of the beguiling faery-witch in his unplanned dream-leap on the dock, he had no idea. It didn't much matter. He had to deal with the end result regardless.

He could only hope to get himself under some semblance of control before he had to stand upright again, as his kilt would do little to conceal his current state of salute. Hadn't he quite enough to deal with at the moment?

So naturally, as Katie chatted with the driver, his thoughts went straight to the kiss they'd shared aboard the ferry. Specifically the one she'd initiated. He wasn't sure what had predicated that shift. Nor had he done anything to put a stop to it. If she hadn't ended it herself, he wasn't quite sure they wouldn't have ended up in the deep shadows behind one of the rescue boats, getting some direct relief for the consistent state of awareness they'd both been in since the prior morning.

It felt like at least a century or two had passed since he'd stood up in her family church and all but ordered her to come away with him. In the interim, it increasingly seemed as if he was incapable of rightly knowing his own mind when he was around her. He listened as the old man chatted away, regaling Katie with some story of a man at the local pub singing a song about a mermaid with a distinct resemblance to Katie's lovely countenance.

It was Graham's turn to privately roll his eyes, but Katie was too engaged in the conversation to notice. Considering the driver was falling in and out of Gaelic as he spoke, his island accent so thick even Graham would have had to pay attention to catch everything the old Scot was saying, Graham doubted Katie had the first clue what was actually being said, and was simply working off whatever clues she could gather.

Graham watched her interact with him as if she understood every last word. She was good with people. He supposed that shouldn't be overly surprising, given her family's business and social standing. She'd probably learned to work a room by the time she could walk. But what he saw was different. She was comfortable, and the conversation was genuine. Or her interest in it was, anyway.

It made him wonder how she'd have handled her arrival in Kinloch. Not that he'd ever thought she couldn't handle it. Back to that family training. She could probably run rings around most of his clanspeople, without them ever being aware they'd been managed. But watching the clear sincerity she felt, and the obvious joy she was taking in what was nothing more than a random meeting, he found himself picturing how she'd handle everyone from Roan and Shay, to old Eliza. Iain, as well, now that he thought on it. It hadn't occurred to him that she could have helped him thwart that threat directly, but he couldn't help but contemplate what might have been.

He'd have enjoyed seeing her work the island. He hadn't met her at her best, and he knew the long days they'd shared had been fatiguing and an emotional scramble for her. But, out there in the islands, packed inside that lorry, he was perhaps truly seeing her for the first time. He realized then, beyond the brief time inside the church, he'd never observed her interact with anyone. He'd done much of the planning and herding them along since then. He noted her natural ebullience, which shone through despite her fatigue. Maybe the stroll on the deck had brought the color back to her cheeks, but listening to her chatter away with the lorry driver, you'd never have guessed how exhausted she was.

The old man was beaming. She had that ability to focus on one person and make them feel like the center of her world. He knew from personal experience. Her wit, her candor, her confidence, and even her vulnerability all combined to form one formidable package.

His people wouldn't have stood a chance with her. She'd have dazzled them all without even trying.

He ducked his chin, corralled his wayward thinking. Again. He had to come up with whatever his new proposition for her was going to be, figure out what he could do for her, to help her along in the next phase of her life, without coming off as patronizing or condescending.

Not that it would likely matter what he offered or the manner in which he delivered it, once he told her he'd changed his mind—he'd dragged her away from her family and across an ocean, on the promise of a haven away from the chaos of her life and a foundation upon which to build a new one, and didn't need her anymore—especially since they were but a ferry ride away from the beginning of it all.

It wasn't true at all, except and only as it pertained to his original reason for taking her there. So much had happened since. He wanted her. On Kinloch, in his life . . . but not because of some ridiculous agreement. However, he sincerely doubted she'd still want to accompany him, once he told her the plan was off.

He figured from what he knew about her she'd toss any alternate offer he made directly back in his face. In fact, he'd be lucky if that was the only thing she directed at his face. He wouldn't lay the least bit of blame on her for that. He'd never treated anyone with less forethought and care. Knowing he'd never meant it to be that way didn't help assuage the guilt.

How in God's name had he let things get so far afield?

"Here we are," the driver announced, still favoring Katie with the very twinkliest of grins. He'd been enamored of her at the slip dock and was downright infatuated after the short ride. Graham wished like hell he couldn't understand that attraction.

"Allow me," the old man said, sliding out of his door faster than his age or girth would have implied was possible. He immediately reached a hand in to help Katie slide across the seat and slip her feet to the ground. She landed with an assisted hop. Graham snapped out of his stupor and managed to get out his side and around to the back of the lorry first. He was unloading her bags before they came around back to stand next to him.

The driver started to step in, flustered that he'd slacked on his duty and was allowing someone he clearly thought of as deserving of his finest service, to tend to that service himself. Graham didn't tread as carefully this time, more interested in finishing the job and getting inside the inn, than coddling the old man's traditional sensibilities. "I've got it," he said, not unkindly, but not brooking any further discussion. "Could you escort Miss McAuley into the inn?" He glanced at Katie. "It will just be a few minutes. Perhaps you could ask what the chances would be of us getting a plate of leftovers from the kitchen at this hour." She would make a far more enchanting beggar than he would.

Once again she looked at him as if he'd been abducted by aliens and replaced with some kind of duplicate she didn't understand. *If she only knew just how accurate that assessment was*, he thought crossly.

Katie didn't respond to him directly, but turned and took the driver's proffered arm and bestowed a particularly beguiling smile in his direction. "Thank you, kind sir," she said, then laughed when the driver bowed with quite the regal flourish, before helping her onto the walkway. Neither of them looked back as they crossed to the heavy, carved door with the stained-glass window that served as the inn's entrance. Graham was left standing there, scowling after them, instead of getting the buggered suitcases out of the damn lorry.

He tried to look on the bright side as he hauled first one stack, and another, then finally another of the matching leather pieces into the foyer of the inn. He'd only have to do that one last time, in the morning.

He pictured the look on Roan's and Shay's faces had he debarked the ferry on Kinloch with Katie by his side, followed by the mountain of luggage. A brief smile quirked the corners of his mouth despite his rather foul mood. They definitely wouldn't have known what to make of her. He shook his head. But, like him, they'd have been intrigued enough to want to find out.

He entered the inn with the last load and deposited it by the rest of the stack. He paid the driver and thanked him for the lift so late at night. The old man was still clearly feeling the effects of his lovely lorry passenger as he quite happily told Graham he'd have done it for free—after he'd pocketed the pound notes into his back pocket, of course.

"Even one as mighty as The MacLeod couldnae hae done better than that one," he said with a wink. "My best to you both."

With an imaginary tip of a hat, the driver let himself out of the lobby before Graham could come up with a suitable reply. He glanced around, but didn't see Katie or the innkeeper. Perhaps she'd taken it upon herself to book the rooms and was presently being shown to hers. The idea that he might have a reprieve before having to confront her about what was going to happen next was an unexpected gift.

But it did not explain the sense of disappointment he felt when he realized that meant not seeing her until morning, and only then to drop the bomb on her and escort her back to the ferry.

"Perverse is wha' ye are," he muttered under his breath. The truth of it was, he wanted to get it over with and her on a boat, train, and plane back to the U.S. and out of his life as soon as possible, so he could focus all his energies on the new obstacle at hand—abolishing the damn law that had started the insanity in the first place. He'd also need to get on with the task of putting her out of his thoughts, and his life, once and for all.

He simply wasn't certain, standing there, which was going to be the harder job in the end.

He'd been fully prepared to talk with Roan later, and tell him everything that had happened. Well, maybe not the part about having full-blown hallucinations like some sort of mental ward patient. But he was thinking, perhaps it was best to simply omit the part about Katie being willing to come to Kinloch all together. Roan would be like a dog with a bone if he knew Graham had come so close to solving the problem by following Roan's lead. And far less willing to do whatever he could to help Graham with the position he'd decided to take.

He'd tell Roan at some point, of course. When Katie was back in Maryland, and after he'd found a way to end that ridiculous race against time. And after Iain left Kinloch. And after everyone returend to their normal lives.

Katie chose that moment to reenter the foyer area, with the innkeeper in tow. She was smiling at something the older woman had said, and though Graham could see the telltale signs of weariness fanning from the corners of her eyes and in the slight stoop of her shoulders, he could also feel the vibrancy she brought to a place just by being in it. There was an energy to Katie like some sort of tractor beam pulling him, from the first when he'd heard her swearing a blue streak in the prayer garden.

Had the circumstances been any different, or had their reasons for spending the bulk of two days together been for reasons remotely normal, he'd have smiled, thinking what a memorable tale their first meeting would make. But it was a tale that wouldn't get told. At least not by him, as there would be no reason for the telling of it.

He didn't think he'd ever forget it.

"Mrs. Ardingall has been lovely enough to agree to prepare two plates to bring up to our room," Katie said, looking happier and far more relaxed than Graham had yet to see her. She was weary, but there was a calm confidence about her. Perhaps because she was finally good and away from home with an end point in view.

He felt like the worst kind of cad . . . because he was. He started thinking about offering to set her up in Castlebay while they worked out what could be done to compensate her for his misguided offer. "Much appreciate that, Mrs. Ardingall," Graham told the older woman, never more sincere.

"I'm afraid it's only a wee bit of stew, but I've some bread and cheese to go with it. We'll be having a good breakfast belowstairs beginning at eight in the morning."

"That sounds wonderful," he told her. A hearty meal would help him swallow the rest of what he had yet to do. Then the rest of what Katie had said played again in his mind and he looked at her. "Room?"

Pink bloomed in her cheeks, but she kept her smile fixed brightly on her pretty face as she hurried to explain. "They've only one at the moment, but it's quite big, fills the uppermost floor. We'll have plenty of space to, uh, spread out." She glanced at her pile of luggage then quickly back to him. "She's agreed to hold most of my bags down here as we'll only be here for the night. She said the ferry leaves at noon, so that leaves us plenty of time to get some extra sleep before coming down to breakfast, then heading to the docks."

She rushed out the explanation without taking a breath and Graham could see she would be embarrassed if he were to make an issue of it. Other than not having to cart the luggage up in a narrow lift, a piece at a time, he didn't find much in the way of good news in the brief outline, but he managed a smile as he turned to the innkeeper. "We're much obliged. If you'd like, I can wait here and bring the food up myself, save you the trip." *And save me from having to have you in our room, even briefly.* Things were awkward enough. And Katie didn't even know the half of it, as yet.

"That would be lovely," Mrs. Ardingall said. "As for the baggage, you can store the ones you dinnae need over there behind the front desk, against the wall if you don't mind, and I'll see to preparin' you both a dish." She smiled kindly, and they nodded and smiled back, as if programmed to do so. Then she turned and disappeared down the hall she and Katie had emerged from minutes before.

As soon as she was out of earshot, Katie crossed to him and whispered, "I'm so sorry, but it was all she had, and I didn't want to try and explain our circumstances, because, frankly, they're beyond explanation, and letting the lorry driver believe what he wanted is one thing, but I just couldn't—"

"'Tis fine," he said, cutting off her nervous chatter, but carefully moving away from the hand she'd been about to lay on his arm during her earnest speech. He began moving the bags. "We're no' here but for a few hours' sleep. We'll make do."

She was quiet for a moment, then picked up two of the smaller valises and helped him by toting them behind the desk herself. "Leave that one," she said, pointing to the mid-sized bag she'd gone through when raiding for fresh clothes. "I can dig through and just bring up what I—"

"We can get the single bag upstairs," he said, knowing he was sounding terse again, just as he knew it wasn't her fault. He couldn't seem to find that last thread of patience he needed—with himself, not her—to be decent and civil. She'd understand soon enough, and he imagined he'd get plenty of terse attitude in return.

She stepped in front of him as he headed toward the lift that was tucked in an alcove across the foyer, next to the wide stairs leading to the floors above. "I'd ask if you were just tired, but I've been with you long enough now to know that it's something more."

"Do ye now," he said, then scowled at himself. What had gotten into him that he couldn't be decent to the one person who deserved his decency most?

She lifted her chin slightly and the light that came into her bright blue eyes then wasn't a merry one, but a warning he knew he'd do well to heed. "I believe so. You've been nothing if not polite this whole time, but since we left the ferry"—she lifted a shoulder, looking more confused than irritated—"something has changed. You're . . . different. Is it just the stress of almost being home and . . . dealing with all of this?" She gestured to the empty foyer, but Graham knew what she was referring to. "I'm nervous and anxious, too, though I imagine yours is for entirely different reasons, as it's your home, your people. But I'm not going to make it more difficult or challenging than it has to be. In fact, I'd like to do whatever I can to make it easier on both of us. To that end, we're a team, Graham. I am on your side." She held her hand up briefly. "It doesn't mean I've decided anything yet. That can't happen until we discuss the actual terms of the proposal. I'm only saying that I'm . . . predisposed, I guess is the word, to be your ally. You're the only person I know here. And, I'm completely dependant on you. So, I'd appreciate it if we could consider this a joint venture, whatever happens, as of now, and act toward each other accordingly."

She reached out to touch his arm again, to reassure him of her sincerity, and he stepped back without thought, instinctively protecting himself against a repeat of whatever the hell had happened on the docks. Her expression fell, and he saw the hurt flash in her eyes before he could think to adjust the knee-jerk action.

"I'm the sorry one," he said, his sigh one of self-directed disgust. "I am—I haven't been right since the docks, but it's no' because of—" He broke off again. He wasn't seriously considering telling her what had happened, was he?

He lifted his gaze to her face then, and found himself instantly lost. Emotions he couldn't completely understand, much less put a name to, swirled in an eddy of confusion inside him. There was pleasure. He felt the punch of it every time he looked at her. The strength was entirely disproportionate to time spent or knowledge gained of each other, as if she was someone he'd long felt affection toward. There was also a sense of unequivocal trust. As if he could tell her anything. As if he'd long made a practice of it. She felt like someone far more bonded to him than a sworn friend or ally. None of that made any sense. Yet every time he looked at her, those were the things he felt.

"Graham—"

"We need to talk, Katie," he said, abruptly putting an end to his silly ruminations and irrational feelings. He didn't need to tell her about the latest vision he'd had on the docks. That would forever stay with him—like a bad dream that forever haunts. "There are things we need to discuss. Now. Before morning."

"What—"

They were interrupted by Mrs. Ardingall, who bustled in with a tray in her arms. "I'll be happy to carry this up," she said, seemingly unaware of the tension in the room.

"No need," Katie said, easily enough, and took the tray from her. "I can take care of it. We appreciate you going to all this trouble."

The woman beamed at the two of them. If she noticed the visible strain, she was professional enough not to let it show. "No trouble a'tall. If there's anything I can do for the two of you, you've only to ring me. Good night."

They nodded, she nodded, and proving her innkeeper skills were long ingrained and second nature, she quietly left them.

"This smells heavenly," Katie said, all but groaning as she took a deep, appreciative sniff. "Maybe we should just eat, get a good night's rest, and talk through things, what comes next, in the morning. I know we'll both feel a lot more human—"

"I've made some decisions. Concerning us. Concerning you." He snagged the handle of the suitcase. "We'll talk upstairs, while we eat."

Chapter 11

Katie wanted to tell Graham he could take his Neanderthal routine and shove it where the sun didn't shine. But given he was the one sponsoring both the bed she was about to sleep in, and the very delicious-smelling meal she was about to eat, she thought better of giving him a piece of her mind right then and there.

But she made no promises for later.

Their room was on the top floor and more long and narrow than the big, more spacious design of hotel rooms back home. Of course it was an inn, not a true hotel, and the narrow, row-house style building it was housed in was likely older than pretty much anything currently standing in the U.S. At that point in her two-day journey, she was thankful it had electricity and running water.

Actually, truth be told, it was rather quaint and lovely, in a provincial sort of way. She was too hungry, though, to give it a thorough checking out. The small sandwich she'd eaten on the ferry had barely taken the edge off her hunger. She'd felt a bit pitchy with the roll of the boat and decided a big meal was probably not a good idea under those circumstances. She knew it was merely fatigue. McAuleys didn't get seasick. Rather than fight it, she'd found a place near the front of the boat to sit and had ended up staying there the entire time. Thinking.

She wished she'd come to more hard, fast conclusions about

the sudden, complete turnaround her life had taken, but the sandwich hadn't taken that big an edge off the fatigue and critical thinking had turned out to be beyond her. Thinking about Graham, however, was not a problem. She'd taken some time away from him to focus on her big-picture issues . . . so what had she done? Spent the whole time away from him, thinking about him.

It had been odd. For a while she was so zoned in on him, the rest of the world simply fell away. She'd recalled those moments out of time with him, the ones that didn't seem to jibe, with the man he was the rest of the time. Both sides of him equally intrigued her. She wished she could make more sense of it, of that . . . connection they seemed to share. One she couldn't seem to shake, even when she finally had some time to herself. It was like she was fixated on the guy.

At the moment, however, she was feeling more pissy than swoony, so she carefully fixated on her stew instead, and one of the quite yummy crusty rolls Mrs. Ardingall had served with it.

"So," he said, at length, after each of them had devoured half of what was on their plates and in their bowls. "First, let me say I've admired you since we first crossed paths."

Katie lowered her spoon as her stomach slowly began to knot. He sounded . . . ominous. "Thank you," she said, not masking her sudden wariness.

"I know we've both been reared in situations that require a lifelong allegiance to something that has been handed to us as a result of our birth, rather than having the opportunity to choose a path based on our own desires. I also know that mine is one I embrace, while I understand why yours is not. Given the lengths your family would go to, to put their needs over your happiness and general welfare, I believe you did the only thing you could have, by extricating yourself from that life, and the obligations that went with it."

Katie stopped pretending she could eat and put her spoon down altogether. "I'm glad you agree. As I am thankful you happened to come along when you did, and provided me with an escape route."

He stopped picking at his roll, and looked directly at her. "Had I no', would you have still fled the chapel?"

"I—" She broke off, and thought back to how she'd felt, why she'd left the church to storm about the prayer garden, as she tried to build a sturdy spine where only a limp noodle had been residing. Even with Graham there, making the offer he did, she'd still opted to go back inside the church with her limp noodle of a spine and marry Blaine anyway. She sighed. "I honestly don't know. I know it was my intent to go through with it. It seemed like the easiest course of action for all concerned, and it was what Blaine wanted. I . . ." She trailed off, then lifted a shoulder as she picked up her own roll and began breaking off bits of the hard crust into what was left of her stew.

The silence continued as he allowed her time to gather her thoughts. Finally, she looked up and met his gaze. "I'd like to think when it came time to actually pledge vows I knew I didn't mean, not in the way they were intended to bond two people together, that I'd have balked. I'd like to think I'd finally found that strength inside myself. But I don't know, Graham. I know with absolute certainty that that's what I *wanted* to do. But that's all I know." She put the shredded roll down. "I don't know how much there is to admire about that. Why do you bring it up?"

He held her gaze, but it was a moment before he said, "Because that is the same courage and strength of spine I should have displayed, when my compatriots were pushing me to fulfill demands put in place over four centuries ago, pushing me to abandon my own beliefs. I knew that running off to another country to track down a woman I'd never met, in order to ask for her hand, was literally the most insane idea anyone had ever proposed to me. At any other time, I wouldnae have considered it for more than the length of time it had taken to spout it. I'd have had a good laugh, then gone back to figuring out how to achieve my goals my own way.

"Yet, in that moment, with the entire island anticipating I'd ensure my continued reign as their leader by doing the right thing, which in their collective minds meant clinging to an outdated and unneeded ancient stricture, followed by Iain's sudden arrival and quite arrogant claim that he intended to best me by doing that very thing . . . suddenly that insane plan sounded like a lifeline. Even then, I didn't want to grab it. I wanted to find a way to accomplish the same goals but in a way I thought better for everyone all around. But I was afraid I'd drown before being allowed the grace time to do so. So I grabbed the lifeline instead."

"What are you saying, Graham?"

"I'm saying I should have stood my ground. I should have shown the exact leadership qualities that a good clan laird must have if he's to guide and lead his clanspeople forward with any kind of true direction. I know the direction we should take. I know it. And—"

"Marrying me isn't it," Katie said, wondering why she felt neither dread nor relief. In fact, she sat there feeling kind of numb.

"No," he said quietly, his expression bleak and apologetic. "No, 'tis no'."

"Graham—"

He lifted a hand to stall her reply. "Allow me to say the rest. For a man charged with seeing to the well-being of an island full of people, I did you a grave disservice by not seeing to yours as well. I should have thought this through more clearly, but time was of the essence, so off I trotted, hoping, I suppose, to figure it out as I went. I assuaged my guilt in heading in a direction I didn't feel one hundred percent certain about, by telling myself I'd propose it as a business arrangement, somehow thinking it would be okay if we both personally benefitted from the legal union. It would seem, on first view, that you'd be the last potential candidate for such an arrangement given the situation you were fleeing. Yet, by the very act of running off, you were immediately put in a position of needing my largesse to reestablish yourself. Miraculous, all around, that the stars would seem to line up to aid and abet something that couldn't possibly be seen as right either here on earth or up in the heavens. Yet, here we both are, considering the insane as if it were actually an okay, forthright, even noble choice."

"What was it that changed your mind back to your original viewpoint?" Katie asked.

His gaze shifted then, taking in each feature of her face, seeming to linger on her mouth, before drifting down over the rest of her. It was as if he was actually touching her, so electric and vibrant were the sensations that followed in the wake of his gaze.

Not so numb any longer.

He looked away, as if realizing belatedly what he was doing, but her body didn't calm down as abruptly. How did he do that? How was it that just a look from the man could rile up her entire system? It wasn't just the hormonal reaction of a woman looking at a hot guy who happened to be looking back with smoldering intent. Though that certainly was part of it. No, it was more of that connection she'd been thinking about earlier. It went further, and deeper . . . though she couldn't begin to explain why, even to herself.

Insanity apparently was not the exclusive mindset of the guy sitting across from her. The one who'd traipsed around the globe and back wearing full, formal kilt regalia.

Graham looked away, just as her nipples tightened to painful buds, and inner thigh muscles quivered as a renewed ache bloomed between them. She took that moment to look down as well, and get herself under some kind of control. But her thoughts, if not her actual gaze, were sliding over to the part of their room where a large brass bed dominated the narrow space. And, as if she had some kind of supernatural powers— which didn't seem as far-fetched in that moment as it should— she watched as Graham's gaze slowly moved toward the bed as well, as if she'd willed his attention there.

She tracked his gaze with hers, and the instant they both landed on the bed, she heard him swear.

"Bloody hell, no' again."

She swung her head back around to look at him, but though he was still staring at the bed, his expression told her his thoughts were obviously elsewhere. Somewhere far, far away, if the lost expression on his face was any indication. She'd seen that expression on him once before, she realized—when they'd been standing down by the slip dock.

She'd been trying to get his attention after the quite charming old man who'd agreed to give them a lift into town waved them over to board his paneled truck. It had been interesting to see Graham cast in the role he was probably quite used to. It might have been harder to wrap her head around the deference that was paid to ancient titles like clan laird, if he hadn't been wearing the kilt and full clan regalia at the time. Instead, in both stature and bearing, he'd appeared every bit the leader and chief who'd command exactly the kind of deference the older man had bestowed upon him.

She'd been around Graham long enough to know that the bowing and scraping hadn't sat well on him. He hadn't wanted to insult the older man, who clearly enjoyed having the chance to be of service to someone he had such traditional respect for, so Graham had let the much smaller, older man scurry about, loading all of her endless pieces of stupid luggage into the back of his truck.

When she'd tried to alert Graham a few minutes later to the fact that Barnaby—at least that's what she thought he'd told her his name was, he was almost impossible to understand—was trying to get them on board, she'd seen the exact same lost-in-thought expression.

"Graham?"

He didn't respond, didn't look at her. Nor had he when she'd spoken to him at the dock. She'd assumed, so close to home, his thoughts had gone to what lay immediately ahead for them. It was right after that, after he'd snapped out of his reverie, that he'd turned grumpy and taciturn. A mood that had clung to him since then.

"Graham?" she said again, with a bit more insistence.

His gaze was locked on the bed, though she'd bet his thoughts were far, far away.

She lifted a hand to touch him, to shake him from that odd stupor, only to curl her fingers inward and pull her hand back. She wasn't sure why she was so certain that touching him would not be a good thing, but there had been a distinct chill that raced down her spine the instant her hand had come close to his arm. Yet it didn't preclude, much less dampen the taut nipples and aching need.

"Graham," she said, again, louder and with a bit of panic thrown in for good measure. She wasn't understanding any of it. She felt rational of thought and perfectly in control . . . yet there was a sense she was teetering on the edge of something else, something far bigger, far greater, and well beyond her control. "Graham!"

It wasn't unusual-odd any longer, it was scary-odd. Graham didn't do so much as blink. It was as if he were in a trance. Panic overrode the warning chill and she took hold of his forearm. "Snap out of it," she ordered, more from fear than from anger.

The next thing she knew he'd yanked her up against his body and strode them both across the room, where he came quite close to tossing her on the bed—except, at the last second he held on and followed her down, the weight of him on top of her oppressive . . . but not at all unwelcome. In fact, where the ache had bloomed, the hot punch of lust was so swift and powerful it took her breath away.

In her head, she was struggling and fighting against his sudden ardor, but in reality, she was clinging to his shoulders and holding on for dear life, as if more afraid of him leaving her, than . . . whatever the hell it was he thought he was going to do.

"What are you about?" he ordered, trapping her face between his hands and staring wildly into her eyes.

Was he awake? Was he still in that weird trance-like place?

She couldn't tell. The laserlike aim of his gaze—all molten lavender at the moment—was intent and quite focused on her.

"I don't know," she said, breathlessly—only partly due to the weight of him bearing her deeply into the soft, down-filled duvet. She dug her fingers deeply into his densely muscled shoulders. "What do you want, Graham?"

"Why are ye plaguing me? Haunting me? What've I done to call you forth? Leave me be, I've enough to worry about, dinnae ye ken?"

"Plaguing you—what?" She realized he was talking to her, imploring her, even angry with her . . . except she didn't think it was her he was really communicating with.

"I'm growing afraid of my own shadow," he continued. "Afraid to breathe, afraid to reach out and touch, for fear you'll drag me back to this place. Just tell me what you want of me so I can do it and be done with ye, done with—this!"

"I-I don't know," she told him, shaken by his intensity. "Graham, it's me. Katie. I—"

"No, it's no' you. It's . . . I dinnae know who or what you are. Ye've her look, her sound, but ye're no' my Katie."

My Katie? My Katie?

"Graham, wake up!" she said, her thoughts as jumbled as her nerves . . . and her hormones. Having two hundred plus pounds of aggressive Scot on top of her was doing all kinds of things to her ability to breathe, and almost none of them had to do with his size. "You're dreaming, or—or something. It's okay, we're in Castlebay, at the inn. You don't have to worry. I understand about your need to do things your way. I'm not going to interfere, Graham."

He snorted at that. "Interfere? Ye've already done that. I want it to stop, I want—"

She managed to free her hands from his shoulders, and placed them on his face gently, but firmly. "Graham, look at me. It's me," she implored. "It's okay."

The instant she touched his face, his gaze sharpened further, and she felt more pinned down by his eyes than she did by his body.

His pupils expanded as a darker desire sprang to life. What had come before paled in comparison. She felt delicate and delectable, about to be thoroughly devoured. She wriggled beneath him in a useless, instinctive attempt to assuage the spear of ache and need arrowing straight through her, which only served to further ignite him.

He angled his mouth over hers, and the minute his lips were crushed against hers, the bed disappeared, the whole room disappeared. She swore her eyes were open, but obviously she'd slipped into some kind of dream world, because she could smell . . . grass. And flowers. And . . . sea air. She could feel the warmth of the sun. Feel the uneven ground under her back.

Graham was kissing her as if his very life depended on it. She clung to him, kissing him back, thinking if she closed her eyes and focused on him, it would sort itself out.

But closing her eyes pulled her in more deeply.

She was both in the moment and watching the moment. She was on a blanket, in a field. There was some kind of old, very old, gray stone building in the distance, the bright blue of the sea behind that. He was on top of her. On top of—a woman. Her. She was confused.

The woman had longer blond hair, and wore clothes that looked like she was part of the cast of a Renaissance Fair. The man wore a kilt, same tartan as the one she'd been staring at for two straight days, only it was . . . different. In the make of it, and the weave. It wasn't as smooth or refined. And it was bunched under a heavy leather belt, the sash a heavier swath over a broad, deeply muscled back. His hair was longer, too. Thick, tangled. Sun streaked. His calves were solid, strong, and his thighs heavily muscled, like his back. There was a sword— sword!—strapped to his hip.

But it was Graham. And that was her. She knew it. Somehow she was also on that woven blanket, in the deep grass, gorgeous flowers blooming like mad all around, the sea in the distance. She could feel the weight of him, his broad hands bracing her face as he took her mouth, took . . . her.

Katie squeezed her eyes shut, but she couldn't kiss Graham, be kissed by Graham, and make any sense of the rest of it.

So she simply stopped trying. She was tired—worn out from too much thinking. What she wanted was peace, quiet, and some long, uninterrupted sleep.

What she wanted, lusted after, deeply and with such need she thought she might die from the lack of it, was the man who was kissing her—Graham, it was Graham—to please, dear God, take her clothes off and drive so hard, so deep—

"Oh," she gasped, against his mouth, as he drew one hand down her cheek, trailed strong fingers along her throat, over her collarbone, then cupped her breast. Her aching, swollen, needy breast. She arched beneath his touch, moaning, not caring in the least what in the hell was going on as long as he didn't stop flicking his fingertip over her taut, throbbing nipple.

She moved under him. She growled. A little. Then she turned his face back to hers and took his mouth, devoured his tongue and suckled on it like she wanted him to suckle her. His fingers tightened on her nipple as she took him, and she relished both.

She felt primal, female, and utterly desirable.

His hand moved lower, over her ribs, her abdomen. She whimpered in the back of her throat at the loss of contact on her breast, then groaned with renewed pleasure when his hand cupped her between her thighs.

She took his tongue harder, and he growled and moved the base of his palm over her until she was moving right back against the sweet, perfect pressure of it.

He shifted his weight a bit more, and started dragging the skirts of her gown—her gown?—up, baring her calves, then her knees. She could feel the sun on her skin and it felt so good. She didn't give a single damn about what made sense and what didn't, as long as that hand presently moving up the inside of her thigh found its—"Oh! Oh, yes."

He took over the kiss. Driving his tongue inside her as his oh-so-clever fingers found the opening in her laced drawers—she had laced drawers, and damn if she didn't like having them—and teased the sensitive skin at the top of her thighs, tickled the curls he found there, before stroking her right across—

"Holy—" She arched hard and strong against the stroke of his finger, then did it again. And again. Until finally, blessedly, mercifully, he slid one inside her. Her groan was long, loud, as she grabbed his shoulders again and arched violently into his hand.

He moved, she pumped, and climbed swiftly toward a dazzling spark of pleasure that was so sharp, so perfect, she thought when it finally splintered she might splinter right along with it. She'd make not a peep of displeasure if it happened, because each and every sliver of what was left of her would be vibrating in pleasure.

But just as the zenith was in her grasp, at the tip of his finger, in fact, he slid it out. She groaned, immediately reaching for him. "Don't—"

His weight settled on her again, and his broad hands were cupping her hips and pulling them up, and she was blissfully, incredibly, and so powerfully filled with him that any thought of what he'd been doing even so much as a second before was obliterated forever from her mind. She could only encapsulate what he was doing, and how he was filling her. Driving her up, driving himself deeper.

She screamed, and it was a rapturous sound. Digging her nails deeply into his back as she held on, found some leverage, any leverage, to meet his thrusts.

He wasn't silent either. The sounds he made as he took her inflamed her further, and she rose to another level.

Maybe she was already in heaven. That had to be it. Some thread of sanity that still existed in the fringes of her mind clung to that rationale. It would, after all, explain everything.

Because this—he—was nothing if not the most blissful and perfect heaven she could have ever possibly imagined.

She was jerked fully back into the moment as she felt him gather, his grip tightening on her hips as he urged her knees up higher, so he could reach just that much deep—"Oh. *Oh!*"

He growled, so low, so gutturally, she was pretty damn sure she felt the vibration of it throughout her entire body as he came in a thundering roar—thundering . . . roar—deep inside her.

She clung to him as he shuddered throughout his release. Or maybe she was the one shaking. It was the single most powerful, most intimate moment she'd ever experienced. Even in her heart-still-pounding, breathless bliss, it had the ability to stun her. How . . . how could she feel . . . so much? It went far past the primal way they'd mated, almost rutting with each other. It could only feel that way with someone who mattered deeply to her. While Graham alternately captivated, charmed, incensed, and enflamed her, she hadn't been with him long enough to elicit the kind of emotions that would need to be there to experience something like that. To feel something like that. Straight to her marrow.

She held him tightly, as he did her, and he gathered her closely while they regained their breath. It was the time to look into his eyes, to ask the questions that so confused her, to understand what was really happening to her. To them.

He pulled her in, tucking her close beneath his chin, against his chest where she felt the heavy thump of his heart. "Katie," he whispered, as she felt him press a kiss to the top of her head.

The gesture, so gentle, so sweet, was too much so for the man who'd just taken her in a mating so earthy, so raw, so wild like the land that surrounded them.

As she shifted to lift her head, to look into his eyes, he rolled from her, to his back. The instant his body left hers, the moment his touch no longer connected them she was suddenly slammed straight back into that brass bed, in their small narrow room in the inn. In Castlebay.

She was sprawled on her back, staring up at the faded, watermarked, painted plaster ceiling. She smoothed her hands down her body, all but groping herself as she checked but— fully clothed—in the same thing she'd worn when she'd checked in. She immediately jerked her head to her left. Graham lay beside her. Also fully clothed. He was on his back, eyes closed. His body tense, like a tightly wound coil ready to spring at the lightest of touches.

"Graham . . . ?"

"Shhh," he said. "Dinnae . . ." But he didn't finish. His voice was raw.

Hers, now that she thought of it, had sounded a bit throaty as well.

"I can't 'shhh,'" she said. "I have to know." She rolled to her side, but at the last second was careful not to touch him. He jerked, as if instinctively driven to prevent the very same thing. That stung a little. While the whole episode had apparently been some kind of rabid hallucination due to extreme mental fatigue and the physical exhaustion of extended travel—sitting upright for two days straight—she was still feeling . . . those feelings. At least an echo of them, anyway.

The reality was he'd carried her to the bed. In that room. And she'd gone . . . somewhere else. She was pretty sure he'd been there already before taking her with him. It was why he'd carried her to the bed. He was the man in the reverie, having gone there ahead of her, talking to . . . her? To someone about her?

She remembered, how it had been Graham on top of her, touching her, kissing her. She'd watched as another man, much like Graham, only not Graham . . . lay down on top of her. But not her. Except it had been.

"Tell me I'm not crazy," she whispered, feeling tears threaten again, from abject confusion and fear.

There was only silence. And the sound of his breathing. She didn't dare touch him. But she didn't get up and leave, either.

Finally, after what felt like eons, he turned his head slowly toward her, until he was looking straight at her, straight into her. Then he said, "I canno'."

Her lips quivered, and her body trembled. Fresh tears filled her eyes. Suddenly, she felt very, very weary. And very, very alone. That felt wrong. Desolately, eternally, wrong.

"I canno' tell you that, Katie," he continued, never so solemn, never so serious, in all the time she'd known him. "Because I very much fear we might both be."

Chapter 12

Graham rolled his head away and stared straight up at the ceiling. He resisted the urge to reach between his legs . . . and make sure. They should talk about it. He knew she knew. Had to know. She'd been there. Kind of. As had he. Kind of.

Only they were in Castlebay. *Back* in Castlebay. Implying they'd been somewhere else. Or . . . had they? How could they *both* know?

He closed his eyes. But he wanted—needed—to look at her face, into her eyes, see . . . whatever it was he was certain was there. Had to be there. "Was there a history, in Annapolis, of witches?"

"What?" He felt rather than saw her roll her head to stare at him. "That's Salem. Massachusetts. Graham, we need to talk about this."

"Oh, aye, that we do." He turned to look at her. "But what comes of that, Katie? Neither of us can explain it." He looked away again. His body was still . . . feeling like the body of a man who'd just had the kind of sex that would have blown the top of his head straight off. And he'd had it with the woman lying next to him . . . except they were both still fully dressed, and, as far as he could tell, untouched. At least in the way he'd been touching her.

Just thinking that aroused him. He wanted to touch her again—more than before. But it was all wrapped up with the dream Graham taking the dream Katie in ways that . . . well, in ways he could only hope to take her in actual real life. But damn if his hunger wasn't every bit as strong as it had been while they'd been transported.

"Have you ever . . ." She trailed off, sighed softly, then rolled to her side, facing him. But not touching him, he noted. "Has this ever happened to you? You're talking witches, but if either of us is from some kind of enchanted, ancient, mystical land, it's not me. Do you have any explanation? Did you . . . I mean, were you there when we—" She rolled abruptly to her back again, and stared at the ceiling.

"I've no explanation. No, I've never experienced anything like this." He turned his head, looked at her. "And aye. I was there, when we . . ." He purposely left the sentence to drift.

Eventually, she turned to look at him.

And that electricity, that pow that socked him right in the gut, was there, just as strong, just as vital, just as demanding, as it was in their other place.

"Did I look like me? I mean, you were you . . . but not you."

The memories of her, in his arms, arching hard against him, as he'd slid his hand up her thigh, felt the slippery wetness of her, slid into her—"Aye," he said, a bit roughly, "it was you. Only . . . a, somewhat different vision of ye. But . . . you."

"That's how I felt, too. Your hair was longer, wilder. And your tartan more roughly woven—not as smoothly worn, more bunched and belted. Y-you had a sword. A big one."

He couldn't help it, he grinned. He was fairly certain he was going insane, so why not laugh? "I'm glad you noticed."

She snorted a laugh, then reached out to swat him. His duck and roll was reflexive and he moved away from her touch before he could think to do otherwise. She'd snatched her hand away as well, as if suddenly in fear of getting burned, but he'd seen the quick flash of hurt cross her face. And he understood it. He didn't much like it when she pulled back from him, either.

"I'm sorry. It's no' that I don't want your touch. I was just trying to avoid another trip into the ether until we've had a chance to sort things out a bit."

She laughed again, but it was a hollow one. "No offense taken," she said, but he knew otherwise. "I don't know what we can do to make sense of this. Or how we can keep it from happening again."

There was a small moment of silence, and he couldn't have said what devil got into him. The bond they shared because of their supernatural journey together gave him a sense of closeness to her that encouraged the devilish smile he didn't try to squelch. "Are we sure we should be tryin' so hard to avoid it? 'Twas confusin', no doubt, but no' exactly such a bad thing otherwise, aye?"

He saw her mouth twitch at the corners, and found himself curling his fingers into his palm to keep from reaching for her.

"Aye," she said, in a dead-on approximation of his accent. "'Twas no' exactly a hardship to endure, no."

"Well, I wouldn't say it wasna hard . . ."

She snickered then. And so did he. One shared glance later, and they both broke out laughing in earnest. They laughed so hard it was impossible to talk, almost to breathe. It felt good, and cleansing, and blessedly normal.

He managed to calm himself before she did, and watched as she enjoyed a final snort and snicker. There was a warmth in his heart then, one he supposed had been growing since he'd encountered her, swathed in white satin while swearing a blue streak, in the prayer garden. How two days and a single night spent together could have brought him to the point of feeling such an honest affection for her, he didn't know. Nor did he much feel the need to quantify it. Something else lurked beneath the surface of their joint adventures, something that spoke of distant times and paths crossed once before.

Suddenly it all started to make a bit of sense to him. Unnerving and fantastical as the merest suspicion of it was, it did make some kind of sense.

"What is it?" she asked.

"What?" he asked, looking to her again.

"You're frowning. And thinking. What just popped into your mind?"

It was different for him, having someone pay such close attention, and be in tune with him so quickly. He didn't normally wear his emotions so plainly, but he supposed they were well past pretending to employ social proprieties.

"I was just . . ." He paused, debated giving voice to the thought, but what the hell. He could hardly sound more daft than he already suspected he was. "I've thought there was a connection between us, since meeting you in the garden. That was no' entirely in line with what I'd be thinking after meeting a complete and total stranger."

She nodded, as if completely understanding the sentiment, and he released the breath he hadn't been aware he'd been holding, which was silly, since he could hardly be worried about wanting her admiration or respect at that point.

"I'm no' sure why I felt compelled to stand up in your chapel, and say the things I did. Of course I wanted you to leave with me, because that was the purpose of my being there, but the way it came out, the intensity of the feelings I had of how wrong it was for you to betroth yourself to another man . . . none of that was a realistic or normal thing to be feeling. And yet, in that moment, I most certainly did."

"It was definitely intense," she said, her lips curving a little, though her expression remained thoughtful and serious. "But it moved me. Called to me, I suppose is a better way of saying it. Something in the conviction you had in your voice, gave me the courage I needed to do what I knew had to be done." She looked at him again. "I suppose that might answer your earlier question. I don't know that I'd have been able to do it without you. Because then—and I know this sounds nuts, but I'm guessing we're past worrying about that now—because then it would have been just for me. I wasn't ever going to be good at putting only my own needs above those of the people I loved. But when you stood, and . . . well, laid claim is the best way I can describe it. There was this feeling, this sense of . . . , finally. That's what it felt like. Finally. Finally, you were there, and I knew the direction I was meant to go. And that direction was toward you."

She lifted a shoulder, and quickly looked away when he rolled to his side and propped up one elbow to rest his head on his curled fist. He said nothing, hoping his silence encouraged her to continue. He realized he needed to hear what she was saying, needed to know what had been going through her mind throughout their journey. The relief he felt in knowing he hadn't been alone, that whatever the insanity was, he wasn't alone inside it, was comforting . . . and he wasn't above taking some of that comfort for himself.

"What should have been the most wrenching decision of my life was somehow not. Not at that moment, anyway. I suppose if I'd had the time to sort it out, I'd have told myself I'd been working toward that moment for a very long time, so the sense of relief and rightness wouldn't have been surprising. But that was only a small part." She paused, took a steadying breath, glanced at him, then looked back to the ceiling, as if it were easier to try and explain if she didn't have to look directly at him while she was doing so.

For some reason, that made him smile, and that warmth, that affection he had for her, grew another notch. He'd give her all the sense of security and strength she needed for herself and more, if he could. In fact, whatever was in his power to give her, he wanted her to have. It felt both selfless and selfish at the same time. He knew he'd put her happiness and general well-being above his own. He also knew the feeling was inspired, at least in part, by the knowledge that it made him feel good—no, great—to be the one charged with seeing to her happiness. Selfishly so. It wasn't the altruistic gesture it might seem. Yet, the absolute joy there was to be had in even thinking he could be that for her was both disquieting and quietly thrilling.

In fact, were he to take his thoughts another step further,

he'd have said the only way anyone could feel things so intensely for a person they'd just met, was if they'd met before. And he felt as if he'd been charged with seeing to her happiness for a very, very long time.

Insanity.

The moment he allowed the thought to take root, a feeling of calm, of rightness, settled somewhere deep within him. As if he'd finally put the puzzle pieces into place, so the picture was being revealed.

The question—or the next piece in the puzzle—was what was he supposed to do about it? He'd decided—they'd agreed—that he needed to move forward with his original plans. Any scheme that included them marrying for any reason other than love, was wrong. For both of them.

A short pain stabbed him near his heart, as if someone had stuck a pin there. So real was the feeling, he reached up and rubbed a fist over it. Though the prick of pain subsided, the lingering ache did not.

"So," she said, "we both felt compelled to join forces, as it were. Since then, on several occasions—escalating in nature each time—we've had . . . episodes, I'll call them, where we've imagined ourselves, or viewed ourselves, or . . . actually been, uh . . . involved." She waved a hand, as if that summed it all up.

He smiled again. He supposed it was as good a summation as he'd have come up with. For some things, there were no words.

"Meaning we have some kind of connection that goes deeper, or began in some other place, some other time, and now that we've crossed paths again, we're caught up in something bigger than ourselves." She slumped a little as she released a breath. "What does it say that I feel a little relief, because it actually makes sense to me?" She rolled her head toward him. "It says I'm crazy. That's what it says."

"Join the club," he said, the smile still playing around the corners of his mouth. He knew he should be far more anxious than he felt. He wasn't exactly at peace with any of it. But the time spent lying on the bed, coupled with the meal they'd had, and the activities he'd internalized in thought, if not deed, were all conspiring to fill him with a sort of languor. It wasn't entirely unwanted or undesirable. In fact, he had an overwhelming desire to tug her across the expanse of bed they'd put between them and tuck her against the larger frame of his body, where she could draw solace from him and he could feel as if he were in his rightful place . . . and they could both find escape in a blissful night's sleep.

Of course, he could do none of those things. They didn't fully understand what would send them hurtling back to that other place. But just as he thought keeping each other safe from another unplanned journey had to be his uppermost concern, another equally strong need was driving him. "Katie," he said, his voice gruff. She looked at him and he held out his hand. "Come here."

She looked from his face, to his hand, then back to his face again, her expression a mixture of fear and . . . longing. It was the latter that sealed his decision.

"If this is the only night we'll share, I'd like to share it without fear of touching you. I'd like to hold you, here, in this bed, in this room."

"But . . . what if—?"

He lifted a shoulder, and his lips quirked. "I dinnae think it will. No' now. But if it did . . . was it such a bad thing?"

Her mouth dropped open, then snapped shut as a pretty pink blush stole across her face.

He wiggled his fingers. "I'm no' intending to try and replicate anything, have no worries. I just . . ." He reached for her. "We've one night. Spend it here," he said, and tugged her close, folding her against his chest. "With me." Their bodies twined with the ease of two people who'd wrapped themselves around each other for many long nights. He didn't question it.

She tipped her chin up to look at him, as he ducked his chin to look at her. "Still with me?" she asked, trying for a teasing tone, but clearly searching his gaze for any telltale signs.

"I'm here." He tipped her chin up further. He would not take advantage, that much he'd meant and would hold to his word. But it didn't mean he had to end their brief time together without tasting her one last time. He lowered his mouth slowly, giving her time and space, to move back if it was a step she wasn't willing to risk.

So it took him aback, and, more disconcertingly, made his heart stutter, when instead, she reached up and cupped his cheek, and drew him down the last inch so she could lay claim to him first.

The brush of her lips was soft, gentle, though not tentative. She paused, broke off enough to look up at him, then smiled so beautifully it fully illuminated her eyes. "Still here," she murmured. Then those eyes drifted shut, and she went back to kissing him.

He was no longer worried about waking dreams and traveling to distant places. In fact, it never even crossed his mind. The only thing he knew, the only thing in his world that mattered at that moment, was Katie curled up in his arms, and her mouth—her sweet mouth—so perfectly on his.

He let her guide the kiss, didn't try to take it over. Oddly, given the level of arousal holding her was doing to him, he wasn't particularly driven to steer that ship. It was wondrous, to discover what she wanted to bring to him, give to him, take from him.

His body raged forth, fully aroused, demanding what it wanted, urging him to take what was so willingly being offered. The demand was strong enough to cloud judgment and defer all rational thought. But there was more going on than the mere slaking of physical need. And that was what he was interested in learning, in experiencing.

So he did.

She explored his mouth slowly, not so much leisurely, but more taking the time to learn each and every nuance of him. He kissed her back when she grew more demanding, followed her lead and took her mouth, let her taste him fully, as she was seeking him out, tasting him. Their kiss was intoxicating in its restraint, and all the more erotic for neither of them giving in to their bodies' demands that they escalate things.

It was only when she grew too breathless to continue that she finally broke off the kiss. He followed after her mouth as she slowly tucked her head under his chin, but checked himself when she slid one hand along his ribs, and under his arm, pulling him a bit closer as she nestled her cheek just against his heart.

He pressed a kiss on the top of her head, and shifted so their bodies aligned fittingly, tucking her legs between his, and sliding his arm around her, his palm up her spine, until he could weave his hand beneath all those curls, and keep her head tucked just as it was.

He let his eyes drift shut, thinking to use the quiet moment to figure out what he should be doing, versus what he wanted to be doing. He'd told her he wasn't taking her to Kinloch, that he'd resolve his problem his own way, and release her from any commitment she might have been willing to make. He needed to think through what he was going to do for her, to help provide a way, for her to begin her new journey, to give her a recourse other than to go back to what she'd struggled so long to leave.

But he wasn't given the chance to do any of those things. Katie sighed, and relaxed fully into him, her fingers, once tensely holding him to her, slackened as sleep finally, mercifully claimed her. No longer forced to sleep upright, to grab winks of sleep while awkwardly leaning from her seat to his shoulder, they could finally stretch out, curl up, and sleep without any motion, noise, or sudden stops and starts.

Those were his final thoughts before he, too, found himself

drifting to that same, blessedly blissful place. No sudden shifts in time or space, no crazy insane things happening that defied all explanation. Just the two of them, exhausted, but comforted by the warmth and solid presence of the other, falling blissfully and quite naturally asleep.

Chapter 13

When Graham next opened his eyes, the sun was barely up, but enough to fill the room with a soft glow. He stretched and flexed his arms, legs, and back, rejoicing in the renewal he felt after a few hours' sleep. It took a few moments for the rest of the story to filter back into his brain. His eyes flew open, his body jerked upright. Katie. The bed was empty except for him, so his gaze darted to each corner. No Katie.

She wouldn't have left. Would she? Wouldn't have gone and not said her good-byes to him. Surely not until they'd discussed how to get her back to the States, or onward to wherever else she wanted to go. It was the very least he could provide given what he'd put her through. Surely she'd have at least accepted that much as payment for the lengths she'd gone to, to even consider his proposal.

"Katie," he called out. Barked. A panic was beginning to swell but he couldn't allow himself to retreat back. It was only forward, for him. She would leave, and he would return to Kinloch alone. Whatever confusing waking dreams they'd shared would also come to an end. Surely they'd put that to its final rest, considering what had happened after they'd checked in, and later, in how they'd managed to sleep the night in each other's arms without any kind of repeat performance, either through their dream state alternate selves, or in that bed.

He slid off the bed and strode to the door, intent on finding Mrs. Ardingall if necessary to find out what she might know of Katie's whereabouts. She could just be getting their morning meal. Except . . .

His gaze tracked back to where her bag had been propped against the wall, left unused last night, given the course of events. Then his head jerked up, and toward the bathroom door. That was it. He sighed, feeling foolish. She'd taken her bag and herself into the bathroom to finally indulge in a good hot shower and a clean change of clothes. Lord knew he was quite looking forward to both of those things himself.

But there was no sound of running water. A short rap on the door brought no response. Anger began to replace the panic. He tugged the door open with a short jerk and stepped into the small washroom. It was empty. As he'd known it would be.

She was gone.

He walked back out, then sank into the chair beside the small table where they'd shared their stew, which was also gone. If it wasn't for the fact that the sun was barely high enough past the horizon to be streaming a soft glow beyond the sill of the window, he'd have worried he had slept the day away and that she'd left out of sheer impatience, waiting for him to awaken.

He thumped his fist on the table. Then again, with more feeling, causing the carved claw and ball feet to chatter a few inches across the wood floor.

Impatient, he shoved to a stand and, after a quick look about—no note that he could see—he grabbed the room key, intending to let himself out the door. He paused and looked back at the bed, then with a quick shake of his head and swearing beneath his breath, he exited the room, locking the door behind him. He wouldn't be coming back.

Downstairs, he found Mrs. Ardingall behind the narrow registration desk at the rear of the foyer entrance.

"Good morning, Mr. MacLeod," she greeted him warmly. No hint whatsoever that she was aware his roommate had already left the premises.

He debated bringing it up, his nature not being one of involving strangers in his personal matters. He almost barked a laugh. He'd done nothing but involve strangers in his personal matters for the past several days.

He strode to the desk and slid the room key. "Thank you for the meal last night."

"Everything was to your liking?"

"It was all fine." He pulled his wallet from his sporran, but the innkeeper lifted her hand to stop him.

"That willnae be necessary. She took care of the room bill when she came down earlier."

Graham checked his wallet, but everything seemed in order. "But how—"

Mrs. Ardingall's smile remained steady and serene, but her cheeks took on the faintest hint of pink. "I dinnae wish to interfere," she said quietly, then leaned slightly forward and lowered her voice again—not that there was anyone in the foyer but them. "I believe she cashed in an airline ticket with Alastair at the excursion office first thing this morning."

"First thing—'tis too early for—" He looked over his shoulder then, through the mullioned glass on either side of the front door. His heart sank when he realized the reason for the pale light. It wasn't due to its being daybreak. It was due to the steady drizzle and overcast skies. He belatedly recalled the weather that had been heading in as they were crossing in the ferry last night.

"What time is it?" he asked. His mobile being dead, he had no idea.

"Quarter past eleven."

"Eleven!"

Her smile ever steady, she nodded. "I believe she was trying to book passage on the ferry. With the weather, it's no' scheduled to leave today until half past noon. Ye've plenty of time."

Graham's heart leapt, which he immediately quelled. "What time does the ferry back to Oban leave?"

"Was to be at ten, but the weather delayed her as well. Should be loading right now. I thought ye were heading onward, to Kinloch."

"I am. Her luggage—"

"She had me contact Barnaby and he came and helped collect her things."

"Barnaby—"

"The gentleman who brought you in last eve."

"Right." Graham had been so distracted by everything that had happened at the slip dock, he hadn't realized he'd never even asked their driver's name. That was unlike him. But hell, what wasn't at the moment?

"Thank you for everything, Mrs. Ardingall."

"Always a pleasure," she said, her smile widening as he sketched a quick bow, before turning on his heels and heading out into the dreary morning.

Bloody hell. He had, in fact, slept half the day away. He wondered when Katie had decided to leave. And why she hadn't at least left him a note. Dammit, he should have asked the innkeeper. But then, surely she'd have passed on anything Katie had told her to tell or give him.

The rain wasn't more than a light patter, but it brought an unseasonal chill to the morning air. He hunched his shoulders, and ignored the grumble in his stomach as he passed by the local pastry, which smelled heavenly. His only goal was getting to the dock before that ferry departed. She might have been fine with concluding their business together in the manner she had, but he wasn't. He hadn't the vaguest of clues what he intended to say to her, but he knew he simply wasn't done with her yet.

Cashed in her honeymoon tickets, had she? He wasn't aware that could be done. Surely she hadn't gotten much for them. And she'd paid for their room, from what little she'd gotten. He already knew her pride would be stung if he tried to pay her back for that, but dammit, she was already facing a significant enough uphill climb. Unless, of course, she'd contacted her family. His grumbling stomach clutched at the thought, though he couldn't have said why. It was her life, her decision to make.

What she did or didn't do with herself had absolutely no bearing on him. So why he was remotely concerned was beyond him.

Except that knot in his gut was telling him exactly why it bothered him. He could tell himself until he was blue in the face that she didn't matter—couldn't matter—to him, given how they'd come to know each other, and why he'd initially wanted her. They couldn't turn things around and pretend it was otherwise. Or she couldn't. And he could hardly blame her.

He could tell himself that. But he would know it was a lie. If he were being honest, it was exactly what he wanted, and he was angry, mad as hell, in fact, that she hadn't been willing to look beyond their ridiculous initial agreement, to see if there was something worthwhile waiting to be discovered between them. Something real, and honest, and true, that had absolutely nothing to do with signed agreements and getting time away to figure out the future.

While he was being honest, he might as well also admit the knot in his gut was more like the squeezing fist of an ache a wee bit more highly centered.

All the more reason to cut his losses before he was played for any more of a fool, book passage to Kinloch, then find a phone. He hadn't communicated with anyone on Kinloch, and they'd have no idea when he was arriving. He thought about that, as he hunched his shoulders a bit more as the misting rain increased to a slight drizzle. Perhaps it was best not to let anyone know of his imminent arrival. He still needed time to think over how best to approach the next step he'd have to take—getting that damned law abolished—before Iain up and married himself off.

He heard the horn of the CalMac and picked up his pace. He should have gotten Mrs. Ardingall to help him with a lift to the docks. It was a bit farther of a trot than he'd remembered from the night before. Of course, all he'd remembered from their trip in was watching Katie as she chatted with Barnaby, and trying like hell to distance himself from the vision he'd had on the dock. If only he'd known just how far into such a vision he would go later on.

He was almost full out running by the time he rounded the lane that headed down to the water. The inn they'd stayed in had faced the waterfront, but winding down to the water's edge and the slip dock itself, was more a circuitous route.

He was too late.

The ferry had debarked as he sprinted the final few meters until the dock came fully into view.

He stopped, bent at the waist, and drew in breath, along with the morning mist, as he watched the ferry chug out into the harbor. He straightened and scanned the rear of the boat, trying to see if she might be at the rail, and if so, would she see that he was there. That he'd run to catch her before she left him. For good.

A healthy dose of hurt mixed in with the anger. She hadn't struck him as the sort to pull such a stunt. But then, given the rather unique complexity of their relationship thus far, perhaps she'd been the wise one to leave as she did. They'd been telling each other they'd keep it business from the moment they'd met, and neither one had been able to hold true to that for more than a five-second span, or so it seemed. Maybe she was the wise one, cutting her losses, before things got any further out of their control. Before they risked any further adventures into whatever that otherworld might still hold in store for them.

Yet . . . he remained annoyed. After all they'd been and done for each other in the intensely focused time they'd spent together, he wouldn't have left her. Regardless of the risks involved. He simply wouldn't have.

He turned then, and headed farther along the waterfront to the other slip. A much, much smaller affair, but then it only had to be functional for the much smaller ferry—compared to the CalMac anyway—that ran across the sound to Kinloch. He knew the schedule fluctuated with the tides and the weather, and that, in the more moderately temperate months, two runs a day was typically the maximum. In the harsher weather, the ferry could go as long as a week or more before making the trip across.

Kinloch wasn't situated that far off, just to the west and south of the smaller Vatarsay, which was connected to Barra by a small causeway. Kinloch was just beyond the sound, but there was a wide enough swath of open sea between them that the least bit of hard weather, combined with the smaller ferry, could make the journey quite treacherous.

He'd long since gotten used to the capricious and unstable nature of their tenuous connection to Barra and the rest of the Outer Hebridean chain, along with the mainland beyond that. Barra did boast an airstrip, Traigh Mhor, which was actually a beach, but in times of emergency, they could make a water landing off Kinloch if someone needed immediate transport for something such as a medical issue. Otherwise, they were dependant on the ferry system not only to ship in any mainland supplies the islanders needed, but also to ship out their baskets.

At the moment, he was just hoping to get himself home.

It was quarter till twelve when he walked inside the small office perched to the side of the smaller slip dock to get his ticket, and also for a bit of respite from the steadily falling rain. He shook his arms and scraped his hair from his face, and offered the man behind the desk a brief smile. "Hullo, Malvy. I need to book passage home."

"Short trip. How'd it go?" Malvy Fraser owned and operated the small, independent ferry that serviced Kinloch and a few of the smaller islands. Though he no longer piloted the boat, having a bad leg and a worse back due to a fishing boat accident a half dozen years back, he could always be found in the office or around the dock.

Malvy had been the one manning the desk when Graham had come through on his way to the U.S., switching ferries to Oban when Roan had been unsuccessful getting him a flight from Traigh Mhor to Glasgow. The flight would have saved him significant time, and allowed him the chance to check in to the small boardinghouse Shay had found in Annapolis, before heading to the chapel. Of course, given how things had all worked out, it was just as well it hadn't happened that way. Although, playing that back through his mind made him realize he'd never called and canceled the room. Bollocks. He'd follow up on that when he dealt with the rental car.

"It went," he told the older man. No one outside Roan and Shay had known about his reasons for leaving the island, though speculation was running hot and heavy by the time he'd boarded the ferry east. Graham had done nothing to thwart the speculation, mainly because, for the most part, they were on the right track. They could do the math in their heads. They knew there were no available McAuley women on the island that he could marry. That, and Iain showing up, had painted a pretty explicit picture. But that was all anyone knew.

Except Malvy. Possibly the only soul living anywhere in the entire Hebridean chain who didn't gossip. Graham had often joked with him, back when Malvy had been the one guiding the ferry into port twice daily on Kinloch, that he'd missed his calling and should have been either a priest or a bartender. Malvy had just laughed and claimed he was a bit of both, and if Graham ever needed spiritual guidance, Malvy could soothe the savage soul . . . providing Graham was pouring the whisky, of course.

During the time Ualraig had been ill and the leadership responsibilities, along with the burden of their crop and economic issues, had increasingly fallen on Graham's shoulders, Malvy had proven to be a good listener with a knack for sound advice. One that Graham had availed himself of on more than one occasion.

It was rare he had reason to leave Kinloch anymore, so he didn't see Malvy often. In fact, when he'd come through on his way to Oban, more than a year had passed since Graham had laid eyes on the man. They'd spent a few minutes catching up, and he'd somehow found himself blurting out the entire preposterous plan. The older man had raised an eyebrow at the idea, but ended up shrugging and saying Graham's own forefathers had certainly bound themselves together for far less. Any further discussion had been interrupted by other passengers coming in to purchase tickets or get Malvy's thoughts on the weather, the fishing, or any number of other things the man seemed to have uncannily accurate knowledge of.

"So . . . ye traveling alone, are ye?" Malvy asked him, as he processed the ticket payment, then handed Graham the slip.

"It would appear so," Graham said, knowing Malvy hadn't meant it as anything other than a statement of fact. He was the most non-judgmental man Graham had ever met, which, combined with the rest of his talents, made him a decent and honorable man, in addition to being a trusted friend.

The older man merely nodded. "We'll be leaving port at half past. Weather's clearing to the west, so you'll be in sunshine by the time ye land on yer own bonny shores."

Graham nodded. "Good." He pocketed the payment slip and ticket, but made no move to leave the small office. It was warm and dry, and though he could pre-board since the ferry was ready and waiting, he knew Malvy wouldn't mind if he hung around until it was time to leave port.

Proving that, the old man lifted his cup. "Tea?" he asked. "Possibly a shot of something to make ye forget you're wearing what smells like wet lamb."

Graham immediately lifted his arm and sniffed, which sent Malvy into a gurgling fit of laughter.

"Get's 'em every time," he said, before covering his mouth as he coughed through the last laugh.

Graham shot him a quelling look. "Aye, well, I'm certain I'd do well for a shower at the moment. It's first on my list when I arrive back, rest assured." He hadn't gotten one the night before, and that morning it hadn't been the first thing on his mind. Chilled and damp from the rain as he was, it was just as well he hadn't wasted the water. Though the soap and a razor wouldn't have been looked at askance.

"Mind explainin' the dress clothes? And wha' happened to your duffel?" Malvy lifted his tea cup and motioned with it.

"I went to church," Graham said simply. "The service demanded something more than work trews and a field shirt. My wardrobe in between the two is a bit wanting."

"How many days ago was that?"

"Amusing," Graham said. "I'm well aware of how I must look."

"Ye're not tellin' me ye got all dressed up and went to church because ye did the deed and tied the knot while ye were there? Wouldn't it need to happen here on Scottish soil? And where is the fair lass?"

"No, I didn't get married."

"More's the pity. What I hear, Iain McAuley is quite the charmer."

Graham's gaze narrowed. "Since when did you join the gossip mill?"

Malvy's smile spread to a grin, but there was a hard light in his eyes. "Since some young buck with more education than sense thinks he can just come along and tear asunder what good-hearted, loyal, hard-working lads like yourself have spent an entire lifetime building up."

Graham's expression smoothed, even as he felt the beginning of a headache thrum along his temples. *And so it is about to start*, he thought. Best he be prepared. "Tell me what ye know."

"What I don't know is what the little lamb thinks he wants with some godforsaken island out in the middle of the sea."

Graham lifted an eyebrow at that description, but Malvy waved him off with a dismissive snort. "One man's treasure island is another man's sinking ship. I know the struggles you and your grandfather faced, and what you will continue to face in years to come. No' much of an inheritance for some posh pup used to the finer things."

"Agreed. So, why do you think he's come? Have you heard anything?"

Malvy lifted a shoulder, took another sip of tea. "Nothing specific. Maybe he thinks he can parlay your basket-making industry to something more, or perhaps he thinks he can sell the whole thing off . . . or worse, back to its own people."

Graham snorted. "He's in for a hell of a disappointment then. We are finally turning the corner toward greater prosperity, but our coffers are filled with the hope of a better future. Not as much with actual money or collateral."

"You and I know that—"

"If he's an educated man, then so would he. It's no' hard to figure out. One walk about the place would show that we're no' exactly living like kings in our own castles. Most especially mine."

Malvy lifted a shoulder again, and drained his teacup. "So you say, and I agree . . . but he's come for something. I dinnae simply believe it's the warm, welcoming arms of a bonny MacLeod lass. I'm certain he's more than his fair share of warm and willing lasses back in Edinburgh."

"To be certain. He's come straight out with it, already, that he's come to claim the island. Stated it baldly in the course of introducing himself. I've just no idea why. But it willnae matter. I plan to put this entire outdated charade to rest, once and for all."

Malvy slid from his stool and limped his permanently hunched body over to the small hot plate where a brass teakettle rested. "So," he said, "if ye've no bride trailing behind ye, then what do ye plan to do to thwart the snot nosed, entitled little arse?"

Graham smiled at Malvy's increasingly annoyed comments regarding Iain. "I appreciate your loyalty," he told the older man as he steeped more tea into his cup, added a bit of honey, and something else from a flask inside his jacket.

"Medicinal," was all he said, when he caught Graham noticing the sly maneuver.

Graham merely shrugged, but said nothing specifically about it. The man wasn't steering boats any longer. "I take it you met him, directly, then." When Malvy nodded, he said, "So, are you basing your low opinion of the man strictly on his status as an interloper?" Graham asked, then held up a hand and smiled briefly. "Not that I've a problem with that."

Malvy took a sip, then settled himself back on his stool. "He's no' one of us," he told him, flatly. "Make no mistake of it, and warn your people. He never will be."

Graham listened to Malvy, and he knew—hoped—that many of his people were forming similar opinions about the man, despite his abundant genetic gifts. Graham's thoughts moved along that line of thought to Katie, and he found himself wondering what her reception would have been. She'd have been well liked, for herself, he thought. But as bride to The MacLeod, with some sway over their futures? He wasn't so certain, listening to Malvy, how well she might have fared. She was also from the posh life. And she wasn't even a Scot. Not Scot-born anyway.

The whole of the matter served to reinforce his idea that he had to get his people to see that not only was the Marriage Pact law antiquated and outdated, but it was actually harmful to their continued forward progress, future successes, and ongoing economic stability. Surely they wouldn't put sentiment over security.

He nodded. "I appreciate the counsel."

Malvy saluted him with his teacup. "Freely given, which is likely what it's worth."

Graham smiled. "It was good to see ye, Malvy."

"The same," he said, flipping open the island paper, the one entirely in Gaelic.

Graham turned and had his hand on the office door, then turned back. "If I had come back with an American McAuley bride on my arm, say one with a similar background as Iain's, would your response have been the same as with him? About never being one of us?"

Malvy paused mid-sip, took a moment to ponder the question, then said, "Depends on the bride."

"Would it? I mean, she wouldn't have been one of us, no matter what she was made of or how well liked she may have been."

"Aye, but she'd be on your arm, as your wife. If you trusted her, perhaps even loved her, it wouldn't be the same at all. Iain McAuley is an interloper with no connection to Kinloch or anyone on it. She'd be on Kinloch as your wife."

"And if McAuley marries someone from the island? Same thing?"

"Again, depends on the bride. But given your standing, the bride ye brought home to work at your side, one who would have your best interests and by extension, your people's best interests at heart, would share the goodwill and good graces ye've earned from a lifetime spent dedicated to those same people. Iain would be husband to an islander, who, while perhaps well liked, or even beloved, wouldn't—couldn't—be of your stature when compared with the entire citizenry."

Graham thought about that. "So, I'd have the edge, is what you're saying. Even if she were an outsider."

"Aye," Malvy said, with a nod. "Even if." Then he leveled an amused smile at Graham. "Is this outsider bride still a possibility?"

Graham shook his head, sorry as he was to dash the obvious pleasure the possibility would have given Malvy. What surprised him was how heavy the weight of disappointment was in his own hopes being dashed as well. But it was a decision already made. By him, initially. And acted upon, by the bride herself. He could only lay the blame with himself. "I think there are better solutions to the problem than marrying a stranger."

"Hmm," Malvy said, as he sipped his fresh cup of tea. "I suppose you'll be having a chance to find that out for yourself."

Graham frowned briefly. Malvy's tone was . . . an amused one, which was a bit surprising, given his very real ire at the thought of Iain's attempted insurgence. "I suppose I will," Graham said, keeping his own tone neutral. He turned again, paused again, debated questioning Malvy on his curious reply, but the horn sounded.

"Safe crossing," Malvy said, and saluted Graham again with

his tea cup as Graham waved good-bye and let himself out of the office.

The rain was lighter, but still steady, so he jogged down to the loading ramp, hoping the passenger list was short and he'd have an empty seat inside the narrow, central interior. Although the chances of not knowing any of the passengers was highly improbable, he found himself hoping the only other people on board were tourists or fishermen. He wasn't ready to talk to anyone, at least not until he spoke with Roan or Shay. He certainly didn't want to answer any speculation about why he was dressed in the manner he was.

With thoughts of getting inside as quickly as possible and finding a far corner to hole up in for the duration of the ride, he put his head down and kept his movement swift and focused on achieving that goal. Not rude, exactly, but not inviting conversation.

It wasn't until he'd managed to find such a corner, that he allowed himself a deep breath, then settled more fully into his seat, turning his head enough to keep his gaze focused outward, toward the rail and beyond, to the horizon. And home.

After a few full minutes had elapsed, a vague image tickled his brain enough for him to pause in his thoughts of planning what to say to Roan and Shay first, then to the rest of the islanders. Slowly he lowered his gaze and scanned the floor to his left.

How could he have missed that . . . that dreaded pile of stitched leather? He'd carried each and every one of those damn things all the way from Annapolis to Castlebay.

He lifted his gaze, even as a rocket punch of adrenaline shot straight to his heart . . . and looked straight into the bright, blue eyes of Katie McAuley.

"Hello, Graham. I saved you a seat."

Chapter 14

Katie had been so worried about what he'd say when he saw her on the ferry, she hadn't taken into consideration how she was going to feel upon seeing him. The morning after. The morning after the intensely primal, thoroughly unforgettable, life-altering sex they didn't really have. A hard knock of lust and . . . something . . . thumped her the instant she laid eyes on him. The lust she was gaining a handle on, at least in terms of expecting it.

But that other part, the something part . . . was a mix of affection and longing, desire and need, all of which had absolutely nothing whatsoever to do with wanting to strip that plaid right off him and climb on his lap right there on the damn ferry. It was that something part that was really scaring the bejesus out of her. The truth of it was, Graham MacLeod mattered to her. That man, that giant, scowling man mattered.

"I thought we'd agreed," he finally said, his expression flattening out until she couldn't get a read on him at all.

Other than that she didn't think he was exactly thrilled to see her. "No," she said, "you decided."

"And what part of that was confusing to ye?"

She leaned back, surprised by the sharp tone. She'd thought he'd be surprised, possibly a little upset that she'd left without saying good-bye, but after last night—not just the during part, but the afterward part, and the after the afterward part, where they'd slept all wrapped around each other all night long—she thought that part would be uppermost in his mind and predispose him to be happy to see her.

Apparently, she'd gotten it all wrong.

"I wasn't confused by any part of it," she said, striving not to sound chilled or hurt, though both were right there for the taking. "I woke up this morning, intent on doing as you'd asked." She didn't mention the part where her heart had ached to the point of breaking at the thought of never seeing him again, and how she'd cried like a baby while in the shower, praying she'd get herself under control before he came in and found her. Mercifully, he'd still been asleep, giving her the critical time she needed to start the process of separating herself from him.

"You know how I feel about asking for handouts, so since you needed the sleep, I figured I would go see about cashing in my honeymoon tickets, at least for enough to stake my trip home. Make a start down the road of standing on my own two feet. I mean, you were going to Kinloch, I was out. I had to start somewhere."

"I'd no' have left you to fend for yourself in Castlebay. Surely you knew that?"

"I don't want to be a responsibility to you, Graham," she said, the hurt squeezing her heart again. There were a lot of things she wanted to be to him, but a responsibility was a distant last. "So I did what felt right. For me. But when it came time to book passage to Oban, I couldn't decide where to go from there. I have no home and the one I did have I'm not willing to go back to. The honeymoon tickets were gone. So that left me with sticking to the plan I had when I left the church. The plan you offered me. At least the part that included time for me to think things through.

"I realize the marriage offer, or the business deal, however you want to define it, is no longer an option. But I thought perhaps you'd be kind enough to make good on the rest of your offer. I can book my own room, and I won't be a bother to you. You don't even have to pretend you know me." She looked down, the burden of trying to remain aloof and unaffected by his out-right rejection wearing thinner, faster than she'd hoped. "I've asked for damn little, Graham, given what you've asked of me. I don't think this is entirely out of line. And I don't see where it can harm your cause."

"Other than the fact that by your very presence, you provide an alternate solution to every traditionalist on the island, which is damn near all of them."

She continued to stare at her hands. She hadn't really thought about it that way. Okay, if she were honest, she hadn't really thought about it much at all, other than knowing that getting on the ferry back to Oban, and onward to the States, had made her feel physically ill, whereas the idea of Kinloch had filled her with a sense of relief.

All right, all right. It also happened if she followed that plan, she didn't have to leave Graham quite yet. It was possible, in her weakest moments, she had fantasized if he saw her, on Kinloch, happy and wanting to be there strictly by choice, and not by some grand scheme, he'd continue on with her. They would have time to discover if there was truly something between them.

Her thoughts flashed to when she'd first woken up that morning—still in his arms, where she'd slept like a baby. There had definitely been something between them then. The rest of him might have been dead asleep, but there was nothing dead about what she'd felt pressing hard between her thighs. She'd been half awake when he'd groaned and moved against her. She responded, kissing his chest and tipping her chin up so she could pull his head down to hers for a long kiss.

Only to come awake enough to realize she wasn't dreaming, and he wasn't awake . . . and she needed to get the hell off that bed before she did something she might regret. Except the only regret she'd had as she'd let herself out of the room was not letting nature take its course. Maybe then they'd have had that very conversation while in a much better frame of mind.

But looking at him, hearing his tone—a tone he'd never once

used with her—made her feel better about not giving in earlier. He might have tossed her out of bed right on her ass.

"I'm sorry," she said. "You're right, I didn't think of that. I'll simply explain to them that I've said no. I'll even champion whatever path it is you want to take."

He looked away and she hated that he didn't feel comfortable making eye contact with her.

"Well," she said, quietly, as the silence grew deafening. Brushing off her pants and smoothing her light sweater, she stood. To think she'd felt well rested and happy after a good night's sleep, hot shower, and a clean set of clothes . . . if still a bit restless from the activities of the night before. Wishing she'd had more of the real thing, she'd hesitated in the doorway, watching him sleep before she'd gone downstairs. "I believe I'll go find myself somewhere else to sit. And don't worry. I'll be on the next ferry out. You won't even have to touch a single suitcase."

She turned away, but hadn't gone two steps when he said, "Why did you leave like you did?"

She looked back. "What?"

"This morning. I woke up and you were gone."

She turned back to face him fully. Was that was this . . . pout of his was all about? His feelings had been hurt? She wasn't sure how she felt about that. Amused, maybe. And surprised he cared enough that her leaving—which he'd asked her to do!—could hurt his feelings.

"I told you, I went to cash my tickets in, and I arranged to have the luggage taken down to the ferry. I came back upstairs then, thinking maybe we'd share a breakfast, say our good-byes."

"Admirable plan. What went wrong?"

Wow, she thought. He was really angry. Furious, if she looked behind the flat gray eyes and even tone.

"You were still dead asleep." *And I was still feeling very restless, and heavily tempted to climb right back in that bed with you and see if visions really can come true,* she thought, but couldn't bring herself to say. "You've had a long couple of days, and I had the ferry to catch. I tried to write you a note. Three times, before I gave up. What was I supposed to say? I couldn't just leave word with Mrs. Ardingall. You're a private man and I knew that wouldn't have been appreciated. She didn't ask any questions when I paid, and I didn't offer any explanations. So . . . I thought, given how things can get with us at times, maybe it was simply better to just go."

"Getting good at that, it appears."

She folded her arms. "Why are you being so rude and hurtful? Yes, I suppose I should have woken you up to say goodbye. But I stood there, watching you sleep, thinking about what had happened the night before, and that's all I could think about."

Graham straightened in his seat and she realized she'd raised her voice a little and worked to tone it down.

"So, if it's honesty you want from me, then here it is. I was afraid. Afraid if I so much as touched you, shook your shoulder, either we'd be catapulted back to where we went last night, or you'd just yank me down on the bed and we'd see what reality was like."

"Why would ye think—"

"Let's just say there were parts of you that were very awake this morning and that made quite an . . . impression on me," she said in a fierce whisper, gratified when his eyes widened a bit and some of the hard lines in his face softened when his jaw relaxed a bit. "Let's just say I was responding to that because I'm female and still breathing. And you were definitely enjoying yourself. But you were asleep. And I knew—" Dammit, her voice caught. She worked hard to swallow the tightness away and keep her composure. McAuleys never lost it in public. "I knew if I kept on down that path, and we did . . . anything else, I'd have a much harder time leaving you than I was already having. Okay? Does that make you happier? So, after much debate, I decided it was best to just go."

"Then you booked passage to Kinloch," he said, but his tone was grudging, the chill gone, if not all the anger.

"I explained that. I went all the way to the other ferry. Barnaby hauled me and my luggage down there. I was in the ticket office. But all I could think was I'd hardly had any time to think about anything, and I wasn't ready yet to go back home and face . . . God knows what. I wanted some time. Needed some time. I thought about finding a room in Oban. Barnaby, he . . ." She lifted a hand, let it drop.

"He what?" Graham's gaze had sharpened again. "What did he do?"

She looked at Graham, into his eyes, surprised at the possessive edge that had crept into his tone, and wondered if he was aware of it. Maybe she was mistaken. Maybe he was still pissed off and worried Barnaby was going to complicate things. "He didn't do anything. But he felt bad, thinking something must have happened between us if I was turning right around and heading back to the mainland. I couldn't tell him the truth."

"What did you tell him?"

"I didn't tell him anything. I let him assume . . . what he assumed. We were at the dock and I wasn't getting out of his truck. He asked me if I thought I was doing the right thing. Of course, he thought we'd had a fight or something. But I took his question seriously anyway. I couldn't help thinking that no, I didn't think I was doing the right thing. So I said that." She slid her folded arms a bit more tightly, more holding herself than making a shield. "And he said maybe it was best to stand my ground, and do whatever I thought I had to do to make things right." She looked away, blew out a sigh, then looked at Graham, who was back to his steady, inscrutable regard of her. "That's when I thought about your offer, and what I still wanted from it. So, I just"—she lifted a shoulder—"I just had him take me to the other dock, and I went to the office and the man there was so nice and friendly—"

"Malvy." Graham swore under his breath. "He knew. The whole time. Smug bastard."

"Don't blame him for anything. He was very polite and helped me take care of everything from the luggage to, well, everything. He—I felt better. Immediately better. I knew it was the right thing. It was too late then, to get back to the inn to tell you what I'd decided to do, and it was raining pretty good. Plus Barnaby had already taken off, so I opted to come aboard and wait for you. I knew you'd be surprised, but I didn't think you'd be angry."

"I'm no'—"

"Oh, but you are. Furious, even. Maybe a little hurt that I didn't say good-bye. I am sorry about that. I'd have felt the same. Maybe worse—if you'd done the same to me."

He looked at her then. "You said you didn't wake me because it would have been harder to say good-bye. Only now you're here . . . prolonging things between us anyway."

She walked over then and sank down in the seat next to him. "I didn't think the rest through. I am sorry for that, too. This isn't any easier for me than it is for you, though I know it's for different reasons. I was thinking about me, and what I wanted. I really didn't think it would matter to you one way or the other since I wasn't going to rely on you for boarding me or anything. I didn't—I didn't think about the rest." She laid a hand on his arm without thinking, then froze. As did he.

Their gazes immediately locked, and neither one so much as breathed. But a beat went by, then another, and they were both still sitting next to each other on the ferry. She let out a shaky breath. "Sorry, I forgot," she murmured, but he covered her hand before she could pull it away.

"No, that would be my line."

She looked up into his face. "What?"

"I'm sorry. It shouldn't have mattered, what you did, or how you chose to take your leave. No one was more surprised than me how angry it made me, to think you could walk away. Despite the fact that we'd already decided to do just that. So I had no cause to be upset with ye."

"But you were. You really were," she added, still surprised, and hurt a little herself at the tone he'd used.

He jerked a nod. "Fiercely so."

It shouldn't have warmed her, that short nod of assent, and the gruff note in his voice. But it did. So complicated, this . . . thing between them. She wished it wasn't but didn't see how they could get to anything normal. Nothing that had happened between them from the moment they met—nothing internally, externally, in the world, or the unexplainable parallel one they'd stumbled into, none of it—approached anything close to normal.

She moved her fingers under his. He tucked his between hers and squeezed. "I am sorry," she said quietly. "I was just . . . confused, I guess. You confuse me, this"—she rubbed her fingers under his—"this confuses me. All of it. I don't know how to act. We're both so afraid of finding one of those trigger things, we never know what to say or do, and I just . . . I tried to leave. I did try." She trailed off and looked down at their joined hands. His so broad and strong, scarred and weather worn. Hers far more delicate, perfectly manicured and well maintained. It was an appropriate metaphor for who they were as people, compared to each other. He'd never fit in her world, and she realized she'd only complicate his. He didn't need that. She didn't know what she needed. No point in making things harder for him, though, while she figured it out.

"Katie," he said quietly and gently. Like the man she'd first met in the garden.

She lifted her gaze to his, and couldn't deny or pretend to ignore the intensity of her relief in seeing openness again, the . . . vulnerability . . . was the word that came to mind. No one looking at Graham MacLeod, hulking in height, square of jaw, broad of shoulder, and heavy of calf, would think he had so much as a chink in his armor. The clan armor he wore only served to strengthen that masculinity, which was interesting, given he was wearing what amounted to a skirt and sash.

She knew he could be fierce. Well, his alter ego, but as of that morning, she knew, firsthand, he was capable of it as well. What she really knew, and understood, was that he was quiet by nature, reflective, thoughtful. He spent more time using his mind to think things through and form workable solutions to problems, than to battering-ram his way through obstacles with his over-sized body.

It was that man she'd found hard to leave. So hard, in fact, that she hadn't.

"What?" she responded, curling the fingers of her free hand inward to keep from reaching up to touch his face. She recalled the kiss they'd shared on the ferry from Oban. Whatever the mystical connection was, however dark and erotic and compelling, their real connection was equally so, for entirely different reasons. She felt . . . accepted by him. Wanted by him. Not for her last name, or her association to money or success. Not because she was the only McAuley eligible to fix his problem. With him, she could fully be herself, no other agenda, and enjoy the knowledge it was not only okay, but desirable.

"I dinnae know what might be ahead. On Kinloch. For me, or for you. Much less as an us."

"I'll stay on the ferry, take it back on the next crossing. I really don't want to complicate—"

He was already shaking his head. "We're no' meant to part, you and me. Don't ye feel that?" He took her hand, turned it over in his so their palms met, then wove his fingers through again and pulled their joined hands up between them. "You stayed. I didn't want ye to go. It's as simple as that."

She smiled then. "Nothing between us is remotely simple."

His lips curved a bit, too, and it made her heart skip a beat, then another, to see the honest affection come to life in his eyes. "Aye, 'tis true enough, I suppose. But at least we're both aware of it. The rest, the parts we can't explain? They're happenin' for a reason, Katie. I cannae help but believe that to be true. It explains, at least in part, why I was so upset with your taking off."

"You wanted me to go," she reminded him.

"In my head, it made rational, logical sense. But that's no' the part of me that was affected by your leaving. No' in that initial moment when I knew you'd gone."

"I didn't mean to hurt you."

"You shouldnae have been able to."

She blinked at that, but knew what he meant. "I suppose not, no. We're still strangers. More or less."

"Only in the measure of time could we consider ourselves that." He lifted her hand, and pressed a kiss to the back of one knuckle, then another. His lips were warm, and so was every inch of her, as a deep well of affection spread through her. "But I think we're timeless, Katherine Elizabeth. I don't know that we've been strangers for a very, very long time."

She could only nod. Anywhere else, with anyone else, she'd be booking an appointment with a very expensive shrink. But, with Graham, surrounded by the sea, and the striking skyline provided by the mountainous islands . . . anything seemed possible. Probable, even. "So, are you saying you want me to stay? On Kinloch?"

"I still think I need to try and have the law changed. I dinnae think it's right to be forced into matrimony."

She smiled. "I can only second that sentiment."

His smile was more a quirk of his lips. "Aye. So, I'll pursue it the way I need to. I'm no' sure what we'll do or say about your presence. But we've the rest of this ferry ride to come up with something."

"We could just tell them the truth."

"What?"

"The truth, Graham." Now that she'd said it, she realized it was exactly what they should do. "Everything. What I was doing when you found me, why I'd decided to run off with you, why we changed our minds, and why I'm on Kinloch anyway. All of it." She ducked her chin briefly and felt a flush creep up her neck. "Okay, so maybe not *all* of it."

He tipped her chin up, and his smile was both knowing and charming as hell. "Aye, perhaps no' all of it. Rather hard to explain."

"Aye," she echoed, her gaze drifting from his eyes to his

mouth, then back to his eyes, which had darkened considerably in those few seconds.

"We should probably agree to keep to ourselves while it's all sorted out, our story, and my pursuit of abolishing the law," he said, his voice all gruff again, only there was an entirely different note behind it.

The kind of note that made the most delicious tingles zip across her skin and down her spine. "We should," she agreed. "Better not to confuse things. People. Us."

"Us," he repeated, voice barely a murmur, his own dark gaze dipping to her mouth.

The look alone made her tremble. "No chance of that . . . thing happening again," she managed, squeezing her thighs together. "Safer that way."

"Safe," he agreed, even as he tipped her chin up a little higher, then shifted slightly in his seat so he could slant his mouth perfectly down onto hers. "So, none of this, then."

"No," she breathed against his mouth. "Absolutely none."

He kissed her like a man dying of thirst, and she was a pool of fresh spring water. He sipped, he dipped his tongue, he tested, tasted, then sipped some more, sighing in abject pleasure with each thirst-quenching swallow.

In turn, she felt like he'd brought the sun and water to a parched, dry desert, and with him, she bloomed into a thriving, vibrant, lush oasis.

The kiss grew in urgency, his fingers shifted to grip her chin, and he released her hand to cup her face as he took the kiss deeper.

She lost all sense of place and time, but reveled in the depth and need of the mating . . . and nary a whisper or hint of anything otherworldly involved. It was purely Graham, real and whole, steady and . . . kissing her like he was branding her for life.

She couldn't help but think, as she clutched at his shoulders, and fell fully and completely under his spell, that perhaps he already had.

Chapter 15

So much for planning and strategy.

Looking up, seeing Katie sitting there, he'd thought it was some new twist to their mystical entwinement. Apparition? Savior? Initially he'd thought the former—that he'd simply willed her there, and her spirit had come to him. Then she'd said his name. The overwhelming sense of relief she hadn't left him after all, that she was truly still there, made her damn near feel like the latter. And that had well and thoroughly pissed him off.

At a time when he needed to be supremely confident and rock steady, in order to get his people to believe in and agree to his plans for the future—theirs and his—he was in some kind of wobbly, emotionally charged netherworld where nothing made sense. He couldn't seem to think straight for more than a moment at a time, largely due to the woman presently in his arms.

The obvious solution was to keep her from being there. They'd just agreed to as much, in fact.

Instead he was kissing her as if his life depended on it.

In that moment, with the taste of her on his mouth, on his tongue, his body rock hard and wanting far more than a taste of her delectable lips, he was hard-pressed to deny the sense that he might die if he didn't find a way to claim her fully. And soon. And often. The urge—the demand—to sink deeply inside her, move, thrust, take, while the sweet, hot core of her wrapped tightly and perfectly around him, milking him until there was nothing left to do but surge forth and pour himself into her . . . yes, that demand, left unfilled, might very well be the death of him.

They both needed to stop pretending it was ever going to be otherwise between them. Until they saw it through, neither was going to be strong enough to tame it, control it.

He left her mouth, kissed her jaw, then tucked her close beneath his chin, both of them gasping a bit for breath. He tried to find his way back to sanity, back to the strength of mind he'd always been able to rely on—until that moment on a garden path, when he'd heard her swear.

His lips curved into a deep smile of their own volition as that moment replayed through his mind. She felt it and pushed back just enough to look at him.

"What's funny?" Her eyes were bright with need, her cheeks flushed from the heat of their kissing.

He wanted to see what the rest of her would look like, flushed with the heat of desire. For real.

"I was just thinking I must be a very perverse man," he said.

"Because you know this isn't what you want, and yet . . ."

"Oh nay, this is what I want." He leaned in and kissed her, hard and fast. "I'm done pretending otherwise."

She blinked a few times as she struggled to find her breath. "Okay."

He grinned. Okay, indeed. "But I said that because I was thinking how I've been drawn to you from the moment I first heard your voice."

"When I was in the prayer garden? But I was angry, very angry, and I'm pretty sure I was, uh, expressing my frustration quite . . . forthrightly when you found me."

"Colorfully so, aye. It was what compelled me up the walk. I wanted to make certain you weren't in need of any assistance. I didn't know if you were ranting to the heavens, or to someone in particular."

"A little of both. Only the someone in particular was me."

She smiled. "You did save me from myself, though, if that makes you feel any better about your perverse Samaritan tendencies."

"Well, I wasn't entirely altruistic. I needed to get inside the church so I could meet the stranger I'd come to marry. When I didn't hear any other voice raised in anger, I decided I'd leave you to your privacy. I must say, I was quite surprised to see the bit of wedding gown flash out as I'd turned to go."

"Is that why you turned back?"

"It made me pause, then I realized if the bride were in the garden, she couldn't be inside getting married, therefore buying me a bit of time to complete my stated mission. However, before I could make good on that decision, we ran into each other, literally."

She looked into his eyes. "I wonder what I'd have done. If you'd never come up the path, I wouldn't have known who you were, why you were there. I wouldn't have known your generosity of spirit—"

"You're too kind. I was stalling."

"You were nice to me, and your attempts to help were sincere, even if they served the dual purpose of putting off a task you weren't all that enthusiastic about taking on. Though I have to say, you sounded pretty enthusiastic once you got inside the church.

"Once I realized she was you."

They both paused, then Katie said, "You know, had you just been some strange man in a kilt, standing up and claiming you and I were destined to be together, I'd have had someone call security, or whatever one does in a church when confronted by a deranged stalker."

"Deranged, now, was I?"

"Well, you have to admit the complete outfit and your heated claims definitely leant the episode an air of—"

"Unique interpretation?"

"I was thinking desperate irrationality, but we can go with that."

"Because of ten or fifteen minutes spent talking to me in the garden, ye thought me perfectly sane?"

"Because of those fifteen minutes, I already knew I was the one you'd crossed an ocean to find . . . I'd had a little time for that to sink in. It was a long walk down that aisle. It felt like miles. I saw you, and I couldn't stop thinking about what you'd said. It was an option, an alternate solution, being dropped into my lap."

"Rather like coming to America to find you was my alternate solution." His smile grew. "To think we both went with the insane plot when given the option."

She smiled as she slid one hand up along the side of his neck and ran her fingers down the side of his stubbled face. "Possibly. But the reason I said yes was because during those fifteen minutes spent in the garden, you'd already treated me with more respect, more honesty, and more compassion than the people inside the church who were supposed to love and support me."

He stared into her eyes. He'd wondered when he'd begun to fall for her. He couldn't imagine a time when he hadn't been thinking of her. "When"—he let the sentence hang, then cleared his throat—"when was the first time you knew . . . about the other part? Between us."

"When was yours?" she countered.

"It's no' the same as the others, no' so much a vision or feeling like ye've been set down in a different time and place. But I know it was there inside me when I stood up in yer chapel. It was like I was compelled to say the things I did, to feel what I felt. Both were way out of proportion to what I'd been planning to say. The intensity of that moment was not a little stunning. Though I was clearly seeing you at the altar, and I was definitely inside that chapel, there was absolutely something greater than myself guiding me, at least in that initial moment." He broke off, looked away for a moment. The few times he'd thought about how he'd behaved in the church had left him feeling a bit ridiculous and mortified. Now he felt anything but. It all felt destined somehow. "Your turn."

"In the limo," she said. "Only it wasn't like—like the thing last night."

Her stuttering had him looking at her again, and he marveled at how pretty a shade of pink her face could become. "Nothing to be embarrassed about, ye ken. About last night, I mean. We, neither of us, had any control over that."

"I've been telling myself that," she said, a dry note in her voice. "Have yours all been, well, not like that, that was—" She couldn't finish. She cleared her throat, then said, "Have they all been, um, highly charged? Like that?"

"If you mean sexually intense, no."

She sat back a bit. "No?"

He couldn't help it, he grinned. "Yours have?"

"Uh, yes." Her blush deepened and his smile grew. "At first, I was more voyeur. I mean, I felt like it was happening to me, but I was more removed. It's hard to explain. Each time after that, it felt more immediate, more . . . real. More detailed. Like all the foggy elements were coming into sharper focus, and I wasn't just watching and feeling. I could smell, and taste, and describe how it felt to touch—" She stopped, blushed again, then laughed. "So, the short answer would be yes."

He was still grinning.

"But not yours?"

"Dinnae look so crushed," he teased.

"I'm—I wasn't. I was just . . . surprised, I guess, because it seems like we've been living out the same thing, experiencing the same thing."

"It's two sides of the same coin, I'm sure of it. Just because I wasn't always dropped down into the midst of us twined together in passion, doesnae mean we weren't just before, or heading straight back to it."

"Has it been like you're dreaming, or just watching? Or have you—you know. Like last night, when we were both there, in the moment, fully together, except . . . not really."

"If you mean could I describe the scents, tastes, feel of things, then the answer is yes. Initially it was as you describe, like I was watching more than feeling it happen simultaneously. But once we landed in Castlebay, it seemed much more detailed, more immediate. As if I was living it, breathing it. The history between us felt very specific."

"History. Yes," she said. "That's it exactly. Well, that last time anyway. It did feel like that. Not just because we were clearly in a different time or place, but . . . there was something familiar about it, though I know I've never been there before or seen anything like it."

"Agreed."

They fell silent for a few moments, but his hands were on her again, and the taste of her was on his tongue, and the shores of Kinloch were fast approaching. He wasn't done. He was so far from being done. "Stay with me," he said. "On Kinloch. Tell me you'll stay."

"What about—"

"I dinnae care what about. I—I know what it felt like when I thought you'd gone. I don't want to feel that again. I want us to have a chance to figure this out. I know it will complicate things, but I'm no' sure I much care. I need to understand this, and for that, I need to understand you."

"Is that why? Because I'm a mystery—or this alternate universe thing between us is a mystery that you simply want solved?"

He tugged her to him and kissed her hard, fast, until they were both breathless when he lifted his head. "I don't want to feel as I did when I thought you'd left me behind. If we do part again, we'll both know the why of it."

Her eyes were huge pools of crystalline blue that could break his heart or make it sing. It was the latter he was after.

"Is the parting inevitable in your mind?" she asked.

"I have no preconceived notions, Katie."

"Are you open to wherever it might lead?"

"Are you?"

Her eyes opened wider, as the horn blew, announcing their arrival in port.

"Ye hadn't thought of your side of it, then?" he said, when she didn't immediately respond. "Only mine?"

"It's your home. I don't want to be there as a curiosity. I only want—"

He waited a beat, but she didn't continue. Instead she broke eye contact and looked down. "Only want what?" he prodded.

She looked up, and he'd never seen her so serious. "I wanted a chance to find out. To figure things out. For myself, yes. But with you, too. I might not have been honest, even with myself, when I decided I wanted to come here. But that is the truth of it. I do want that chance."

"You're taking the bigger gamble," he told her. "I'm home, my life is here. I'll be able to continue on, much as before, with my work, my goals. You . . . you've just left a life in chaos, without clear direction for the next steps on your path."

"I'd say that puts you at as great a risk, then. Getting involved with someone who is neither steady nor grounded. Nor even knows what she wants to be when she grows up. Certainly, at the very least, it carries the potential of risk that I'll want to go back home. At some point."

"Aye, I suppose it does."

The horn blew again, startling her. He held her, knowing what they said here, decided here, was critical to whatever would come afterward.

"Are we being selfish, wanting to explore this?" she asked. "Maybe you were right the first time and it's wiser to cut our losses, so you can go do what you need to do to take care of your people, and yourself. While I go . . . figure out, well, my entire life. We could always try again later, if that's what we still wanted. When the rest is clear and it's not so complicated."

"It's rare I've let myself want anything that wasn't also about achieving things for others," he told her, keeping her face turned to his, his eyes steady on hers. "I'm no' sure 'tis wise, this want I have for you. And aye, it could lead to heartache, I suppose. But I'm not willing to leave it up to fate, again, that our paths can cross in the future. We're both here now. I'd rather know I tried, and failed, than turn tail and run from it." He pulled her closer, until his mouth was near on to hers. "Because there could be a great glory to be had in this, Katherine Elizabeth Georgina Rosemary. Greater glory than surely I've known or felt until this time. One we'll never know if we don't try."

"I want to know," she whispered. "I want to find out."

"Then find out we shall, *mo chridhe*. Find out we shall."

They were still kissing as the boat bumped along the pilings into the slip dock.

Graham finally broke apart, and gently set her back in her seat. "We look well and thoroughly ravished," he said with a smile, knowing he should care a great deal more than he did, how they initially presented themselves to everyone. "I'm no' thinking anyone looking at the two of us at the moment is going to buy the explanation that ye've turned my offer down flat, and have simply come along on a personal sabbatical."

"But I am on a personal sabbatical." She leaned forward and planted a full out kiss of her own, then shifted back, straightened her clothes and hair, before standing up and picking up the jacket she'd left on her seat. "It just happens to be very, very personal." A short, perfect smile curved her lips and her eyes glowed as she looked at him, then she turned and smoothed her expression, squared her shoulders, and draped her neatly folded jacket over her arm.

She looked every bit the McAuley of McAuley-Sheffield. He found himself thinking, it was also the very same look he'd imagine she'd bring as The McAuley, which is exactly what she'd be if paired with The MacLeod. It was a tantalizing realization. The idea of a true partnership. Fanciful, in this case. Foolish, even. Given she had nothing invested in the island or the people, or they her.

Yet he watched as she walked over to where Malvy's grandson, young Colm, stood with the heavy ropes at the ready, to tie the ferry to the dock, bright smile on her face. He watched as she gestured to the pile of luggage and discussed whatever arrangements she needed to make to get them off the boat.

He could have told her he'd arrange all of that and save her the trouble. But he realized while his decision to withdraw the marriage business proposal was the right one for him to make—especially as they decided to move ahead with exploring the personal direction their continued relationship was taking—Katie reclaiming a part of herself by staking her independence, was the right one for her. So he let her go about figuring out her luggage issues, bemused by the immediate broad smile from Colm, who Graham knew to be rather taciturn and quiet by nature. The bright smile looked good on the young man, as did the flush it brought to his otherwise pale, narrow face. No sooner had they tied at the dock than Colm was leading the way to the pile of luggage, eager to help as if he were on a personal mission.

Graham smiled, thinking it would be lovely indeed if all the hearts on Kinloch could be won so easily. Odd, how he was so certain it was the right thing to do, abolishing the Marriage Pact, and thereby abolishing his need to marry anyone, ever, if he chose . . . that whenever he looked at her, watched her, he couldn't seem to stop seeing her in that very role.

Perverse, to be certain.

He stood to help young Colm, who'd surely get a hernia if he tried to move the entire mountain at once, which clearly seemed to be his aim, hoping to impress Katie with his manly skills, no doubt. Katie was already tackling some on her own, so Graham took a few as well, assuming as a group effort it wouldn't be seen as usurping her independence in any way.

Colm led the charge across the ramp to the dock. The rain had let up, but was still there in the form of a heavy mist hanging damply in the cool afternoon air. The sun was making an effort to break completely through, but was losing the battle more often than winning it. Graham motioned Katie on in front of him, then he brought up the rear. It was only when they stopped on the dock and unloaded, so they could go back for a

second round, that Graham realized in all their breathless, hor-
monally charged chatter, they hadn't actually decided on how
they were going to approach things in the village.

It was one thing to beg her to stay with him, which is exactly
where he wanted her, and quite another to bring her to Kinloch, introduce her as a McAuley, then install her in his home
while he went about trying to get them to agree to abolish the
Marriage Pact law. It wasn't the complication of doing that
while having her under his roof giving him pause, but how such
an arrangement might alter the perception his clanspeople would
have of her—and not in a favorable way. He never wanted her
to be anything less than well respected, well liked, and, hopefully, well loved. He didn't want to sabotage the one chance she
had there because he couldn't keep his hands off her.

So . . . did he explain as much and get her a room? Of
course, she'd insist on paying for it. If circumstances were different, he wouldn't mind her taking care of her own needs if
that's what she wanted to do. He had no idea how much
money she'd gotten back for the aborted honeymoon. Given
her stay was open-ended, he doubted it was enough to fund a
room for any extended time, and leave much for essentials—
food and the sort. All of which he'd be more than happy to help
with, if she'd let him. But he wasn't holding out much hope on
that front.

"Wait here with the bags," he said. "I'll go back with Colm
and get the last of it."

"I can—"

"I know you can," he said, smiling, "but I'm willing. And
they're the biggest ones left."

"Okay," she said with a smile. "If you insist."

"See?" he teased. "No' so hard as all that."

She stuck her tongue out at him, making him chuckle. "Is
there someone I can talk to about arranging transportation into
town," she asked, "or—"

"Dinnae worry about it, there will be someone to help with
that."

"Like Barnaby-type help?" she asked, sincerely curious about the older man's willing, if embarrassing obeisance.

He supposed it was a curious thing to her, the role he played there. He was long used to the respect accorded to the person in his position. Even though he'd never been completely comfortable with it, he'd learned to graciously accept what they considered gestures of respect. He realized in doing so, he was showing them respect in return, proving he could be trusted to take the role as seriously as they did.

"It is a way of life here," he told her, "that social structure, so it's possible, yes. Does that bother you?" he asked, also sincere.

She shook her head. "I think it's rather sweet, especially as it seems sincere and not a false front put on because of social dictates. You have no idea how refreshing that is to me."

His smile flashed more broadly. "Good. Keep that in mind as we head into the village."

She laughed. "I'll do my best."

He stepped closer, so he could speak and only be heard by her. "I was thinking that perhaps we should consider getting you a room in the village, at first. No' because I dinnae want you with me, and no' because of the abolishment proceedings. But so you can go about meeting everyone and—"

"Make a good first impression before I start shacking up with their leader?" She laughed when his eyes widened. "You're very cute when you're embarrassed. But that is what you meant, right?"

"Um, aye. I suppose. Though I might have worded it differently."

"You really are adorable when flustered. It makes you an easy target. I'm just saying."

He smiled, charmed by her despite the heat he could feel in his face. "I'll consider myself forewarned then."

"So, do you have any recommendations on where I should stay?"

"Well, lad, if ye dinnae have the answer to that one, perhaps I could be of greater service."

Graham hadn't even seen him approach. "Roan," he called out as his trusted friend came up the dock. He felt momentarily disconcerted, which was silly given that Roan was going to be one of the easiest hearts she'd have the opportunity to win.

His friend gave him a hug and a back slap. "That was a fast turnaround, mate." He turned to face Katie. "Miss Katie McAuley, I presume?" He nudged Graham in the side. "I must admit," he said from the side of his mouth, "I didn't think ye'd pull this off. Owe Shay money now, I do." He stepped forward before Graham could respond, extending his hand as he did. "A great pleasure to meet you," he said, his charm on full tilt. "Welcome to Kinloch."

Katie's gaze darted from Roan, to Graham, and back to Roan as he stopped directly in front of her. She shook his hand. "Thank you. The pleasure is mine, I assure you. You're a good friend of Graham's, right?"

Roan covered his heart. "He's no' been tellin' tales, has he? I swear, I'm no' half so bad as he's made me out to be."

Katie smiled. "He's said nothing of the sort."

Looking at Roan's joyous expression told Graham his friend thought it was all tidily sewn up. He was going to have to arrange a private meeting and quickly.

"Roan McAuley," he introduced himself. "We're distant relatives, in fact."

Her smile widened. "That's wonderful."

Roan took her arm and turned her toward the road that led into the village, and beyond to Graham's ancestral properties. "I've brought the lorry, so we can get ye out to Graham's and settled," he was saying as he simply left Graham behind, ostensibly to handle the luggage.

Graham scowled. Roan was famous for managing to be elsewhere when the heavy lifting began, claiming he was best employed as the brains of any organized effort. He overheard what Roan was saying, and jumped forward to correct his mistaken assumption, only to hear Katie say, "Thank you for the assistance. It's appreciated. I have a bit more luggage than you might imagine, so I hope there's room."

Roan shot a look at Graham over his shoulder and winked broadly, then smiled back to Katie chattering away, as he escorted her toward the side of the road where he'd parked his lorry.

Colm came up to stand beside Graham. "This is the rest of them."

Graham turned to find the lad had brought up the last two bags while he'd been watching Roan and Katie. "Good." He pulled out a few pound notes and folded them into Colm's hand. "I'd appreciate some help gettin' Miss McAuley's luggage out to Roan's lorry."

Colm nodded, quite serious once again. He handed the money back to Graham. "No need to pay me," he said, then looked past Graham to where Katie stood, laughing and talking with Roan as if they were old friends. "Will she be stayin' on here?"

Graham looked from Katie to Colm's face, and sighed inwardly. Poor pup was already stricken with it. Graham would have been amused, if he wasn't feeling much the same way. "Aye," he said. "That she will."

Colm sighed. "She's quite beautiful. Like a fairy and a goddess, all wrapped into one."

"How very . . . poetic of you," Graham said, his lips quirking. The threat of the smile faded as he turned to look at Katie once again. Her hair looked gilded in the early afternoon sun, as it peeked out at last from behind the receding clouds. Her smile was bright, and he could see how brightly blue her eyes were, even from that distance. He felt a sharp tug in the vicinity of his heart. "And most accurate," he added.

Colm nodded, and both men sighed before turning to put their backs into hauling Katie's luggage. One last time.

Chapter 16

The lorry ride was similar to the last one she'd taken with Barnaby. She was squeezed between two men, thigh to hip with Graham, who appeared a bit moody, just as before, and there was a charming man telling charming stories—although she could actually understand almost everything Roan was saying. The only difference was Roan McAuley was not a short, stout, balding leprechaun of a man, as Barnaby was. Quite the opposite.

He was an inch or two shorter than Graham, so still topping six feet, but whereas Graham was a big, brawny guy, Roan was lanky and lean, with a whipcord look to him. His hair was dark, like Graham's, but he had lively green eyes, a fast smile, and dimples to die for. He was quick to laugh, and quicker still to make her laugh. In fact, the only laughter not filling the crammed cab of his truck was Graham's.

She thought he'd be happy to be home, happy to be back in the embrace of friends and familiar faces. While he wasn't scowling, or upset, he was letting his friend do all the talking.

Roan had known who she was, and she remembered he was the one to track down her whereabouts, so that made sense. Still, it was odd to think they had blood relatives in common, however ancient the tie might be. As they were driving through the land of her ancestors, Roan kept up a running commentary, telling her everything she could ever want to know about the island, its stormy history, even the legend behind the Marriage Pact.

She'd felt Graham tense beside her during that brief part of the conversation, but had already figured out it was not the time to tell Roan they weren't going to honor the pact. In fact, Graham wanted to have the whole thing repealed. She'd leave that for Graham, as she'd assumed he'd want her to.

They drove through the port village of, well, she was still calling it Port Joy. She hadn't been able to clearly get it from hearing Roan say the name. The port village was the only one on the small island. From there, the island road wound through the short, narrow valley created by the twin peaks that rose from either end of the island. One was much taller and larger than the other, but the convenient arrangement of that topography led to growing the flax that was harvested, spun, and died into a thick, waxy thread and woven into the baskets the small island was becoming famous for. She hadn't understood, beyond the unique thread used, what made their baskets so special. Listening to Roan describe their beauty in much greater detail, she found herself anxious to see some of the handiwork.

"Ahead is Graham's property. The low stone walls are an auld mark of the property lines, but essentially everything from the west end of the valley, over the mountain and out to the shore belongs to The MacLeod."

She took in the view. It was awesome in the purest sense of the word. She turned to Graham. "It's beautiful, your home."

His attention had been fixed out the side window, and he nodded, said a quiet, "thank you," but continued to keep his own counsel. She wondered if he was upset that she'd allowed Roan's assumption that she was staying with Graham go un-challenged. Despite being touched by Graham's gentlemanly sensibilities, the truth of the matter was, they were unattached adults and it was the twenty-first century.

Roan didn't seem remotely put out by the notion of them staying together and had, in fact, assumed it quite naturally and easily. It had seemed to her, rather than mount any kind of pretense they weren't interested in each other personally— they'd been ever-so-successful with that so far—she'd grabbed the opportunity that had arisen.

It was not the time to pursue whatever the reason was for his reticence. She turned back to Roan. "When the other clan has the chief in power, do they take this property?"

He shook his head. "The McAuley has property that mirrors this, at the other end of the valley. It wraps around Ben Domchaidh, the smaller of the two peaks. MacLeod's valley has the flax crops and supports the crofters, while The McAuley oversees the fishing boats and the village."

"Sounds like a fair split. How is it determined which clan laird is in power?"

"It always passes down through family first, and only changes over when there is no direct heir."

"How long has it been since a McAuley laird was in power?"

"Nigh on three quarters of a century. Before Graham's great grandfather, 'twas a McAuley then."

"There's no competitive thing going on between them?"

"No, the Marriage Pact sees to that."

"Because whoever is in power is always married to someone from the other clan."

"Precisely."

Katie quickly changed the subject before Roan could push it in a more personal direction. "So, tell me, what is it that you do here? Graham said something about marketing. Is that for your basket industry?"

"Aye. I see to the marketing of our baskets worldwide. We've grown leaps and bounds since the advent of the Internet. I do my best to get us into the various travel guides as well as the Scottish heritage shopping networks, which are legion. They are especially popular in your country, and north, in Canada. Because the marketing ties so closely with the tourism angle, I also oversee that element as well."

"In terms of promotion?"

"In terms of all of it. I'll help visitors book their stay, whatever excursions they might find of interest, as well as their extended travel plans in the rest of the U.K. if necessary."

"Does Kinloch do a heavy tourist trade?"

"Fair, but it's no' the backbone of our economy. That would be the artisan baskets. Frankly, it's the baskets that are the tourist lure. We're a wee island without much more to offer, no' in comparison to the chain as it extends north. So, the two are truly a joint venture."

Katie nodded, taking it all in. "Well, it's a beautiful home you have here," she said, meaning it sincerely. "All of Kinloch." What she'd seen of the island was like a perfect little Highland paradise, with the mountains soaring left and right, but an island paradise, too, surrounded by the beautiful blue sea.

"Thank you," Roan said, clearly pleased with her assessment.

Katie cast a quick glance at Graham, but he seemed quite absorbed by the view beyond his passenger window, which was field after field of the flax they grew to support their industry. *His crops,* she thought, realizing he was probably already fast back to work in his head. Not that she could blame him.

No one had said a word about Iain. She wasn't going to be the one to bring him up, but she was dying to know what his status was. Roan had been quite the gentleman concerning the reasons for her arrival on the island, too. She wasn't about to bring that up, either.

"Do you have a catalogue, or a website for the baskets? I'd love to see—" She broke off on a gasp as they came around a tight bend in the road, wrapping almost right up to the base of the mountain. A sudden push up into a higher plateau of the valley appeared, wedged narrow and tight between a gouge-like crease in the mountain. In the center sat an ancient stone castle, with fortress-like walls, cornered with tall, skinny turrets, flat along the boundary tops. The chimneys and peaks of the building—or buildings within the four walls—barely peeked over the tops. "Wow."

"That's *Flaithbheartach*," Roan announced, rather proudly and grandly, even for him. "Graham's ancestral abode."

"I'm not even going to try and pronounce that," she said on a laugh.

"Gaelic, for lordly dominion. More or less." Roan said it again, slowly sounding it out.

"Fly-vyurk-tuck?"

Roan chuckled. "You'll have it in no time."

She smiled. "I'll take your word on that." She looked back to the castle. It was forbidding, to say the least. Certainly not a fairy castle or anything Disney would have dreamt up. It was a fortress, intended as a defense first, practical if not exactly a romantic vision. Positioned as it was, she could see how well and truly it would have accomplished that job. It might not have been the fancy, flag waving, multi-mullioned castle that dreams were made of, but there was something about the place, the valley, the fortress castle, all of it, that made something deep and powerful rumble through her. "It's stunning," she said, feeling her heart rate kick up as they drew ever closer.

"It's crumbling." Graham said the first words he'd uttered of his own volition since they'd climbed in the truck.

"How old is it?" she asked him, not wanting him to retreat back to silence, now that he'd decided to join in. Though she'd thoroughly enjoyed Roan's sunny, cruise director disposition, the viewpoint she truly wanted, was Graham's. "Has it been in MacLeod possession continuously?"

"For the past six and a quarter centuries, aye."

"I can't wrap my head around that, not truly. My family is considered one of the oldest in Maryland, and we're just in our third century as Americans, though we've only had the current family home and property since the turn of the last century. That is considered old—really old." She laughed, then sighed again as she watched the castle come into clear view as they climbed up toward it. "More than twice the time of our entire history . . . and under the conditions of a much harsher time. I can't even imagine."

"'Tis a compelling story," Roan began, but Katie cut him off with a brief touch on his arm.

She wanted to hear that story from Graham. It was *his* home, *his* history. Everything about it compelled her to share it with him. She didn't question that certainty too much, not wanting to distract herself from what had thus far been a lovely final leg to her long journey.

"Does the McAuley clan have something similar at the other end of the island?" she asked Roan, hoping he didn't think her rude for interrupting.

"No, this is the island stronghold. Both clans have used it as defense against outside aggression, but the direct line of ownership has always been MacLeod. We have what amounts to a rather extended manor home, with all sorts of wings and floors and such added and built onto it over the centuries. It doesn't have the same battle history as *Flaithbheartach* and only the core part of the house is still the original structure. Fire, flood, and extreme weather has no' been kind to the McAuley stronghold, but we've the abbey and the tower that falls under our purview to maintain. The tower dates back to the fifteenth century, same as this stronghold, but the abbey is even older, built in the twelfth century. It's since been discovered that it was built on top of what was once a Pictish henge."

"There's but a pile of rocks left to it now," Graham added.

"Aye," Roan readily agreed.

"I know what an abbey is, but what is the tower? The remains of some other, older castle?"

"No," Roan replied. "The tower was built as exactly that. It was the stronghold prison, for lack of a better term."

"So you had the jail next to the church?"

"Well, the church is actually just off the coast, on a wee strip of land, but the windows cut into the tower all share the same view."

"The abbey?"

He nodded. "When you're about to be hung or beheaded, what better time to pray for your mortal soul?"

She gulped. "True. I guess. Yikes."

"We have a lot of that kind of history here," Roan said dryly.

The conversation faded at that point, as they crossed over a steep crevasse on a flat bridge connecting the road to the castle. Katie peered out the window to see how far down the gorge went, but couldn't see it from her vantage point. She assumed she'd have plenty of time for that later. The lorry trundled through the arched passageway into the courtyard.

She couldn't take in everything at once. There was a central building, built from the same gray stone, though it was obvious from the various different colors it had been repaired and re-built a number of times. Parts of it had crumbled, but to her it was more amazing any of it still stood, much less was still liv-able. The central building was the tallest, topped by a single square turret that had seen better centuries. Numerous smaller buildings crowded up along the outside perimeter of that build-ing. Several more were tucked in the far corners of the walled courtyard, in varying stages of ruin.

Roan pulled around the side of the main building, inching between two lower, squat stone buildings, and put the lorry in park next to a set of rather inconspicuous double doors. Not a grand entrance, considering the breadth and scope of the place. Closer up she wasn't entirely certain how much of it was, in fact, livable.

Roan climbed out as did Graham, but it was Graham who leaned in to reach for her hand.

Relieved by the gesture after the somewhat awkward silence on the way in, she gladly took his hand and slid out of the front seat. He kept her hand tucked in his as he turned to Roan. "I've another favor to ask. If you wouldn't mind tucking her luggage inside the main vestibule, we've had a rather long go of it and I'd like to take Katie in and get her settled. I'll be down to talk with you and Shay in an hour or two."

Roan looked surprised by the request, but after a glance at Graham's implacable expression and Katie's thankful smile, he merely nodded. "I can do that." He looked to Katie. "I hope after you settle in, you'll come down to the village and allow us to introduce you around. I'm glad you're here, Katie."

She nodded. "I am, too," she said, never more sincere.

He looked to Graham then. "You'll have time for a chat?"

Graham nodded. "We'll need some time. We have much to discuss."

Roan grinned widely, but sobered upon seeing something in Graham's expression or hearing it in his tone. "Okay. I'll arrange it." Roan sketched a quick bow and walked to the back of the lorry.

Graham was opening the narrow door when she heard Roan whistle under his breath. "She comes with baggage," he murmured.

"You've no idea," Katie said, so quietly only Graham could hear.

Rather than chuckle, he merely pushed the door open and gestured for her to step inside. "Mind yer head, and the step down."

It was damp and dark inside. So dark, in fact, she could see nothing beyond the several feet inside the door illuminated by the light outside. She felt him step in behind her.

"Should we be helping him? I hate that he has to—"

"He'll manage fine. He's due for some manly labor."

Okay, Katie thought.

She heard the scrape of something, then a moment later, a flame shot to life behind her, startling a little squeal from her as she spun around in time to see Graham lifting an old-fashioned oil lamp. A moment later, it was lit, followed by another one.

"Here," he told her, "hold it by the centerpiece of the handle, and keep it out in front of you, as the metal framing will get hot."

She took the square lamp, surprised by how heavy it was for a relatively small thing.

He left the door open behind him, ostensibly, so Roan could cart her bags in.

"Follow me," he told her. Lifting his lamp, he stepped in front of her and headed down the dimly illuminated passageway.

She followed behind him, holding the lamp out to the side so as not to inadvertently bang it into Graham if he suddenly stopped or changed directions. She couldn't tell if it was an actual hallway, or more a true passageway to some other part of the building. It was soft under her feet, but hard at the same time, as if there were several layers of rug on the ancient stone floor she assumed was beneath.

"Why didn't you ever tell me?" she asked, as they continued onward, and eventually up a narrow set of stairs.

"Tell you what?"

At least he's talking now, she thought, trying to keep an open mind about his less-than-delightful demeanor. "That you lived in an ancient castle."

"Ye never asked."

"Very funny."

"We're at the top," he told her, "so hold where you are for a moment."

Her hand was on the side railing mounted to the stone wall to her right. She did as he said, then listened for a moment as there was some scraping, then a loud squeak. He was broad enough that she couldn't see around him, especially as he was two steps above her. Then a door swung open at the top.

"Oh," she said, somewhat startled, not only by the sudden doorway appearing, but by the fact that there was light beyond it. The regular kind of lighting, at least as far as she could tell.

He extinguished his lamp and hung it on an iron hook set into the stone wall at the top of the stairs. Then he turned and reached for hers. Keeping one hand on the rail, she handed it up to him. He shut hers out and hung it on the hook on the opposite wall, on the other side of the doorway.

She thought she heard him sigh, then he climbed the remaining steps and entered the room, turning and extending a hand toward her.

She took the broad hand, which he closed instantly around hers. It was the first time, even after standing outside, that she'd felt truly welcomed by him.

He tugged her up the last step and through the doorway. "Be it ever so humble . . ."

She stepped in behind him and he moved so she could see the room beyond. "Oh . . . Graham. It's . . . magnificent."

He barked a laugh, which echoed throughout the tall, cavernous chamber. "It's hardly that. In fact, you're looking at the only habitable part of the entire endeavor. When I said it was crumbling, I wasn't being modest."

She turned slowly and took in the entire space. It was obvious they were in the center tower, which was far more massive in breadth on the inside than it had appeared from the outside. Graham's living space took up the entire open floorplan, though it had been divided into sections, largely by the furniture or things placed in each section. "It's sort of like a medieval one-room cabin." She looked up toward the top of the tower, which soared openly to the peak, several stories above her head.

The tower was square, as was the living space. A quarter of it was filled with tables and an assortment of interesting-looking equipment, piles of books, charts, and an amazing array of photographs. Little bags containing sprouted seedlings were tacked up and down the far stone wall, with duct tape. To her right a smaller section held his bed, an oversized, high-backed leather chair mounded with cast-off clothing, mostly pants, T-shirts, and work shirts, all of them muddy. Boots of varying ages and types cluttered the floor. The bed itself was a massive thing, with heavy corner posts and an even heavier carved headboard. It looked like something Paul Bunyan would sleep in, but then, as she thought about it, she supposed that made it perfect for Graham.

Another section was crammed with bookshelves that extended up the wall so high the tops were lost in shadows. There was a rolling ladder, but it didn't reach that high. A wood-burning stove dominated another section, and just beyond was a narrow door, and the even narrower kitchen area. A small stove, fridge, sink, and cabinet counter made up the entire unit. All the appliances had seen better days. Centuries, perhaps. Given the clutter of dishes, apparently they were still functional. A heavy plank table sat in the center of the room, and it, too, was covered in maps, diagrams, papers, books, and more of the curious seedling baggies.

She finally got all the way back around to where Graham was standing, silently watching her. He hadn't tried to explain or introduce any part of the place to her, allowing her to take it all in on her own.

"I wasn't expectin' company when I left," was all he said.

It struck her then, why he'd been so quiet in the car, and allowed Roan to do all the talking. Was it possible he was embarrassed to have her there? He'd invited her to stay with him, but perhaps he'd meant they'd stay in town, or—she wasn't entirely sure. Other than openly fidget and shift his weight on his feet, he couldn't be feeling any more obviously awkward.

"Graham, don't you dare apologize for this amazing place you have the privilege to call home."

He looked at her like she'd sprouted a second head.

"I think it's unbelievable that any of this remains, habitable or not. I cannot imagine having this kind of responsibility handed down to me." She turned around again. "You truly live here."

"Aye, it's my family home."

"No, I don't mean it like that. I mean it like"—she swept an arm in front of her—"you *live* here."

He was obviously confused by her meaning. "Well, I've nowhere else to go, exactly."

She shook her head. "In my world, I don't even get to pick out my own nightstand. I mean, I get consulted on possible color schemes, and surely, it's fine with me if they change everything, from carpet to wall hangings, every several years, because, 'darling, you simply cannot have things grow stale or out of style,'" she said, in what she knew was a dead-on impersonation of her mother. "Only in my dorm did I get the chance to create anything close to this."

"You mean clutter and controlled chaos?"

"I mean my own space. I only had the dorm—actually, it was a room in the sorority house—for one semester before Father insisted on installing me in an off-campus apartment. I haven't picked out so much as a toothbrush holder since."

"If you'd wanted something different, why not simply demand it?" he asked. "Surely that wouldn't have been a threat to the family business, or family harmony. Unless, of course, your sense of taste and style is atrocious."

It took her two full beats to realize he was joking. She smiled on a half laugh. "I've been wondering where you've been."

"I've never left your side," he said, sounding a tiny bit more like himself.

She closed the distance between them. "I'm flattered," she said, "that you'd bring me here."

"You've an odd sense then, of what it is to be honored."

"Graham, I don't want this to be awkward. I'll stay in town. I know you won't understand, but I've never been more sincere . . . I like it here. It's warm, and human, and . . . lived in. Gloriously, imperfectly, socks-left-on-the-floor lived in."

"I'm beginning to see why your mother wouldn't allow you to choose your room design scheme," he said, but the twinkle was almost back.

She stepped closer still, until she had to arch her neck to look up into his face. He looked down into hers. "I've wanted you here, thought of you here, dreamt of you here. Possibly I was caught up inside some hormonal fog, because it wasn't until we were entering the valley from the village I realized you were actually going to step foot in here. The *actual* here, not my dream here, where we tumble into some lovely bed, with lovely linens, and heaps of pillows . . . and there's maid service."

She laughed. "You're adorable, you know that."

"I know I'm somewhat mortified that I'm a thirty-one-year-old man, living in a decaying castle like the last bachelor on some kind of horrible B movie set."

She laughed. "There's no reason for it, you know."

"I canno' believe you aren't cringing in horror."

"I left because I wanted to live. And breathe. I can do that here."

"No' too deeply. With the breathing, I mean. There's mold. Though I've created this washing solution that seems to have done the trick on the interior walls. I haven't had the time to develop it more as the crop studies take up most of my time, but—"

"Is that what all the bagged seedlings are for? Crop studies?"

He nodded. "Specimens. I'm trying to find a hybrid that will stay true to the ancestral integrity of the flax we've always grown, while making it genetically more impervious to blight and infestation."

"And, are you finding success?"

He smiled then, and it was the first time she'd seen true pride show on his face since they'd been on the ferry to Barra and she'd swooned at the sight of his island home.

"Aye. 'Tis a time-consuming, arduously slow process, that's taken me years, but yes, we're seeing improvement with each and every growth cycle."

"Will you show me?"

"You want to see seedling specimens?"

"I want to see everything you have going on." She grinned up at him then, and he grew the tiniest bit flustered at her obvious admiration—which made him that much more adorable. "I guess I knew you were a scientist. Maybe it's the formal wear you've been sporting the entire time I've known you, but I haven't really pictured it. Until now."

"You'll be happy to know I do have running water. A full shower and loo." He motioned to the narrow door beside the kitchen. "It's beyond there. We had to bring the piping up for the kitchen—propane appliances—and keep everything clustered. It's no' much—"

"Electricity, too."

"Aye, backed up by generator. Mostly so I don't lose any power with my seed incubators. Plus, with only the occasional turret hole for light, it does get a wee bit dark in here when the lights go off."

She looked at him then and slowly smiled.

It took him a moment to get past his own personal discon-certment with everything that was happening, and on to under-standing her full meaning. "Right," he said, then again, with more feeling. "Right."

"You're different here. In your own space."

"If you mean bumbling, dotty-minded professor, you wouldn't be far from wrong."

"Intensely-focused-to-the-exclusion-of-all-else professor may-be, but that wasn't my meaning. I can see you here, working, thinking."

It was his turn to close the remaining bit of distance between them. He tipped up her chin, then let his hand drop. "You're not as I thought you'd be."

"In what way?"

"I was worried the islanders wouldn't be open to you, to ac-cepting you, because of your background, your wealth, no' being one of us. We're crofters and fishermen, weavers, and shopkeepers."

"Surely you thought more highly of your own people than that."

"I do. They are the best people you could ever hope to meet. I'm ashamed to say I feared you'd be judged and found want-ing. Yet, the one who did the judging, was me."

"You really thought I wouldn't understand you have a dif-ferent lifestyle than me?"

"You might understand it, but that doesnae mean you wouldn't want to run screaming from it when faced with the idea of liv-ing it yourself."

"You really do underestimate me, then," she said, trying not to be hurt, because she understood the bias to be general more than personal. Still, it stung a little bit. "Have I come off as a person who sees things in terms of money and status?"

"No, no' at all, but—"

"Then you're right. Shame on you, Graham MacLeod."

A flush crept up his neck, but he surprised her by smiling.

"What's funny about you being a jerk?" She said it mildly, but it didn't dampen his smile one whit.

"I like that you don't worry about what you say to me. I find I like being called to task. By you, anyway."

"Others don't? Your friends?"

"Oh, they are fearless to the point of boorishness when it comes to calling me out. But I'm no' interested in taking them to bed, or inviting them to live under my roof." He looked up. "Such as it is."

"As you are in me, you mean."

"Aye," he said, his gaze warming as he looked back at her, his smile turning to one of wonder and honest affection that made her toes curl just a little. "As I am with you."

"So, are ye sayin' I can stay here with ye, Graham MacLeod?"

"I'd be honored, if you think you could stomach it. I would even go so far as to promise to shovel out a layer or two, so you can find a surface to perch on. Now and again."

"Is it okay, really?" she asked, dropping the teasing banter and asking him honestly.

"It's only because it does seem okay, very okay, that I can even imagine asking you to. It's no' just because I know you're used to fine things, Katie. It's that I see you as deserving of being kept in that manner and much more."

"Well, we both know I'm no longer a kept woman, by my family, or by you. If you're inviting me to stay as your guest because it's me, personally, not some image of me . . . that you'd like to have—"

That's as far as she got.

Graham lifted her directly off her feet, and up against his chest, wrapped in his arms, face to face, where he took her mouth with his with the kind of focused intensity she'd been trying to describe about his work lab.

He made her feel nothing like a lab specimen, and everything like a desirable woman who was about to be thoroughly ravished.

She was definitely happy with that particular plan.

So she kissed him back.

Chapter 17

Graham had so many thoughts and feelings running through him as he'd watched Katie look at his home, his life, himself, really, for the first time, he didn't know how to begin processing it all. He'd worried, on the whole trip out, about having her there. What had he been thinking? He should have booked them into a room in town.

But he didn't want to share her, that first time of being in one place, his home. In the village, there would have been no peace. Quite the opposite, it would have been like conducting his courtship of her on a grand stage, with everyone watching and giving advice. So, in that respect, his home was perfect.

But it was the only thing he'd felt was perfect, the closer they got.

Then she'd come inside, and been more perfectly suited and beautifully accepting of his world, and him, than he could have ever hoped for. She'd humbled him, well and truly, with her sincere enthusiasm and honest need for the very real life he conducted there. Every chaotic, messy, crammed-full-of-crap inch of it.

She was there. And it mattered. So much more than he'd thought it would.

He'd wanted her in his arms almost from the moment she'd first spun around and taken it all in with such obvious joy.

Then he'd wondered, worried, if being there would transport them again, if they tried to . . . do anything.

By the end of her introduction to his home, he simply hadn't cared. She was there. And for a while, she was his. He intended to see they had whatever time it took to find out what happened next.

He turned and backed her against the nearest bookshelf, pulling her legs up around his hips, so she could wrap them around his waist as he kept her pinned there with his body, freeing his hands to cup her cheeks, and take their kiss deeper still.

"How is it I've missed you so much," she said against his mouth, "when I've never had you. And never left you. I mean—"

"I know what you mean," he said. He was dying for her, to feel her under him, over him, to be inside her. He felt starved for it, as if deprived for eons, and yet it was to be their first time.

"Hold on," he told her. He swung her away and carried her to his bed. "I'd thought to shower, to tidy up, to—"

"Take me to bed, Graham MacLeod," she whispered against his throat, her voice so tight with need, the rest, all of it, simply vanished from his thoughts.

He kicked boots from his path and held her to him with one arm while he ripped the bedspread from his bed, taking assorted and sundry clothes along with it. The one decadence he had allowed himself was the bed. It wasn't an heirloom. There hadn't been beds big enough in his accumulated family history to comfortably suit him. He had had it made for him using parts and bits of heirlooms that had otherwise fallen to ruin. It was sturdy, and would likely become an heirloom if the place were to hold up for a few centuries more. The bed most certainly would.

He followed her down onto the thick, feather-stuffed mattress, sending pillows flying as he moved her up the bed, so their bodies aligned more perfectly.

He groaned, or maybe it was Katie, as their hips met and legs entwined. She was already pulling at his tartan as he was her blouse. "Allow me," he said, moving her hands, and removing the clan crest with shaky hands, so he could unwrap himself from the rest.

"My turn," she said, and tackled the front of his white linen, so limp and crumpled from his travels, there wasn't much fine left to it. She didn't seem to mind as her nimble fingers made fast work of the fastenings.

She pushed it aside and moaned softly as she finally put her hands on his bare chest. "A scientist with the body of a god. It's like winning the lottery."

He laughed and felt the back of his neck burn at the same time. "Field work," he said, by way of explanation.

"Who knew making little seedlings grow could bring about such delightful results," she murmured, as she lifted her head to press her lips to the center of his chest. "You are . . ." She let her lips, and her tongue, continue that thought for her.

Graham groaned, as every muscle fiber in his body began to twitch under her very thorough exploration. When he could take it no longer, he reared back and straddled her hips, careful to keep the weight from crushing her, while pinning her hands to the bed.

"Clever hands," he said, "but I'd like a turn at it as well." He didn't make fast work with her blouse buttons, mostly because unveiling her slowly was the best kind of torture—for them both, if her slowly writhing hips were any gauge. He peeled back the exquisitely tailored shirt fronts to uncover the most delectable looking scrap of white lace. "Now that's what I call a delightful result." He scooted down, so he could bring his mouth in line with those lovely, plump nipples of hers, pressing up hard against the silk. He braced himself on his elbows, then took his turn with slow, thorough exploration. He suckled her through the expensive silk, making her arch off the bed, then alternately tugged and nipped, each motion gentle enough to bring pleasure, but just taught enough to make her gasp and begin to writhe in earnest.

So responsive, his Katie. "I believe I've found a new field of study," he said, as he slid one hand behind her, unfastened the hooks, then slid the bra from her so he could return to his earlier ministrations, with no barrier between them.

Her gasps became shallow pants, as he drove her higher, and higher still. "In fact," he said, between kisses as he left one damp nipple, and worked his way slowly over to the other. "It could take me years of field work to document all the ways I can make you—" His mouth closed over her and tugged just hard enough that she arched violently off the bed. Her fingers were in his hair, her nails digging into his scalp, holding him there, while he marveled at the reality that she was actually going to climax just from that kind of stimulation.

"Graham, just keep—oh . . . *oh*!" With her hips pistoning under him, he found he was rapidly losing what little control he had.

He slid down and unsnapped her trousers, sliding them down legs that were as delectably creamy as the rest of her. They would have to wait until a later time to be given their own due. His kilt and linen shirt slid to the floor along with her trousers and shoes.

He climbed back over her lovely, luscious form. "What was it you were saying about discovering riches?" he asked. "Because I am a very wealthy man right now."

He watched her eyes widen as she ran her gaze over him . . . all of him.

"Graham, I'm not sure—"

"I'm no' goin' to hurt ye," he said, knowing her stature and frame were much smaller and narrower than his. He gentled his touch and slid an arm under her waist to lift her up to his body. "Relax, we'll take it slowly and—"

She grabbed his hips and pulled him to her, lifting her legs at the same time so he pushed into her. "To hell with slow," she said, and dug her heels into his back.

The stunning feel of her wrapped fully, tightly around him, was so abrupt, so perfect. "God . . . oh, God." Control snapped, and she did little to help him regain it.

She moved under him, writhing like a woman seeking one thing and one thing only.

He was happy to oblige. His hips were moving, thrusting him deep, then deeper still.

It was as if she were made just for him. She arched, they both groaned, she took him, held him, and oh did she squeeze— "Katie, darlin', I'm no' so sure ye should be doin' that if you dinnae want me to—"

"Oh, but I do want you to," she said, almost on a growl.

"Well, in that case," he said, and simply gave himself completely over to her. "Never let it be said I didnae give you everything you want."

From that point on, the air was filled with moans and gasps, growls and sighs. He wasn't sure who was thrusting most against whom and he wasn't certain he cared.

There was nothing remotely civil or even thoughtful about that rutting match between them. They both reveled in the sheer animal intensity of it. He'd never thought to find someone so earthy, raw, and elemental. He certainly hadn't expected it from one so finely made as his Katie. She was a boundless well of surprises, and none were so happily discovered as that one.

Her nails raked his back as she screamed her way through her climax, which had the very lovely result of yanking him fast and hard over the edge. He was fairly certain the twinkly lights in his range of vision truly were stars, as he'd easily been catapulted into the cosmos by the primal union such as theirs was.

His muscles had not a whit of strength left in them after he'd finished pulsing himself into her. He rolled away to keep from collapsing on top of her, earning him a little mewing sound of despair, but neither had enough energy or strength left to do much about it.

"I'd collapse on ye," he grunted, struggling to get his heart rate down before it simply pumped right through his chest wall.

"What a way to go," she breathed, and he could hear the absolute joy threading through the exhaustion. "That was . . ." She sighed with gusto. "I have no words."

"The sigh told me enough," he said, realizing he had quite the Cheshire smile of his own curving his sweaty mug.

"Good. Because there's more where that came from."

He simply lay there and kept grinning, happier than he could recall being. Ever. The physical release was just one part of it, albeit a damned brilliant one. "So," he said, at length, "welcome home."

She laughed. It was more of a giggle, a joyful bubble of sound that made him happy—deep in places he hadn't known he had to fill. And that, he realized, was what was truly brilliant. She fit. She fit him, she fit here. She fit.

He rolled to his side, as she did the same. Their bodies, still slicked with sweat, collided chest to shoulders, and they both laughed. He braced her so she wouldn't fall against him, but apparently she didn't so much mind slick skin and heated embraces, because she slipped right into his embrace, much as she had the night before in Castlebay.

He pulled her close, marveling again at the way their bodies, so disparate in size, could move so naturally together as they did. "Why is it that every twenty-four-hour span of time with you feels much, much longer? It's no' possible to me, that it was only early, early this morning that we were in Castlebay."

"And only two days ago, that you sat beside me in a beautiful church garden, and explained why it was you'd come to get me and take me home."

He was silent then, for a long moment, but held her close when she tried to lean back enough to look at him.

"I wasn't trying to ruin the mood," she said, quietly, kissing that spot in the center of his chest that made him weak in the knees, each and every time she did it. "In fact . . ." she started, then trailed off. Then she, too, fell silent.

"In fact," he prodded. "What? What is on your mind, Katie?" He pushed back enough to tip her face up to his. He brushed the tangle of spun silk that was her hair from her face. Her eyes he thought to be sparkling blue, were nothing short of brilliant. "One of the things I most enjoy about us, is that we speak our minds."

"How many days did you say you had until you had to be married to a McAuley, or lose your leadership here?"

He had no idea what she'd been about to ask him, but that caught him off guard. "Dinnae worry about—"

"I'm not worrying. I'm asking. How many days?"

" 'Twas forty when I went to America."

"And if Iain marries before then? He wins?"

"No, that is no' how it works. I have until the end of the autumnal equinox. After that, 'tis whoever takes a bride first. So if he finds someone willing, he has only to wait until then to make it official. He can marry at midnight that night, and Kinloch will be his to rule."

"How long, being brutally honest, do you think it will take to convince everyone here that abolishing the Pact is the smarter way to go? How many holdouts do you think you'll have?"

"The percentage will no' be low. Not at first. I am going to sit down with Roan and Shay this evening, and we'll start formalizing a strategy that will put the idea forth in the best possible light."

"And then what? I mean, with no law, how will future leaders be decided?"

"As they always have been. By birth. If I have no rightful heir by the time of my passing, with no siblings, the leadership passes to the current McAuley. And so forth. We will simply cease to require the inter-clan bond of marriage. Unless they wish to, of course, but it wouldn't be grounds for removal from power."

"Hmm," was all she said.

"Why do you ask?" he finally asked.

She nudged him to his back, then sprawled half across his chest, propping her chin up on her folded hands. It was that very ease she had with him that bowled him over, time and time again. He hoped he never tired of it. Couldn't imagine doing so.

"What if . . ." She closed her eyes.

"Katie," he said, alarm creeping in, despite the absolute languor filling his every body part.

She flashed her eyes open. "Sorry, no, I didn't mean to make you think I'd gone . . . you know, off."

He pulled her up and kissed her on the forehead, the tip of her nose, and her mouth. "I suppose we should be grateful it didn't happen here. Now."

"I know. But . . . you know what, it's funny."

"It is?"

She smiled and bussed him on the mouth, before pushing him back on the bed, and resuming her place, chin propped on his chest. He fervently hoped they conducted every meeting they ever had, just like this.

"It didn't feel like *that other* was out there, on the fringes, waiting in the wings. It has felt like that—like it was always there—but it doesn't feel like it's there now. What we did felt . . . separate from that. Like it was its own moment."

He let his head relax into the pillows. "Perhaps. I don't know."

She looked up then, and her eyes went wide. Whatever she'd been about to say was lost as she gasped and scrambled fully off him, all the way to the foot of the bed.

He immediately sat up and reached for her. "What's wrong? Katie?"

She pointed at the headboard, then swung around as she took in the entire bed, all four posts, then the headboard again. "It was here."

"What was here?"

"My first vision. It was us. I mean the current us." She waved a hand. "You know what I mean. You and I were entwined, right here, on this bed. When you rolled off, it was you, *you*. Not otherworld you. And it was me. We were here. *Here*, Graham. Right *here*. How old is this bed?"

"I had it made. From other family pieces, but it's new in my lifetime. Not even a decade old."

"Hunh." She kept studying the headboard, then finally closed her eyes. "So wild," she murmured. "But maybe"—she looked at him again—"maybe that's why there was no hint of that other world. Because we were fulfilling—" She waved a hand, at a loss for the right words. "We did what we were supposed to do."

Graham couldn't help it, he grinned. "Well, if that's the case, then I wish we'd traveled there a lot more often."

She swatted at his leg, but she laughed, too.

He lay there thinking she had absolutely no concerns about sitting there, quite casually and stunningly naked, as they laughed and talked about things that others would have been carted away to the nutbin for even thinking. Felt perfectly natural.

"Why are you grinning?" she asked, smiling, completely unaffected by their current circumstance.

"Because I'm happy," he said, and realized the truth of it. "I've felt like I've led a blessed life, because I was given a clear purpose, and a path that would help people. Not everyone gets that."

"Yes," she said, softly, "I know."

"I didnae mean—"

"No, I know that," she said. "But I also know, from personal experience, that you're very, very right. It's lovely, beautiful even, that you see it exactly as you do. I have such respect for that. I hope I figure out the same path for myself. It's good to see it in front of you. That helps, you know? It's out there in front of me somewhere. I just have to find it."

"See, that's just it," he said. "I am blessed." He sat up, took her arms, and pulled her gently down on top of him, until they were laying fully back on the bed again. "But it wasn't until I met you, that I understood what it was to be happy. Truly happy."

She beamed a smile so bright and so . . . well, charming came to mind. He was pretty sure he'd just made her blush. "I'm glad," she said. "In fact, that might be the best accomplishment I've achieved so far." She leaned in, kissed him soundly, and sat up. "I have a long way to go yet, but thank you."

"For?" he asked, pulling her back down.

"For giving me such a lovely place to start."

He smiled then, and pulled her in for another kiss. It had been all hunger and blatant seduction before. It was no longer about assuaging sexual need. I was about communicating a different need entirely. As they kissed, the union, slow and sweet, was every bit as intimate, if not more so.

When she finally lifted her head, she kissed the tip of his nose, then the scar on his chin.

"What was that for?" he asked, his voice a pleasant rumble. He felt so completely and perfectly sated, on every level a man could feel it, he could happily have ascended to heaven right then and feel like he'd lived a full life.

"Because I could," she said, "which makes *me* incredibly happy."

He smiled, and tucked her closely against him as pleasure warred with fatigue. It was a pleasant, comfortable languor. He rolled them a little, so they could nestle better amongst the pillows. A little sleep would be wonderful. When they awoke they'd shower, find something to eat—if he had anything edible—before he went into town to talk to Roan and Shay. He suddenly remembered something else. "Hey," he said, kissing her temple as he let his body fully relax and the urge to sleep take over.

"Hmm," she said, already drowsily drifting off.

"Why did you ask? About the number of days."

"Mmm, that," she said, and he could feel her smiling against his chest. She slipped her arm around his waist, and tucked her leg between his, curling her foot around his calf. "Because that's how many days I have to get you to agree to marry me."

Chapter 18

"Wait a minute," Roan said as he paced. "You bring the most delightful, beautiful creature ever to grace our shores home with you . . . and she just happens to be—because you are the luckiest son of a bitch alive—the one woman in all of Christendom who will fulfill the Marriage Pact . . . and you dinnae want to marry her?" He spun on his heel and reached out toward Shay. "Does that make any sense to you?"

"I've no' had the chance to make her lovely acquaintance, but, on the surface, no." Shay looked squarely at Graham. "No, I'm afraid it doesn't."

"And!" Roan went on, fully revved, "He wants the citizenry to vote down our most traditional of all laws. It's akin to asking them to vote down one of the Ten Commandments. You dinnae have to do it, because *she's right here on our island*!"

"I want it repealed because it's wrong—even if I were to marry Katie—or anyone else," he added, trying not to fan those flames. He was already feeling pretty roasted himself. Reeling right over the spit, in fact, from what Katie had said to him right before she dropped into the sleep of the dead. In fact, she was still lights out to the world when he'd left to come down to see Roan and Shay.

He had left a note.

"I want the opportunity, and should be afforded one, to marry whomever I choose."

"But, it could be Katie." Spoken, surprisingly, by Shay.

He looked to his other, calmer friend. "That's not the point. It could be anyone."

"It's entirely the point. Because I will tell you, you haven't a hope in hell of getting this thing voted down. If you think no one is going to know who she is or what her role here could be, you're even more daft than you're being right now."

"What I dinnae understand, is why ye still want to change things," Roan said. "Pursue the easy solution."

Graham swung his head in Roan's direction. "I beg your pardon."

Roan immediately lifted his hands up, but shot a saucy wink in Shay's direction. "See? He's protective as all bloody hell. Jealous, too. Hardly said two words on the drive out. Clearly concerned that I might win her over with my charming wit and easy laugh."

"Clearly concerned that if you're no' careful, you'll have a few less teeth to keep gleaming white," Graham responded.

Shay quickly resumed his no nonsense counsel. "Loathe as I am to agree with him when he's being a horse's arse, he does have a point."

"Aye, right on top of his little, narrow head."

"Ye're protective of her, Graham," Shay said, like it explained everything.

"She's here as my guest, of course I'm going to protect her." He scowled at Roan. "Clearly she'll be in need of it."

"Now, now," Roan said, totally unfazed by Graham's mood.

"If she's someone you have any feelings for," Shay said, "then that's far more than others in your position have been fortunate enough to have in the beginning. If there is room for growth there, then hallelujah. But, regardless of that, she's here. Let's make her our offer—"

"I've seen how she looks at him, Shay," Roan said. "You

willnae be needing to draw up any documents. I've a feeling she won't be demanding much more than singular access to our idiot friend here. Though the why of it has me completely baffled."

"Do ye no' see that this is about more than the restrictions being placed on me? It would remove the issue from ever being a problem, again."

"That's just it," Shay said, quite seriously. "You're the only one who thinks it's a problem."

Graham opened his mouth to argue, then shut it again. He wasn't sure how to argue that one. He finally sank into one of the chairs in front of Roan's desk. "Bring me up to date on our friend, Iain," he said, opting to change the subject until he could better determine how to get them to understand his desire. "I can tell ye, I spoke with Malvy, and he has nothing good to say about him."

"He doesnae belong here," Shay said. "I'm the one who believes in inclusion, so—"

"Malvy said almost the exact same thing." Graham wasn't anxious to bring Katie back into the discussion, but his need to get some feedback outweighed his common sense. It was a running theme with him where she was concerned, but apparently this time wasn't going to be any different. "Roan, you've met Katie. Your own personal feelings aside, do you think she'll meet the same kind of resistance that Iain is meeting? Or is that no' the case with him?" He looked to Shay. "Are your feelings typical of the masses?"

Roan responded first. "Initially, and please keep your fist out of my pretty face when I say this, I'd imagine members of the opposite sex in either case will be fairly predisposed to think favorably of their candidate."

Graham looked to Shay again. "Is Iain finding favor with the women here?"

Shay lifted a shoulder in an unenthusiastic shrug. "I'd like to say otherwise, but he is turning a head or two."

"It's more than one or two," Roan put in. "But ye'd have an equal shot in that race."

"I dinnae want a race," Graham barked, then immediately waved his hand. "I'm sorry. Why doesn't anyone see this for the insanity it is? I am next in line, I've devoted my whole life to this, willingly and with great love. Why must I compromise the rest of my life? And why is anyone willing to even consider allowing Iain to gain a toehold?" He stood. "I understand about your feelings on the abolishment, but I'm calling a council. Shay, post the banns. Day after tomorrow. I might not have any luck in getting anyone to change their mind, but I'm going to speak my own. So when they move forward with this silly contest, and I refuse to play, they'll know well in advance what their choice will be bringing them." He walked to the door. "And it's no' going to be me."

"Then what do you plan to do?" Shay asked.

Graham turned back. "I haven't a clue. But I'm no' devoting my life to a group of people who have such little respect for mine. Who knows, maybe I'll head back to Annapolis with Katie."

"You wouldn't," Roan said, truly stunned.

"Have ye no' heard anything I've said? I'm not toying with this. I've never been more sincere."

"I dinnae think the people see it as such a live-or-die issue," Shay said. "To them it's exciting, something to gossip about. It appeals to their romantic side."

"Romantic? What in the hell is romantic about this?"

"When they find out you're back with an eligible McAuley staying under your roof, it will only gain more momentum," Roan said.

"It's human drama, Graham," Shay said. "And it ends with a wedding. I dinnae think they see the greater picture as you do. The fact that there might be a real romance is secondary to the historic romance of the situation."

"Oh, there's romance."

Graham looked at Roan. "Iain?"

"No, you idiot. You."

"I told ye—"

Roan laughed. "You can keep telling me, mate, until you cease to draw breath. But I've seen the two of you." He looked at Shay and mouthed, "*Romance*," then made a sign with his hands showing it was a big one.

Shay turned to Graham and said, "Why did you want to know if we'd accept Katie?"

Graham didn't answer that directly. Instead, he looked between his two friends. "I wanted your support in this," he said.

"I know," Shay said, "and we'd be behind you. We are behind you. But we dinnae want ye wasting time. You're bucking four hundred years of tradition, with the answer to the Marriage Pact sleeping under your roof." He held up his hand to stop Graham's reply. "With the contract, if needed. I'm no' saying just because she's here, she's willing."

"She's willing," Roan muttered.

When Graham shot him a quelling look, he didn't back down. "You know, I understand about the sacrifice, about wanting to lead your own life. Aye, ye do enough for the people here, and they revere you for it. But not a single person on this island, most especially those of us who would be happy to find any port in a very lonely storm, are going to feel sorry for you. You have her. I don't care how it happened, or why you found her. But you did. Why don't you stop focusing on how wrong this stupid law is, and start focusing on what's standing right in front of ye."

Graham ducked his head, wishing like hell Roan's argument didn't move him. But it did. He looked to Shay. "How long?" he asked.

"Thirty-six days."

"I meant until we could legally part ways—if we married."

Roan swore under his breath and sat down behind his desk. He swung his chair around so it faced the window, folded his arms, and propped his feet up on the printer stand.

Graham kept his attention on Shay.

"It doesnae say. I suppose you could do it at any time. But you'll lose the faith of your people if ye don't at least give it a try."

"I won't stop working for what's best for all of us. Whether I'm married or not isn't going to make any difference in that."

"It's not all about healthy crops, Graham," Roan stated flatly.

"It's about hope," Shay added.

"That's what healthy crops give us," Graham said.

"What I'm trying to get through your thick skull is that without love, we don't care if we have prosperity. What's the point?" Roan said.

"Which is why this is so ludicrous. No one cares about love, just about the wedding. It's a hollow victory."

"Not one couple has ever split up. That's the history of the Marriage Pact. They believe in it. They think if love isn't there in the beginning, it grows. Four hundred years, Graham. Not one split. That's hope."

"That's romance," Roan added.

"If they think Iain can give them that, then the rest, everything else I've worked for, is meaningless?"

"No, of course not," Roan said. "They'll root for ye. They'll want it to be ye. But if it's no', then they'll take it as a sign that it's time for a change."

"And just like that, they'll blindly follow some bloke who's never set foot on the island until three days ago."

"They'll take the leap of faith. It's—"

"Tradition, I hear you. I guess I just dinnae understand—"

"That's because ye work in a lab with mathematical equations all day," Roan said. "Not all things are linear, with a calculable solution at the end. We've managed to survive over four centuries doing it this way, and taking those leaps when they come along. Maybe ye're the one who has to have faith in them. In their beliefs."

"And if doing that means the end to Kinloch?"

"Then it was a good run," Roan said.

Graham shook his head. "Fine." He looked to Shay. "Put the notice out. Joint clan council. Two days from now. In the village square."

He walked out and closed the door behind him.

Chapter 19

Katie stretched like the proverbial cat in the windowsill. When her legs stretched beyond the length of the down-filled duvet covering her, she snatched them right back in again. It was a damn chilly windowsill.

She snuggled under the covers and enjoyed the luxury of waking up slowly, without any wheels moving under her. She had no idea how long she'd been asleep, but she knew exactly where she was. She turned her head and opened her eyes, but Graham's side of the bed was empty. She pouted, then laughed when she saw the note propped on his pillow with her name on it in big letters.

She pulled it over and opened it. Before she even read the first word, she took a moment to look at his handwriting. There was something intimate about a handwritten note. His was legible, but that was the most she could say for it. She smiled, charmed by the slanted scrawl. She read: *Darling Katie, this is so you know I've not left you and run off to the nearest ferry.* "Very funny." But it was funny. And she rather liked the Darling Katie part. She could hear his accent as she read and made the appropriate adjustments in her mind. *I've gone into Aoibhneas to meet with Roan and Shay.* "So, that's how you'd spell that," she murmured. Not a big help. She was going to stick with Port Joy. *I will bring sustenance with me upon my return. You may want to wait on the shower.* She wiggled her eyebrows at that and smiled to herself, thinking he wanted a little shower recreation. She was okay with that plan. Then she read on: *It's a bit tricky and I don't want you scalding yourself.* "Right." She sighed. "Sometimes, you're such a scientist."

She was smiling as she rolled out of bed, then danced a little on the cold stone floor until she jumped to a rug. "Clothes would be a very good thing right now." She thought about all her luggage down in the entry vestibule, and cringed at the idea of getting it all up there. She thought maybe she'd just bring it up an armful of clothes at a time, until she had what she needed. "But will I be able to light the lantern thingies and not burn the place to the ground, that's the question."

"Were ye plannin' on going up and down the stairs in your all together?"

She squealed and turned to find Graham standing just inside the door to the stairs. Only it hardly looked like him.

"I'm rather liking this kind of homecoming. Will be the first time I'll be wantin' to leave the fields early. Or just stay in."

She would have grabbed the duvet, or searched for her clothes, wherever the hell they'd been flung to, but she was too busy standing there, goggling at Graham's drastically changed appearance, to care much about her own nudity. "Wow," she said. Not pithy, but it did sum things up.

He took a moment, then realized she was staring at him with the same avid fascination he was staring at her but for a totally different reason. At that, he looked down at himself, then back at her. "Is something the matter?"

"I—uh, no. Not at all." She couldn't take her eyes off him. "I've only seen you in your tartan." *Well, and stunningly naked.*

"Oh," he said, "aye. I hadn't thought of that." He made a fast gesture at himself, then crossed to the kitchen area and sat down a large cloth sack, sliding the long straps from his shoulder.

He was so cute, she thought, all self-conscious. Look at him. What was there to be self-conscious about? The man was wearing trousers, a heavy cream button-down work shirt with a thin burgundy plaid stripe running through it, and heavy work boots. He was possibly the hottest thing she'd ever seen. The loose fitting khaki pants accentuated his narrow waist and crazy muscular thighs. And that shirt? What it did for his broad shoulders. She was a fan. But what really had her wanting to drag him straight back to bed was the way he'd pulled his hair back in a queue at his neck and the wire-rim scientist glasses.

Seriously. Hottest thing she'd ever seen.

He slid the glasses off as he tipped the bag on its side.

"No," she said. "Don't do that."

"Ye're no' hungry?"

She walked right into the kitchen, naked as a jaybird, quite thankful, for once, for no picture windows, and pushed his glasses back up onto his face.

"What—"

"I'm hungry."

"I'm no' surprised, but I need to get—"

She started undoing the buttons on his shirt.

"Oh," he said, letting go of the bag.

"Aye," she said, pushing the shirt back off his shoulders.

He reached to take the band from his hair.

"Really, just leave things alone."

He lifted his hand away, held them both up, as if in surrender. But he was smiling. "Had I known ye liked the lonely scientist farmer look, I'd have left the tartan at home."

She was licking his chest at the moment, but paused long enough to shake her head. "Oh, I'm having that kilt bronzed."

He laughed, then scooped her up and over his shoulder.

She squealed and smacked his ass. "Wow. Remind me again why we thought we shouldn't be doing this?"

He tossed her gently into the center of the bed, then leapt in after. "Because we weren't in our right minds."

"Right," she said, pulling him over on top of her. "I'm so glad we have our wits about us now."

"Aye. Wits." He tugged her mouth down to his and the conversation dwindled.

The laughter, however, did not. This time it was playful and fun. If her heart hadn't been in jeopardy before, when he looked up from where he'd been feasting quite lingeringly over her nipples, as his glasses fogged, and he slid them down his nose to wiggle his eyebrows at her, she knew she was lost.

"Come here," she said, laughing even as her throat closed over with sudden emotion. She tugged him up until he was on top of her, then carefully, slowly, slid his glasses off and gently set them somewhere back over her head. "Not booking passage to Oban this morning might be the best decision I've ever made in my life."

"You mean after the one that had me carrying you out of the chapel."

"Well, that, too," she said, and leaned up to kiss his chin.

Playful and fun, suddenly shifted to gentle and sweet, as he dipped his mouth and kissed her slowly, with a mild rather than ravenous hunger. She could feel how ready his body was for her, and yet he took his time, lingering at the corners of her mouth, dropping sweet kisses along the side of her jaw. Teasing her earlobe, making her gasp, softly, as he kissed the pulse on the side of her neck.

In his home, surrounded by the things that truly mattered to him, it was easy to imagine him as the quiet, sensitive lover. It wasn't as if she hadn't seem glimpses of that side of him all along. But she'd seen the fierce protector in him, felt the warrior conqueror when he took her earlier. And she was falling for both men.

He moved his way back to her mouth, and when he pulled her more fully under him, he moved between her thighs, and took her in one, slow, deep thrust. She arched, gasped, and felt her body climb straight up that peak. But rather than build on that, and take her faster, thrust harder, he kept it slow, steady, climbing her up slowly, sweetly, until she thought she might sob from the need for release.

"Graham," she said, on a choked plea.

"Shh," he said, against the side of her neck. "We've all the time in the world. Let me . . ."

Love you.

Those were the words she heard, and it made her own heart take flight. He hadn't said them, but she knew, in that moment, it was what she wanted. Wherever her path took her—if she could find a way to stay on Kinloch—that was her intention. She wasn't giving up without the fight of her life. One thing McAuleys were really good at, was going after what they wanted. And getting it.

He slid an arm beneath her back and pulled her up that last bit, so he could slide the rest of the way. "Oh. That is . . ."

"I know," he whispered against her neck.

She felt him gather, his body tensed, and he grew fuller, yet continued his slow, steady strokes.

"Graham," she whispered.

"Darling Katie," he said, then arched his back and groaned, long and low, as he pulsed into her until he shuddered from the strength of the release.

Her body shook right along with his. When he tried to move away, she held on tight. "Stay," she asked him. "With me."

His hold on her tightened until she thought she might faint, but it was the sweetest, instinctive hug she'd ever received. It was as honest a response as she could have hoped for.

When they could both finally breathe, he slipped from her, rolled to his side, and pulled her with him, keeping her close. "That was . . ."

"I know," she said, pressing a kiss to his chest.

"I dinnae want to move. I think all my limbs have been turned to water."

"I know exactly how you feel."

"Let me catch my breath, then I'll take ye into the shower—"

"If you show me how it works—"

He tipped her face up to his. "I want to go on record right now."

"Okay," she said, fighting a smile at his oh so serious tone. It was the twinkle in his eyes, though, that really caught at her heart. They were back to fun, but there was another layer to it.

A more poignant tug in her chest, and the deep affection that had been growing for him all along, had reached a fully new plateau. "Go on."

"You'll always be an independent free spirit, it's who you are. But I am finding that I enjoy, a great deal, taking care of you. In ways big and small. So if you can understand by allowing me these small pleasures, you're making me happy, perhaps it will-nae be such a challenge for you to let go a little bit."

"Would these little things include scrubbing my back in the shower?"

"It would be a most delightful place to start, aye."

"Then I believe I am willing to give it a go."

He grinned. "This is a partnership that might have a bit of merit."

"I'm happy you feel that way," she teased back.

He hadn't said a word about her earlier declaration, about wanting him to marry her. He'd played it as a joke at the time, but she was pretty sure he knew she'd never been more serious. Every moment they spent with each other served to strengthen what they could have together. She was going to have to trust that, trust him.

"How did the meeting go, with Roan and Shay?"

She'd expected, perhaps, a bit of frustration on his part, as she'd known he was a bit worried that his friends wouldn't support his desire to see the end to the Marriage Pact, but she hadn't been prepared for the way his expression immediately shuttered. Not when they'd made such huge strides in reaching a new level of trust with one another.

"Don't do that," she said, but softly.

"Do what?"

"Shut yourself off. I take it the chat didn't go as you'd hoped." She pushed up a little, and framed his hard jaw with her hand. "I'd like to think you could talk to me about everything. I'd like to have that freedom with you. I'll try and always keep an open mind, but you'll also know I will tell you how I honestly feel. I'd hope for the same trust and feedback from you." She smiled at him. "I'm no' just looking for a partner in the shower, ye ken."

His lips twitched, and she felt like she'd just made a major inroad.

"You're uncanny with that, ye know."

"I've Scot blood in me."

"You've a few things Scot in you, as a matter of fact."

His comment elicited a surprised burble of laughter from her, and she swatted him. "I can't believe you just said that."

"If I'm to trust you with the serious topics, then I should know I can trust you to handle my bawdy humor as well. What?" he asked, when she looked at him askance. "Do I no' strike you as the type?"

"I'm not so sure there is really anything you could do or say that would surprise me. You're an amazing dichotomy of so many different things. I haven't learned them all yet, so you might catch me off guard from time to time."

"I find I dinnae mind that so much. You blush the most becoming shade of pink."

She lifted up and kissed him on the chin. "So do you. So I understand the attraction. Just remember, fair's fair."

"What have I done?" he said with mock horror.

"If you think it's successfully changing the topic, you'll find you're mistaken," she told him. "So, tell me what went on with Roan and Shay. I take it they weren't receptive to your abolitionist ideas."

"Not entirely, no."

"Do you think they'll come around? Will you be able to persuade them?"

"They made a pretty good case for keeping the Pact intact."

Surprise had her pushing up to a half sit so she could see his face more fully. "Really? Did that make you see things differently as well?"

He shook his head. "No' in the way they'd hoped. But they did make me think on the part of my job I talked to you about the other day."

"That being?"

"Feeling as if I have a sense of what my people need from me in terms of personal direction. As I said, I understand economics, and keeping us a successful, thriving island in terms of our bottom line."

"But you feared you didn't have a sense of how to maintain the emotional balance. You said you thought they were happy with your performance, though."

"No one has said anything, no. But I fear if I pursue this path I am on, it will become an issue and swiftly. I dinnae want to disappoint them, and Roan and Shay made a case for giving them hope."

"By marrying someone you don't love?"

His arms tightened around her, surprising her with the instinctive gesture. She tried not to react to it, but it made every part of her want to sing for joy, knowing he truly did want her. He might not be prepared to admit the full breadth of it yet, but some part of him already knew what was there, what could be there, between them.

"Perhaps they can explain it to you. I suppose it makes sense, if you look at it through their filter. It just doesnae happen to be the way I think. I'm no' sure if a compromise, in this case, is what I should do. I feel that I would be cheating us both."

"So, what are you going to do?"

"I had Shay post the banns for a clan council meeting. Two days hence."

"You'll put it to a vote? So soon?"

"No. I just want the opportunity to tell them why I feel as I do, and listen to what they have to say. I'm hoping that will guide me in what I should do next."

"Would you really walk away? End your work here?"

"If they decide that fate is the ultimate decider, and Iain ends up the victor, then I dinnae see how I could stay on. If they truly believe that life and their future is best left to the whims of fate, then they'll embrace the path that doesnae have me on it. They can't have it both ways."

"What about you then? I mean, where would you go? What would you do?"

He smiled then, and it surprised her. "Asks the woman on the brink of making the same journey. It's no' like this is all I can be, Katie. It's just what I want to be. But perhaps my fate is to take a new direction as well."

She curled back beside him, her mind racing in all new directions. She hadn't expected the reaction to his desire to end the Pact to be a positive one, certainly not initially anyway. But it was all rapidly growing far more complicated than she would have expected.

So she pushed, when she otherwise would have counseled herself not to. She had a feeling once the two of them essentially reentered Kinloch society, things were going to move swiftly toward one conclusion or another. She didn't trust they'd have much of a chance to control things once everybody else began to have a say. So she had her say, while she still had his complete and focused attention.

She scooted up, until their faces were level, and cupped his face until he turned to look fully into her eyes. "I know it is with the best of intentions you want to move your people past an ancient restriction you feel would serve not only the current generation, but generations to come—in a better, more freely adaptable way. It also honors your own feelings."

"Aye, you've just stated it far more clearly than I could. Perhaps I should have had you with me at the meeting."

She smiled at that. "I'm a hell of a negotiator."

"I'll tuck that fact away," he said, smiling too, but she saw the strain around the edges.

"But there is a third option."

"What do you mean?"

"You want the Pact abolished. Your friends seem to think not only will that not happen, but that the law, as it stands is still more benefit than detriment to the people of Kinloch."

"That is the crux of it, aye."

"If the time constraint elapses, what are the chances that Iain will make good on his threat?"

"According to Roan, high to near on a certainty."

"So let me propose to you a third option."

"Please do," he said, pulling her hand presently cupping his cheek around to his mouth, where he pressed a rather hot and bothersome little kiss to the palm of her hand, which she then snatched away.

"No distracting the negotiator."

He grinned unrepentantly. "I'm merely trying to gauge just how finely honed those skills of yours are. If I'm going to take you into battle, a clan leader needs to know these things."

She wiggled her eyebrows at him, but when she spoke, she'd never been more serious. "That is exactly my proposition. Take me into battle with you."

"Meaning what?"

"Meaning you give your people what they want." She took his hand then, and pressed a hot, sweet kiss of her own to the center of his palm. He didn't jerk it away, but his expression definitely changed to one not so confident as before.

"What are you plotting inside that lovely blond head of yours?"

"I'm just saying we're not exactly repulsed by each other."

"Ye can safely make that argument, aye."

"Why don't we end Iain's reign of potential terror. Give your people the wedding they want. Then continue on with your quest to abolish the law, for those who come after." She held up her hand. "Let me get it all out there, then you can shoot me down. Doing it that way you wouldn't be working under any time constraints, and you'd have me there, pitching the battle with you."

"Why on earth would they want to repeal something they see is still working?"

That made her heart sing just a little, but she kept it under wraps. "If we talk to them, implore them to search their hearts, and free their future leaders to be allowed to follow theirs . . . I think together we might make a stronger case. Precisely because we did follow the law, but still want to seek freedom for those who come after. And . . ." What she'd said so far was the easy part. What she had to say next was the hard part, the part she really didn't want to point out, or put on the table. But it had to be said if she was to ultimately get what she wanted— Graham wanting her as freely and fully as she wanted him. "If the law is abolished, you would be free to dissolve our union, and still seek the partner of your choice. And show them for real, what that would give them, and give to you."

She knew it was the best possible solution to the problem, but she didn't want him to actually take her up on that last part. She didn't want to see his reaction to that comment.

So, it made her heart decidedly heavier, when he seemed to take it under serious consideration. "You'd do that? We wouldn't be able to judge how long it might take."

"I want time here, to sort through my future options. I've nowhere I have to be. If the situation becomes untenable, then you can simply divorce me, and move on in whatever manner you wish, Pact or no Pact."

"Not one union has ever been dissolved. Four hundred years."

"You want to dissolve it all, so ending the lengthy streak is hardly a sin by comparison."

His expression shuttered a bit, but she didn't call him out on it. She wasn't feeling quite as generous as she'd been feeling minutes ago, when she thought he'd balk at the idea of letting her go. Or had certainly hoped he would.

Surely they were on the path to that destination—marriage— already. But, her confidence a bit shaken, she wasn't as happily ready to skip down the aisle. Yet she either had conviction in her own plans, or she did not. She could hardly ask that of him, and not be willing to trust in her own vision. There were no guarantees in any event.

"Ye've given me a lot to think on," he said.

She nodded, wishing she had a bit less on her mind at the

moment. But it was all part of the same thing. She needed him to be as sure of her, as she felt she was about him. It was just the beginning . . . she needed to keep the faith.

"You know," she told him, "I am suddenly ravenous. Why don't you show me the mysteries of your shower and I'll clean up while you put together whatever goodies you brought back with you from . . ."

"Port Joy?" he offered when she didn't attempt to mangle the village name. A glimpse of the teasing smile curved his lips. Clearly his thoughts were on other things. Like whether or not he was game to marry and divorce her to make a point with his people.

Oh, Katherine Elizabeth, what have you gone and done now?

Chapter 20

"They are truly works of art," Katie breathed, as she looked from one basket to the next, lining the showcases in Roan's office. "My God, I had no idea." She turned to face him. "These are made right here on the island? All of them? How many do you ship, say, in a month?"

He pulled out a spread sheet and handed it to her. She looked over the numbers and her mouth fell open. "Oh, my word." She looked up to find Roan smiling quite proudly.

"We're only back up to sixty-seven percent consistent crop production. We could push the market further, but we have to be confident we could continuously fulfill the demand."

Katie laid the spreadsheet back on the desk and picked up the small catalog that showcased their work. "How often do the pieces change?"

"Continuously. Mostly the catalog is a means of showing what our range is. Many of our customers want the unique, the one-of-a-kind."

"You do that? Custom baskets?"

"In a sense. We can take recommendations of color schemes and quote a price range, but the weaver has the freedom to create whatever she wants, so long as it meets the criterion of the agreed upon price."

"What is the percentage of customer dissatisfaction?"

Roan handed her another spreadsheet. "Third column is the rate of return or refusal for the past corporate year."

"Wow," she said, seriously impressed. "I guess your reputation helps in that regard a lot. With such a subjective product, that's really an amazingly low figure."

"We're proud of it, aye."

"Still, the marketing challenges you face with that kind of stock fluctuation—"

"Are indeed challenging. It's my job to come up with solutions." He cocked his head and studied her as she handed the folder back to him. "Would it be presumptuous of me to assume your role in McAuley-Sheffield was in some way parallel to my, admittedly, much smaller role here?"

"You may assume that, yes," she said with a smile. "I don't know that I can honestly say I had the same honest passion for it that you do for yours, but I can say with a fair amount of confidence that I was pretty damn good at it."

"Good," Roan said, clapping the folder shut in increased excitement. Considering he'd been pretty much a zero-to-sixty sort whenever they'd spent time together, that was saying a lot. "Would you be remotely receptive to seeing some ideas I've been playing around with, for the fall and winter campaigns?"

"Sure," she said, surprised to realize she meant it. It was entirely different than back at home. She truly was free to do what she wanted. The knowledge that she might contribute something made her feel energized about trying. No one was more surprised than she was. She'd thought she hated her job.

Maybe it was just her employer.

He handed her another file. "Look these over. If you can pry Graham out of his lab, hijack his computer and go to the website listed on the front sheet. That's us. Look and see what's going on now, to understand better where I'd like us to be."

"I can do that," she said, slowly flipping through the pages, already excited about having something to sink her teeth into.

She'd been on Kinloch for a week, and it was her first time going solo.

For the first couple days, she'd stayed at Graham's, initially waiting until after his clan council meeting, which had gone about as well as Roan and Shay had predicted it would. Then he'd taken her into the village to meet everyone, and that part had actually gone quite well. She knew she was like the oddity at the circus, but they certainly hadn't made her feel that way. In fact, to a man, or woman, they'd been nothing but cordial and kind.

She'd found them to be exactly as Graham had said they'd be, the nicest people to know. However, she wasn't fool enough, to think for one second, there wasn't gossip raging like wildfire behind her back. She didn't take offense at it. After all, in their position, she'd surely be doing the same thing.

But she didn't go off and hide. Graham had taken her on extensive tours of the fields. He'd shown her how they converted the plants she saw into the thread they wove into the baskets. It wasn't until this morning, though, that she'd seen the end results, firsthand. Roan was going to take her to meet some of the weavers so she could see up close what they were all so deeply connected to. So far, she'd found each part of the process absolutely fascinating. She was equally intrigued by the contents of the folder she held in her hand.

Roan stood. "Are ye ready to go check out some of the weaver's studios?"

"You're sure they won't mind?"

Roan barked one of his infectious laughs. "You are joking, right? You are the hot commodity on the island right now. There were actual arguments over who would hostess you and who would have to wait."

"You're putting me on."

"I'm doing nothing of the sort."

"Be honest, it's because I'm a curiosity, right? I'm the McAuley that The MacLeod is keeping in his castle, but won't make an honest woman of, isn't that the draw?"

Roan rubbed his hands together. "Absolutely, darlin'. That's what makes this so delicious."

She laughed. He was so outrageous and yet so completely harmless she could hardly call him on it.

"So," he said, putting a friendly arm about her shoulder as he guided her through the front office and out to his truck, parked in front. "How is your personal campaign coming along?"

She nudged him in the ribs. "Honestly, not here, where God and everyone are listening in."

He laughed. "In the getaway car then, Mrs. Peel, and quickly."

She rolled her eyes and climbed in the opposite side. She'd yet to drive herself anywhere, but she was slowly acclimating herself to the whole wrong side of the road concept. She looked over at her cohort in crime, and felt that little pang of home-sickness she felt each time they set off on a new adventure. Actually, it wasn't so much homesickness as it was Blaine-sickness. She missed her best friend. There had been no word, no contact made. She was starting to wonder how long was long enough, to risk checking in with her very best friend. Mostly to see how he was doing, but also, if she were honest, to find out what all had transpired since she'd left Annapolis. She'd been tempted on more than one occasion to get on Graham's computer or Roan's laptop and see what news stories had leaked out after her aborted wedding fiasco, but she'd chickened out each time, feeling what she didn't know, couldn't hurt her.

She was well aware that the friendship she'd instantly struck up with Roan had very much become a bit of a placebo for what she was missing with Blaine. Other than the very obvious difference that Roan was quite emphatically heterosexual, he really was the closest thing she had to a gay best friend. To her, Roan was like the big brother she'd never had. Or maybe the big cousin he truly was. Playful, and at times flirtatious, but al-ways with the understanding that she didn't regard him the least bit a contender for her affections.

It made him behave that much more outrageously around her, which she found pretty adorable. Making that fact clear to him was her amusement. It drove him crazy that he couldn't get a rise out of her.

That was Graham's exclusive domain. She was quite secure in the fact, and, thankfully, so was he. Graham might find his friend's barrage of playful sexual innuendo around Katie tiresome and juvenile, two words he'd used often in Roan's presence, but what it didn't make him was jealous.

Katie found that immensely refreshing. He trusted Roan and her implicitly. She liked knowing she'd gained that level of trust with Graham. It meant a great deal. Between the crops, industry business, island business, and the general demands on Graham's time, having Roan around to keep her distracted had also kept her sane.

It had been five days since the epic failure of the clan council meeting, and Graham still hadn't given her an answer to her offer.

"Okay," Roan said, as he pulled out on the narrow village track. "You share first. Is he cracking at all?"

Katie lifted a shoulder. "I don't know. We spent the couple days it took us to get here, and my first full day here, pretty much joined at the hip." *And a few other places,* she thought, but despite Roan's sense of humor, she didn't say it out loud. "He's been understandably busy and distracted the past few days, but we've spent meals together, supper, at least, and there has been time to talk."

"He's said nothing about your Marriage Pact proposal?"

She shook her head. She hadn't told Roan about the other proposal she'd made. Given that the Pact proposal she'd made had come after, she assumed Graham thought it was something she'd said in the heat of the moment. She'd never been more clear thinking, but she'd been willing to leave that aside for the time being, in favor of getting him to say something, anything, about his plans for the deadline, which was four short weeks away.

Odd how the time she'd known him felt like a lifetime, yet since arriving there, time felt as if it were flying by.

"Has he said anything more to you about what his plans are? Has he talked to you or Shay since the council?"

Roan shook his head. "Shay is still in Edinburgh and likely won't be back until sometime next week, if then."

Katie hadn't had the chance to meet Graham's other close friend, as he'd been gone by the time she'd gone into the village. In addition to seeing to everyone's legal needs on Kinloch, he also ran the small firm his father had started on the mainland. From time to time, he had to go there to work on or oversee a particularly difficult case. "It's kind of ironic," she said, "that Graham is here trying to figure out how to make the Marriage Pact functional, and Shay is in Edinburgh, trying to find a way to conclude the divorce case for two very dysfunctional people." She looked over at Roan. "What are his views on the Marriage Pact?"

"Shay is a good mediator, because he can see both the merits of and the detractions of any kind of union. He happens to be very good at disassembling the marital kind, but he believes the Marriage Pact should stay."

"Really?"

Roan nodded. I think he likes the continuity of it, of what it's stood for. He likes to have faith where he can. Don't fix what's not broken is his motto. There are already enough broken things."

"And you?"

"Maybe not for the same reasons, but pretty much the same outcome."

"Do you think we should marry and leave the Pact be?"

"I think Graham should follow his heart in both matters. I'm just no' certain he knows his own heart." He glanced over to her, a kind smile on his face. "He hasn't had to use it much. He's a thinker by nature, a researcher and an investigator. He accumulates data and extrapolates theories. He's not much for leap of faith moments. Except, perhaps where you were concerned. Very unlike him, that. So you'll probably have to give him time to do it his way."

"Which is?"

Roan's smile spread to a grin. "Accumulate data and extrapolate theories."

"About marriage?"

"About you."

Katie folded her arms over her suddenly knotted stomach. "Lovely." She had to pray that when Graham added up all his data and came up with an equation, she was the sum of all the various parts.

"I'm taking you around the east end of the island. You'll get to see the tower, and the abbey. Most of the weavers are on the MacLeod end of the island, but we have one artist in particular whose work I think you'll find fascinating."

"Has she been weaving a long time?"

Roan shook his head. "No, in fact, she's new here."

Katie hadn't known Roan for very long, but she'd known Blaine her whole life. When Tag's name had first started to enter their conversations, ever so casually, she'd come to recognize a certain look on Blaine's face when he spoke about him. Right from the start, Katie knew, even before Blaine did, that Tag was The One. Roan had a very similar look on his face at the moment. She smiled. "So, what is her name?"

"There's the tower, there," Roan pointed, drawing her attention away from uncovering Roan's possible secret love, and directing it to the dark, imposing tower built from the same stone, it appeared, as Graham's stronghold castle.

"It's held up as well as the castle has, it appears."

"Aye, it's rather defied the odds. The castle is somewhat protected, wedged in the high valley between the two mountains as it is. The weather on this end of the island is much fiercer and there's less protection as a good part of the east end extends well past the mountain itself."

"Oh," Katie exclaimed. "Look at all the flowers."

"That's the machair. It's a very unique, natural formation that runs just above a beach line, but below the actual strip of solid land."

"It's stunning and those flowers look so exotic." There was a tickle at the edge of her mind, but it was easily ignored as they drove past the tower and along the machair, heading toward the bend in the road where the mountain eased out again and butted up against the track. It wasn't until they'd gone past the tower and she'd turned her attention from the startling wall of mountain to her left, back to the flowery machair to her right, that she gasped, then said, "Stop the car."

"What? Why? What's wrong?"

"Nothing, just—" She didn't finish. The moment he'd coasted to a stop, she'd hopped out of the cab of the truck.

"Wait, where are you—"

"That building," she shouted back over the wind, as Roan climbed out his side of the car, "out there on that spit of land. That's the abbey?"

"Aye, 'tis. Why do ye ask?"

"Nothing, it's just . . ." She walked away from him, her gaze fixed on the spot beyond the end of the machair, where the grass tufted up brilliant and green, a rocky tumble just beyond . . . and in the distance, what had been at one time, she knew for a fact, a stone abbey. She could have drawn it from memory. "It wasn't always out in the water, was it? The abbey?" She turned to find that Roan was still back by the truck, and couldn't hear her. Didn't matter. She knew the answer. She was staring at the place where Graham had first made love to her. Or to some past version of her. "Right over there." She wandered into the grass, tentative at first, then more boldly. Since the time she and Graham had consummated their relationship, neither of them had had a vision, not even a feeling of one.

They'd talked about it briefly, late one night, when she'd been looking at the carved headboard. They'd talked about her first vision in more detail, and she'd asked him what he thought the visions meant, and why they'd stopped. He hadn't given her a specific answer, saying he was still confounded by the whole thing, but happy they'd stopped and neither of them had to worry about touching the other any longer.

"That makes two places. Both here on Kinloch." Katie had her own theories. One was, by both of them coming back to Kinloch and joining together, the reasons for the visions had ceased to exist. She firmly believed they'd been some kind of spiritual message, sent to tell them they belonged together.

It was easy to believe that, because *she* believed they belonged together. As fantastical as the visions had been, they'd both had them. They couldn't deny they existed, no matter how inexplicable and unbelievable they might have been. They'd only continued on while their future together had been in limbo.

She wondered what would happen, in a month, if Graham decided to send her away and reject both the Marriage Pact, and her. Unless . . . he didn't think she was planning to stay on regardless, did he? Actually, he'd said he didn't plan to stay on, because that would mean Iain would be in power.

As if she'd conjured him up, another car pulled in behind Roan's truck, and out of it climbed the movie star handsome Iain McAuley.

She started back across the grass, but she'd gone a bit farther afield than she'd realized. He'd already approached Roan before she could get close enough to hear what they were saying. The wind snatched most of it away, anyway. However, Roan's body posture and flat expression said it all. And it took a lot to dim the natural light that was Roan McAuley.

She'd had the misfortune to cross paths twice with the contender for Graham's place on Kinloch. She'd like to think she would have found his charm and natural gregariousness cloying and overbearing even if she hadn't had a personal stake in not liking the man. But the truth of it was, he was a very likable guy, which only served to confound her—and many of the islanders, it appeared—who would be much happier if he was simply vile and easy to hate.

The islanders of Kinloch were a people whose nature it was to throw open their doors, and welcome everyone as if they were a friend. It was easy to see why tourism was flourishing.

Iain would have otherwise likely been easily loved by the people. He was very good looking, had an easy wit, and never met a person he couldn't charm. The exception being the man she was currently living with, and his two closest friends.

She wanted to think Iain smug and smarmy, but thus far, he'd seemed sincerely friendly.

None of that explained what he was doing on the island, or why he wanted to take over Kinloch. Nice, friendly people just didn't do that for no reason.

"Hullo, Katie," he called out. "Beautiful day for a stroll."

Other than herself, he was the only blond on the island. It was rather disconcerting, but worse was he felt it lent them some kind of special bond. She didn't agree. His accent was highly refined, making him sound almost more English than Scot. She liked to think it made him sound entitled. But she knew she was reaching for reasons not to like the man.

"Yes, it's a nice day," she agreed, then turned to Roan. "We should continue on. Thanks for letting me stretch my legs. A pleasure seeing you again, Mr. McAuley."

He looked surprised by her easy dismissal, as if he was used to people wanting more of his time, not less. It was perversely why she took great pleasure in cutting him off whenever he showed up. Although she couldn't exactly point to a specific flaw, the fact remained he was a weasel of some stripe who was trying to thwart Graham's continued work on the island. Just because the stripe wasn't apparent to the naked eye, didn't mean he wasn't sporting one.

Roan opened her door and she climbed in without another look in his direction. "Good day," Roan said to him, a rather satisfied smile on his face as he shut the door and climbed in his own side.

"Thanks," Iain said. "And it's Iain," he called out to Katie.

She would never call him that, just to continue to piss him off.

"Still no idea why he's really here?" she asked Roan as they got back on the single-track lane and continued on their journey.

"None. I've done about all the digging I can do. Shay has also done his share, given he's in Edinburgh, but he's found nothing other than that Iain has worked for the same firm since getting out of school, and his mumsy left him quite well off when she kicked the proverbial bucket. I have no clue what he wants from us, or why he's taken such an extended sabbatical to do it."

"Hmm," Katie said, but what she was thinking was the same thing she'd been thinking for the past few days now. There was one person she knew who could dig the dirt on the queen herself if given the time and proper motivation.

Roan's phone chirped and he fished it out of his jacket pocket. "Aye, Eliza, what is it, my darlin'?"

"Dinnae ye darlin' me, ye scamp."

Roan and Katie shared a quick grin. Roan's teasing of Katie was a new hobby of his, whereas he'd spent a lifetime getting a rise, and the occasional blush, out of his office assistant, who was easily old enough to be his grandmother.

"Don't tell me you're jealous because I am off gallivanting the countryside with a beautiful woman. You know yer first in my heart, and—"

"Actually, 'tis Katie I am trying to track down."

Roan glanced at Katie again. "Oh? Can I pass along a message, or do ye need to speak to her?"

"Well . . ."

Eliza had a stout voice to go with her stout figure, so Katie had heard every word.

"What is it, Mrs. McAuley?" she called out. "I'm right here."

"It seems ye have a visitor. Just in off the ferry."

Katie felt her face go pale. Had her parents found her so quickly? "I do?" she croaked.

"Aye, and he claims to be yer husband. Oh, and Graham just came in. Shall I tell them both to wait here for ye?"

Roan had already turned the truck around. In fact, they passed Iain, who'd climbed back in his car, and was following them back into town.

"Well, things just got interesting," Roan said.

"You don't know the half of it." Katie slumped down in her seat and started to swear.

Chapter 21

"I beg your pardon, Mr. Sheffield, but Katie is no' your wife. I know this, I was there." Graham had stepped into the office as Eliza was on the phone announcing the very fact.

He'd had a long, frustrating day—arguing with one of their seed suppliers, mediating a sheep-stealing issue between two of his crofters, then his lorry had blown a tire on the way in—and he was supposed to be there to talk with Roan, who was out and about with Katie. Again.

When he saw the two of them pull up out front followed by that arse in swine's clothing, Iain McAuley, Graham came very close to simply chucking it all and catching the next ferry to anywhere but Kinloch. They could have the damn place. Let pretty boy run it into the ground.

"You!" Blaine said, stabbing a finger at Graham. "What the hell have you done with my Katie?"

"You might want to lower that finger before I snap it off," Graham said with exaggerated politeness. "I've done nothing with yer Katie." *Except all the things you can't do with her*, he'd wanted to add, but that was his foul mood talking. He managed to keep his tongue. "She'll be here in a moment to prove it."

Roan held open the door and Katie rushed in. "Blaine? What are you doing here? How did you—"

"It wasn't easy," he said, with a relieved sigh as he swept her into a tight bear hug. "Took me almost a week. I believe that's a record."

"Speaking of that, I'm glad you're here." She grabbed his hand and pulled him toward Roan's office. "Follow me, everyone." She looked at Eliza. "Please, if you want Graham to continue keeping everyone on Kinloch happy and successful, do whatever you must, but keep that guy out of Roan's office." She nodded to Iain, who was stepping up to the front door as she spoke.

She didn't wait to see what Eliza did, but hurriedly shuffled them all into Roan's office and shut the door behind her, then locked it for good measure.

"Blaine, this is Roan and Graham. Well, you've met Graham. Sort of. Roan, this is—"

"The guy ye didn't marry. Not good sport telling lies, ol' chap," he said to Blaine. "I have second dibs on her if Graham here proves himself to be a complete idiot and blows the best thing he's ever been lucky enough to find. I'm thinking ye're a distant third now. Especially seeing as there are some aspects of her new relationship that, let's just say, might have been lacking in her last one."

"Roan!" Katie gasped. "I'm never telling you anything ever again."

Roan shrugged, unrepentant.

Graham watched the entire thing like a tennis match gone mad. "Care to explain your theatrics?" he said, before they could burst into simultaneous chatter once again.

"You mean me?" Katie asked, once she realized he was talking to her and not Blaine. "It's not theatrics." She turned to Blaine. "I wanted to call. A thousand times. And a hundred times that. I would have. But I needed to resolve things here first."

"Here? You just got here. What could possibly need resolving?"

"I'll fill you in later, and you can do the same for me. My parents?"

He just shook his head.

Katie winced. "That bad?"

"Armageddon is bad. This? Much, much worse."

She flinched. "I'm sorry. You—did you—and Tag . . . ?"

Blaine looked to Roan and Graham, then back to her. "As you said, we'll catch up later."

"Katie—" Graham began.

"I know, I know." She looked to Graham. "I made another discovery today. About—uh, things. We'll talk later."

"Can I get in on this date night schedule?" Roan asked.

"Shut up, Roan," both Katie and Graham said simultaneously.

He lifted his hands. "Just trying to keep up."

"As I was looking at my . . . discovery, Iain pulled up."

"What did he want?" Graham asked.

"What does he ever want? I have no idea. We blew him off and got back in the truck, and I asked Roan if he or Shay had gotten any dirt on Iain, which they haven't, and that made me think of"—she turned to Blaine—"you. And now here you are. I really think there is something to the visions, Graham."

"Visions," Roan and Blaine said at the same time.

"It's nothing, don't worry," she told them. "But you're here, Blaine, and just in time."

"We need to talk, Katie. You need to come home with me."

"We do need to talk. Blaine, I'm not coming home"—she looked straight at Graham—"if I have anything to say about it. And, if a certain thickheaded man on this island will ever pull said thickhead out of his overly scientific ass long enough to see the good thing he already has right in front of him, and how damn lucky he is to have it, this will be my home."

Roan hooted. Blaine spluttered. Graham . . . *finally* spurred into action.

He stepped forward, and very calmly, but deliberately, put his hand out for Katie. "It seems there is a lot of talking to be done with a number of different people. I'd like to pull rank here and talk with you right now. If you dinnae mind."

"I'm sorry," she told him. "Wait. No, I'm not. Graham—"

"Alone," he said. "Please."

She held his gaze for a long moment, mutiny in her eyes. Then her shoulders slumped and she nodded. "Fine, fine, but first." She turned to the other two men introducing them again. "Blaine Sheffield, Roan McAuley. Roan? This is the man who will find the answer to our most perplexing question."

"He can tell me why you're chasing after that idiot when I'd marry you in a heartbeat?"

"Funny. We can't marry. We're like second cousins."

"Right, second cousins, two centuries removed."

"Well, you're like a cousin to me."

"Ouch."

"Katie, honestly," this from Blaine. "We really don't have time—"

"No, we don't. In fact, time is running out fast. Blaine, Roan will give you the details, but there is a man here, right out in that office, in fact, who is trying to take over this island, only none of us can figure out why."

"What does that have to do with me?"

"I want you to find out. If anyone can do it, you can. Come on, Blaine. You owe me."

"I most certainly do not. You left me standing at the altar!"

"Okay, poor choice of words. But I did that for your own good, as well as for mine. I didn't know what it would lead to"—she looked to Graham—"but I do now. After telling everyone including myself how independent I am now, I've done exactly what I always do. Sit back and don't rock the boat." She took a step closer to Graham. "Well, I'm rocking it now. So look out. Blaine, please, if you've ever loved me, then help me. I promise, other than coming back to Maryland, I'll do whatever I can to help you."

She took Graham's hand, and went to the door. Graham wasn't sure who started clapping, but he was pretty sure it wasn't Sheffield.

Graham, on the other hand, had just spent the past five minutes going from confusion, to fury, to disconcertment . . . to pride. As they passed Iain, he sketched a quick salute.

Surprised, given Graham had generally pretended the man was invisible to him, it took Iain a moment to snap to attention and take advantage of the occasion. "Graham, I've come to discuss—"

"Sorry," Graham called back over his shoulder as Katie continued marching him out the front door. "Can't chat now. But rest assured we're all probably going to have a big chat later on."

It was the first time he'd ever seen Iain frown.

"Where are we—"

"Mind your head," she told him as she shoved him into Roan's front seat with a strength that belied her much smaller frame.

He barely managed to duck in time to keep his skull from being cracked on the frame, and had just closed his door when she climbed in the driver's side and shut the door. "Has Roan been giving you driving lessons?"

"No," she said, then peeled away from the curb.

Graham grabbed both dash and door handle. "Ye, uh, mind telling me what's going on? Or where we're goin'?"

She didn't answer, but her expression rivaled that of the fiercest Valkyrie. He wisely held his tongue, thinking he'd figure it out in due time. The island wasn't that big.

Still, it was a surprise to him when she drove away from the castle and across to the McAuley side of the island. Just past the machair, she pulled over and parked. Well, it was more a controlled swerve and slamming of the brakes, but he was happy enough to be alive and in one piece. He didn't quibble.

"Come on," she said, and climbed out. "I want to show you something." She started off across the green.

He did as she asked. With his long strides, he was beside her in a few steps. "What is it, Katie?" He reached for her arm, but she leapt to the side to avoid his touch.

Neither of them had done that in days. Since she'd come to his castle, in fact. It stung more than a little.

"Not here. You'll understand in just a—" She stopped and pointed. "There. Look there." She pointed first to where the machair met the grass line. Then she pointed out to sea. "And there."

Graham glanced from the grass, to the ruins of the abbey, and back to the grass, but he was still confounded. "I dinnae understand. What are ye—" Then he froze, and very slowly turned to look once again at the abbey, then the grassy knoll. Then, finally, at Katie. "It was here."

She slumped in obvious relief. "Aye."

"But . . . why? What is it you think this means?"

She started walking again, and stopped when she was standing directly over the spot where the two of them, or some previous version of them, had lain on a blanket, wrapped in a passion he'd only known from watching it. His gaze lifted to hers, and he felt his heart fill. "Now, I know it for real."

"So do I." She stepped closer. "Graham, don't you see? You were going to buck the tradition. You were going to end the chain. I think . . . I think we've been . . . a part of that chain. Before. I don't know how many times. This is what you're meant to do. What *we're* meant to do. As long as we've been heading in that direction"—she lifted her shoulders—"No more visions, no more messages."

"So, I'm supposed to what? Ask for your hand to keep the visions at bay?"

She sighed and shook her head, but there was no hurt in her eyes, only frustration. "No. You're supposed to take the leap of faith like your forebears did." She stepped closer still. "Don't you see, Graham? That's what all of this is. That's what life is. A huge leap of faith. Otherwise why get up in the morning? Why even try to improve your lot in life? Because you believe there will continue to be a life worth improving, that's why. Leap of faith."

"Katie—"

"No, let me finish. I was going to wait, to let you make up your own mind—because I wanted you to want this, want me, want the future with me, because *you* truly wanted it. Not because of the Pact, not to thwart the Pact. But because I was worth the leap."

"But you—"

"I'm not done. Taking off from the church, leaving that life behind, was the only time in my life I've ever dared leap. Then what did I do? I came here . . . and went right back to sitting on the sidelines, allowing others to call the shots. Shots that involved me, and my life, and my future. Well, I'm not doing that anymore." She boldly walked right up to him and put her hands on his shoulders.

They both paused a moment, stock still, but nothing happened.

"I didn't know what I *wanted* when I left Annapolis. Only what I *didn't* want. But in that chapel, you stood there and said, 'You're supposed to be mine.' Graham, I don't know how, or why or what forces really led you to that church on that day. But for every second since the moment you strode into that garden, I am absolutely convinced you are supposed to be mine. I don't want to help you abolish the Marriage Pact. I think that any law, any . . . belief, that has lasted as long as that one has, with its brilliant and unassailable results, has to be something worth taking a leap of faith for. I told you I would convince you to marry me before the time was up. But if you don't already know, don't already believe, somewhere in your heart—in the place not ruled by data and equations, research and documentation—that I really am supposed to be yours, then waiting another four weeks isn't going to change that."

"Are ye quite done now?" he asked, when she seemed to finally run out of steam.

She started to pull her hands from his shoulders but he covered them with his own, and pulled them down between them, so he could weave their fingers together. Then he held on tight—as tight as he'd ever held on to anything in his life.

"I've spent my life figuring out solutions to complex problems by applying logic and rational thought. I don't know that intuition ever came into play. My head has always ruled my gut, and my heart. It wasn't even a contest. So ye can see why this Pact went against everything I believed in. It wasn't logical." He pulled their joined hands up between them. "An act of desperation sent me across an ocean, sent me to find you. From that moment on, nothing in my life has been orderly or rational. No amount of logical problem solving is giving me the absolute answer I am seeking. It was easier to break down the unexplainable, than it was to confront it. The visions, the Pact . . . I just wanted them to go away, so I didn't have to deal with what I didn't—couldn't—understand."

"It's—"

He shook his head. "I gave ye yer moment."

She held his gaze, then nodded.

"Roan and Shay tried to explain the Pact, the leap of faith required, as giving hope. They told me that no one here would ever vote it asunder, because no one wanted to stop believing in its promise, which is a lifetime bond. Four hundred years' worth of them. It gave them hope. Taking that away would have been more brutal, more cruel, and more devastating than a blight that would forever obliterate our crops. That would be an act of God. Of fate. Destroying the Pact would have been an act of man. Namely this one."

"When . . . when did you understand?"

"I think a part of me always did. I was simply too afraid to reach for it, to hand such an important piece of my life . . . of myself, to something I couldn't absolutely quantify."

"What changed?"

"You. I never wanted you to leave. If we'd have wed, I'd have never willingly divorced you. That's why I couldn't answer you, about your offer to help with the Pact. That you'd even do that, for me . . . was humbling and made me feel even less worthy."

"For what it's worth, I wouldn't have been able to go through with it. I've known that from the moment the words left my mouth. My only hope was the same as yours, that once we'd tied the knot, nothing would ever be able to unravel it."

"I know that. Have known that."

"When were you going to get around to telling me?" she said, the first hint of a smile curving her beautiful lips.

"I dinnae know. I was working my way up to it. It's why I've spent so much time away the past few days. I can't seem to think straight when I'm around you. I needed to figure out how I was going to tell you, once again, that I'd changed my thinkin'—Without you thinkin' me so fickle you'd run from the proof of it."

"I'd never run. The only running I ever did, was toward you."

He tugged her closer, then lifted her up against him so he could kiss her, long, and lingering. "I know," he said, against the side of her cheek, before letting her slide to the ground. "I watched you, just now, in Roan's office, and that was when I knew I was done waiting. You were . . . you are magnificent. And you're absolutely right. I've been a complete horse's arse."

"Well, maybe not a complete one."

He smiled . . . and then he got down on one knee.

"Oh," she gasped, and tugged one hand free to cover first her mouth, then her heart. "Graham—"

"Well, the part of me that's not a complete horse's patootie would like to take a step . . . a leap, in fact."

Her eyes—eyes he planned to look into for the rest of his life—went glassy, and her hand clutched at his, even as she clutched at her heart. "Hurry," she said, hoarsely, "I might not be able to keep my knees locked much longer."

"Katherine Elizabeth Georgina Rosemary McAuley, I would consider it an honor, one I vow to spend the rest of my life proving I'm worthy of holding, if you'd consider giving me your hand in marriage." He lifted his hand, turned her palm over in his, and traced a heart there, before closing her fingers around it. "You've had mine since the day I met you. I love you, Katie. I'm fairly certain I've said these words to you for centuries, but I'd like the pleasure of saying them for at least another fifty or so more years. Will you marry me, darling Katie mine?"

"Aye," she choked out. "Come here."

He stood and swept her into his arms.

"I love you, Graham MacLeod. We'll stand in this very spot again, across time. I know it. But I love you in this life, and I want every day of it. So yes, I'll marry you." Then she thumped him on the chest. "I thought you'd never ask."

He laughed, then took her mouth in a bold, deep, claiming kiss as if he'd never kissed her before. She was well and truly his.

"If you dinnae mind, I'd like ye to choose another wedding dress," he said, as she kissed the side of his neck, then pressed her cheek against his chest.

"Do I have to wear a dress?" She looked up at him then, and grinned.

"I was thinkin' I'd like to claim you, and say my vows, in front of both God, and my friends and clansmen. We can always play naked bride and groom later, though."

She laughed, then tugged his head down for a claiming kiss of her own. "Deal," she said, making him laugh in return. "You know, maybe something that's a little throwback to another era."

"You mean like that dress you were wearing when we—"

She nodded.

And he cleared the sudden dryness from his throat. "Aye, that would be acceptable, indeed it would. Though we'll perhaps have to put off naked bride and groom night."

"Why?"

"Because we're going to play vision re-creation night, first."

"Oh," she said, then her eyes widened and her grin widened as well. "Oh!"

"Aye."

"Perhaps you should take me home. We might want to practice a bit."

"Our vows?"

"Our honeymoon."

"What of your friend? Back at Roan's? Shouldn't we—" He stopped and grinned. Broadly.

"What?"

"I believe perhaps we should stop back by. Ye and Blaine can set a time to talk and I can tell one Mr. Iain McAuley to book the next ferry passage home."

"Indeed," she said. "Sounds like a plan." She looked down and he followed her gaze.

"What is it?"

She lifted her gaze to his. "I was just thinking, it's a shame we don't have a blanket."

He laughed as he turned with her still in his arms, to head back to Roan's truck. "I'll make certain I have one stowed in every vehicle on the island. A new decree."

Her laughter was interrupted by a rousing cheer.

They turned their heads toward the road, where at least a dozen cars and three times that many people were clapping and cheering wildly. In the center were Roan and Eliza. Roan cheering, Eliza fanning her face and dabbing at the corners of her eyes. No sign of Blaine. Or Iain.

The cheering grew, as did the crowd, as Graham carried her back toward them. To think he'd been worried they wouldn't accept her. What was not to love?

"Welcome home, *mo chridhe*," he said, settling her in his arms, beaming broadly as he carried his bride-to-be to the people who loved them both. That was what true happiness was all about.

Epilogue

"It doesnae matter, really, does it? Iain's gone now."

"I suppose not," Katie told her soon-to-be husband. "But Blaine thinks he hit upon something. He needs Shay to do a little bit of digging, some fact-checking while he's still in Edinburgh."

"Iain has no power here now, witnessed by the fact that he took the first boat out once news of our engagement swept the island. You can tell Blaine we're very thankful, but it's no longer something we need to worry about."

Katie wasn't so certain as Graham, but then his intuition was a bit rustic compared to hers. If Blaine thought he could get some definitive answers by talking to Shay, she didn't see the harm in it.

"What of Blaine?" Graham asked. "Has he decided if he's staying on for the wedding?"

"I don't know. We're . . . talking about it."

"Tag is welcome to come as well."

She smiled and rolled her stool over to his and bussed him loudly on the cheek. It had been two weeks since he'd proposed, and two days after—when he'd found her working up some sketches for Roan to look over regarding upgrades to both their catalog design and their website—he'd repurposed a section of his lab. He'd cobbled together a drafting table and had even rustled up some basic supplies. When he was at home, they often worked side by side. She'd found she was enjoying her return to graphic design, but she was *really* enjoying collaborating with Roan on ideas and ways they could expand their marketing plan.

"Yet another reason I adore you. I'll tell Blaine. But that's still a sore subject."

"Maybe he's the one next in line for the leap of faith lesson."

"Maybe," Katie said, wishing fervently that would be true. "Maybe I'll have Shay and Roan give him the same talking-to they gave you."

Graham shuddered lightly, then went back to studying the seed specimen he'd just slid under his microscope. "I think I'll be givin' the encore performance a pass. But dinnae let that stop ye from askin'."

"Oh, I won't." She started to sketch again, then stopped. "What would you say if I invited my mother and father?"

He immediately lifted his head and looked at her in disbelief. "Do you really think that's a wise idea? I'd like to actually get through the entire ceremony without fear of your father shooting me."

"My mother has the far more deadly aim."

"Good to know. Another reason to think this one through." He sobered then when he realized she was serious. "They've yet to accept your calls."

"They won't talk to me until I come home."

"Could make issuing an invitation to the wedding rather tricky."

"Aye, I know. But I think I want to try. I'd regret it if I didn't at least extend the branch. Maybe if they realize I'm really never coming home, that disowning me isn't exactly a threat that holds any power over me, they'll reconsider."

"Do ye really believe that?"

She smiled, a bit sadly, a tad wistfully. "No. I know better. But the gesture will be extended. Okay?"

He nodded. "I'll look into Kevlar tartans immediately."

She swatted him, and laughed, then leaned over a moment later and whispered, "Thank you."

"What for?" he whispered back, already looking at his seedling.

"Letting me continue to stumble along my own path, my own way."

Without looking up he hooked his booted foot around her stool and wheeled her closer. Then he sat up, spun her around, took her face in his hands, and kissed her soundly on the mouth. Then did so again. And a third time. When he finally lifted his head, she was both a bit breathless and a lot wide-eyed.

"What was that for, Mr. MacLeod?"

"That was to remind you there's only one thing I can truly 'let' you do."

"And that is?"

"Encourage you to let me kiss you, so I can let you kiss me back."

She thought about that for a moment.

"If it's important to you, it's your decision, Katie. I may not always agree, but I'll always back you. You'll find your own way, as I will continue to find mine. We'll at least have each other to cling to, to celebrate the victories and commiserate over the more misguided attempts."

"When did you get so smart, anyway?"

He pretended to think about it. "I'm pretty sure it was right about the time I opted to head into a certain prayer garden and play Good Samaritan to a bride in need."

"Hmm." She pretended to think about that, then stood up . . . and plopped herself down right in his lap, straddling him, very carefully sliding his glasses off and setting them on the lab station behind her.

"As it happens," she told him, "you've yet again managed to stumble across a bride in need."

"Have I now?"

"What do you propose to do about it?"

"What I should have done the first time it happened." With that he surged up to a stand, making her squeal as he slid her over his shoulder and wrapped his arms around the backs of her thighs to hold her there.

"And what, pray tell," she said, between gasps of laughter, "would that be?"

"To claim her as my own in every way I know how."

"Oh," she said, as he followed her down on to the bed.

"Oh, indeed," he replied.

"How does one claim a bride, exactly?"

"Like this," he said . . . proceeding to show her. In detail. For a very, very long time.

Grab BEAST BEHAVING BADLY, the latest in the Pride series from Shelly Laurenston, out now from Brava!

Bo shot through the goal crease and slammed the puck into the net.

"Morning!"

That voice cut through his focus, and without breaking his stride, Bo changed direction and skated over to the rink entrance. He stopped hard, ice spraying out from his skates, and stood in front of the wolfdog.

He stared down at her and she stared up at him. She kept smiling even when he didn't. Finally he asked, "What time did we agree on?"

"Seven," she replied with a cheery note that put his teeth on edge.

"And what time is it?"

"Uh . . ." She dug into her jeans pocket and pulled out a cell phone. The fact that she still had on that damn, useless watch made his head want to explode. How did one function—as an adult anyway—without a goddamn watch?

Grinning so that he could see all those perfectly aligned teeth, she said, "Six forty-five!"

"And what time did we agree on?"

She blinked and her smile faded. After a moment, "Seven."

"Is it seven?"

"No." When he only continued to stare at her, she softly asked, "Want to meet me at the track at seven?"

He continued to stare at her until she nodded and said, "Okay." She walked out and Bo went back to work.

Fifteen minutes later, Bo walked into the small arena at seven a.m. Blayne, looking comfortable in dark blue leggings, sweatshirt, and skates, turned to face him. He expected her to be mad at him or, even worse, for her to get that wounded look he often got from people when he was blatantly direct. But having to deal with either of those scenarios was a price Bo was always willing to pay to ensure that the people in his life understood how he worked from the beginning. This way, there were no surprises later. It was called "boundaries," and he read about it in a book.

Yet when Blayne saw him, she grinned and held up a Starbucks cup. "Coffee," she said when he got close. "I got you the house brand because I had no idea what you would like. And they had cinnamon twists, so I got you a few of those."

He took the coffee, watching her close. Where was it? The anger? The resentment? Was she plotting something?

Blayne held the bag of sweets out for him and Bo took them. "Thank you," he said, still suspicious even as he sipped his perfectly brewed coffee.

"You're welcome." And there went that grin again. Big and brighter than the damn sun. "And I get it. Seven means seven. Eight means eight, et cetera, et cetera. Got it and I'm on it. It won't happen again." She said all that without a trace of bitterness or annoyance, dazzling Bo with her understanding more than she'd dazzled him with those legs.

"So"—she put her hands on her hips—"what do you want me to do first?"

Marry me? Wait. No, no. Incorrect response. It'll just weird her out and make her run again. Normal. Be normal. You can do this. You're not just a great skater. You're a normal *great skater.*

When Bo knew he had his shit together, he said, "Let's work on your focus first. And, um, should I ask what happened to your face?" She had a bunch of cuts on her cheeks. Gouges. Like something small had pawed at her.

"Nope!" she chirped, pulling off her sweatshirt. She wore a worn blue T-shirt underneath with B&G PLUMBING scrawled across it. With sweatshirt in hand, Blayne skated over to the bleachers, stopped, shook her head, skated over to another section of bleachers, stopped, looked at the sweatshirt, turned around, and skated over to the railing. "I should leave it here," she explained. "In case I get chilly."

It occurred to Bo he'd just lost two minutes of his life watching her try to figure out where to place a damn sweatshirt. Two minutes that he'd never get back.

"Woo-hoo!" she called out once she hit the track. "Let's go!"

She was skating backward as she urged him to join her with both hands.

He pointed behind her. "Watch the—"

"Ow!"

"—pole."

Christ, what had he gotten himself into?

Christ almighty, what had she gotten herself into?

Twenty minutes in and she wanted to smash the man's head against a wall. She wanted to go back in time and kick the shit out of Genghis Khan before turning on his brothers, Larry and Moe. Okay. That wasn't their names but she could barely remember Genghis's name on a good day, how the hell was she supposed to remember his brothers'? But whatever the Khan kin's names may be, Blayne wanted to hurt them all for cursing her world with this . . . this . . . Visigoth!

Even worse, she knew he didn't even take what she did seriously. He insisted on calling it a chick sport. If he were a sexist pig across the board, Blayne could overlook it as a mere flaw in his upbringing. But, she soon discovered, Novikov had a very high degree of respect for female athletes . . . as long as they were athletes and not just "hot chicks in cute outfits, roughing each other up. All you guys need is some hot oil or mud and you'd have a real moneymaker on your hands."

And yet, even while he didn't respect her sport as a sport, he still worked her like he was getting her ready for the Olympics.

After thirty minutes, she wanted nothing more but to lie on her side and pant. She doubted the hybrid would let her get away with that, though.

Shooting around the track, Novikov stopped her in a way that she was finding extremely annoying—grabbing her head with that big hand of his and holding her in place.

He shoved her back with one good push, and Blayne fought not to fall on her ass at that speed. When someone shoved her like that, they were usually pissed. He wasn't.

"I need to see something," he said, still nursing that cup of coffee. He'd finished off the cinnamon twists in less than five minutes while she was warming up. "Come at me as hard as you can."

"Are you sure?" she asked, looking him over. He didn't have any of his protective gear on, somehow managing to change into sweatpants and T-shirt and still make it down to the track exactly at seven. "I don't want to hurt you," she told him honestly.

The laughter that followed, however, made her think she did want to hurt him. She wanted to hurt him a lot. When he realized she wasn't laughing with him—or, in this case, laughing at *herself* since he was obviously laughing *at* her—Novikov blinked and said, "Oh. You're not kidding."

"No. I'm not kidding."

"Oh. Oh! Um . . . I'll be fine. Hit me with your best shot."

"Like Pat Benatar?" she joked, but when he only stared at her, she said, "Forget it."

Blayne sized up the behemoth in front of her and decided to move back a few more feet so she could get a really fast start. She got into position and took one more scrutinizing look. It was a skill her father had taught her. To size up weakness. Whether the weakness of a person or a building or whatever. Of

course, Blayne often used this skill for good, finding out someone's weakness and then working to help them overcome it.
Her father, however, used it to destroy.

Lowering her body, Blayne took a breath, tightened her fists,
and took off. She lost some speed on the turn but picked it up
as she cut inside. As Blayne approached Novikov, she sized him
up one more time as he stood there casually, sipping his coffee
and watching her move around the track. Based on that last as-
sessing look, she slightly adjusted her position and slammed
into him with everything she had.

And, yeah, she knocked herself out cold, but it was totally
worth it when the behemoth went down with her.

Catch THE DEVIL SHE KNOWS, the latest from Diane Whiteside, out now from Brava!

"This is no place for a lady," he observed, ancient eyes studying Gareth without fear.

"She has a suite booked at the best European hotel—and I will continue to keep her safe."

"Most excellent." He bowed. "Peace be upon you."

"And upon you be peace," Gareth returned in equally excellent Arabic.

Portia could read nothing in Gareth's face after they'd left, unlike her wedding day, the last time they'd met. She sighed, wishing for so many things.

"Hmm?" Gareth asked noncommittally, just as he would have when she was twelve. Back then, he'd been surprised at her presence on his expeditions out of Uncle William's house. But he'd never refused to take her along and he'd always answered her questions, even if he didn't start any conversations. At least in the beginning, he hadn't.

"He looks so helpless, unlike the charming—"

"Charming?" Gareth's tone sharpened fractionally. He turned toward the large, comfortable barouche that Sidonie had just climbed aboard.

"Parrot? Or maybe a mynah bird?" Portia spread her hands a little helplessly, before following his lead. A seagull soared overhead, effortlessly free, unlike herself. "Abdul Hamid always reminded me of a tropical creature, with his vivid waistcoats and eternal, colorful chatter. Seeing him crumpled up like this makes him look like a broken bird."

"I doubt there's any serious damage." Warmth softened Gareth's eyes for the first time until they gleamed blue as the water behind him. He offered her his hand and she took the first step up into the carriage.

"Are you sure?" Standing on the metal step, she was almost at eye level with him.

"They didn't have enough time to tie him up and truly start working him over. The police here have a pattern they like to follow." His expression hardened for a moment then he kissed the tips of her fingers. "But that didn't happen. Once he sees a good doctor, is bandaged up, and has a long rest, he should be fine."

"Are you truly certain?" She searched his face. They had never, ever lied to each other.

"As much as I can be."

"Very well then." She tightened her fingers around his, feeling his strength flood into hers once again. "Thank you for rescuing us."

"It was my pleasure, Portia." He kissed her hand again, brushing his lips across her knuckles. It was still no contact at all, nothing like all the men who'd tried to seduce her into an affair while she was married, saying she needed to distract herself from St. Arles. She'd always refused them, telling herself and them it was because St. Arles would never tolerate a cuckoo in the nest. He'd have known in a minute if another man had sired his heir and heaven knows, the son of a bitch kept hauling himself back to her bed to breed one.

She hadn't realized until now it was because no other man made her bones shiver, even when her skin hadn't been touched.

Don't miss Cynthia Eden's I'LL BE SLAYING YOU, out next month from Brava!

"Let me buy you a drink."

She'd ignored the men beside her. Greeted the few come-ons she'd gotten with silence. But that voice—

Dee glanced to the left. Tall, Dark, and Sexy was back.

And he was smiling down at her. A big, wide grin that showed off a weird little dint in his right cheek. Not a dimple, too hard for that. She hadn't noticed that curve last night, now with the hunt and kill distracting her.

Shit, but he was hot.

Thanks to the spotlights over the bar, she could see him so much better tonight. No shadows to hide behind now.

Hard angles, strong jaw, sexy man.

She licked her lips. "Already got one." Dee held up her glass.

"Babe, that's water." He motioned to the bartender. "Let me get you something with bite."

She'd spent the night looking for a bite. Hadn't found it yet. Her fingers snagged his. "I'm working." Booze couldn't slow her down. Not with the one she hunted.

Black brows shot up. Then he leaned in close. So close that she caught the scent of his aftershave. "You gonna kill another woman tonight?" A whisper that blew against her.

Her lips tightened. "Vampire," she said quietly.

He blinked. Those eyes of his were eerie. Like a smoky fog staring back at her.

"I hunted a vampire last night," Dee told him, keeping her voice hushed because in a place like this, you never knew who was listening. "And, technically, she'd already been killed once before I got to her."

His fingers locked around her upper arm. She'd yanked on a black T-shirt before heading out, and his fingertips skimmed her flesh. "Guess you're right," he murmured and leaned in even closer.

His lips were about two inches—maybe just one—away from hers.

What would he taste like?

It'd been too long since she'd had a lover, and this guy fit all of her criteria. Big, strong, sexy, and aware of the score in the city.

"Wanna dance with me?" Such dark words. No accent at all underlined the whisper. Just a rich purr of sex.

Oh but she bet the guy was fantastic in the sack.

Find out. A not-so-weak challenge in her mind. Why not? She wasn't seeing anyone. He seemed up for it and—

Dee brought her left hand up between them and pushed against his chest. "I don't dance." Especially not to that too-fast, pounding music that made her head ache.

He didn't retreat. His eyes bored into hers. "Pity." His fingers skated down her arm and caught her wrist. He took her glass away and placed it on the bar top with a clink.

She cocked her head and studied him. "Are you following me?" Two nights. First one, sure, that could have been coincidence. A coincidence she was grudgingly grateful for, but tonight—

The faintest curl hinted on his lips. "What if I am?"

His thighs brushed against her. Big, strong thighs. Thick with muscle.

Dee swallowed. So not the time.

But the man was tempting.

She couldn't afford a distraction. Not then. "Then you'd better be very, very careful." Dee shoved against him. Hard.

He stumbled back a step and his smile widened. "You keep

playing hard to get, and I'm gonna start thinking you're not in-terested in me, Sandra Dee."

Who was this guy? Dee jumped off the bar stool. "You'd be thinking right, buddy."

He took her wrist again with strong, roughened fingers. The guy towered over her. Always the way of it. When you couldn't even skim five foot six with big-ass heels, most men towered over you. And since Dee had never worn heels in her life . . .

The guy bent toward her when he said, "I see the way you look at me."

What did that mean?

"Curious . . . but more. Like maybe you got a wild side lurk-ing in you. A side that wants out."

Maybe she did. The guy sure looked like he could play. *After the case.*

"I don't know you, Chase," she finally told him, too aware of his touch on her skin. Too aware that her nipples were tightening and she was leaning toward him as her nostrils flared and she tried to suck up more of his scent. "I don't know—"

"I saved your life." A fallen angel's smile. "Doesn't that count for something?"